FORBIDDEN FLAME

He was kissing her full on the mouth again, this time without tenderness. His kiss demanded more, much more, from her. His arms drew her ever closer against his muscular body. She sensed the heat, the desire, emanating from him, but before she could respond, his hands were suddenly withdrawn from behind her head as he stepped away.

"Damn!" he swore. "Go back to bed, Gem."

"Chase, I—"

"Do you hear me? Leave me alone. Go back to bed." Anger and loathing laced each word.

She didn't understand what she had done. Tears welled and spilled over. "Chase," she pleaded.

"Don't you understand? I don't have anything for you."

Other *Leisure Books* by Robin Lee Hatcher:

ROBIN LEE HATCHER

GEMFIRE

To Fela Dawson Scott & Gloria Pedersen,
dearest friends and fellow authors
who share my ups and downs, joys and sorrows,
successes and failures...
not to mention more than our share of pie at
Plush Pippin
I love you.

And to my editor,
Alicia Condon,
for making such a difference.
Thanks

A Centurion Book®

Published by special arrangement with Dorchester
Publishing Co., Inc.

Printed in the United States of America.

1

A smoky haze filled the saloon, making Gem's eyes smart and tear as she stood behind her father staring down at his cards. Lucky McBride was holding a flush, queen high, the best darned hand he'd had in a long time. She could feel his excitement mounting. The pot in the middle of the table was a rich one, richer than any Lucky had been in before. She tried not to think of the things they could buy if her father won.

Gem's aquamarine eyes flicked to the other men seated around the table. Three had already thrown in their cards. The remaining players were her father and two others. A man called Barnes was seated directly across the table from Lucky. He was about her father's age. He was unshaven with long black hair and a twitch in his right cheek. There was something about his dark eyes—shifting, wary, close-set eyes—that gave her an instant antipathy for the man.

1

The other player was younger, perhaps twenty-one or twenty-two, and from the way he was dressed she guessed he was a cowboy. He'd said very little throughout the game, his startling sapphire eyes observing his opponents without giving away his own thoughts.

"You gonna play or not, McBride?" Barnes growled.

Gem turned her attention back to the game. With a start, she realized that Barnes had raised once again. Five dollars this time. Everything Lucky and Gem McBride owned was already lying in the center of that green felt table. If he threw in his cards now, they were left with nothing except the clothes on their backs. Their money, their horses, their saddles, everything. They would lose it all.

"Will you take my IOU?"

Barnes laughed and shook his head. "Forget it, McBride." He turned his attention toward the younger man, waiting expectantly.

"Hey, Lucky," a miner yelled from the bar. "Why not throw in Gem? She oughta be worth a dollar or two."

Lucky was sweating. Gem could see the trickles leaving damp tracks down the back of his neck. Her father turned and looked up at her, then suddenly snatched the scruffy hat from her head, revealing her short, strawberry blonde curls.

"What about it?" he asked the men at the table. "She ain't much to look at, I'll give you that. But she's a hard worker and she ain't used to much pamperin'."

Gem felt the hard gaze of the older man studying her. She swallowed the frightened taste of bile that rose in her throat and hoped her fear didn't show.

"She's near 'bout fifteen years old, more or less," Lucky continued. "Be a woman 'fore you know it, even if she ain't much higher than buffalo grass. She might even pretty up some."

Gem wanted to cry. She wanted to run off and hide. Men were looking at her from every corner of the saloon. Some were sniggering as they came to stand nearer the card table. There she stood, in a dress so old and worn it had no color or shape left in it. The bodice was too snug over her developing breasts, and the skirt was too short, revealing the shabby boots that pinched her toes. She knew she wasn't pretty. She hated the way her strange bluish-green eyes tipped up at the outside corners. Like a cat's eyes, she'd always thought. Freckles darkened her pert nose and high cheeks, and her baby-fine red-gold hair was too short and curly. No, she was a far sight from pretty, and now every man-jack of them was looking at her and knowing it too. How could her father humiliate her like this?

"Fifteen, you say?" Barnes inquired, a smile baring yellowed teeth. "Don't look more'n ten."

"It's just 'cause she's so tiny."

"All right, McBride. You're still in."

Gem didn't look at the other player at the table for confirmation of his acceptance. She was too busy praying the floor would open up and swallow her whole. Lucky McBride had never been much of a father. He'd been dragging her from cow town to gold rush town and then off to another for as long as she could remember. They'd slept more often under the stars than in a bed, and she'd been hungry more often than full. But she wouldn't have thought he'd do anything like this to her. She squeezed her eyes shut, holding in the tears and shutting out everything else.

"A flush. Queen high." Her father's voice was jubilant.

"Not so fast, you old fool. I say you're a cheat, and I don't hold with no cheatin'."

Suddenly the room exploded with gunfire. Gem's eyes flew open in time to see her father slump over the table. Barnes was standing up, a look of surprise on his face. His gun slipped from his fingers, clattering to the floor. Then, almost in slow motion, he followed it, his head just missing the edge of the table. His eyes were still open, but he wasn't seeing anything—and never would again.

"Pa?" Gem touched her father's shoulder. "Pa?" His head rolled to the side.

"I think he's dead, miss."

She turned her stunned gaze on the blue-eyed man. He was standing back from the table, his chair overturned on the floor. He still gripped his revolver in his right hand.

"You *killed* him?"

He shook his head as he holstered his Peacemaker. "No. Barnes there shot your pa. I just made sure he didn't shoot anybody else."

"Well, I'll be," a voice said from behind her. "Never thought Barnes was that big of a fool."

"Looks like somebody needs to claim the pot."

"Devil take the pot. I'll take Gem. Might grow into somethin' yet."

Gem could hear the chuckles and lewd jokes. She was frightened, but she wasn't going to show it. She reached over her father's body and began to scoop up Lucky's last winnings. At least she wouldn't go hungry.

"Sorry, miss. The pot's mine." Sapphire eyes watched her as he spread out four kings across the green felt. "You'd better come with me."

She couldn't believe this was happening. First her father gambled away everything he owned in the world, including his only daughter; then he was shot and killed, falsely accused of being a cheat; his murderer lay dead on the floor; and now this man was telling her to come with him.

"I won't." Defiantly, she crossed her arms across the bodice of her faded calico dress.

He shrugged. "As you wish."

He swept up his winnings and put them in his saddlebags. She thought he was leaving, but with a sudden turn, he caught her up and tossed her on her stomach over his left shoulder. Raucous laughter broke out in the saloon.

Gem was silent for a moment, shock numbing her from action. But when he carried her outside and started to step up into his saddle, she began to complain—loudly. "Put me down, you two-bit murderin' sonofa—"

He whacked her backside with his right hand. "Quiet, little girl. I don't hold with being sworn at by children."

Surprised, she obeyed.

He turned his head away from her, looking over at the man with a gray beard who was standing outside the saloon. "Silva, tell the sheriff what happened, and see that McBride gets a proper funeral. Four Winds will pay for it. Tell the sheriff I'm taking the girl out to Aunt Enid. If he's got questions, he can ride out, but I think there's enough witnesses inside so he'll know what happened."

Silva nodded mutely.

"See if you can round up her things and send them out to the ranch." Her captor turned his horse and jogged out of town.

Her stomach bouncing against his shoulder, Gem was too busy trying to draw a full breath to voice any further complaints, but once he urged his mount into a smoother gait, she proceeded to tell him just what she thought of him. She pounded on his back with her fists and kicked her feet. She swore at him like a drunken trailhand on his first night off the Chisholm. She did everything she could think of to make as big a nuisance of herself as possible.

Suddenly he jerked his horse to a stop and dropped her in a heap on the ground. His jaw was set in a hard line and his blue eyes snapped angrily. "Look, I told you to be quiet. I'm not going to hurt you. I'm just trying to help."

"Help?" Gem scrambled to her feet. Frowning, she rubbed her aching backside, then put her hands on her hips and tipped her head back to flash angry eyes up at him. "Help me how? By draggin' me out in the middle a' nowhere? By takin' the money my pa would've won? Why, you mangy, good for nothin'—"

"Young lady, if you swear at me again I'll tan your backside until you can't sit down for a month of Sundays." He sounded like he meant just what he said. "Even if you had that money, would you rather I'd left you back in that saloon? If so, start walking.

It's not so far. You'll make it by dark. I'm sure there's more than one or two cowpokes or gold diggers in that town who'd be glad to put you up for a night."

Tears blinded her. She didn't know what to do. She knew what was likely to happen to her if she went back to Virginia City. In no time at all, her money would be gone or her horses probably stolen—or perhaps something much worse—and then where would she be? She was alone and friendless. She had no place to go.

"Here. Use this." He had dismounted and was standing before her, holding out his neckerchief.

She took it from him and dried her eyes, then blew her nose. "Where . . . where're you takin' me?" she asked in a small, shaky voice, hating herself for crying and for sounding weak.

"To my uncle's ranch. The Four Winds. My Aunt Enid will see that you're taken care of." He offered a smile. "They're nice folks. Will you come?"

Gem looked up at him and saw that he actually didn't look like he meant to do her any harm. Despite towering over her by at least a foot, he didn't seem as threatening as he once had. In fact, his expression looked almost tender.

She sniffed. "I ain't lookin' for charity, you know."

"I know." He swung up into his saddle, then held out his hand toward her. "Will you come with me?"

She held her breath a moment as she stared at the friendly sparkle in his eyes. Her decision was made. "What's your name anyhow?" she asked as she took hold of his hand.

"Chase Dupre. Pleased to make your acquaintance, Miss McBride."

He pulled her up behind him, and with a touch of his spurs to the horse's sides, they shot forward. To keep from falling off, Gem grabbed hold of his waist and held on tight, tears starting up all over again.

Chase wondered what on earth he was doing, riding out of Virginia City with a strawberry-haired waif clinging to him from behind the saddle. If he had gone straight to Stewart's place instead of slipping up to Virginia for a few games of cards . . .

The old man had already been sitting at the table with Barnes and the others when Chase came in and asked if he could join them for a hand or two. He hadn't noticed the girl until he'd been dealt in. There wasn't much of her he could see with that hat pulled down to her ears and her standing right up against Lucky's back. Once, when she'd glanced over at him, he'd caught a glimpse of a freckled nose, but that was all he'd noticed until somebody suggested that Lucky throw her into the pot.

Chase had grown cold with anger as the father casually gambled his daughter away. He'd looked at the four kings and known he was going to win the rich stakes in the center of the table, but what on earth was he going to do with that little girl? But he'd been just mad enough to take her. The last thing in the world he'd wanted to do was put her back in the old man's care. Care? From the looks of her, he hadn't spent much time caring for her.

He'd seen Barnes reaching for his gun and had jumped to his feet, drawing his own revolver, but it had already been too late for the old drifter. Lucky McBride had been dead even before Barnes hit the floor.

And now here was Chase, taking Gem home with him. He knew Aunt Enid would welcome her with open arms. And Uncle Frank? He would raise an eyebrow and look stern, but there was sure to be a twinkle in his eye. Chase didn't know of two more giving, loving people than his aunt and uncle. If Gem stuck around, Aunt Enid would have her cleaned up and talking like a lady in no time. He'd bet on it.

He chuckled to himself. Betting was what had got him into this predicament in the first place. Maybe his aunt was right about the evils of the game. He'd better stay out of Virginia City, or next thing he knew he'd have himself his own orphanage.

It was well over an hour, even closer to two, before the horse they were riding approached the clapboard house at Four Winds. Gem peeked around Chase to look at the cluster of outbuildings. Then her gaze settled on the ranch house itself. The large, two-story home was painted French gray. It had a red roof and red shutters at the windows and three chimneys. Gem didn't think she'd ever seen anything so pretty in her life and was once again gripped by fear. As they approached, a woman stepped out on the porch, wiping her hands on her apron. She was tall and slender, like the young man in front of Gem. Her hair was gray and she had a weathered but friendly face.

"What in Sam Hill are you doing back, Chase? I thought you were going over to see Len Stewart and check out that new bull of his." Her gray eyes slid to Gem. "And what's this you've brought back with you?"

Chase helped Gem dismount. "It's a long story, Aunt Enid, but the fact is I won her in a poker game. Her name's Gem McBride. Her pa was shot in Virginia City. She didn't seem to have anybody else, so I brought her to you." He shrugged. "Thought it's what you'd want me to do."

Enid Dupre hurried down the steps from the porch and gathered Gem in her arms like a protective mother hen. "Why, you poor child. How terrible for you." Looking up at Chase, she said, "You did the right thing." She turned toward the house, drawing Gem with her, then glanced back over her shoulder. "Aren't you coming in?"

"No, I'd better get on over to Stewart's before Uncle Frank finds out I made a stop in Virginia." He grinned. "I'm not sure what he'll think of my day's winnings."

Enid waved him away as her arm tightened once more around Gem's shoulders. "Don't you pay Chase any mind, girl. You just come on in the house and I'll make us some tea. It'll make you feel better."

Gem fought the rise of tears. She didn't hold much with crying and never had, but it seemed to be all she wanted to do today, especially with this woman's arm around her shoulders and the tender concern in her voice. Gem couldn't remember the last time anyone had been so kind to her. It made her feel warm and safe, and she desperately wanted to feel warm and safe, if only for a little while. Tomorrow she would have to make plans. Tomorrow she would have to decide what she was going to do, where she was going to go, but for now she would let someone take care of her.

Gem awakened in the large, soft bed in the second-story bedroom. At first when she opened her eyes, she thought she must still be dreaming. But no. This was better than a dream. This was real.

She pushed herself up against the pillows at her back and allowed her eyes to drift around the room. Thick rugs covered the hardwood floor. Sheer curtains draped the large window. A pink and cream pitcher and basin sat on a nearby table. Clean fluffy towels were draped over the edge of a chair next to the washstand. The four-poster bed in which she was lying was covered with thick comforters to protect against the cold Montana nights.

Gem had never spent a night in such luxury, and she was reluctant to leave it. She remembered the hot bath that had been prepared for her the night before. The Dupres had their own bathing room, and Enid had given her a bar of the sweetest smelling bath soap. The soap had left Gem's skin and hair feeling so soft and clean. She couldn't remember a nicer feeling.

And then she had been bustled up to this room and put into bed and brought a bowl of hot soup and fresh-baked bread, and before she had known it, she was drifting off to sleep, into a slumber filled with pleasant dreams.

But now it was morning and she had to face reality. She was fifteen years old, her father was dead, and she was penniless and alone. She had no other family, no friends in Montana. Her father had been a drifter and a two-bit gambler. Her mother, dead since Gem was four, was just a faded memory.

Gem drew her knees up to her chin and wrapped her arms around her legs. She stared toward the window where the morning sunlight was spilling onto the rug, but she didn't really see the golden rays as she contemplated her situation. Supposedly, Gem belonged to Chase Dupre now. Her father had put her up in a poker game, and like it or not, Chase had held the winning hand. Technically, she knew he couldn't own her, but still . . . Perhaps it had something to do with pride. She didn't want him to think that a McBride would welch on a bet.

So what she had to do now was pay off her debt. She had to find out just how much she was worth, according to the stakes of the game, and work it off.

Gem threw off the bedcovers, intent on finding her clothes, but they weren't where she'd left them the night before. In their place was a soft pink dress with tiny rosebud buttons up the front. There were even some undergarments and a pair of pretty pink slippers. Her aquamarine eyes widened as she gingerly picked up the dress and rubbed it against her cheek, amazed by the soft texture of the fabric. Almost reverently, she shed the borrowed nightshirt and dressed in the clothes left for her.

There was a brush on the dressing table. As she reached for it, her hand stopped in midair. She stared disbelieving at her reflection in the mirror. Was that her? Was that really Gem McBride looking back at her? If it weren't for the wretched freckles across the bridge of her small nose, the girl staring back at her in those fine clothes was almost pretty, even though her fine, curly, red-gold hair was too short. She leaned closer. Yes, she was almost . . .

Suddenly she snorted at her meandering thoughts. She might be a lot of things but pretty wasn't one of them. She ran the brush hastily through her shorn locks, then hurried out of the bedroom. She had to find Chase before he started his morning chores.

Gem descended the stairs and turned toward the back of the house, following the narrow hallway toward the kitchen and bypassing the cavernous parlor that constituted a major portion of the main floor. Delicious odors of frying bacon and eggs and flapjacks tickled her nose and made her stomach growl as she stepped into the kitchen.

Enid looked up and greeted her. "Good morning, Gem. And would you look at you! Don't you look pretty this morning? I was hoping those clothes would fit. I had an idea you'd be about the size of my Chantal, though she was a mite younger when she wore that dress. I'm so glad they fit."

"Thank you, Mrs. Dupre. The clothes are right pretty, and I thank you for loanin' 'em to me. I was—"

"None of this Mrs. Dupre business. Since you're going to be living here with us, you must call me Aunt Enid. And I'm not loaning the clothes. They're yours."

Living here? Aunt Enid? This was getting out of hand. "I need to speak with your nephew. Is he up yet?"

"Chase? Oh, my word, yes." She jerked her head toward the front of the house. "I think you'll find him in the barn. He's got a mare about to foal, and he's out there first thing every morning." She turned back to the food on the stove. "Why don't you go out and tell him his breakfast is ready, and you can talk over whatever's on your mind."

Gem thanked her as she turned and left the kitchen.

The barn was filled with the sweet scent of hay mingled with the earthier smells of animal dung, sweat, and dust. Gem found Chase in a stall with a pinto mare, her belly distended with the foal she carried. He was rubbing her back and talking softly to her. Gem paused to observe the scene a moment before speaking.

"It won't be long now, girl," he said to the mare. "You're going to have a fine colt with long, wobbly legs and an enormous appetite. Before you know it, he'll be running circles around you." He bent down to check her udder. "Probably tonight."

"How can you tell?"

Chase looked up without apparent surprise at her appearance. "Come here and look at her udder. See how swollen it is and what looks like wax on her teats? That means it won't be long."

As Gem straightened, her eyes met Chase's; she felt a strange sensation in her stomach, as if it had just been twisted and shaken. Her mouth felt dry and numb as she spoke. "I didn't see you again last night." She decided right then that she liked his dark looks and his friendly blue eyes.

"It's a long ride to Stewart's place."

Tiny tingles ran up and down her arm when he spoke. She felt different, almost silly. "Your aunt said to tell you your breakfast is ready."

"I imagine it's your breakfast too. Come on."

He grinned at her as he headed toward the house with long, yard-eating strides.

"Wait!" Gem hurried after him, suddenly remembering why she'd sought him out.

Chase stopped and looked back at her, one eyebrow raised.

"I . . . I needed to talk to you."

"Can't we talk over breakfast?" he asked as he started to turn.

Gem caught him by the arm. "No, please. You don't understand. Your aunt seems to think I'm going to be stayin' here. For a long time, I mean. I think we need to talk."

He waited patiently for her to continue.

"Look, I know you won me in that poker game, and I'm not about to welch on my pa's bet. You just tell me what I need to repay you, and I'll work off the debt. But I can't do that if your aunt is thinking I'm just a guest here."

Chase's smile broadened. His hand reached out to tousle her hair. "Okay, kid. I'll think about it. Now let's go get some breakfast. I'm starved."

The Dupres were a tall family. Gem sat down at the kitchen table, feeling dwarfed and insignificant in their midst. She sat facing Enid with Chase on her left and Frank, who she had met when she and Chase entered the house, on her right. Chase and his uncle attacked the serving platters with relish, piling their plates high with flapjacks and pork and eggs.

"How's your mare doing?" Frank asked before taking his first bite.

Gem didn't listen to his reply. She was busy

studying the family, one by one, beginning with Chase. Yesterday all she'd really noticed about him were his deep-set blue eyes. But there was more to his strikingly handsome appearance than just the startling sapphire shade of his eyes or the dark, expressive brows that capped them. His shaggy, dark brown hair was streaked by the sun, and his oval face with its firm jaw and chiseled nose was bronzed from working outdoors. She already knew the strength of his broad shoulders and muscled arms, hidden beneath the blue shirt he was wearing, but his strength went deeper than that. She sensed it in his warm humor, his confident walk, even in the deep timbre of his voice.

Chase's glance met hers and she felt herself growing warm. She dropped her gaze to her plate and began to eat, not tasting anything she put in her mouth. When she felt the blush fading from her cheeks, she looked up again, this time turning her studious eyes upon Frank Dupre. An older copy of Chase, his face, though just as handsome, was weathered by time and the elements, and his brown hair was thinning and graying at the temples, but his six-foot frame was still straight and strong. His blue eyes were a darker shade; she read in them a calm wisdom. This man would never fear what tomorrow might bring. He had learned to accept life, both the joys and the hardships.

Gem had already experienced the kindness of Enid Dupre. In someone else's face, gray eyes would have seemed cold, even forbidding, but Enid's were warm and loving, and she had the same easy smile of her husband and nephew. She was a thin, wiry woman, much taller than Gem's petite height of five

feet. Here again was a strength and calm assurance
that was foreign to Gem's experience.

"Uncle Frank, Gem here wants it known that
she's not a guest and wants to know what she can do
to repay her debt and earn her keep."

Gem swallowed hard, brought back to the conversation by Chase's words. She looked at him without noticing the humorous twitch at the corner of his
mouth as he fought a smile. Then her gaze darted
quickly past Enid and stopped on Frank.

The older man was staring at her, his brows
drawn tight in a frown. "Don't you worry your head
about that, Gem. Nobody here is thinking of you as a
guest."

Gem clenched her hands beneath the table,
quelling the sudden fear that was making her stomach flip-flop. Just how did they think of her? What
would they require of her to give her her freedom?

"You better make up your mind right now that
you're a part of this family, and this family all works
hard to make the Four Winds a success. You'll earn
your keep as long as you do one thing." The frown
vanished suddenly, replaced by a teasing smile. "You
call me Uncle Frank and we'll get on just fine."

"And I already told you to call me Aunt Enid."

Chase speared another stack of flapjacks. "Guess
that makes me your cousin. Welcome to the Dupre
family, Gem."

"But—" Her gaze moved from one face to the
next. "But you don't know anything about me," she
protested. "I might . . . I might be a thief. I might
rob you blind in the night. You can't just take me in
like . . . like—" She felt tears welling up again and
had to stop talking to bring them under control.

"It's too late, my dear. We've already decided you're to stay here." Gem saw Enid's smile through watery eyes. "We *want* you to stay."

It made no sense. Why should this family, who had so much, bring her into their midst and make her a part of them? People didn't do that sort of thing. She shouldn't trust their kindness. There had to be a reason for it. Yet, for some reason, she wanted to trust them. She wanted to be a part of their family, of this ranch. She wanted it more than anything she'd ever wanted in her life.

"I'll stay," she answered softly. "But I won't promise for how long," she added with a determined, independent lift of her chin.

Frank chuckled and turned his attention back to his breakfast. "That's fair enough. You try us out for a while. I think we'll grow on you."

It might have taken a long time for them to grow on her. In fact, it might never have happened. She was thinking she would leave the next day. She was just going to forget the wager her father had made and get out while she could. She'd never lived in a home, not since her mother died. She'd never stayed in one place very long. How could she allow herself to be lulled into staying? She didn't belong in their fine house and to be treated like one of them. She was Gem McBride, daughter of Lucky McBride, an orphan with only as much education as she'd been able to pick up from the few books she'd read. Oh, she'd worked on making her speech sound nice, but when she forgot herself she could swear as good as any trail hand. No, she didn't belong with the Dupres.

She was going to leave. She was planning how and when. And she would have left, too, except for one small complication. She fell in love with the Dupres that very same night. No, not the Dupres. It was Chase Dupre who stole her heart that second night at Four Winds.

2

Chase's mare went into labor near midnight. He had been out to check on her several times through-out the evening. Gem knew because, unable to sleep, she was watching from her bedroom window. When he didn't return from the barn as he had on previous trips, her curiosity got the better of her and she followed after him.

The June night was chilly, but inside the barn, the animals and hay made it warm. The pinto was lying on her side, breathing heavily. Every so often she would fling her head back and nip at her swollen side. Chase was hunkered down behind her, watching and waiting.

"The foal, it's coming?" Gem asked as his gaze lifted to meet hers.

"Should be soon."

"May I stay?"

"Sure. But come around and stay in the corner. Sometimes it makes a mare nervous to be watched when she's foaling."

Gem did as she was told, moving silently to the far side of the stall. She folded her legs beneath her and settled into the clean straw that was strewn over the floor.

"Easy, Kansas," Chase crooned soothingly to the mare.

"Is that her name? Kansas?"

He nodded.

The minutes ticked away in silence. Gem didn't know what made Chase start talking to her. Perhaps it was to break the waiting. Perhaps it was the warm confines of the stall that made it seem as if they were the only two people in the world. Whatever it was, she was glad for it. She liked the sound of his voice.

"Uncle Frank was my father's brother, and Aunt Enid was my mother's sister. Uncle Frank and Aunt Enid met at my parents' wedding. Aunt Enid was supposed to marry someone else—" A shadow passed over his face, as if he'd just remembered a very unpleasant thought, then it vanished as he continued speaking. "But she ran away with my uncle Frank a few days later. The four of them went to California to seek their fortunes. They didn't find much gold, but they found out it could be profitable selling cattle to hungry miners."

Chase grinned as he glanced over at her. "I used to love to hear them tell stories about those years in California. It was quite the place then. Wild and lawless, Aunt Enid calls it, but I can tell she liked parts of it too. I was born in San Francisco, but we moved up to Oregon Territory before I was old

enough to remember. My father—his name was
Jean—he and Uncle Frank built their herd by trading
one fat cow for two thin, worn-out ones to folks
coming across the trail to California and Oregon.
After the gold strikes were made up here in Montana,
they decided to bring their families and build a ranch
here. My father had been up to this Madison River
country and liked it. Thought it would make good
cattle country." He stroked the mare's side gently.
"My mother never could have any more children
after me, but Aunt Enid had a son and a daughter, my
cousins, Paul and Chantal."

"Chantal . . . Aunt Enid told me these used to
be her clothes I'm wearing. Where is she now?"

"They all died in the winter of sixty-six."

She watched his face in the yellow glow of the
lantern hanging from a nail above the stall door.
There was sorrow but no bitterness.

"My mother—her name was Denise—she was
the prettiest woman you ever laid eyes on, gentle and
fun, but she wasn't as strong as Aunt Enid. When we
all took sick with the fever, she was the first to go. I've
always thought my father just died so he could be
with her."

Gem had never heard anyone talk that way
before. She couldn't imagine people loving someone
so much they'd want to die when the other did. And
then she found herself thinking maybe she did understand it when Chase glanced in her direction and
smiled, and she felt the strange fluttering of her heart.

Chase couldn't remember the last time he'd
talked so much in one stretch. He wasn't sure what it
was about Gem, but she sure had a way of getting to

him. He couldn't help wondering what kind of life she had lived, with a father like Lucky McBride and all. He was sorry things had happened the way they did, but at least now things would go better for her. Gem would be good for Aunt Enid, too. His aunt had always needed a girl to mother. And the kid was in need of some mothering from the looks of things.

Gem offered him a hesitant smile, and he returned it. Come to think of it, it might be fun to have her around the place. She had grit, that was for certain. And she was kind of cute, now that she was all cleaned up. Chase had done most of his growing up without other children around. It might be fun having a little cousin. He could be on the teaching end, instead of always the student. Yes, it just might have been a good thing all around, his trip into Virginia City that morning.

"It's coming."

"What?"

"The foal," Chase answered softly. "It's coming."

It took her a moment to pull her gaze away from him and turn her attention to the laboring mare. The legs and nose came first, disguised in the membrane that had nurtured the foal for months. In what seemed like ages but was only a matter of minutes, the birthing was over. Kansas lifted her head to look back at the foal and, moments later, was on her feet, sniffing and prodding the newborn. The foal's nose broke through the membrane.

"Look!" Gem exclaimed, excited now. "It's a pinto, just like Kansas. Oh, it's beautiful, Chase. Look at it!" The black and white foal was wet from nose to tail and looked to be all head and legs, but Gem thought it the most beautiful, wonderful thing she'd ever seen.

Chase was watching Gem's unabashed excitement. "You like it, huh?"

"Oh, yes."

"Then it's yours if you promise to take good care of it."

"Mine?" She looked up at him with rounded eyes. "Oh, Chase, I couldn't. I mean . . . you see, I don't—"

He grinned that grin of his and reached down to ruffle her unruly curls as he'd done once before. "It's okay, kid. I want you to have it. Think of it as a gift from your new cousin."

The summer stretched out before Gem, filled with promise in her new life. She was happier than she'd ever been before—and more miserable than she'd ever been either. She was fifteen and in love for the first time, but to Chase she was just a "kid" with raucous curls, a new cousin to tease and laugh at and with.

From the start, though, he was good to her. He taught her how to ride like a cowboy, how to train a horse to cut out a steer from the herd. He showed her how to read signs on the trail and how to judge the weather before a sudden summer storm came. He even tried to teach her how to shoot, first with his Colt Peacemaker .45 and then with his Winchester .44-.40, but Gem didn't think she'd ever be very good with a gun, no matter how many lessons he gave her. She just couldn't concentrate on the target when he had his arms around her, his chin nearly resting on her shoulder, his breath in her ear. To make things worse, he never knew what his nearness was doing to her. He just teased her about her bad eye.

The only time she ever bettered Chase was in poker. He called her the luckiest gal with a deck of cards he'd ever seen. He never did catch on that she was cheating him blind. Lucky might not have taught her much else, but he'd taught her how to read and write and how to cheat at cards. Always said it helped to know how to cheat so you could catch someone else at it. And while she could have said a lot of bad things about her father, she could say honestly that she'd never known him to cheat in a real game of cards. It was ironic that he had died an accused cheater. If he'd cheated, they wouldn't have been so broke all the time because there were few men better at cards than Lucky McBride had been.

As for the other Dupres, she cared for them deeply. Gem wanted very much to please Enid. Enid was an honest, hardworking woman, and she loved Gem and Gem knew it. She would have liked to be the kind of daughter Enid had lost, but she just couldn't do it. When she tried to help Enid with the cooking, she learned that even her limited skills with the Peacemaker outshone her cooking talents. And she wasn't much of a lady either. Enid made her several pretty dresses and gave her more of Chantal's things that had been packed away for years, but Gem always felt more comfortable in the soft leather skirt, split for riding astride, which was one of the Dupres' earliest gifts to her. Gem didn't have time for ribbons and frills, not when she wanted to be spending her time with Chase and he was out working the range.

On the other hand, it was easy to please Frank.

His passion was for the horses at Four Winds. When he saw her with Kansas's filly, which Gem christened Wichita, he knew he'd met a kindred spirit. Whether he was doctoring or training, Gem loved to help him with his beloved animals. She could learn more about horses in ten minutes with Frank Dupre than most people ever knew about anything.

In addition to the Dupre family, she became a favorite with the cowboys who worked the Four Winds range, kind of a mascot, and even earned herself an admirer or two amongst them, although she paid their flirtations no heed. From Pike Matthews, a crusty old cowboy who'd been with the Dupres from the start of the Four Winds ranch, she learned how to crack a bullwhip and lasso a fence post, and Teddy Hubbs spent a few evenings giving her lessons on the mouth organ.

Except for Chase's blindness when it came to her budding woman's love for him, there was only one thing that marred Gem's first month with the Dupres. Powell Daniels. She wouldn't likely ever forget the first time they met.

It was hotter than Hades in the middle of July. Gem had finished her chores around the house and had quickly tossed a saddle over a horse's back and gone in search of Chase. Instead of Chase, she met up with Powell near a creek that ran out of the mountains and cut a winding trail toward the Madison River on the other side of the valley. She had dismounted and was taking a drink when she heard his voice.

"What have we here?"

She gasped and jumped to her feet.

He was an enormous man, not as tall as Chase

but heavier with massive chest and arms. His bulk dwarfed the sorrel gelding he was riding. His hazel eyes narrowed as he stared at her over his prominent nose.

"Who are you? What are you doing on Four Winds?" she demanded, taking the offensive.

"That's just what I was about to ask you, little lady." He swung down from his horse as he spoke.

Gem edged closer to her mount, wondering if she could reach her rifle. "I live here."

"You?" He raised his bushy eyebrows. "Now, I wouldn't forget seein' a pretty little thing like you here before."

"And I don't remember seein' you either." Instinct told her that this man had seen what Chase had failed to see, that she was a young woman and not a child. She didn't like the gleam in his eyes as he stepped surreptitiously closer.

His beefy hand fell onto the back of her horse's saddle. "I was just on my way to see Chase. If you're stayin' there, why don't we ride together?" He showed her a crooked grin. "My pa would be won-derin' where my manners went. I ain't even told you my name. I'm Powell Daniels of the Big Pine. We're neighbors, little lady."

Somehow she knew he wasn't a friend of the Dupre family. She sensed he was a dangerous man. She was frightened by the way his eyes perused her, but she wasn't about to show her fear. "Take your hand off my horse, mister."

"No call to be snappish, little girl." He edged closer.

"I'm warning you—"

He laughed, and his face darkened. "What is it

you think I want? Oh . . . So that's it. You think I'd waste my time with a skinny little thing like you?" He laughed again, softer this time. "Come to think of it, maybe it'd be interestin' at that." He moved to caress her face.

Without forethought, her hand shot out, and she slapped him hard.

His eyes narrowed. "Why, you little—"

"You touch me and I'll kill you." She had no weapon except fury, but she didn't speak idly. She meant what she said.

He seemed to consider her warning, then stepped back from her. He raised his hands in a sign of surrender. "We'll let it pass this time, little girl, but I'll be around. Powell Daniels never takes a no. Not from any man or woman." He grinned wickedly.

At just that moment, Chase cantered over the rise and pulled his stallion to a sudden halt on the other side of the stream. His eyes darkened when he recognized Powell.

"What are you doing here, Daniels?" Chase's voice was as cold as water in a mountain spring.

Gem knew it. Powell was no friend of the Dupres.

"I was just talkin' to this pretty little gal here. She says she's stayin' at Four Winds. Now, Chase, if that's true, it just ain't right to not let the rest of us lonely boys know. There's a whole mess of fellas who would've been by to say howdy and welcome her to the valley."

"You stay away from Gem." Chase's horse forged the creek as he spoke. "In fact, stay away from Four Winds altogether, and we'll all be happier."

"No call to be unfriendly, Chase." Powell's ruddy face belied the calm protest. He glanced back at Gem, impaling her with his hazel eyes. "We'll meet again, Miss Gem. I promise. We'll become *good* friends."

"When cows can fly. I'd rather be friends with hogs in their wallow than with the likes of you."

With her last remark, she had succeeded in making him angry. She could see it in his eyes. "I promise you," he said in a low voice so only she could hear, "you won't be able to avoid me forever. There'll come a time and a place for us to settle this."

Gem stepped back from him as if he'd struck her, suddenly frightened by the threatening tone of his voice. She didn't know what she could have done to avoid it, but she knew she had made a powerful enemy.

With surprising quickness for a man of his size, Powell remounted his gelding and rode away from the creek without another word.

Chase reined in beside her. "Look out for him, Gem. He's no good." He waited while she swung up onto her horse. "There's not a decent man left at Big Pine since Rod left, and how Josh Daniels ever sired him I'll never know."

"Rodney Daniels? He's related to Powell?" She couldn't believe it. Rodney, who worked for the Dupres, was a wiry, slender-built cowboy, maybe five inches taller than Gem, with blond hair, laughing brown eyes, and a bright smile.

"Powell is Rod's older brother. Rod must take after his mother in looks, God rest her pitiful soul, but Powell is the spitting image of his father." Chase turned his horse toward the ranch house. "Just remember, except for Rod, the Daniels bunch is a bad lot. We put up with them during roundups, but if I had it my way, I'd tell them the next time they set foot on Four Winds I'd greet them with rifle fire. Uncle Frank says we need to be neighborly. He just doesn't know what I know about Josh Daniels and his son."

This was a side of Chase she'd never seen. There was more than just distrust or anger in his voice. There was hate, and it frightened her. She remembered how fast he was with a gun, and she wondered if Powell Daniels might be faster.

Gem's gaze moved to follow the departing horse and rider. "I'll be careful."

It would be many years before Gem understood the bad blood that ran between the Dupre and the Daniels families, and she would see much of it shed before the hate had run its course.

3

Gem's unpleasant run-in with Powell was soon forgotten amid the frantic preparations for the annual Four Winds barbecue and dance. As the big day drew closer, the men tried to absent themselves from the house as early as possible before Aunt Enid could give them one more job to do. Gem didn't mind helping, but she grew more nervous with each passing day. She'd never been to such a grand party. She knew she wouldn't fit in, yet she couldn't disappoint Aunt Enid by saying she'd rather not be there, especially when Enid presented her with a special new gown for the party.

The day of the barbecue dawned with clear skies and the promise of blistering heat. Guests started arriving before noon. Gem stood between Frank and Enid, greeting folks and being introduced to practically everyone who lived within a hundred miles—or at least it seemed that way. Gem felt shy and unsure of herself. She was wearing the gown of fine lawn, honeysuckle yellow in color, that Enid had made for her. The matching satin slippers pinched her toes; she sorely missed her comfortable riding skirt and familiar boots. She would have much preferred to be out tending cattle than at this party where she felt like a fish out of water.

She kept hoping things would get better, that she would soon feel more at ease, but the promise of a miserable day to come was fulfilled with the arrival of the Mills family from Virginia City.

Enid made the introductions. "Mr. Mills, this is Gem McBride. She's come to live with us, and we couldn't be happier about it. She's like the niece we never had. Gem, this is Jedidiah Mills. He's an attorney in Virginia City."

"I'm pleased to meet you, Miss McBride." Mr. Mills nodded formally to Gem. "And this is my wife, Christina, and our lovely daughter, Carol Anne. I expect you girls will become good friends."

Gem's eyes met Carol Anne's large brown ones and knew instantly that he was wrong. Carol Anne was a beautiful, tall young woman, perhaps two or three years older than Gem, with high cheekbones, a lovely pale complexion, and a rosy mouth. Her long brunette tresses were pulled back from her face, then fell in a luxurious cascade of waves down her back. Her smile was mocking as she acknowledged the introduction.

"Gem McBride? Why, you must be the little waif that Chase won in the poker game." Her voice was soft and cultured, belying the sting of her words. "All of Virginia laughed about it for days. I had no idea you had stayed on at Four Winds. But the Dupres are such charitable people, aren't they? And, of course, Chase has always taken in strays."

Carol Anne moved off in a flurry of petticoats, leaving Gem to stare after her in surprise and then fury. Her temper didn't improve when she witnessed Carol Anne, moments later, strolling through the yard, parasol shading her delicate skin, her arm linked with Chase's.

The afternoon crept by at a snail's pace for Gem. Carol Anne was never away from Chase. She was always touching his arm or his hand, always gazing up at him with adoring eyes, a sweet smile curving her lips. Even in the day's terrible heat, Carol Anne appeared cool and unruffled, while Gem felt sweaty and sticky and terribly lonely.

Gem slipped away from the partyers late in the afternoon, seeking solace in the corral with Kansas and Wichita.

"She's a witch," Gem whispered in the filly's ear as she stroked Wichita's neck. "You'd think he'd be able to see through her simperin' and flirtin'. I'd've thought he was smarter than that."

Kansas snorted and bobbed her head as if in agreement.

"Oh, Chase," Gem mocked in a high-pitched voice, fluttering her eyes, "I just *love* comin' to your barbecue every year. I wish Father would bring us to visit more often, but it's such a long buggy ride and he's *so* busy in town. And, of course, I just couldn't ride out here all alone. It just wouldn't be proper." Her face grew dark as she turned away in a huff. "Stupidest thing I've ever seen, goin' all mushy-eyed over some man, and him standin' there, drinkin' it all in." She hiked her skirts above her knees and crawled through the fence rails.

Walking back toward the house, she heard laughter coming from the bunkhouse. The friendly sounds drew her closer. She paused at the door and looked inside. Several cowboys were seated around a long table, playing cards.

Rodney Daniels looked up just then. "We got us some men here that think they know how to play poker. Care to sit in, Gem?"

Gem glanced over her shoulder at the crowd of people spilling out of the house and spreading over the lawn. She wished she belonged there. She wanted to belong wherever Chase was. But she didn't and she might as well accept it, at least for now.

"Sure. I'd love to sit in."

Chase was bored silly by all Carol Anne's chatter. He wished he could find some way to slip from her grasp, but she had stuck to him like glue all day long. He looked around, squinting his eyes against the glare of the hot sun. Another group of riders approached the house. He stiffened as they rode nearer. It was Josh and Powell Daniels and some of the men from the Big Pine spread.

He turned his head, searching out his aunt and uncle. They, too, had seen the new arrivals and were walking together to greet them. He watched as Frank shook hands with Josh and felt a hot rage building inside his chest. He should have told his uncle about Josh a long time ago, but Enid wouldn't hear of it. At the time, Frank was still sick with the fever and lying near death. Enid said it should be forgotten. Even once Frank was well, she made Chase promise not to speak of it. She said if Frank knew it would only make trouble, and it was better left alone.

But Chase hadn't forgotten . . .

"Chase?" Carol Anne's voice pulled him away from the old unpleasant memories. "I would so like another one of your aunt's delicious ices." She paused artfully, then tugged gently on his arm. "Would you be good enough to get me one?" She fluttered her lashes once again. "I'd be ever so grateful."

"Sure, Carol Anne. You wait right here."

Glad for an excuse to get away from her, even for only a brief respite, Chase headed for the long tables set up beneath the tall shade trees. One of the young Stewart boys was lingering near the food, keeping a watchful eye out for his mother. Chase grinned at the red-haired lad as he snatched up another tiny sandwich and shoved it into his mouth.

"Say, Todd."

Todd Stewart gulped down the sandwich guiltily as he heard his name spoken so close beside him.

"How about takin' one of these ices over to Miss Mills." He pointed. "Over there on the lawn beneath that big box elder. You tell her I'll be back in a minute. Just need to talk to a few folks."

But he didn't head toward any of the guests. Instead, he escaped to the back of the house for a quiet smoke. Usually he enjoyed this barbecue. Come to think of it, usually he enjoyed Carol Anne. At least, he'd always thought he enjoyed her. Had she changed that much or had he? He wasn't sure. All he knew was she bored him. And he was smart enough to know she only had one thing on her mind. Marriage, with a capital M. Someday she might turn into a fine wife for somebody . . . but not for him. He had yet to meet the woman who would make him think of marriage.

And until he did, he'd prefer the honest, good-natured company of a girl like Gem to a flirtatious little fool like Carol Anne.

"Hiding out, boy, or can I join you?"

Chase looked up, nodding at his uncle. "Sure. Come on and set a spell."

Frank rolled a smoke, then sat down next to Chase. He struck a match against the sole of his boot, lighting his cigarette with thoughtful puffs. "It is a mite quieter here. Never did understand why women-folk enjoy such things."

For several minutes, they sat side by side on the back steps, smoking and staring up at the mountains that rose gracefully toward the pale blue sky. There was a comfortable companionship shared between uncle and nephew. Neither felt the need to fill the silence with talk unless there was something that needed to be said.

That something came from Frank. "I've been meaning to speak to you about the ranch."

Chase turned his head to look at the serious set of his uncle's face.

"Four Winds is growing. We've done a good job these past few years. Got us some good hands and the weather's been good to the cows. We keep getting top dollar for our herd. But if we're going to keep on growing, we're going to have to bring in more cows, build this place up. We've got more than five hundred thousand acres of prime grassland out there. Room for a lot more cows than we're running. I'd like you to take a look down Texas way." The grin he cast toward his nephew made deep ridges in his leatherlike skin. "Be good for you, boy. Time you saw more of this country than just this valley, anyhow. Traveling makes a better man of you."

"You mean you're not coming with me?"

"*Nooo*." Frank drew out the word as he shook his head. "Enid would have my head if I left her here to watch out for things alone for so long. Not that she couldn't do it." He chuckled and slapped his knee. "That woman of mine could run this whole territory by herself if she took it into her mind she wanted to." He sobered. "No, I want you to do this on your own, Chase. Take your time. Stay a year if you want. Take a look see at some other spreads. Then find the best darn bunch of cows you can and bring them back to Four Winds."

It was a lot to think about. He'd never really considered leaving Four Winds, other than on the cattle drive each fall. But the idea quickly grew on him. A chance to see the cattle kingdoms in Texas. It was too good to pass up. "I won't let you down, Uncle Frank."

"Lord, boy. I know that." Frank patted Chase's back as he turned his gaze back on the mountains. "You know, Chase, I keep calling you boy, but no one knows better than me that you're a man. This ranch is as much yours as it is mine. Your father would've been right proud to know he's got such a son."

Once again, they fell into thoughtful silence, the bond grown closer between them.

* * *

"Read 'em and weep, fellas." Gem spread her cards across the rough pine table, grinning from ear to ear.

"I say we don't let her play anymore," Teddy Hubbs grumbled, but she knew he was only jesting.

As the afternoon had turned into evening and the air had cooled, Gem had almost forgotten Chase and the clinging Carol Anne. She was in her element here, among the cowboys, cards in hand. She didn't have to worry about saying something that would announce to the world she was less than a lady. She didn't have to worry about embarrassing Enid or Frank. These men were her friends. They liked her just the way she was, and they made her feel good. They made her forget Chase and . . .

Well, she could almost forget.

"Hey, Jimmy, this is where the real action is."

Gem looked up as Powell and two other men entered the bunkhouse. His eyes latched onto her immediately.

"Are you lookin' for a couple more players?" Powell asked her.

"Not if you're one of them." There was no mistaking her feelings in the tone of her voice. She hadn't liked him that day by the stream, and she didn't like him any better now. She'd been glad she'd been able to avoid meeting up with him for so long. Now here he was at Four Winds, ruining the only good time she'd had all day. At least here she wasn't alone.

Powell chuckled. "Hey there, little darlin'. What kinda way is that to treat your guests?" He grabbed a stool and pulled it up to the table beside Gem as his eyes slid suggestively over the front of her gown. "Deal me in, honey."

"Watch your mouth, Powell," Rodney warned.

Powell's jaw hardened as he swung his head around. "What's the matter, baby brother? Have you staked a claim here? I'd say she'd need a real man, not some mealymouthed punk without enough sense to live with his own kind."

"Daniels, why don't you go get yourself something to eat and drink?" Pike Matthews suggested calmly, but his blue eyes flashed a warning. "There's plenty of things going on here today to keep everyone happy. If you don't like our company, I suggest you go find somewhere else to play cards."

Powell ignored Pike as he turned toward Gem once again. "And how about you, honey? You don't want me to leave, do you?" His arm went around her shoulders. "Give me a kiss and show 'em we're friends."

Rodney flew across the table with such fury no one was prepared for it. He knocked Powell backward off his stool and the two brothers rolled across the bunkhouse floor. There was a moment of shocked silence before the other two cowhands from Big Pine began swinging, and suddenly the bunkhouse was in an uproar. Gem stumbled backward against the wall, watching the fray with wide eyes.

Rodney had had the advantage of surprise over his larger, older brother when the fight began, but that advantage was quickly slipping away, giving ground to Powell's superior size and strength. Powell punched Rodney several times in the face, then struck him in the midsection, sending Rodney sailing across the room. As the older Daniels stalked across the bunkhouse, intent on bludgeoning his brother a few more times with his meaty fists, Gem picked up a nearby stool. Without conscious thought, she went after him with it. Every ounce of strength she possessed was used as she brought it crashing down on his head. Powell stopped and turned toward her, his look one of dumb surprise. Then his eyes rolled back in his head, and he crumpled to the floor like a house of cards.

Gem was nearly as surprised as Powell had been. She stared down at his still form, not yet believing she had felled him. Then, with a wicked gleam in her eye, she tightened her grip on the stool. She was filled with power. She would show those no-good cowpokes from the Big Pines. She would smash every one of them over their thick heads. She would leave them all lying on the floor like sacks of flour. She turned quickly . . . and stepped right into a swinging fist.

The world tipped and she went sliding off of it into darkness.

"Gem. Gem, are you all right? Open your eyes, Gem."

She heard Chase's voice calling to her. It was all part of a lovely dream. They'd been dancing, the two of them, twirling and twirling and twirling, and he'd told her he loved her and she'd told him she loved him, and everything was beautiful and fine and wonderful.

"Gem. Come on. Look at me."

She forced her eyes open and looked into his worried sapphire gaze. "You don't really like her, do you? And you're not in love with her either, are you,

Chase?" She sighed and offered up a dizzy smile. The room beyond him was still spinning crazily, just like when they were dancing.

"What?"

"You wouldn't marry a girl like her, would you?"

"Marry who? What are you talking about?"

His face was fading from view. "You'd rather marry me, wouldn't you, Chase?"

"Marry you?" There was a lengthy pause as he considered her question. Then he replied in a tender, amused voice, "Sure, kid. I'll marry you." His hand ruffled her hair. "If you still want me when you grow up, I'll marry you."

4

Four Winds Ranch, Montana, 1880

Gem watched the orange-red sun slip slowly behind the western horizon. Darkness settled quickly over the house and yard. She pushed a stray wisp of hair from her face as she turned and entered the house.

Seated near a lamp, her mending in her lap, Aunt Enid looked up when she heard the door close. "No sign of them?"

Gem shook her head.

"We might as well turn in then. They won't be back tonight."

"Do you suppose they got it?" Gem walked over to the window and pushed aside the curtains for one last look. "We can't afford to lose any more cows to that damn bear."

"Gem—" came Enid's gentle rebuke.

"Sorry, Aunt Enid." She did her best not to swear, but sometimes . . .

Enid laid her mending in the basket beside her chair and got wearily to her feet. "Your standing there won't help them trap and kill it. Let's get to bed. With no men around the place again, we'll have ourselves a busy day tomorrow." She kissed Gem's cheek, then headed for the stairs.

"I'll put out the lights and be right up," Gem said as she let the curtains fall closed. "Say good night to Uncle Frank for me."

"I'll do that, dear."

Gem listened as Enid's footsteps faded. She heard the bedroom door close. The house was draped in silence. She sighed deeply and went to turn down the lamp. If only she could have gone with the men this morning. She hated the waiting, not knowing what was happening. She longed for the chance to see that bear killed. She would have liked a chance to shoot it herself. The grizzly had slaughtered livestock up and down the valley all last summer and again this spring. The men had tracked it for days on end, but always it eluded them. A few men had seen it up close. Only one man, Charlie Brothers, had been lucky enough to survive the encounter, and he'd been left with only one leg.

Gem climbed the stairs in the dark. She could hear soft voices coming from Enid and Frank's room at the end of the hall. Poor Uncle Frank. It was hard on him, being unable to ride out with the others. Her heart nearly broke every time she saw him, yet she never heard him complain.

She turned into her own bedroom, pausing to lean against the closed door. As she stood there, the rising moon topped the eastern mountain peaks, sending silvery moonlight to filter through her windows. She walked across the room and sat in a window seat, resting her chin on folded arms. Her eyes fell on the silent bunkhouse. Again she sighed.

Unbidden, the memory returned. The night of the barbecue. The card game in the bunkhouse. Powell Daniels. The fight. She saw it all again with such clarity. And then, as always, she heard Chase saying, "Sure, kid. I'll marry you."

She had clung to that promise when he'd left for Texas a few days later. She'd been clinging to it for nearly five years. She knew it was foolish. She realized now that he'd just been humoring her, that he'd seen her as a mere child. And he was right. She *had* been a child. She should have outgrown her infatuation for him after all these years. All these years without seeing him. All these years without hearing from him. But she hadn't outgrown it. She had become a woman while he was away, and her love for him had grown too.

"Damn you, Chase Dupre," she swore under her breath. She closed her eyes as tears welled up in them. "Damn you." Sometimes being angry helped a little. Sometimes . . .

One letter. One letter in five years. He was staying a little longer in Texas, it had said. Don't worry about him, it had said. He would have a surprise for them when he returned, it had said. But still he hadn't come.

Gem rose from the window seat, beginning to unbutton her blouse as she moved toward the bed. She had just slipped out of her skirt and was reaching for her nightgown when she heard the galloping hooves and whoops of the voices.

They got the bear, she thought as she whirled around and raced to the window, pulling on her nightgown as she moved.

There were three of them, all carrying torches. As she watched, one of them rode into the barn, then rode out again, this time without his torch. A second man threw his up into the opening of the loft. She watched in disbelief as the third man added his torch to the already flaming barn.

"Aunt Enid!" She raced from her room and down the hall, throwing open their bedroom door before her. "The vandals! They're here!" she blurted, then turned without waiting for a response.

Gem flew down the stairs, pausing only long enough to grab a rifle from the case just outside Frank's study. She was drawing a bead on one of the men even as she came out the door. She fired. She thought she saw him jerk to one side, as if struck in the shoulder, but he didn't fall from the horse. She swung the rifle toward a second man just as a bullet whizzed past her ear. She dropped to the porch.

"Let's go!" one of them shouted.

She fired one more shot as they galloped into the night.

Gem scrambled to her feet and ran toward the barn. Orange tongues were already licking the sides of the window in the loft, and dense smoke belched skyward. She pulled the barn door open wide, coughing as the choking smoke filled her lungs. She paused only a second before plunging inside. She had to get the horses out while there was still time.

The frightened cries of the trapped animals filled the barn. Gem, ignoring her own fear, grabbed a blanket and threw it over the head of the horse in the first stall.

"Easy, boy. Easy."

She led him out of his stall, turning him loose as soon as they reached the barn door, then hurried back inside.

In just those precious few moments it had taken her to free one horse, the fire had grown in intensity. She had to move faster. There were still three more horses in the barn. One of them was Wichita. She had to save Wichita.

Her eyes burned and tears ran down her cheeks as she stumbled toward the pinto's stall. Wichita's black eyes rolled in her head, and she reared and struck at the stall door, then kicked the wall with her hind feet. Gem tried to open the door, but flying hooves kept her back.

"Easy, Wichita. Let me in, girl," she cried against the crackle and snap of the fire.

She jerked open the door and quickly entered. She grabbed the mare's halter with one hand and was pulled off the ground as Wichita reared once more. Desperately, she hung on as a sharp, tearing pain shot through her left arm and shoulder. She gritted her teeth and ignored the pain as she swung the blanket over the pinto's head with her other hand.

"Come on, girl. We've got to get out of here. Easy now. Come on, Wichita. Come on."

An arch of flames lit the doorway. Gem felt terror nipping at her, telling her to stay back, to hide in the barn, not to go any further. Panic swelled, but she fought it off and ran toward the flaming doorway, leading the mare beside her. Enid was waiting outside

when she got there. Rod's wife, Katie, stood not far behind her, clutching her crying child in her arms.

"Take Wichita. I'm going back for—"

Enid's hand grabbed her arm. "You're not going back in there, Gem," she shouted. "There's nothing more you can do."

"But the horses—"

"It's too late, Gem. You can't go back."

Gem turned to look at the barn. The doorway was obscured by flames. Fiery fingers clawed through the roof of the barn, destroying everything within reach. The terrified cries of the two trapped animals mingled with the roar of the growing fire.

Enid's hand pulled her further away from the inferno. "There's nothing more we can do," she repeated.

The three women retreated to a safe distance and watched it burn.

She didn't sleep all night. Sometime after midnight, when they were certain a wind wouldn't rise and spread the fire to the bunkhouse or the main house, when there was little else for the dying fire to consume, Enid had retired to her room, insisting that Gem do the same. But Gem couldn't sleep. She paced her room until nearly dawn.

Finally she heated some water and filled the tub. She bathed away the soot and ash that covered her from head to toe, hoping she could also wash away the anguish, the frustration, and the anger that filled her heart and soul. Yes, she was angry. Angry at her own helplessness. Angry at the men who had wrought such senseless destruction. Angry at Chase for once again not being there when they needed him.

In her room once more, she slipped into a clean, white nightgown and returned to the window seat. She pulled her long red-gold tresses over her shoulder and began brushing out the snarls. But her thoughts drew her eyes back to the smoldering remains of the barn.

She was certain in her heart that Powell had led the vandals. Anytime there was trouble in this valley, he was sure to be a part of it. One day she would catch him at it. Powell Daniels seemed to live to make trouble, especially for anyone at Four Winds. He'd been a thorn in her side since the first day they met, and some day she would bring him low.

Her eyes seemed to focus once again, and she saw the two horsemen loping toward the ranch house. In the distance, they were just shadows in the pewter light of early dawn.

"I'll be horsewhipped if you'll get away with it twice, Powell Daniels," she muttered, jumping to her feet. "I'll be damned if I do."

She didn't waste time to pull on a robe over her nightgown. They wouldn't have a chance to burn the house like they had the barn. She ran from her room and down the stairs, picking up the rifle just as she had before. Only this time she wasn't going to give them the chance to shoot back at her. She went to a window in the parlor and tossed it open. Then she leveled the weapon expertly at her shoulder and drew aim on the first rider just as light began peaking over the mountain tops.

*   *   *

Chase had ridden most of the night to get home. He'd been impatient to reach Four Winds now that he was so close. But instead of feeling the joy he had expected, he was alert to trouble. He had smelled the smoke long before he could see the charred remains of the barn. He had been afraid he would find even worse. He'd been afraid it would be the house. He began to relax now that he could see the house was safe.

The last thing in the world Chase would have expected at that moment was to have his hat shot from his head.

"What the—" He reined in abruptly.

"Don't bother to come any closer," a woman's voice shouted from inside. "Just turn those horses around and ride out, and we'll forget you were ever here."

"Who is that, *amigo*?" Julio asked.

Chase glanced quickly over at his friend, then back toward the house. "I don't know, but I mean to find out." He nudged his horse forward.

Dust shot up in front of them as a bullet ricocheted off the ground.

"I mean it, mister. The next one has your name on it. Now ride out."

Chase frowned. Where was Aunt Enid? Uncle Frank? He glanced toward the bunkhouse. All was quiet. Even with the shooting, no one had come running out. Turning his head to the right, he glanced again at the burned barn, pieces of wood still smoldering. Something was terribly wrong.

He raised himself in his saddle. "I'm here to see Frank Dupre," he yelled back. "Where is he?"

There was a moment's hesitation. When the voice replied, it was softer. "What business do you have with him?"

"He's my uncle. My name is Chase Dupre."

Chase saw the movement of the curtains as the rifle was withdrawn from the parlor window. A moment later the door opened, but whoever stood there was still hidden in the shadows of the house. He urged his mount slowly forward, and this time there was no rifle fire to stop him. Still some distance from the house, he dismounted and stood beside his horse, waiting to see what would happen.

She stepped out onto the porch, a pixie vision in white, strawberry-gold hair swirling around her shoulders. Suddenly she dropped the rifle that was hanging at her side and came running across the yard. She was in his arms before he knew what was happening.

"Chase, you're home. You're really home," he heard her whisper as her arms encircled his neck.

And then she was kissing him. For a moment, he stood stiffly, confused and uncertain. Then, almost of their own volition, his arms tightened around her back, and he drew her closer, savoring the sweetness of her lips. Even as he wondered who she was, he allowed himself to enjoy her unbridled emotions.

He sensed a sudden shyness as her lips slipped away from him. She took a step backward, looking up at him, a quivering smile on her pink mouth. "We've missed you, Chase."

His eyes widened in surprise. "Holy smoke!" It was Gem McBride.

Her red-blonde hair fell nearly to her hips, rippling in gentle waves instead of the short, tight curls he remembered. The freckles had disappeared from her pert nose. Now her complexion was alabaster clear, accentuating her tip-tilted aquamarine eyes and the rosy pink of her heart-shaped mouth. She was still tiny, no more than five feet tall and looking as if a strong wind could blow her from here and gone. But beneath her white nightgown, he could see there was nothing left of the child he remembered.

"You grew up while I was gone," he said, feeling stupid even as the words left his mouth.

"I had to," she answered, blushing prettily. "You said you'd marry me when I did, so I had to grow up."

"Marry her, *amigo*?"

As Gem's eyes moved toward Julio, Chase turned around. "Julio, this is my . . . cousin."

Julio swung down from the back of his black stallion and removed his hat as he stepped forward. "I don't believe you ever told me about her, Chase. If so, I would have brought your cattle up without you long before now." He took Gem's hand and raised it to his lips, looking over her knuckles as he kissed them, his dark brown eyes twinkling at her.

"I'm not really his cousin," Gem whispered as she drew her hand away, the rush of color deepening in her cheeks.

"Chase!"

He spun around at the sound of his name. His aunt was standing on the porch, holding onto the rail. He stepped around Gem and hurried toward the house.

"Aunt Enid," he murmured as he gathered her against him in a tight embrace. When he released her, he kissed her cheek, then studied her face for as many changes as he'd found in Gem. But she was unchanged, except for a few more lines around the corners of her eyes. "What's happened here? Where's Uncle Frank?"

"Come inside, Chase. I'll fix some coffee and we'll talk. You've been gone a long time." She looked around him as Gem and Julio approached the house. "Gem, you'd better get dressed, my dear. You'll catch your death."

Gem paled as her gaze fell to her flimsy attire, then the blush returned in a blaze of color. Suddenly she bolted around them and rushed up the stairs.

Chase's eyes followed after her, and he shook his head. Who would have thought Gem would blossom into such a beauty? He'd nearly forgotten her. If he *had* thought of her, he would have thought she'd left Four Winds by now. That summer seemed such a long time ago. A happier time. A better time.

Again he shook his head, then glanced back at his aunt. "Where's Uncle Frank?" he repeated.

"He's upstairs," she replied, "but I must tell you something before you go up to see him." She hooked her arm through his and drew him inside. "Come along. You can sit at the table while I make the coffee. Your friend, too." Her eyes flicked toward Julio.

"Sorry. Aunt Enid, this is Julio Valdez. Julio, my aunt, Enid Dupre."

"It is a pleasure, senora," Julio said with a polite bow. "I have heard much about you these past years."

"I wish I could say the same." Enid's eyes gently chastised her nephew, but she said no more about his lengthy absence.

The kitchen was warm. A fire was already burning in the stove, and a pot of coffee was beginning to brew. The friendly smell and the morning sun streaming into the room made him feel good inside, made him feel at home again.

"Katie must have heard you arrive. She's put the coffee on for us."

"Katie?" Chase raised an eyebrow in question.

"Rod's wife. She helps me around the place. They live in the little house out back."

"Rod's wife . . . You don't mean Rodney Daniels?"

Enid laughed softly. "You'll find a lot of things have changed around here, Chase. Wait till you see Rod and Katie's little girl."

"Well, I'll be—" he muttered as he pulled out a chair and sat at the kitchen table.

For some reason he'd thought things would stay the same at Four Winds. Five years. He'd been gone five years. Gem had grown up. Rod had taken a wife and had a daughter. Things had stayed no more the same here than he was still the same man who'd ridden away.

Chase raked his fingers through his hair. "Tell me what's happened, Aunt Enid? Why isn't Uncle Frank down here to greet me? What happened to the barn? Where are the men?"

Silent, Enid brought the pot of coffee over to the table and filled two cups for the men, then poured a cup for herself and sat down. She took a long sip, watching Chase over the edge with alert gray eyes. Then she began to speak. "Trouble started about two years ago. The cattle you'd sent up from Texas with your letter were in good shape, and we had a fine crop of calves that spring. But then the rustling started. We've lost countless head in the past two years to those thieving bandits."

"Any idea who they are?"

"Oh, I've got my theories, same as everybody else, but we've got no proof. But rustling hasn't been our only problem. There's a grizzly been coming down out of the mountains and killing cows. And he doesn't stop with cattle either. Wade Irvine was killed last summer, and Charlie Brothers down at the Golden Bar lost his leg from being mauled by that devil. Tore it right off. It's a miracle Charlie's even alive."

Chase exchanged a frowning glance with Julio.

"Then, this spring, the vandals started riding. They've been hitting farms and ranches from the Golden Bar all the way up to Gallatin, burning barns, tearing down fences, running off stock. Doesn't seem to be any reason for it. Pure destruction, that's all they're after. They've managed to drive off a few families."

Chase's hand tightened around his coffee cup. "Is that what happened here? To the barn?"

"Last night. They rode in late, the three of them, and set fire to it."

"Didn't the men try to stop them?" he asked, incredulous. "Didn't anybody even get a shot at them?"

"Weren't any men here. We'd gotten word that the grizzly was down from the hills, about ten miles south of here, and I sent the men after it. We were in bed when they rode in. Gem saw them from her window. She got off a couple shots before they rode away, and she thinks she may have hit one of them, but it was too late. Once they were gone, Gem got a couple horses out before—" Her voice trailed off and her eyes glazed over as she seemed to replay the fiery scene in her mind.

Chase felt an impotent anger flaring up in his stomach as he imagined the three women trying to save the burning barn alone, trying hopelessly to save the stock that was inside. Then the anger faded as he realized his uncle's name had not yet been mentioned. Aunt Enid had ignored his question purposefully. He dreaded to ask again, sensing he wouldn't like the answer. "Where was Uncle Frank?"

His aunt rose from the table and walked slowly to the stove. Her shoulders were suddenly slumped; her posture looked to be that of an old, old woman. She started to pick up the coffee pot, but her hand fell back to her side. She shook her head.

"Uncle Frank is paralyzed."

Chase swiveled on his chair toward the kitchen doorway. Gem was standing there, her eyes sparking with the anger he'd heard in her voice. She had swept her hair back and caught it at the nape with a ribbon. The white blouse and split leather skirt affirmed the woman's figure he had ascertained through her night attire, but he didn't have the chance nor inclination to ponder the transformation.

"It happened during spring roundup," Gem continued. "Powell Daniels dared Uncle Frank to ride Old Whitey. Bet him his best stallion Uncle Frank couldn't do it. You know how he is about horses. He wanted that stallion, and he also wanted to prove he could still ride a bronc."

Chase could remember Old Whitey. He'd tried to ride him once himself. "But no one's ever ridden that horse."

"Powell held the bronc while Uncle Frank got up in the saddle. As soon as he turned loose, Old Whitey shot straight up and twisted right out from under Uncle Frank. The bronc's hind hoof hit him square in the back on his way down." Gem left the kitchen doorway and walked across the room to Enid. She laid a gentle hand on the older woman's back, then glanced around at Chase, her eyes smoldering with barely checked anger. "Aunt Enid and I were there. She grabbed a rifle and went into the corral and shot Old Whitey right between the eyes, but it didn't change the fact that Uncle Frank's back was broken. Doctor says he'll never walk again."

"God almighty," Chase whispered, dropping his head into his hands, his elbows resting on the table. He felt a twisting pain in his chest, just like someone turning a knife.

Suddenly Gem's fists struck the table. Chase's head jerked up, and his eyes clashed with the fury in hers.

"Where the hell have you been, Chase Dupre?" she shouted. "What gave you the right to desert your aunt and uncle for five years? Five years, damn you! We've all waited and wondered and worried. You should have been here with us. You should have been here where you belonged. If you'd been here—"

"No, Gem. Gem—" Enid's hands clasped Gem's shoulders and drew her back away from the table.

Her eyes accused him. "You could have written."

"I wrote," he protested.

"One letter. One lousy letter in five years. A letter that told us nothing except you weren't coming home yet."

Gem was crying now. Enid held her tightly against her breast and let her sob out her hurt and frustration.

"I wrote more than once," Chase said softly in his own defense, then was flooded with guilt when he realized how few letters he had written. Just three. Just three letters in five years.

"We never got them." Gem choked on a sob.

Chase got to his feet, feeling his own helplessness and frustration. "You don't understand, Gem," he said softly. "I wanted to come back sooner but—" He paused for a moment, waiting for a response. When there was none, he said, "I'm going up to see Uncle Frank."

Enid nodded mutely, her tender gaze telling him she loved him and his reasons for staying away didn't matter to her.

With a weighted heart, Chase ascended the stairs.

She shouldn't have attacked him that way. She shouldn't have blamed him for what had happened while he was away. His homecoming had been difficult enough, finding Uncle Frank a cripple, the barn destroyed, and the rest of the problems that had plagued the Four Winds and the other ranchers these past two years.

Gem found Chase leaning on the corral fence.

He was gazing sightlessly at the charred remains of the barn. His handsome bronzed face looked haggard. There was a tiredness in his blue eyes that went beyond fatigue. It was an exhaustion of the soul.

"Chase?" She touched his arm lightly, and he looked at her. For a moment she thought he didn't know who she was. It was as if he were lost in a fog somewhere, and the sensation alarmed her. "Chase, I'm sorry for what I said."

His gaze cleared. He smiled sadly. "It's okay, kid. I think I deserved it."

Her hand tightened on his sleeve. "No. No, you didn't. It's just we've all missed you terribly." She dropped her hand and turned away, saying in a choked voice, "You were gone such a long time."

"Why'd you stay, Gem? I'd have thought you'd've been long gone by now."

It hurt that he hadn't known she would be here, that he had given her so little thought. Where else would she have waited for him to return? "This is my home," she answered softly.

"I didn't mean it that way. I know it's your home. I meant I thought you'd have married some lucky fellow by now."

I was waiting for you, Chase. She turned toward him again but kept her eyes averted. She knew if she looked at him he would have to see the love she felt for him. Now wasn't the time to reveal what she felt. Later, once he was settled in and things returned to normal, then she would declare her heart.

"I never expected you to grow up so pretty."

Now there was a real smile in his teasing voice, and it drew her eyes to his face. "Can you still beat all the hands at poker?"

She met his grin. "Of course."

Suddenly the smile faded and he pointed at her, aghast. "You? It was *you*?"

"What was me?"

"*You* shot my hat off?"

He was so incredulous, she had to laugh. "It was me."

"You could have *killed* me," he accused.

"Not likely. I hit just exactly what I was aiming at."

Chase shook his head. "You forget. I tried to teach you how to shoot. I know what a terrible shot you are. You had the worst eye in the entire territory."

Softly, she replied, "It's you who forget, Chase. I had a very fine teacher, and I've had nearly five years to practice since the lessons stopped."

Maybe she was wrong. Maybe now *would* be a good time to tell him, to show him. Her fingers ached to touch him. She wanted to run her fingers over his cheek and sweep his shaggy brown hair back from his face. She'd like to rub the tension from his forehead. And more than anything, she wanted to press her lips against his. She wanted him to take her in his arms and crush her against him.

"Chase—"

She sensed him stiffen and watched as clouds gathered in his eyes as he gazed into the distance. She turned to see what had stolen the gentle humor they had shared only moments before. A wagon was approaching.

"Who is it, Chase?"

With a voice devoid of emotion, he answered, "It's my wife."

5

His wife.

Gem watched as Chase walked over to the wagon and extended a hand to the woman, helping her down from her high perch.

His wife.

A sinking feeling dragged at her heart. There was a mind-numbing buzz in her ears.

His wife.

With his hand in the small of her back, Chase guided the Latin beauty toward Gem. As she watched their approach, Gem felt herself growing smaller, more pale, and oh so very plain.

"Gem, this is my wife, Consuela."

"How do you do." Gem's voice was barely audible as she hesitantly held out a hand in welcome.

Black eyes, very round and trimmed with long

sable lashes, perused Gem's face, then dropped to her proffered hand.

Chase completed the introduction. "Consuela, my cousin, Gem McBride."

Consuela touched Gem's fingers lightly. Her voice when she spoke was as sweet and smooth as warm honey, her Spanish accent beguiling. "Senora McBride. I did not know Chase had a cousin."

"We're happy to have you here." It was a lie. Gem wasn't happy to have her there. She hated her flawless olive skin, her high sculpted cheekbones, and her full red mouth. She hated the shiny blue-black hair tucked in a tidy bun beneath the attractive red bonnet. She hated the possessive gloved fingers which lay in the crook of Chase's arm. "And I'm not married," she added with just a trifling hint of defiance.

Consuela's smile failed to reach her eyes. "*Gracias*, senorita." She turned her head, gracefully tilting it to look up at Chase. "It has been a long day, Chase. I would like to wash off the trail dust and lie down."

"Of course. I'll take you to our room. Excuse us, Gem."

Their room. The thought cut like a knife. They would be sharing Chase's room. How often in the past five years had Gem entered that room, dusting and polishing, keeping it ready for his return, always with the hope of someday sharing it with him.

She felt a surge of anger heating her cheeks and raised her hands to touch them. She would like to scratch that woman's eyes out. And she would like to hit Chase too. She'd like to pummel him with her fists until he cried for mercy. He had betrayed her!

Then as quickly as it had come, the anger faded, leaving a sharp pain to pierce her heart. No, he hadn't betrayed her. He had never loved her. She had to face it. This time she had to face the truth and accept it.

Gem straightened her shoulders and turned toward the house, drawing in a deep breath and making a solemn, silent vow that no one would ever know she had loved him. She would treat him like the cousin he professed to be. She would become a friend to his wife. She would do it all . . . even if it killed her.

As she stood there, drawing in her resolve, the front door opened and Julio stepped outside. He paused on the porch and settled his dark, sugar-loaf sombrero over his black hair, then looked up to find her watching him. He flashed her a smile, showing a row of straight white teeth as he stepped down from the porch and walked toward her.

"Senorita," he said with a polite nod.

She acknowledged it with one of her own.

"My friend did not finish our introductions this morning. Perhaps he was still nervous from being shot at, no?" His smile broadened.

Reluctantly, she returned it.

Again he bowed, this time very low with a broad sweep of his hand. "I am Julio Manuel Enrique Valdez of Casa de Oro. At your service, senorita."

This time her smile was genuine.

"That is much better. You have a lovely smile, and you must use it often. Now tell me, Senorita Dupre. How is it you are a Dupre but not a cousin?"

"I'm not a Dupre." The words came painfully from her lips.

Not a Dupre . . . For so long she had thought, hoped, dreamed that one day she would be called Gem Dupre. And now it would never happen. Valiantly she disguised the pain that pierced her heart, keeping the smile on her mouth as she executed an exaggerated curtsy.

"Gem Elizabeth McBride, Senor Valdez. I'm pleased to make your acquaintance."

Julio continued to peruse her, his smile fading slightly. He seemed to see beneath her facade to the hurt she wanted to hide. Then his black eyes flicked toward the south. "I am riding out to the herd. Would you like to come?"

Whether he knew it or not, he was offering her a means of escape, some time away from the house before she had to face Chase and Consuela again. She needed more time to gather her thoughts and emotions before she viewed them again as a married couple. "Yes, Mr. Valdez. I would like that very much."

"Please, senorita. If we are to be friends, you must call me Julio."

"Okay, Julio. And you must call me Gem." That settled, she added, "I'll saddle my horse." She hurried off toward the corral.

Chase watched the interchange from the window of his bedroom and allowed his thoughts to drift back in time, back to the summer when she followed him around the ranch like a stray puppy, back to the summer when she delighted over the foal he gave her, back to the summer when she hit Powell Daniels over the head with a stool and then was knocked out herself. He smiled when he remembered the black eye she'd sported just before he left for Texas.

Texas. Consuela.

He turned from the window and leaned against the sill as he watched his wife brushing her long hair. She was sitting on the side of the bed, clad only in chemise and petticoat, her head tipped forward and to the side. Her hair fell over her shoulder and past her knees, and she stroked it with a steady rhythm, bringing out the glossy sheen he had always admired. Her generous breasts swelled above the white fabric of the chemise. It had been a long time since they had shared a room, a long time since he had seen her this way. There was an almost forgotten stirring in his loins.

Consuela threw her hair over her shoulder and looked up, finding his eyes upon her. Her mouth narrowed. "If you think, just because we have arrived at your ranch, that you can have your way with me, you are much mistaken, Senor Dupre. Now, I am tired. Please go away and let me sleep."

The beginnings of desire died quickly, frustration and anger sweeping through him. "Have no fear, Mrs. Dupre," he snapped as he grabbed his hat from the chair near the door. "I won't trouble you with my presence any longer."

Silently cursing all womanhood, he stormed out of the house, glad his aunt was nowhere to be seen. She would only have questioned him, if not with her voice then with her eyes, and he was in no mood to explain to anyone about his marriage to the beautiful Consuela Valdez Dupre.

* * *

Julio and Gem rode in silence, cantering their horses across the valley. Long grass swayed gently in the June breeze. The land undulated with high ground and low. Creeks wended from the mountains toward the river, copses of cottonwood and shrubs nestled near their banks. To the east and west, mountain ranges, covered with tall pines, rose with rugged majesty toward an expansive blue sky. It was a land meant for cattle, rich with feed and water, a land of challenge and promise.

Gem heard a shout and turned her head toward the east, then drew in the reins and brought Wichita to a halt. Julio followed suit. She squinted against the midday sun and watched in silence as the cowboys rode toward them.

Rodney was in the lead. She could see the tired slope of his shoulders and knew he had probably had little sleep since he and the others had galloped away from the ranch in search of the killer grizzly. Her gaze moved to the others, counting silently. Five. They were all there. She breathed a quick prayer of thanks for their safety.

"Any luck, Rod?" she called as they drew nearer.

Rodney's horse stopped, its head drooping wearily. "Nothing. We tracked him and thought we had him cornered." His eyes moved to Julio, silently questioning his identity. "But he outsmarted us. Lucky he didn't backtrack on us." His gaze swept back to Gem.

"Well, I've got some good news for you. Chase is home. And he's brought another herd up with him."

Five tired faces perked up.

"Chase is back?" Rodney echoed. "Hey, Teddy.

You hear that? Chase is back."

"I heard. When'd he get in, Gem?"

"This morning." She glanced toward Julio. "This is his friend, Julio Valdez. We're on our way out to the herd now."

"Need us to come along?" Rodney asked.

Julio shook his head. "No, senor. Our men can bring them in."

"Then if it's all right, Gem, we'll be getting on back to the house. Doggone if it won't be good to see Chase again." Rodney turned his horse's head and nudged it with his boot.

"Rodney, there's more you should know."

He pulled in the reins and glanced back at her.

"The vandals hit us last night. They burned the barn."

"Anyone hurt? Katie and the baby?"

"Katie and Maggie are both fine," she assured him.

Rodney nodded his thanks and led the men off toward the ranch house.

Gem watched them go. "They've all been with the Four Winds for a long time. They'll be glad to have Chase back."

"But no more than you, senorita. Am I not right?"

"No, Julio," she replied softly. "No more than me." She couldn't bring herself to look at him, knowing her eyes would reveal too much.

"That is good. Chase has wanted to return to Four Winds for a long time. It is good to be welcomed home by so many."

In unison they turned their horses and urged

them into a lope, ending any further conversation. But silently she questioned him. If Chase had wanted to return, why hadn't he done it sooner? What had kept him from his family, from those who loved him, for so long?

And why, oh why, did he have to return with a wife?

Evening was fast approaching when Gem and Julio returned. Chase was standing on the porch, leaning against the post, his eyes scanning the rolling landscape that stretched away from the ranch house. A whiff of sowbelly and beans drifted from the bunkhouse on the evening breeze, carrying with it the men's voices in good-natured banter. Inside the house, he could hear Aunt Enid and Katie talking as they prepared supper for the family.

He had been standing there for a long time, just drinking in the goodness of being home again, allowing the tensions to drain out and forgetting, for at least a little while, the troubles that faced him. It was easy to forget when you found yourself surrounded by friends and family, when you knew you were where you belonged. It was easy to forget when men were slapping you on the back and reminding each other of times they had all shared. It would stay easy to forget—until Consuela came down from the bedroom.

Gem and Julio jogged their horses across the yard, stopping near the porch. Gem hopped down from the saddle and tossed the reins over the hitching post. She pushed the broad-brimmed hat back from her head, letting it hang against her back, held in place by the tie around her throat. Her face was flushed from the ride and covered with dust . . . and surprisingly pretty.

"Oh, Chase, I've just seen the cattle. And the horses, too. Uncle Frank will be so pleased."

Her enthusiasm brought him fresh pleasure.

"You know how Uncle Frank is about his horses. When he sees those new mares—" She turned toward Julio, still sitting astride his black stallion. "And Julio promised we could breed Kansas and Wichita with Diablo." As if in confirmation, the stallion nodded his head and snorted.

"Kansas? I thought she must be dead by this time. She wasn't in the corral."

"No, Pike's using her this week. They're up by Cottonwood Creek. He and Red Saunders."

"Rodney told me Pike was working up that way." His gaze drifted to her saddle horse. "Well, I'll be. That's Wichita, isn't it?" He stepped off the porch and laid his hand on the mare's shiny neck. His gaze traveled over her sturdy chest and well-muscled shoulders, then down her sleek legs. "She grew up even better than I thought she would." He spoke more to himself than to Gem. Then his eyes met hers across Wichita's back, and he thought, *So did you*.

Julio swung down from his saddle. "I'll put the horses in the corral, *amigo*." Unobtrusively he reached for the reins and led the saddle horses away, leaving Gem and Chase momentarily alone.

"I like Julio. He seems very nice," Gem said, her eyes not straying from his.

"He's been a good friend to me."

"Will he stay on at Four Winds?"

"I don't know. His father owns a ranch in Texas, but he's got several older brothers who are still there. There's no hurry for him to return."

"But you're here to stay. Aren't you, Chase?" Her voice was barely more than a whisper, hardly more than a prayer.

"Nothing could get me to leave here again." He suddenly remembered the way she had kissed him that very morning, and he wished she would do it again. He wished . . .

"Chase?" His aunt's voice preceded her through the door. "Consuela is calling for you."

He stepped back from Gem, awash with guilt. He had no right to think about her that way.

"When you go up," Enid continued as she turned toward the kitchen once more, "tell her supper will be on the table in ten minutes. We hope she's rested enough to join us."

"I'll see you at supper," Chase mumbled to Gem.

He turned on his heel and entered the house, climbing the stairs without haste. There had been a time when Consuela could whisper his name and he would race to her side. How quickly that had changed. How cruelly his love had been destroyed.

Consuela looked up from the dressing table as he entered. She was wearing a bright yellow sateen gown. The V neck of the bodice accentuated the fullness of her bosom and the narrowness of her waist. She had swept her long hair into a coiled chignon and fastened it with a comb, revealing her white throat and delicate ears. He recalled the first time he had seen her so. He'd never seen anyone so beautiful. But he saw through that beauty now, and

he knew that what lay beneath the surface was far
from lovely.

"Chase, why did you not come when I called?"
she scolded, drawing her pretty mouth into a pout. "I
thought you meant to leave me forever in this dismal
little room."

His eyes scanned his bedroom, the room he had
longed for so many times in these past years. It was
anything but little or dismal. It was spacious, filled
with a massive four-poster bed, plush carpets brought
here from the East, a mahogany chiffonier, and the
dressing table brought in from Chantal's old room. It
was different from the room they had shared in the
Valdez hacienda, but it was a fine room nonetheless.

When his gaze returned to Consuela, he discovered he felt no anger, only fatigue and a deep sense of
failure and sorrow. He sighed heavily. "Aunt Enid
says supper is ready and hopes you'll feel rested
enough to join us. They're all eager to get to know
you."

"Of course they wish to know me. I am now
mistress of this little ranch, no? I will not disappoint
them, my love."

Gem had only enough time for a quick wash and
a hasty brush through her wind-tangled hair before
supper was on the table. She had come to the table
often enough in the past still dusty from a day in the
saddle, but the instant Consuela entered the room on
Chase's arm, looking as bright as a buttercup, she
knew that today was not a good day to have done so.
She immediately imagined herself as others would see
her in comparison with Chase's elegant wife. She
wanted to slink away into hiding.

Once again Consuela was introduced to all the new faces. Aunt Enid greeted her with a kiss on the cheek. Uncle Frank said he was pleased to have such a pretty new niece and apologized for not being able to get up off his cot which Chase and Julio had carried downstairs.

And then it was Gem's turn. She reminded herself of her vow to become Consuela's friend, no matter what it took. She held out her hand. "I'm pleased you're here," she said with a forced smile. "I . . . I hope we'll be more than friends. I hope we'll be like sisters."

"But of course. I think I should like that. With so many brothers at the Casa de Oro, I would be very happy to have a little *hermana*." She looked at Julio, standing beside Gem. "You see. Even here in Montana Territory, I cannot escape my brothers."

"Julio is your brother?"

"*Si*." Consuela looped her arm through Chase's and leaned into him. "My husband has a great fondness for all the Valdez family. Is that not true, Chase?"

Something flashed in Chase's expression, something Gem couldn't quite define, and then it was gone and he was guiding his wife across the room toward the large table. He pulled out a chair for her. She sat down, lifting a glowing face up to him and whispering an inaudible endearment. He made no reply but turned and came back to the others. He and Julio once again lifted Frank's cot and carried it close to the table, setting it near Enid's chair.

When they were all seated and the serving dishes were being passed, Enid spoke again. "You must tell

us about your home, Consuela. What does Casa de
Oro mean?"

"It means nothing to me, senora," came her
abrupt reply.

Her statement was followed by an uncomfort-
able silence.

"Please forgive my sister, Senora Dupre," Julio
said softly. "She sometimes forgets the manners my
mother taught her when she was a little girl." He
turned a stern black gaze upon Consuela. "I think she
was too spoiled by all those brothers she spoke of. Do
you not agree, *nina*?"

Consuela only glared back at him.

The anger faded from Julio's eyes as he turned
toward his hostess once more. "Casa de Oro means
golden house. My mother, Dominica Valdez, named
it when my father first took her there as his bride. The
sun was setting, and she said it turned the house all
gold and knew it was a good sign. That it would be a
house of great joy and she would give her husband
many sons to build a great hacienda."

Gem allowed her gaze to move around the table
as Julio spoke. She could read pride and love in
Julio's expression. In Chase, she saw agreement and
sensed that he'd been happy at Casa de Oro. But
Consuela's look was petulant, even bitter. She
wondered . . .

"No, Senor Dupre," Julio replied to a question
which Gem hadn't heard as she mused. "My mother
died two years ago." He looked at Chase. "That is
one reason your nephew did not return sooner. He
stayed to help us. My father was beyond solace for
many months."

"I'm sorry to hear that, Julio." Enid placed a hand over his and squeezed it. "We understand about losing loved ones around here."

"*Gracias*, senora. I now see why Chase is the kind of friend he is."

Enid was visibly pleased by his compliment. "Julio, you must stop this 'senora' business. I'm Enid or Aunt Enid to everyone for miles around. You do the same and we'll all get along fine." She turned a warm smile on Consuela. "That goes for you too, my dear."

Gem felt another stab of anger shoot through her. She remembered so clearly the day Enid had said nearly the same words to her, making her a part of the family. She felt usurped, replaced. She'd like to kick somebody. She turned her snapping eyes upon her plate, hoping to conceal the petty rage that broiled within.

6

Gem couldn't sleep. She tossed and turned, wrinkling the sheets, rumpling the blankets, until the bed was a shambles. The night plodded by with torturous inertia. Silvered moonbeams streamed through the lace curtains at her windows, teasing her with the feeling of day when she knew she should be sleeping.

But how could she sleep when thoughts of Chase plagued her mind? A hundred different pictures flashed before her closed eyelids, all from just that day, all of them of Chase. Chase smiling. Chase frowning. Chase laughing. Chase with Consuela.

He wasn't happy. She knew it beyond doubt. And it was Consuela's fault.

One more reason to dislike her.

But he loved Consuela once. He must have loved

her or he wouldn't be so hurt now.

How do you know he's hurt?

He's hurt, all right. You can see it all over him.

I could make him stop hurting. I know I could.

No, you couldn't. You're just his little cousin. You'll always be just his little cousin. Just a dumb, infatuated little kid.

But if he doesn't love her anymore . . .

You don't know that.

But . . .

You can't have him. He's married to Consuela and that's that. There's no undoing it.

Oh, Chase. I could make you happy. I love you so.

Gem threw off the covers and dressed quickly. She pulled on her boots in the last rays of moonlight, then hurried from her room as if pursued by demons.

Perhaps she *was* pursued by demons. Her arguing thoughts stayed with her, taunting and teasing and torturing.

"Oh, Chase," she whispered.

"Gem? What are you doing out here?"

She jumped back with a startled squeal, her hand hitting her chest as if to stop her heart from flying out in fright.

He stepped forward and caught her arm. "You okay?"

"Yes. Yes," she answered breathlessly, willing her heart to stop pounding in her ears. She looked up at him. "You just startled me is all."

"Sorry. When I heard you say my name, I figured you knew I was here. I thought—" He let his sentence drift into silence.

"I needed to take a walk. I couldn't sleep." She

knew it didn't explain why she had whispered his
name. But what could she tell him? She shouldn't let
him know that thoughts of him made her sleepless,
yet how could she deny the truth? "I couldn't sleep,"
she repeated needlessly.

"Me either."

The moon was gone, but a soft glow lingered
over the earth, just bright enough for them to see the
other's shadow but too dark to see the other's face.

She searched her mind for something to say,
anything to say as the silence lingered and his hand
remained on her arm, seeming to sear the flesh
beneath her blouse. "We're all so glad you're home,
Chase." How many times had he heard that today?

"Me too."

Gem couldn't seem to help herself. She stepped
closer to him. Her fingers trembled as they moved
from her chest to his. She could feel the heat of his
body through his shirt. A sudden weakness flowed
through her legs and brought a shortness of breath.
She tilted her head back. Her eyelids drifted half-
closed. She willed him to hold her, to kiss her, to love
her, and for a moment she thought he was going to
do all three.

He leaned toward her. She sensed the rising
tension between them. Then she heard his stifled
moan as he turned abruptly and began walking,
pulling her along with him.

She searched for something to say to hide her
own shame and embarrassment. "I . . . I think
Consuela will be happy here. I mean, how could she
help but be?"

His hand dropped away, but he kept walking.
She had to take nearly two steps for every one of his.

She was almost running to keep up with him as they left the house and the corrals, the bunkhouse, and the outbuildings behind them, heading up the sloping hillside that led to the mountains. He was quickly leaving her behind.

"Chase!"

He stopped suddenly. She knew he was looking down at her, trying to study her in the darkness before dawn. She knew without a doubt that he was wearing that same frown she had noticed on his brow so often during the day. She wanted to reach up and smooth it away.

"I don't want to talk about Consuela with you, Gem. Do you understand me? My wife is my business. If you want to be friends with her, that's fine. You two go ahead and be friends. But don't ask her about me and don't ask me about her."

His gruffness brought tears to her eyes. "Sure, Chase." Her words were clipped in a throat tight with emotion as she fought the unwelcome moisture.

He drew a deep breath, then let it out with a sigh. His hand stretched out and he ruffled her hair. "I'm sorry, kid. I didn't mean to take it out on you." Then his fingers cupped her chin and he lifted her face toward his. "Hey, you're not crying, are you? Not the girl that knocked Powell Daniels colder than a Montana blizzard last time I saw her?"

Gem swallowed hard. "No, Chase. I'm not crying."

"Liar," he scolded softly. His finger touched her cheek, flicking away a renegade tear. "Ah, kid, I'm really sorry. Sometimes I forget you're not just one of the guys."

If he'd meant to comfort her, that was definitely not the way. She didn't want to be just one of the guys any more than she wanted to be just a kid.

"I think I'd better walk on alone," he continued. "I'm not fit company for anybody tonight."

"That's okay, Chase." She turned, ready to hurry back to the house before a fresh wave of tears hit her.

"Gem." Her name from his lips, spoken softly in the pre-morning air, halted her retreat. "We're going to bring the cattle up tomorrow. I want Uncle Frank to get to see the herd before we turn them out on the range. You going to come along and help?"

She tossed a strangled reply over her shoulder. "Sure. I'd love to come, Chase. See you in the morning." Then she hurried away.

Pull yourself up by your own bootstraps. That's one thing she'd been taught by her shiftless father. It's what she did that morning before going down for breakfast. She vowed nobody'd ever know how miserable she was.

As she stepped into the hallway, she could hear angry words being spoken behind the closed door of Chase's room. She tried to will herself to move on. She tried to will herself not to listen.

"Is this the ranch you were so proud of, so eager to return to that you forced my father to reject me? Did you drag me across this wretched country for *this*? Do you not have the *vaqueros* to work it that you must go too? Am I not miserable enough that you should leave me here all alone?"

"Consuela, I've always worked this range right alongside the cowpokes. I don't mean to do it different now. And you're not alone. Aunt Enid and Uncle Frank are here. See if you can't give them a hand."

"You are nothing, Chase Dupre. I spit on you. Go! Chase your stupid cows. Get out! Get out of my room. Get out of my sight. And don't think I'll ever invite you back into my bed. You are not man enough for me."

The door opened.

"Do you understand me, Senor Dupre? I won't have your hands on me. I never wanted you. Never!"

Chase stepped quickly out of the room. His eyes darted to the top of the stairs where Gem stood eavesdropping. She felt herself blushing furiously as he drew up short, knowing she had heard everything. She dropped her gaze and hurried down the stairs.

Aunt Enid was in the kitchen, busily frying up a breakfast of eggs and beef steaks. Gem made for the coffee pot on the stove and filled a cup to the rim, then moved to the back door which stood open to the morning breeze. Looking out, she didn't turn around when she heard Chase's footsteps. She couldn't look him in the face.

"Mornin', Chase." Enid turned from the stove. "Julio eating with us this morning?"

"I think he ate in the bunkhouse. Don't fix too much. I don't have much of an appetite."

Gem heard the scrape of the chair as it slid away from the table.

"Nonsense," Enid replied. "You're going out to do a full day's work, and you're going to start out with a full stomach. Now sit there and eat what I cook for you. Gem?"

Gem looked over her shoulder.

"Get over here and start eating if you're planning to go with them."

They ate quickly, neither Chase nor Gem looking up from their plates, letting Aunt Enid do all the
talking. Gem was first to finish.

"I'm going out to saddle Wichita," she said as
she rose from the table. She dropped a kiss on Enid's
head and wished she could do the same to Chase.

As she reached the door, she heard Chase saying,
"Tell Uncle Frank we'll have them here by late in the
afternoon. We'll carry him out and let him have a
look."

"I'll tell him, dear." There was a special tenderness in Enid's voice this morning.

She heard, too, Gem thought, and it made her feel
even worse. She left the kitchen behind her, wishing
that she'd never stopped to listen to the hurtful,
angry words, wishing she'd never seen Chase's anguish.

Julio knew as soon as he saw his friend's face that
his sister had once again caused him sorrow. He
wished he could take her over his knee and paddle
some sense into her, but it was already too late. She
had taken Chase's love and twisted it, then thrown it
in his face in the cruelest of fashions. Any other man
would have left her after what she had done. Even her
own father had rejected her. But Chase was too
honorable for that. He had married her, and he
would make the best of living with her.

As Julio swung onto Diablo's back, he saw Gem
leading her mare from the corral, and a smile slipped
into place on his mouth. Her long strawberry-blonde
hair was hanging in a thick braid down the back of her

jacket. A dusty hat shaded her eyes, and she walked with the same free, easy gait as the other cowpokes.

"*Buenos dias*, Gem," he called to her.

"Good morning, Julio." But even as she spoke to him, her glance flicked toward Chase.

"You will watch us drive in the cattle today, *amiga*?"

"I'm here to help bring them in, Julio, not watch."

"You have done this before? It is not an easy job."

Gem laughed, and her eyes sparkled. "Julio, I've ridden drag and point and everything in-between on the drives to Cheyenne for the last two years, and I've helped with every roundup since I came to Four Winds. I've eaten enough dust to start my own dirt farm." She swung up onto the saddle, then looked over at him again. She cocked her head sideways and winked, speaking louder this time. "I'm probably a better cowhand than Chase."

It was obvious to Julio that she was baiting his friend, and it worked. Chase looked up from cinching his gelding's saddle. His brow was still drawn together in a frown, but this one was different. He had heard a challenge and was considering it. There was even a glint of humor in his bright blue eyes.

"Better than me, Gem?" Chase leaned his arms across the rump of his horse and tipped his hat brim back.

She tossed her head in a sassy manner. "You might be better here or there, Chase, just 'cause you're a little stronger, but I'd be willin' to wager that all around—"

"Wager, huh? Does that include a hand or two of poker?"

"Nice way to end a day, don't you think?"

She's in love with him. It was so clear to Julio. Not a cousin's love. A woman's love.

"All right, Gem McBride," Chase responded, a real grin brightening his face as he mounted his cowpony. "We get to the herd, we'll have ourselves a little contest."

Gem leaned over in the saddle and held out her hand to him. "Deal."

"Deal."

They shook on it.

But Chase doesn't know she loves him, Julio concluded with a shake of his head.

He could see there was even more trouble ahead for them all.

Wichita darted after the stray cow, her head low, her body tense. Every time the cow changed directions, she was ready and spurted after it. Gem had little to do but hang on and be ready with the lariat. As the longhorn spun again, Gem let loose with the rope, letting it sing through her leather-gloved fingers and settle over the animal's head. She made a quick dally around the horn of the saddle. The men whooped it up behind her as Teddy looped the rear leg and finished the job. Her hat had fallen off her head and was dangling against her back. Stray wisps of hair clung in damp curls around the edge of her dusty face.

She turned a triumphant smile in Chase's direction. "If I'm not mistaken, Mr. Dupre, this test is mine." She felt a special gladness welling inside her as he returned her smile.

"Agreed, Miss McBride."

The dust cleared from between them just as the overheard argument of that morning had vanished in the freedom of the day. Gem handed her lasso to another cowboy, then trotted Wichita over to where Chase and Julio had watched her performance.

There was no teasing or jesting in Chase's voice as he said, "You did a fine job training Wichita. I don't think I've ever seen a better cowpony."

"Thanks, Chase." She blushed with pleasure. "Uncle Frank helped a lot." She patted the mare's sweaty neck and murmured a "Good girl."

"We'd better move on. Uncle Frank'll be wondering what happened to us." Chase turned away and cantered toward the front of the herd.

Teddy freed the cow and looped Gem's lariat around his arm as he walked toward her. He handed it up to her, grinning all the while. "I think you surprised him."

She nodded, her eyes still following after Chase, his words of praise making her glow inside.

"*Amiga?*"

Gem reluctantly pulled her gaze away from Chase.

"May I give you a word of advice?"

"Sure, Julio."

"Be careful not to let Consuela see how you feel about him. She will cut you to ribbons."

She started to deny it. "I don't know what—" But she stopped the words short. There was no point in lying to Julio. "Does it show that much?"

"To me. Not to Chase."

Gem turned her head toward the sea of moving cattle, seeking out Chase's buckskin gelding. "I guess it's better that way," she said sadly.

"*Si*. It is better that way."

"I promised myself I'd be a good friend to Consuela since she's Chase's wife. But after what I heard this morning . . ." Her eyes returned to Julio. ". . . I don't know if I can be her friend."

"I am sorry to say this about my own sister, Gem, but don't waste your time. She will not accept your offer of friendship. I know her well. She only takes. She never gives."

"He loves her a great deal, doesn't he, Julio?" It hurt to ask. She wasn't sure she even wanted to know the answer.

"He loved her once. The love has been dead a long time now. I think he wants no more of love."

Gem felt as if her heart were breaking into a million tiny pieces. "Consuela's done that to him?"

"She has done even worse than that to him, senorita." Julio's reply was spoken in a hushed voice, barely audible above the clacking of horns and bawling of cattle as the herd moved by them.

"What exactly has she done, Julio? I need to understand."

"When he wants you to know, *amiga*, he will tell you. But do not ask him until he is ready."

There were five of them around the table in the bunkhouse—Chase, Julio, Gem, Rodney, and Teddy. A bluish-gray haze hung in a cloud over their heads as the men smoked their cheroots and cigarettes. Outside, someone was strumming a guitar and singing in a low, peaceful voice. It was the conclusion of a satisfying day for Chase. The look on Uncle Frank's face was something he would remember for a long time to come, especially when he saw the fine herd of horses.

"Another two bits," Teddy said, tossing his coin into the center of the table.

Chase looked back at his hand, then picked up two bits and followed suit.

"I'll see that," Gem said softly, "and raise another two bits."

The little snippet is really on a roll tonight, Chase thought as he looked at the neat stacks of coins in front of Gem. She was cleaning them all out.

She had changed out of her trail garb into a soft teal blouse that nearly matched her eyes in color. Her hair was pulled back at the sides and caught with a barrette at the back of her head. It fell in soft waves around her shoulders, and the light from the lanterns seemed to dance in golden reflection from each shaft. Her lips were pressed together in concentration, a look he found both amusing and enchanting. How very different, yet how very much the same was this young woman from the scruffy, feisty waif he'd brought home to Four Winds five years ago.

She looked up from her cards and found him watching her. She smiled, and it lit up her whole face. He felt warm and welcome here. He returned the smile.

"It's up to you, Chase," she said, reminding him that they were in the midst of a poker game.

He glanced again at his hand, then laid the cards face down on the table. "I'm out."

The playing went on, the pot growing by two

bits here, fifty cents there. Chase wasn't following the game, however; he just sat back and enjoyed watching the others and listening to the familiar sounds outside.

The men who had come up the trail with them from Texas would be paid in the morning. Most of them would move on. A few would choose to stay in these parts. Chase hoped Julio would be among those who would stay.

"Sorry, fellas." Gem laid down her cards. "Full house."

A general groan arose from the men.

"Senorita, I think you are too lucky at the cards." Julio leaned his head toward hers. "You would not cheat these honest, hardworking men, would you?"

She grinned. "Cheat my friends? Never!" Then she turned away from Julio, glancing at Chase. "But I had a point to make with Mr. Dupre here. Now, sir. Do you admit defeat?"

"Miss McBride." His voice matched her bantering tone. "I do indeed admit defeat. I confess you are a top cowhand, one of the best it's been my pleasure to know, not to mention one of the prettiest. And, by the way, you're one hell of a poker player, too."

"Thank you." She bobbed her head, then pushed her chair back from the table. "Now, if you boys will excuse me, this cowhand is looking forward to a long, good night's sleep in a soft bed." She scooped her winnings into her hat.

"I'll walk with you." Chase rose from the table at the same time she did. "Good night, boys."

"Night, Chase. Night, Gem."

They walked with unhurried steps toward the main house. Soft lights glowed in the windows of Enid's and Frank's room.

"You certainly made Uncle Frank happy with those mares. And when he saw the size of the herd, he nearly burst with pride. You've made his dream for this ranch come true."

"We're not there yet," Chase replied, glancing down at her as they walked, "but we're headed in the right direction." He was silent for a moment, then added, "I just wish it hadn't taken me so long to get it done."

"You're back now, Chase. That's all that counts."

They reached the porch and stopped in unison as their feet touched the top step. Chase was suddenly aware of what a pleasant feeling it was to be walking in the evening with Gem, heading for the house together. Then his thoughts moved on up to his room where Consuela awaited him, and the pleasant feeling vanished.

"I think I'll sit out here awhile." He leaned against the porch rail. "Good night, Gem."

She hesitated a moment, surprised by his abrupt dismissal. Then she moved toward the door. "Good night, Chase," she said softly just before she disappeared into the house.

Chase listened to her footsteps as she climbed the stairs. He heard the gentle closing of her door, and he imagined her lighting the lamp and then sitting on the edge of the bed while she brushed her hair. It made a pretty picture in his mind. What an odd combination she was. Beautiful young woman and rough-and-tumble cowpoke, all mixed up into one. In just two days he'd felt the warmth of her smile and the wrath of her tongue. There was something very special about . . .

He shook his head, clearing his mind. There were more important things that should be occupying his thoughts now. He turned his gaze toward the darkness of night as he pulled a cheroot from his pocket. He struck a match against the porch rail and brought it toward his face, drawing deeply on the small cigar. Tomorrow they'd start work on the barn, clearing away the debris. He'd ride into Virginia City and order some new lumber from the mill. And while he was there, he'd talk to the sheriff and find out what was being done about the vandals and rustlers. He wasn't going to sit back and let that continue. Not on Four Winds. Not now that he was home.

7

Gem didn't get to town very often. Although there were a few in Virginia City she didn't care much to see—folks like Carol Anne Mills and her stuffy father, Jedidiah—for the most part she enjoyed an excursion into town, so she was both pleased and excited when Chase asked her if she'd like to go with him. She agreed quickly, and then regretted it when she learned Consuela would be going too.

The morning sky was a clear blue when the buggy left Four Winds, Chase holding the reins and the horse trotting along at a brisk pace while Gem and Julio followed on horseback. Consuela's gay chatter drifted back to Gem, who noticed that Chase rarely answered. Neither did Gem try to converse with Julio. Instead she let one silent mile after another fall behind them while she pondered Chase's relationship with his wife. She couldn't help wondering what Consuela had done to destroy his love. From what little Julio had said, she knew it must have been something terrible.

The foursome entered Virginia City's dusty streets close to noon, and Chase led the way to the opposite end of town, stopping in front of Mrs. Culverson's Restaurant. He hopped down and offered a hand to Consuela, who descended gracefully to the street.

"We'll get something to eat," Chase said to Julio, "then Gem can show Consuela around town while we ride out to the lumber mill."

Gem would have preferred to go with Chase and Julio to the mill but knew she couldn't say so. She would just have to keep that promise to herself. She would do her utmost to befriend Consuela, despite what she knew or suspected.

"Maybe you'd like to visit one of the dress shops," she offered to Consuela as they sat down at a table.

"*Si*, I would like that. I am tired of the clothes I brought with me. They remind me of all those miserable months I have spent following the cows. If we had stayed at Casa de Oro—"

"Buy whatever you like, Consuela," Chase interrupted gruffly. "And you too, Gem."

"*Gracias, mi amor*." Consuela leaned against his arm and kissed his cheek. "You are *so* good to me."

Gem stared at her folded hands, clenched tightly in her lap, not wanting to see or hear the exchange between them. There was so much that was unsaid, lurking beneath the surface. *Mi amor*, Consuela had called him. *My love*. But Gem sensed the words were said to hurt him, not as a term of endearment.

The men ate their meal quickly. As soon as they were finished, Chase and Julio stood up and excused themselves, promising to meet the women in two hours at the buggy. Consuela nodded and sipped her coffee while Gem watched Chase weaving his way through the tables and out of the restaurant.

"Senorita?"

"Hmmm?"

"Remember that he is *my* husband."

Gem's head snapped back, returning her gaze to Consuela. "Whatever do you mean?" she asked, but knew exactly what Consuela meant.

"I may not want him, but no one else shall have him." Consuela smiled. "Do you understand me?"

Gem straightened in her chair and lifted her chin. "Why do you want to hurt him so?"

Consuela shrugged, a cruel smile on her full lips.

"And besides," Gem continued, "you've mistaken my feelings for Chase. He's like a cousin to me. I love him 'cause he's family."

"As you wish, senorita. But I warn you, do not try to interfere between us." She stood up. "Now, let us go shopping."

They were leaving Hattie's Millinery Shop nearly two hours later, Gem's arms loaded with Consuela's purchases, when they met up with Josh and Powell Daniels.

"Why, Miss McBride. What a pleasure seeing you here," Powell said with a grin. His hazel eyes perused Consuela. "And who is your friend here?"

Gem tried to step around him without answering, but Josh blocked her path. "Here now. You don't have to be in such a hurry. Why not let me and my boy help you carry all those packages?"

"That's not necessary, Mr. Daniels. We can manage just fine."

Consuela was meeting Powell's gaze with a direct one of her own. "Do not be silly, Gem. Let the gentlemen help us." She handed her packages to Powell. "*Gracias*, senor."

"You're welcome, senorita." As he turned, Powell glanced at Gem. "Are you gonna introduce us or not?"

Reluctantly, she made the introductions. "Consuela, this is Powell Daniels and his father, Josh, from the Big Pine. Consuela is Chase's *wife*." She put a heavy emphasis on the word, hoping it would make a difference. "They just got up from Texas a couple days ago."

"Well, I'll be—" Powell grinned again in open admiration. "Whatever did you see in Chase Dupre to make you want to be his missus?" He offered her his elbow.

"At the moment, senor, I cannot remember." Consuela slipped her hand into the crook of his elbow, and the two of them proceeded toward Mrs. Culverson's.

Gem stood rooted to the boardwalk, anger welling up and heating her cheeks. Of all people for Consuela to be flirting with, it had to be Powell Daniels. Powell had been pestering Gem ever since they first met, and she disliked him with unparalleled intensity. What's more, she knew that Chase disliked him for reasons of his own. If Chase saw Consuela walking with Powell . . . She bolted forward, still holding onto her own things rather than passing them to Josh.

Luckily, Chase and Julio hadn't arrived yet.

Powell placed the hat boxes and other packages in the back of the buggy, then assisted Consuela up to her seat. He touched his hat brim with two fingers. "It sure was a pleasure, Mrs. Dupre. I hope we'll be seein' each other again soon."

"It is my wish also, Senor Daniels."

Gem watched the two big men stroll away, helpless rage leaving her momentarily speechless. Suddenly she threw her packages into the buggy. Her hands on her hips, she raised defiant eyes toward Consuela. "Look here, Consuela. Don't you ever speak to that man again. You hear me? He's no friend of the Dupres, him or his pa. Chase and Powell can't stand the sight of each other. I don't have any proof, but it wouldn't surprise me if he wasn't the one that burned down the barn."

Consuela slowly opened her fan and began moving it in front of her face. "You cannot tell me what to do, *muchacha*."

A string of curses that Gem had learned long ago in saloons and bunkhouses filled her head and clung to the tip of her tongue, ready to spill forth in wrath. But Aunt Enid's admonitions about swearing wouldn't let her utter them in the middle of the main street, no matter how tempted she was. In frustration, she could only grit out a high-pitched, "Oooh!" before hurrying to her tethered horse and mounting quickly. "Tell Chase I left to go back to the ranch." She didn't wait for Consuela's reply.

* * *

Chase found her in the meadow where they used to go for target practice. She was shooting at a row of pine cones she'd lined up along the top of a fallen tree. She didn't realize he was even there until she holstered her revolver and started walking toward the log to set up another line of pine cones.

"Mighty good shooting," he called from the edge of the trees.

She stopped, looked over her shoulder at him, still scowling. "Thanks."

He nudged his horse forward. "You mad about something?"

"About something."

"Care to tell me what'd make you mad enough to leave town without us?"

"No."

"Was it Consuela?" he asked, softer this time, causing her to stop and look back at him once again. Chase drew his horse up beside her. "Was it Consuela?" he repeated.

Gem sighed. "Doesn't matter."

He swung down. "I didn't bring her to Montana to make everyone else miserable."

She shrugged. "She's your wife. She belongs here as much as anyone else. More'n some."

"What did she do, Gem?"

She couldn't help herself. The sadness in his voice drew her like a magnet. She turned and her hand reached out to touch his cheek, lingering there in a gentle caress. Pools gathered in aquamarine orbs, clinging precariously to long lashes. "What did she do to *you*, Chase?" she asked.

For a moment it seemed he would respond to

the love in her eyes. He stared down at her, unmoving, his gaze flickering over her face, and it seemed as if she could see right into his heart, and shared his despair. Then the open wound of his soul was hidden from view, swallowed up by a hardened facade that warned her not to get too close. His fingers closed around her wrist, and he slowly moved her hand away from his cheek. He stepped back from her.

"Chase—" She still held out her hand toward him, offering friendship, devotion, love—whatever he would accept from her. "Maybe it would help to talk about it."

"It wouldn't help," he answered gruffly, then turned his back on her.

"Julio said—"

"Julio talks too much." He shoved his hands into the pockets of his blue denims.

Gem looked at the taut back, quelling the urge to go to him once more. It wasn't her place to do so. For her own sake, for Chase's sake, she'd be better off to leave him alone. She spun on her heel and walked swiftly toward the log. She picked up pine cones from around the tree and lined them neatly in a row atop the log. As she headed back in Chase's direction, she pulled her revolver from its holster and loaded the chambers.

"Care to see my fast draw?" Her voice was intentionally light and cheerful.

Chase glanced over his shoulder.

"Care to see?" she repeated.

He turned around.

Gem spun toward the log and began firing

rapidly. Pine cones and pieces of pine cones flew in all directions as she shot them off the log with scarcely a second between one shot and the next.

Take that, Consuela, she thought with each pull of the trigger, *and that and that and that*.

If only he understood that she loved him, but he thought she felt sorry for him and his pride would never allow him to accept pity. She knew that was what he thought, and she understood it. She didn't want anyone feeling sorry for her either, loving Chase as she did and him too blind to see it. And even if he did see it, what good would it do? She should leave Four Winds. She should go away from here. But where would she go and what would she do to support herself? She couldn't run cattle anywhere else. No one was going to hire a woman to do a man's job, even if she was capable of doing it, even if she could prove it as she had yesterday. But what else could she do?

A long silence passed between them as these thoughts raced through her mind. She wasn't even aware that Chase had turned away and mounted his horse again.

"I'll speak to Consuela, try to get her to—"

"No!" She jammed the Peacemaker into the holster. "Don't you dare say a word to her about me, Chase Dupre. I'll fight my own battles. If Consuela and I have a problem, it's between us, same as things between you and her are between you two."

The shadow of a smile passed over his mouth. "Okay, kid. Whatever you say." He pulled his horse around.

"Chase."

"Yeah?" He stopped and glanced back.

"I'm not a kid any more."

"So I'm beginning to see."

"I think we oughta pay a call on Chase and his pretty new wife, Pa. It's just the neighborly thing to do." Leaning against the hitching post, Powell struck a match and watched it burn down, tossing it into the dust at his feet just before it burned his fingers.

"Don't imagine we'd be too welcome. That boy never did think much of the Daniels family." Josh pushed himself out of his chair and walked over to the porch rail, letting his gaze sweep over the panoramic view before him.

Powell knew the direction of his father's thoughts. He had come here after Enid Dupre. He'd stayed because of Enid Dupre. He'd built this ranch, hoping that one day she would be its mistress. Well, Enid Dupre didn't want anything more to do with the Danielses than Chase did. She had spurned his father, and it grated on Powell's nerves to know that anyone could do that and get away with it. But his pa didn't seem to be angry about it any more. He seemed content with things as they were, with this ranch and this house and their cattle.

But it wasn't enough for Powell. This was good land, and he wanted more of it. He wanted to own it all, all the way down to Yellowstone, and some day he would. He meant to be the biggest cattle rancher in Montana. He wasn't a man who gave up what he wanted. He wasn't going to be like his pa. He'd own this land no matter what he had to do to get it, and he wasn't going to let anyone stand in his way, especially a Dupre.

He lit another match, staring into the tiny flame, mesmerized for that moment by the flickering yellow-orange glow. A strange excitement spread through him. It was almost sexual, and he reveled in its tingling warmth. Of course, the excitement was greater the bigger the fire. Say when a barn was burning, for example.

"I suppose it wouldn't hurt to make a call," Josh said suddenly. "Give us a chance to see your brother and Katie and Maggie."

Powell grunted. He didn't have much use for his baby brother or his family.

The sons of Josh Daniels were as different as night and day. While Powell was a near duplicate of his father—exactly the same height at five feet nine, hazel eyes, brown hair, ruddy complexion, and prominent nose—Rodney had taken after their mother with his slight build, blond hair, and handsome, almost delicate features. But even more than the physical differences were the differences in the brothers' personalities. Here again Powell was more like his father. He was determined and bull-headed, quick to anger, and dangerous in a fight. Rodney, on the other hand, was more even-tempered and avoided violence when possible. It was his easygoing nature and sense of fair play and honesty that had driven him from the Big Pine Ranch. He'd always objected to Powell's ruthless methods in gaining whatever he wanted. It seemed only fitting that Rodney had gone to work for the Dupres. He was more like them than a Daniels.

Good riddance, Powell thought now as he struck

another match and watched it burn. He thought again of the barn at Four Winds, and he grinned in satisfaction.

"It's not Rod or Chase I want to see. It's that new Mrs. Dupre."

"Boy, I'm tellin' you. Don't go messin' with another man's wife. It'll only cause you grief."

Powell snorted. "Is that sage advice from one who knows?" His eyes clashed with his father's. "Let me tell you something, Pa. If it was me hankerin' after another man's wife, there wouldn't be anything that'd keep us apart, not even her. And one day those Dupres are going to find out what happens to those that look down their noses at us."

"It ain't always that simple, Powell."

He pushed away from the hitching post. "It's simple enough when you're man enough to take care of it." He pointed his finger at his father. "And one day I'm goin' to do your job for you."

Josh shook his head slowly as he ran his fingers through his graying brown hair. "I taught you too much hate, boy. It's going to eat you up inside."

Powell laughed harshly, then hit out for the barn. He was eager to get over to Four Winds and reacquaint himself with the lovely Consuela Dupre.

8

Chase had stripped off his shirt, the heat of the June sun beating down on his back as he nailed another board on the new barn. He paused for a moment, wiping the sweat from his forehead with the back of his hand. His muscles ached and he was tired, but it was a good kind of tired. The barn was nearing completion. He could see the work of his own hands, standing strong and sure, ready to shelter the livestock against the harsh Montana winters.

Squinting against the sun, he glanced toward the house. Consuela and Aunt Enid were sitting in the shade of the porch. Aunt Enid's hands were busy with something, probably darning or patching, but Consuela sat idle, occasionally flicking her fan in front of her face. He felt irritation rising like bile in his throat. Why should it surprise him that she did

nothing to help? She had always been waited on at
Casa de Oro. She was the cherished baby sister, the
only daughter of aging parents. She had been brought
up to grace a home with beauty and laughter, nothing
more. Wasn't that what had drawn him to her at the
start? Her beauty, her laughter, her innocence. He'd
loved her, loved her so much he hadn't returned to
Montana that first year as he'd promised . . . or the
next year or the next. He'd loved her until it hurt.

But it didn't hurt any more. There was nothing
left to hurt. Anger, yes. He still felt anger. Anger at
her selfishness. Anger at her deceptions. And sometimes sadness over the futility of his life.

He picked up the hammer and started working
again. He didn't have time to feel sorry for himself.
He was married to her, and he would have to make
the best of it. Perhaps some time away from her would
help. Tomorrow he would ride out to inspect the line
cabins. It was early still, but winter had a way of
sneaking up on you in this country.

"Julio, hand me a few more nails, will you?"

Chase's gaze followed the sound of Gem's voice.
She was kneeling at the corner of the barn, hammer-
ing away with the best of them. Something warm
touched his heart as he watched her. What was it? The
feeling was there so briefly he didn't have a chance to
examine it. But he did know this. In the days since
he'd returned to Four Winds, she'd been a bright
spot in his life.

Julio approached her and dropped some nails
into her outstretched hand. He said something to
her, and she laughed up at him, her eyes sparkling.
Julio touched the tip of her pert nose, wiping away a
smudge of dirt. Gem batted at his hand playfully, and

they laughed in unison. Chase was surprised by the sudden burst of jealousy that raised its ugly green head as he watched them.

Julio turned to walk away from her, then stopped, his eyes narrowing as he peered up the road. Chase's own gaze followed Julio's.

It had been five years since Chase had seen them, since the night of the barbecue and the bunkhouse brawl, but he recognized Josh and Powell immediately, even before they were close enough to see their faces. He straightened, a frown creasing his sweat-streaked forehead. In an instant it was winter again. Winter, and he was a small, sick boy . . .

The snow was piled in frigid drifts against the sides of the old log house. Chase thought he'd never heard the wind howl so fiercely or for so long as he lay in his bed, his young body still weakened by the fever that had raged through it for days. Aunt Enid had seemed to always be hovering over him, giving him something cool to drink or coaxing him to take another sip of hot broth.

He was alone in his loft bedroom when voices drifted up and awakened him. He lay still, trying to recall how much time had passed since he'd fallen ill. He remembered his mother was the first. She'd fainted in the kitchen and his father had put her to bed. Then cousin Chantal had complained of a sore throat and how she hurt all over. Chase must have been next, but he couldn't remember how or when. He wondered how his mother and Chantal were doing. Were they still sick? And the others. Why hadn't he seen his father or Uncle Frank or his younger cousin, Paul?

He swung his legs over the side of the bed and tried to stand, but his limbs crumpled beneath him. His head swam wickedly for a moment. He took a deep breath, then drew himself up onto his knees and began to crawl toward the ladder leading from the loft. The voices grew louder and clearer.

"I'd thank you kindly to leave here, Josh. I've sick folk to tend to."

"Let them tend themselves, Enid. Come away with me before you take sick yourself." It was a stranger's voice. A man's voice.

"You forget it's my husband you're asking me to leave."

"I'm not forgettin'. My wife's dead and Frank's going to die soon enough. I've followed you a long way, a long time, and I don't intend to leave this valley without you."

"Take your hand off me." His aunt's voice was frigid. "You don't seem to understand, Josh Daniels. I love my husband. Even if he was dead, I wouldn't go anywhere with you. I told you that back East, and I'm tellin' you now."

"I don't ever lose what's mine."

"I was never yours."

Chase reached the top of the ladder just as the man pulled his aunt into his arms and kissed her harshly.

"Take your filthy hands off her!" Chase shouted.

The man stepped back from Enid and gazed up at Chase with undisguised disdain. "Is that Frank's whelp?"

"He's Denise's boy." As she spoke, Enid moved quickly away from him, reaching for the rifle that rested near the door. "Now, Josh, I want you to go.

I'm going to forget this ever happened. You just go on and leave us be."

Josh glared in Chase's direction a moment longer, then turned his gaze upon Enid. A smile slit a crooked path across his face. "I don't ever lose what's mine, Enid. I'll go, but I won't go far. I can be patient. Me and my boys can wait."

He left then, and Enid hurried to help Chase back to bed.

"Who was he? What did he want here?" he demanded.

Enid studied his serious, boyish face, thin and haggard from the fever, but a face quickly approaching manhood. She seemed to be weighing what she should tell him. When she answered, it was with quiet honesty. "I knew him before I met your uncle Frank. His parents and mine had agreed that their oldest children should marry, but I never liked him. Still, I suppose I would have done it to please them if Frank hadn't come along. I guess Josh has been looking for me ever since I eloped with your uncle."

"Does Uncle Frank know?"

"No, dear, and you mustn't tell him. Not ever. I want you to promise."

Chase frowned. He hadn't liked that man, and he thought Uncle Frank should know about him. As long as he was around, there would be trouble. Chase was sure of it.

"Promise me, Chase Dupre. Your uncle is a sick man, and I won't have him worried. Now you give me your word."

Reluctantly, he agreed. "All right, Aunt Enid. I promise. But I don't like it. I don't like it one bit."

* * *

Chase still didn't like it. The two log cabins were gone, replaced by this fine two-story home. The small ranch had grown bigger, as had the boy who had told Josh to get his filthy hands off his aunt. Much had changed since that day, but not Chase's feelings toward Josh Daniels or his oldest son. There had always been enmity between Powell and Chase. Perhaps it had been born into each of them.

"Afternoon, Chase. Heard you were back." Powell drew in the reins of his horse.

Josh dismounted. "We met your wife in town the other day. We'd about given up on you coming back to Montana. I guess your aunt was mighty pleased to see you." He held out his hand. "Good to have you back."

Chase looked at the proffered hand with suspicion. He couldn't remember Josh Daniels ever having a good word to say to him. Finally he took hold of it and gave it a brief squeeze. As he released it, he said, "It's good to be back, Josh, and I'm here to stay. Brought back a fine herd of cows with me."

"So I heard." Josh glanced toward the barn. "Looks like you've had a bit of trouble."

"Nothing we can't handle."

Josh ignored Chase's gruff tone as he looked over at his son. "Well, get down, boy, and give Chase a welcome."

"My welcome's as good from here, Pa."

Josh squinted up at the sun. "Sure is a hot one for June, ain't it?" He dropped his gaze and turned his head toward the porch. "Don't suppose you'd offer us somethin' cool to drink."

Gem had walked over to stand beside Chase, and now she spoke for him. "There's lemonade up at the house. Wouldn't be neighborly if we didn't invite you to stay for some on a hot day like this."

It wasn't exactly a warm invitation, but it was better than anything Chase could have done. Still, Chase knew Gem was right. Aunt Enid would be ashamed of their manners if they didn't invite the two men to stay. Her hospitality didn't allow her to be unfriendly even to the likes of them.

Gem walked between Chase and Josh. Powell stayed in the saddle, waiting until he'd reached the hitching post near the front steps before he dismounted. Consuela and Aunt Enid had both risen from their chairs and come to the edge of the porch.

"Afternoon, Enid." Josh removed his hat as he spoke. "We came to say our welcome backs to Chase here."

"That's kind of you, Josh. Won't you come in and say hello to Frank? He gets terribly bored these days. He'd certainly like to pass some time with an old friend."

Old friend? The words grated on Chase's nerves. Josh was no friend of Frank's. He was just waiting around for Frank to die so he could steal his wife.

"Be happy to," Josh answered.

Enid touched Consuela's arm. "This is my new niece, Consuela Dupre. She's come up from Texas with Chase."

"We had the pleasure in Virginia City. Pleased to see you again so soon, Mrs. Dupre."

"The pleasure is mine, Senor Daniels," Consuela responded sweetly. Then her dark eyes swept away from the older man to linger on Powell. "And you, too, Senor Powell."

Chase watched her flirtation and waited to feel

angry or jealous, but nothing happened. He had witnessed this same scene too many times. Consuela was a born flirt. She couldn't help herself. If a man was near, she needed to conquer him, to add him to her list of admirers. It was a part of her nature, something he doubted would ever change. And men couldn't help responding to her. He certainly hadn't been able to when he met her. The only part that bothered him now was that it was Powell who returned her flirtatious glances.

Powell nodded toward Consuela, then looked at Chase. "Your wife here has made Montana prettier just by her comin'. Never figured you'd be so lucky, Dupre."

Lucky? Yeah, I'm lucky, all right.

Gem stepped up onto the porch. "You men sit down. I'll bring out the lemonade."

Her eyes met with Chase's, and he knew in that instant that she shared his feelings about having the Danielses on Four Winds. She distrusted them as heartily as he did. He wondered if anything had happened between Powell and Gem in the years he'd been away, and then felt a pang of guilt for not being here to protect her from him.

"Sometime I must have my husband bring me over to your ranch, Senor Daniels." Consuela's voice drew Chase's attention away from Gem. She had hooked her arm through Powell's and was drawing him toward the chairs on the porch. "It sounds very beautiful."

"Anytime you want to see it, you just come on over, with or without Chase," Powell responded with a broad grin.

"Oh, I will, senor. I promise."

Chase ground his teeth and joined them on the porch.

It had been the most disgusting thing she had ever witnessed, Consuela preening before the likes of Powell Daniels. It made Gem's blood boil just to think of it. She wished Chase would have put him in his place. She wished he would have punched him senseless. But Chase had sat there drinking lemonade, acting as if nothing was out of the ordinary. Still, she had been aware of the undercurrent of distrust and dislike he felt, having Powell Daniels sitting on his front porch. Yet, for some reason she didn't quite understand, she was certain he didn't care that his wife had fawned over his longtime enemy and had flirted with those long lashes of hers, giggling all the while like a silly schoolgirl.

But Gem had minded. She had minded a great deal. If she hadn't already disliked Consuela Valdez Dupre, that afternoon would have done the trick.

9

Gem was already saddling Wichita when Chase stepped out of the house the next morning. Out of the corner of her eye she saw him walking toward the corral, but didn't stop what she was doing. She leaned under Wichita's belly and grabbed the cinch, beginning to loop the latigo through the ring.

"Where are you off to so early?" Chase asked as he paused on the other side of the corral fence.

"I'm going with you."

"Oh? First I'd heard of it."

She turned around to look at him. There was a tiredness in his eyes that seemed never to go away. "I thought you might like company," she said.

"I would, but I'm going to be staying out for a few days."

Gem shrugged her shoulders. "So I'll head back early."

What she had wanted to say was she would stay with him, but she hadn't the nerve. With a shiver she wondered what would it be like to spend the night beneath the stars alone with Chase? Her stomach did a funny flip-flop.

"Well, let's get going then." He slipped between the fence rails and headed for his buckskin. They were both mounted and leaving Four Winds' house and outbuildings behind them in a matter of minutes.

It was going to be another scorcher. The grasses of the valley were already beginning to turn brown beneath the relentless summer rays. The sun peeking over the tips of the craggy mountains was already carrying an unusual warmth, chasing away the crispness of morning.

"If we don't get some rain soon—" Chase let his voice trail off as they cantered south, following the edge of the mountain range.

"It could be a long, hot summer," Gem responded.

They rode in companionable silence for an hour or so before stopping to water their horses. The stream plunged down the side of the mountain, still fed by melting snow.

Gem knelt beside the creek and cupped her hands for a drink. When she had quenched her thirst, she splashed some of the cold water on her cheeks, then shook her head, scattering droplets around her. She drew in a deep breath and sat back on her heels as she reopened her eyes. She loved the pungent green smell of the pines. The scent tickled her nostrils and trickled down inside of her, leaving her feeling fresh and clean, like a morning after the rain. She picked up her hat from the ground beside her and got to her feet, turning to discover Chase watching her.

He smiled, and the lines around his eyes crinkled up in pleasure. "It doesn't smell the same anywhere else I've been."

"I didn't think it could." She returned the smile.

For that moment, so very brief and poignant, it was as if they shared the same soul, same mind. Both of them loving this land with a depth few could understand, but they understood and it drew them closer.

Chase broke the spell as he put his hat back over his hair. "We'd better get going. We've got lots of ground to cover, and you'll have to ride for home soon enough."

She nodded and mounted her mare.

It was several hours later, just past the second line cabin, when they found the carcass of the steer and the tracks of the grizzly. It was a fresh kill, but there wasn't much left of the longhorn.

"I was hoping we'd seen the last of this," Gem said while Chase dismounted and hunkered down to study the large prints left in the dirt.

"Hasn't been that long since it was here."

"Are you sure?" Gem felt a tingle of fear icing its way up her spine. Her eyes darted toward the pines that thickened as the mountain climbed toward its jagged peak.

Chase pushed his hat back on his head. "I'm sure." He straightened, his gaze aimed in the same direction as hers. "It's up there, Gem, waiting to take out more of our cows, and I didn't drive that herd all those miles just to feed some grizzly. Somebody's got to get it."

"We've tried."

"I haven't." He raised his eyes to meet hers. "Gem, I want you to ride back to the ranch. Tell whoever is around to get out here. I'm going to go after it while the trail is fresh."

"Chase, you can't go after that bear alone. It's already killed more than one man, including Wade. Charlie's a cripple 'cause he went out alone. It's smart and it backtracks on everybody."

Chase swung onto his horse. "You're wasting time. Get going." He pulled his rifle from its sheath and turned the buckskin up the mountainside.

Gem watched him go, panic rising in her chest. The bear was a killer. If Chase ran into him alone . . .

She jerked Wichita's head around and dug her spurs into the mare's sides, sending her flying in the opposite direction. She leaned low in the saddle and talked to the horse, urging more speed from her thundering hooves, but her thoughts were back at the spot where she had last seen Chase. He didn't know what he was riding into. He couldn't. He hadn't been there when they found Wade's body. But she had, and she would never forget the grisly scene, not if she lived to be a hundred. If it hadn't been for his gun and the few scraps of clothes, they might never have known who it was. His face had been gone, torn away by mighty claws and furious teeth.

She shuddered. "Hurry up, Wichita," she shouted, and touched her spurs to the mare's ribs once again.

"I don't think Chase likes Powell or his father. Why is that, senora?" Consuela sat in a chair pulled near the back door of the kitchen, fanning herself, while Enid washed clothes in a tub outside.

Enid lifted her face from her work. Her eyes narrowed as she observed the lounging woman in the doorway. She brushed some stray hairs away from her forehead, then leaned back over the washtub. "There was a time when Josh fancied himself in love with me."

"And you, señora? Did you love him?"

"Saints alive, no! There's not another man for me but Frank Dupre. Never was, never will be."

Enid continued scrubbing the shirt, but her thoughts turned to Frank. She'd always thought she'd kept Josh's pursuit a secret, thought Frank hadn't seen the way he pestered her when she was in town or the way he looked at her when he came visiting at Four Winds. Frank's insistence that Josh Daniels might be unlikable but he was still a neighbor made her believe her subterfuge was successful. She smiled to herself.

That man of hers! He'd not been as blind as she'd thought. He'd seen what Josh was doing, and he didn't wait for Josh to plant a bullet in his back out on the range. He'd ridden up to the Big Pine and he'd put Josh Daniels in his place. He had let him know that Enid was a Dupre and a Dupre she was going to stay, and Josh might as well get that straight in his mind right then. She didn't know all the details of what had happened that day, but there'd been a change in Josh's attitude toward her. While she still, to this very day, felt a little uneasy around him and his son, she wasn't threatened by them. And though a friendship never formed between the two men, a grudging respect had been born somewhere through the years.

"But, senora," Consuela persisted, breaking into her private musings, "why does Chase dislike Powell so? It's not his fault if Senor Daniels loved you."

Enid straightened and carried the shirts to the clothesline. "Powell and Chase have had it in for each other since they were boys. I reckon Chase has got his reasons. I don't know what they are, and I don't reckon it's got to be my business to know them. I do know that Powell's about as worthless as they come, and I don't doubt but what he's behind most of the trouble that happens hereabouts." She turned, placing her hands on her hips, her forehead scrunched up as she frowned into the sun. "Consuela, I don't know what the trouble is between you and Chase, and I don't want to know. That's between a man and wife and isn't no one's concern but yours and his. But you hear me now, and you hear me good. You keep away from Powell Daniels. He'll only bring grief to you and this family. You mark my words."

Consuela stood slowly. Her dark eyes were wide with innocence and surprise. "I do not know what you mean, senora. I was only being friendly. After all, I thought they were your friends. They came to welcome Chase home, and you took Senor Daniels up to see Senor Dupre."

Enid was ashamed of herself. Consuela almost looked as if she would cry. "Josh and I made our peace a few years back," she said in explanation, "but that don't mean I want them here or involved with my family. You've got a good man in Chase. You'd better be workin' at making him happy."

"I do not seem to be very good at making anyone happy, senora." Consuela sniffed as she fled into the house.

Enid stood silently for a moment, then walked back to the washtub and began scrubbing another shirt. Try as she might, she just couldn't quite believe that Consuela's tears were real. She might have had more patience with the girl's laziness if she thought Consuela loved Chase or was good to him.

Why couldn't he have married a girl like Gem? Better yet, why couldn't he have married Gem?

Chase left his gelding behind and proceeded on foot. The foliage was dense, and he was having a difficult time following the bear's trail. His ears were alert to any sound of breaking twigs and rustling brush. He had heard enough stories of this grizzly since his return to keep him aware of the beast's craftiness. He didn't have any desire to be the next victim.

The minutes dragged slowly by as he continued to climb, his eyes peering carefully at every sign, still listening for any telltale sound that would warn him of the bear's presence. His shirt was damp with his own sweat, and he was thankful for the shade offered by the tall pines. He paused long enough to remove his hat and wipe the perspiration from his forehead, then glanced back behind him.

It was then he heard the snap of a branch and the rumbling snort. He turned swiftly, bringing up his rifle, but was stopped cold by the sight of the majestic grizzly, standing above him on an outcropping of rocks. It stood on its hind legs, its forearms stretched out in front of its massive chest. The yellow-brown hairs of its coat were tipped with silver, giving it the grizzled look that gave it its name. It shook its head slowly from side to side, nose pointed toward the sky, and a low growling rumbled up from its chest. It was easily seven feet tall and probably weighed a thousand pounds. Chase would have sworn he could smell its foul breath even from this distance.

"That coat of yours is gonna look mighty fine on my wall." Chase raised the rifle to his shoulder.

The bear suddenly roared, dropping to all fours and disappearing from the edge of the cliff before Chase could fire. Tensely, he waited. Would it come up behind him? Or would it come straight down the mountainside? He turned his head, scanning for possible paths the bear might take. He was scarcely breathing now, tension filling his veins as he waited.

Consuela couldn't stand to be in that house one more minute. If she stayed, she would start screaming. She didn't know much about hitching a horse to a buggy, but she figured she could manage it if she had to. Luckily she found one of the cowhands in the new barn, working on some tack.

"Senor?"

He glanced up at her.

"I want to go for a ride in the buggy. Would you please prepare it for me?"

"It's mighty hot, ma'am. Maybe you'd best wait till evenin'."

"I do not wish to wait," she answered petulantly. "Now, will you do it, or must I try myself?"

The grizzled old cowboy sighed. "No, ma'am. If you want to go out in this heat, I don't aim to be one to stop you." He rose slowly from the barrel he'd been sitting on and went to do her bidding. When the horse was in harness and the buggy ready to go, the cowboy helped her up to the seat, then stepped back. "I better come along, ma'am. Don't want you gettin' into no trouble."

"I have no intention of getting into trouble, gringo." With the sarcasm still lingering in the air, she snapped the whip over the horse's rump and trotted out of the barn.

Consuela knew exactly in which direction she was headed. Powell had pointed out the way to the Big Pine spread, and she wanted to see if his home was as grand as he'd said. She wondered if it could be as wonderful as Casa de Oro. No, nothing could be that grand.

How she missed her home. She missed her brothers, Pedro and Juan and Iago and Fidel. And Pedro's wife, Maria, and her friends, Dulcinea and Alicia and Pepita. And Padre.

"No, I don't miss Padre," she whispered angrily. "I *won't* miss Padre."

The last time he'd spoken to her came rushing back, unwelcome but unavoidable . . .

"You would do such a thing? You would do that to me and to your husband?" Manuel Valdez stood across the room from her, his short, stocky frame outlined by the sunlight pouring through the window.

"Padre, I could not bear to leave you. It is not my fault. Chase was going to take me away from Casa de Oro. I had to do something to keep him from leaving. I had to do something!"

"You knew you would be leaving your home when you married him. You knew his place was in Montana."

"But, Padre, I did not think he would ever really

leave Texas. I thought if he loved me enough he would stay here. I thought if he really loved me he—"

"Enough! No more excuses. Thank God your mama did not live to see this day. It would have killed her."

Consuela was crying now. It wasn't her fault. It wasn't her fault. If Chase hadn't wanted to leave . . .

Manuel left his place by the window and walked toward the door. His hand on the latch, he turned to look back at her. "When your husband is ready to leave with his cattle, you will go with him. Casa de Oro is no longer your home, and Manuel Valdez is no longer your father. Manuel Valdez has no daughter."

"Padre!"

The door slammed, and she was left alone . . .

It was all Chase's fault. If he hadn't talked her into marrying him . . . If he hadn't insisted that they come to Montana . . . If he hadn't gotten her pregnant . . .

Wichita gave everything she had left to carry Gem back to the site where she'd left Chase. The game little mare was lathered in sweat when Gem finally drew back on the reins and brought her to a halt.

"Up that way." She pointed up the mountain. "He was following the tracks up that way."

Teddy dismounted and studied the tracks a moment, then nodded and stepped back up in the saddle. "Gem, you better stay here and rest that horse of yours. Julio and me'll go after him."

"No. I'm going too."

"Amiga, you are going to kill your little horse if you ride her any more." Julio's voice was gentle but persuasive. "Look at her."

He was right, of course. Wichita was ready to drop in her tracks. She was quivering with exhaustion. Reluctantly Gem nodded.

"We'll fire three fast shots when we find him," Teddy told her, and the two men rode up toward the trees.

Gem hopped to the ground and freed Wichita's cinch, pulling the saddle and blankets from the mare's back and laying them on the ground. Then she began walking.

She spoke softly to the mare as she led her in a wide, slow circle. "Better get you cooled down, girl. I didn't mean to be so hard on you, but—"

She wasn't thinking about the mare. She was thinking about Chase and that grizzly. What had happened while she was away? It had taken forever before she'd come across Teddy and Julio. Anything could have happened. Chase could even be . . .

"Stop it!" she said aloud, scolding herself for her morbid train of thought.

With determined steps she set off toward the nearby creek to water her cooling mare. She allowed Wichita to bury her muzzle in the water for a moment or two, then pulled her head up.

"Not too much too fast, girl."

She pulled the reluctant mare away from the stream, resuming their slow walk, her eyes returning to the mountainside. Where were they? Where was Chase? What was happening?

With a sudden whinny of fright, Wichita threw her head back and reared up on her hind legs. Gem was jerked off her feet, but she managed to hang onto the reins, keeping the wild-eyed mare from bolting. Her own heart was pounding in her throat. She knew

without seeing what must be frightening the horse. It
had to be the grizzly.

She clasped the reins and hauled the mare forward with all her strength, glancing in all directions
as she hurried toward her saddle and the rifle resting
in its scabbard. Just as she reached it, the enormous
bear burst from the forest, perhaps a hundred yards
south of her. It was lumbering on all fours, oblivious
of or just unconcerned by her presence. Gem yanked
the rifle from its sheath and leveled it against her
shoulder, squinting down the sights. But already the
bear was out of range. She lowered the weapon and
watched as he galloped out of sight.

Wichita was still quivering and dancing nervously behind her. Gem turned and placed a soothing
hand on the mare's black and white neck. "Easy,
girl," she crooned. "Easy."

The mare settled a little at the sound of Gem's
voice, but her tail continued to twitch and she
snorted and pawed the dust.

Gem felt the same way as she waited for a sign
from the men.

Chase was standing beside his buckskin gelding
when Julio and Teddy found him. The gelding was
dead.

Julio stepped down from his saddle and stood
beside his friend.

"I was lucky," Chase said in a low voice. "If he'd
wanted, he probably could've had me instead of my
horse."

"Did you shoot him, *amigo*?"

"No. I saw him about an hour or so ago up the
ridge there. He was standing over me on a spur of

rock. I should have had a shot at him then, but all I could do was look. He's the biggest dang bear I ever saw."

Teddy cocked his rifle and fired, then fired again and again.

Chase looked at him in question.

"We promised to let Gem know when we found you," Teddy replied.

"She's waiting?"

"*Si.* We left her near the creek."

Chase turned away from his fallen buckskin. "Let's get down there. No telling where that grizzly is by now."

The waiting was worse once she heard the shots. Did it mean he was all right? Or did it mean something far worse? Gem began walking Wichita again, this time more for herself than for the mare. Carrying the rifle at her side, she paced back to the stream and let the horse drink her fill. Then she walked back to where the saddle lay. The waiting had become unbearable. With an oath muttered under her breath, she threw the saddle onto Wichita's back, cinched it with experienced fingers, swung up into the saddle, and headed up the mountainside.

"*Amiga!*"

Julio's voice carried down through the pines. Gem stopped Wichita and raised her eyes, scanning the forest until she spied the three riders.

Julio waved. "He is with us," he called, pointing to Chase who was riding behind him. "He is safe."

She raised an arm and returned his wave, then hurried Wichita in their direction. Something inside of her demanded proof that he was unharmed. She wanted to see it with her own eyes. She wanted to touch him and know that he was whole.

But, of course, she couldn't touch him, no matter how much she wanted to. All she could do once they reached each other was ask, "What happened to your horse?"

"The grizzly got him."

Her eyes flicked quickly over him. There was no blood. He seemed to be all right. But if his horse had been killed . . .

"I'd left him behind and gone on foot. I wasn't even there when it happened," he said, reading the worry in her eyes. "We don't know where the bear is now."

Their eyes remained locked together.

"He came out of the mountains and headed west toward the river."

Chase tensed. "You saw him?"

"I would have shot him, but I wasn't anywhere near my rifle."

"You could have been killed," Chase said softly.

"So could you," she answered, even more softly, sensing that something special was being shared between them.

Chase was the first to look away. He glanced up at the sky. "We'd better be heading toward the ranch. We've got a big day ahead of us tomorrow if we're going to trap that bear."

"We're going after him so soon?"

"Not *we*," Chase answered with an emphatic shake of his head. "The men."

"I'm as good a shot as—" she began.

"Don't argue with me, Gem."

She pressed her lips tightly together. They'd just see who got left behind.

"Chase, I did not think you would be back tonight."

He closed the bedroom door behind him. "Sorry to disappoint you, Consuela." He moved to the chair beside the bed and sat down, immediately starting to remove his boots.

She twisted around on the stool at her dressing table. Her long black hair shimmered in the lantern light and lay in a soft mass around her shoulders and down the back of her filmy negligee. Her lower lip protruded slightly as she rose from the stool. "Why do you say that, Chase? I am not disappointed to have you with me. I wish you would spend more time with me. We could go into Virginia City again. Or we could have a party. Oh, I would love a party. Please, Chase. I am so bored."

"I have work to do, Consuela." He dropped his boots on the floor as he looked up at her. He could see her voluptuous body beneath the soft fabric of her nightgown but was unstirred by it.

"Oh! You and your stupid cows. You are the most selfish man I know. Whatever possessed me to marry you?" She tossed her hair behind her shoulders. "Why did you ever bring me to this terrible place if only to leave me alone all the time?"

Chase stood up too. "As I recall, Consuela, it's you who wanted me to leave you alone."

"I do not want you to desert me, *mi amor*. Am I not still the woman you desired?" When he merely looked at her with disinterest, her black eyes snapped.

"It is in our bed where I want you to leave me alone, senor."

"Then you're about to get your wish, senora, because that's the last place I want you." With that, he removed his shirt and denims. She tossed some Spanish curses in his direction, but he ignored them as he stretched out on his side of their bed and closed his eyes.

Still muttering angry epithets, Consuela put out the light and lay down beside him, both of them hugging their own edge of the bed.

Surprisingly, Chase didn't fall quickly to sleep as he'd assumed he would. He found himself remembering other nights he'd shared with Consuela, nights when she had welcomed him to her bed and into her arms. Or at least he had thought she was welcoming him. But it had all been an act for Consuela. Everything was an act for Consuela. He knew that now. Consuela would never need or want anyone except herself. But it didn't matter any more. What he had once felt for her was gone. There was no more love, no more desire. Why not forget it? Let it go. Consuela would never change. She would flirt with him, but she would also flirt with every man she met. She would demand his attention, but she would scorn him as a lover, choosing that way to punish him for all the wrongs she felt he had done her, not understanding that since he no longer loved her he also no longer desired her.

He rolled onto his back and stared at the ceiling in the darkness, pondering those years in Texas. If he'd done anything differently, would Consuela have loved him? Would they be happy now?

No, he answered himself. They had never been happy and they could never be happy. He knew that, and he must accept it. But it might have been easier to accept, perhaps, if his son had lived.

His son?

It was a question that would never find an answer.

10

Gem and Consuela both stood on the porch as the men saddled their horses and prepared to ride out at the crack of dawn. Each was making her own plans for the day but was keeping them a secret from Chase Dupre.

Gem had no intention of being left behind while the men went in search of the grizzly. She'd done enough waiting, worrying, and wondering yesterday. Chase could say what he wanted. She was as good a shot as any of the men who were going with him, and a better shot than some. Once they were on their way, she would saddle up Wichita and follow after them. Once they were in the bear's vicinity, they couldn't make her go back. They'd have to let her stay and help.

Consuela's plans had nothing to do with a grizzly. However, the bear of a man who occupied her thoughts could be every bit as dangerous. She had sat in her buggy the day before, staring at the main house at the Big Pine Ranch, intrigued by what she knew about Powell—and even more by what she didn't know about him. *This* she knew for certain— Chase didn't like him, and that was enough to make him appealing to Consuela. She intended to get even with Chase for taking her away from her family, for alienating her from her father, for bringing her to this foreign land, and Powell Daniels seemed a good place to start.

"We may be gone several days, Aunt Enid," Chase said as he hugged her. "Don't you go worrying about us. This time we're going to get him."

"You take care, boy." She patted his cheek with a weathered hand, then stepped away from him.

Chase glanced up at the porch. "Consuela—"

"*Hasta luego*, Chase. I will be waiting for your return." Her tone was one of dismissal.

He turned next to Gem. "Take care of everyone while we're away. Red and Corky'll be around if you need them."

"We'll be fine," she answered, guilt making her voice sound husky. She cleared her throat. "You just take care of yourself."

He nodded, then turned and swung into the saddle. "Let's go, men."

They galloped out of the yard, leaving the three women in a swirl of dust.

Aunt Enid stared after them for quite a while before turning her gaze upward. "Might have us some rain before nightfall," she said as she wiped her hands on her apron. Then she walked past Consuela and Gem and entered the house.

"Rain?" Consuela echoed. "There is not a cloud in the sky. How can she say it will rain?"

"Feels it in her bones, I suppose." Gem also turned and headed into the house, too preoccupied with her own plans to pretend any politeness to Consuela.

She hurried up the stairs to her room and finished throwing a few things into her saddle bags, including a slicker. If Aunt Enid said it might rain, then she was going to be ready for it. She had already packed some food the night before, enough to last her a couple of days or so. Everything ready, she dashed off a quick note to Enid, explaining where she was going.

I just couldn't stay behind and worry, she wrote as she closed. *I have to be doing whatever I can to help. Love, Gem* .

She propped the paper up on her pillow, then slung her bags over her shoulder and hurried out to the barn.

Consuela's plans weren't quite as definite, but she was getting ready just as quickly. She intended to return to the Big Pine today, but this time she was going to ride right up to the house. She knew Powell was interested in her. She had seen that same gleam in many an eye since she turned thirteen or fourteen years old, and she had learned at a very early age how to turn that interest to her advantage.

She swept her dark hair up into a thick bun, then hid it beneath a riding bonnet of red felt with a large black plume. She dressed in her best riding habit, also a bright red. She wanted Powell to see her coming.

Although not a terrific horsewoman, she was a capable enough rider. She was even able to saddle her own mount when she was forced to, and this was to be one of those times. Those men not on the bear hunt were out riding line. She wasn't about to ask Gem to help her, nor did she want Enid to know she was going for a ride. She would just have to do it herself. She slipped from the house unobserved and hurried to the barn. She led out the docile mare that Chase had brought up with them from Texas and soon had her under saddle.

As she jogged away from Four Winds, she discovered that her heart was beating rapidly. She felt a great surge of excitement and breathless anticipation. She also felt a sense of danger, of treading where other women would fear to tread. A smile tilted the corners of her mouth.

"You see, Senor Dupre? I do not need you. I do not need *mi padre*. I will do as I please."

The rains came at nightfall. The men were too far up the mountain from one of the line shacks, so they were forced to make camp beneath the trees, seeking what little shelter they provided to keep them dry. As Chase sat silently beside the hissing and spitting fire that struggled valiantly to stay aflame, he pondered the foe he pursued. He wasn't a man given to fear, but he knew that the big grizzly was formidable and wily. This wasn't a turkey shoot they were on.

His gaze lifted from the fire as he got to his feet and turned to stare out into the darkness. He wondered if the bear was out there now, waiting for them to fall asleep. He listened, but all he could hear was the patter of rain on the trees above. He squinted, trying to seek out any strange movements in the stormy blackness that surrounded them.

And then he saw the flicker of light. He stepped farther away from his own campfire. There was no mistaking it. Someone was out there.

"Julio."

"*Si, amigo*?" His friend was quickly beside him.

"We've got company."

"You know who it might be?"

Chase nodded, his mouth set in a grim line. "I've got a pretty good idea."

Julio waited for Chase to reveal the stranger's identity.

"I'll bet you the next calf born at Four Winds that that's Gem out there."

"Gem?" Julio was incredulous. "Surely she—"

With grudging admiration, Chase said, "Oh, yes, she would. Darn fool doesn't have the sense to be afraid of anything. Let's go get her." He turned toward the others. "I think Gem's been following us. Julio and I are going to go bring her back to camp."

"Well, if that don't beat all." Zeke chuckled beneath his beard. "That girl is somethin', ain't she."

Chase and Julio mounted up and started off into the drizzly night, their hats pulled low over their heads.

She heard them long before she could make them out. Just as their slightly darker forms became evident amidst the shadows of the trees, Gem leveled the rifle against her shoulder and called out loudly,

"Stop right there." She paused a moment, fighting back the quiver that wanted to invade her voice. "Identify yourself."

"Don't shoot, kid. It's just us."

Chase! Her heart skipped a beat. She was so glad to hear his voice. She hadn't realized how lonely it would be at night up here on the mountainside.

The horses moved forward until the orange flicker of firelight danced on their sodden coats. Gem lowered her rifle and looked guiltily up into Chase's frowning countenance.

He leaned forward, resting an arm on the horn of his saddle. "Thought I told you to stay at home."

"I couldn't." She cocked her head to one side and peered up at him, a challenge in her eyes. "I'm not used to sitting back while others do the work."

Chase pushed his hat back on his head, unable to stifle a grin. "Get your horse, Gem. I can see there's no sending you back."

"Darn right there's not," she muttered as she quickly turned to pick up her saddle.

Chase slid from his horse and kicked out the fire as she tightened the cinch under her mare's belly. He stepped up beside her just as she turned around. Her hand came up to his chest to catch herself before walking into him. He grabbed her arm at the same time for apparently the same reason.

She couldn't see his face, but she sensed the spark that passed between them as they touched. It made her stomach jump and her heart flutter. She was thankful for the darkness. She didn't want him to see what she felt. She didn't want to be pitied for loving him.

"Do you ever do what you're told?" Chase asked softly.

"If it seems right."

There was a breathless pause.

"Well, I'm telling you, Gem. If you're going with us on this bear hunt, you've got to promise you'll do just as you're told. I don't want you hurt. You hear me, Gem?"

She moved her palm from his chest. "I hear you, Chase."

"Senora Dupre will be very worried," Consuela said as she stared into the stormy night.

"Don't worry, Consuela. I've already sent one of my men to tell her you are here, safe and sound."

Consuela turned from the window, pushing the skirt of her red habit out of the way with a dainty foot. She raised a dark eyebrow and asked coyly, "Safe, senor?" She stepped closer to him. "I am not so sure any woman would be safe with you."

Even without looking up at him, she knew he was staring at her voluptuous bosom, carefully exposed above the neckline of her bodice. She smiled, knowing that she was causing him some discomfort. It was a dangerous game she played, but she had always delighted in it. It made her feel special, in control. She loved it when men desired her but were helpless to take what they wanted.

Powell's fingers closed around her upper arm, and he drew her toward him. She looked up into his eyes and felt a flicker of fear. Perhaps this game was *too* dangerous.

"You're right, ma'am. A woman like you isn't

safe with me." He chuckled. "Know what else? A woman like you is glad she's not safe."

"My husband would not like to see you holding me this way." Her words were carefully calculated to make him jealous, perhaps even angry.

"But he ain't here to see it. Besides, Mrs. Dupre, I never have cared much what your husband likes or dislikes." His other hand gripped her as he pulled her up against him. "And I don't reckon you care much either. Am I right?"

For a moment, she merely stared up at him, scarcely breathing. Slowly, a self-pleased smile tilted her mouth. "You do not like my husband, senor?"

"Not for a minute."

"Then you may kiss me, senor."

"I plan to do more than kissin'." His mouth covered hers roughly.

She'd never been kissed like this before. Always the man with whom she had teased and flirted had been gentle, their words of praise filled with flowery promises of lifelong devotion. She had convinced them that she was shy and innocent. And the few who had bedded her before she married Chase had all believed her a virgin. Men were such fools. Stupid, rutting fools.

She pushed away from Powell, straightening her hair and her bodice as she did so. "You presume too much, senor." Consuela turned to walk away from him.

Once again his fingers closed around her arm. Once again she was pulled roughly against him. His face close to hers, he ground out a warning. "I don't presume nothin', Consuela. I read you like a book. You think you can tease me and get me all riled up and then just walk away, smilin' to yourself and thinkin' you're pretty smart. Well, that don't suit me none. You come here to make that husband of yours mad. Why's your reason and none of mine. But how is up to me." Again he kissed her, and his free hand roamed possessively over her body.

Consuela struggled against him, and he laughed into her mouth. When he released her, she gasped for air.

Powell laughed again. "All right, little lady, you make the choice. You want to start somethin', that's fine with me, but don't start it if you don't mean to finish it." His eyes dropped to her heaving breasts. "And you know what I mean by finishin' it."

She knew. This was more than a silly flirtation. This was more than even a quick tussle in the hay. This man was dangerous. He might even be a cruel lover. But he was Chase's enemy, and somehow that made the risks all worthwhile. She would make Chase sorry for taking her from Casa de Oro. If it was the last thing she ever did, she would make him sorry.

"*Si*, senor." Her voice was low and suggestive. She tilted her head to one side and gazed up at his face. "I know what you mean."

In the soft glow of the dying embers, Chase watched Gem's sleeping face. He felt a warm tugging at his heart.

"She is very special, *mi amigo*."

Chase glanced over at Julio where he leaned against a tree, smoking a cheroot. "Yes. Gem's special."

"I would give a lot for such a woman's love."

Chase nodded as he turned his eyes back on

Gem. She slept with her head cradled in one arm. Her mouth was set as if in deep concentration. Her strawberry hair brushed her neck just above her blanket, the shafts reflecting the light of the hot coals. The warm tugging at his heart turned to a twisting in his belly. He'd give a lot for such a woman's love, too.

And then what? he wondered, a scowl knitting his eyebrows. He had enough problems with the wife he had without taking on another female, especially when there was no hope for a future.

He lay down, turning his back toward the fire and Gem, resting his head on his saddle. "Nothing stopping you from going after her, Julio," he said gruffly and squeezed his eyes closed.

"Nothing, *amigo?*" his friend asked in a whisper.

"Nothing."

11

The mountain air was cold after the night of rain. The hunters shivered beneath their coats as they broke camp the next morning, saddling their horses, checking their supplies.

"We'll meet back here before nightfall. Make sure you stay with your partners. And watch your backs." Chase slipped his rifle into the scabbard, then swung effortlessly onto the saddle. "Gem, you ride with Ben and me."

Already mounted, Gem nodded.

Julio led his horse over beside hers. "You take care of my *amigo*, Gem," he told her, grinning all the while.

She returned his smile. "Why else do you think he wants me with him? He knows I'm the best darn shot of the whole bunch."

Catching her by surprise, Julio took her hand and lifted the backs of her fingers to his lips. His mouth still hovering over them, he looked up at her. "Most of all, senorita, take care of yourself."

Gem didn't know what to say or how to respond. The tender look in his dark brown eyes was so unexpected. There was more than just friendship there. There were feelings she didn't want to deal with. She glanced away from him, and her gaze collided with Chase's.

"Let's go," he said gruffly.

Julio squeezed her fingers, then released her.

The party split up into three groups of three, each heading in a different direction. Gem fell in behind Ben, trailing the two men as they headed up the side of the wooded mountain. She shrugged deep inside her coat. She felt miserable, not from the cold but from the confusion that raged inside her head.

Had she ever done anything to make Julio think there might be something more than friendship between them? She didn't think so. After all, he was the one person who knew she was in love with Chase. Wasn't that enough for him to know she wouldn't return any stronger feelings than those she already felt for him?

And then there was Chase. Why had he growled at her? For a while last night, she'd thought he was almost happy to see her. This morning he had been like a bear himself.

You're a fool, Gem McBride. What do you want from him? He's married, after all. Even if she isn't right for him, even if she does make him miserable and unhappy, there's not a thing you can do about it. Do you want to make him feel even worse?

Oh, how she wished they could go back to what it was before. Before he'd gone down to Texas and met Consuela. Back when they could ride together and laugh and shoot and play cards in the bunkhouse. Back when she could idolize him. Back when she thought him perfect in every way. Back when she was made miserable and ecstatic at the same time by that terrible, wonderful teen-age crush she had carried around for him, and Chase as blind as a bat even then.

She looked past Ben's head, watching Chase's back as the horses followed the winding trail through the dense trees, climbing, always climbing.

Why, she wondered, was it so easy for him to follow the tracks of a wild animal, but so impossible for him to see what she felt for him? But, of course, it was still a hopeless situation, whether or not he knew how she felt.

You ought to leave Four Winds, she told herself, not for the first time. But what could she do and where could she go? Besides, here she could see him each day, even if another woman shared his room. At least here she could hunt bears with him and ride herd and talk over dinner. Was it worse to be near and unable to have, or was it worse to be far away and unable to have?

There were no answers, and Gem's mood blackened as the day stretched out behind them.

The sun was beginning to burn off the morning mist when Chase lifted his hand and brought his horse to a halt. He stepped to the ground and hunkered down, his mount's reins trailing through his fingers.

"Look at this," he said to Ben. "He's been this way this morning."

Gem nudged her mare forward. "Are you sure?" she asked as she leaned over in the saddle.

Chase removed his hat and ran the sleeve of his shirt across his forehead. "I'm sure. Maybe an hour or two ago." Without looking at her, he straightened and remounted. "Keep a sharp eye out. He could be closer than we think."

Powell escorted Consuela back to Four Winds in his own carriage. It had been a most satisfying night. While she was not the most enthusiastic lover he had ever taken to his bed, she didn't shrink away from him either. He understood it wasn't desire that brought her to him. She was doing it for reasons of her own. Reasons he didn't completely understand. Or maybe he did. Wasn't part of the reason he wanted her because she was Chase's wife? To know he was cuckolding a Dupre . . . It was a satisfying feeling.

Enid Dupre was waiting for them on the porch as they pulled up in front of the house.

"Consuela! I've been so worried. I've had Corky out looking for you since before dawn."

"Didn't my man get here last night, Mrs. Dupre?"

Enid cast a suspicious glance in Powell's direction. "What man?"

"Consuela's horse took a fall near the Big Pine. It was ready to storm, so Pa and me thought she'd better stay the night. We put her up in the guest room, all nice and cozy, and Mrs. Blake took care of her." It was a nice touch, adding that Josh and the housekeeper had been there, when in fact Josh had been in Virginia City last night and Powell had sent the housekeeper packing to her own quarters as soon as Consuela arrived.

"Oh, senora." Consuela paled as he helped her out of the carriage. "I was so frightened. I do not know what I would have done without the kind help of Senor Daniels. I went for a ride and got lost. I could not remember which way was the ranch, and the storm was coming. I was so frightened, Aunt Enid. And then my horse stumbled and hurt his leg. If I had not seen the lights from Senor Daniels' hacienda—"

Well done, my little Spanish harlot, Powell thought, hiding his grin from Enid's wary eyes. What a performance.

Powell tipped his hat to Enid and then to Consuela. "I won't be stayin'. Just glad I could see Chase's wife home without any harm done. We'll send her horse back soon as its leg firms up."

The suspicion lingered in Enid's eyes even as she said, "Thanks, Powell. We're grateful for your help."

"No trouble at all, ma'am. Good day, Mrs. Dupre," he added to Consuela.

"*Buenos dios*, Senor Daniels."

Powell slapped the reins across the backs of his matching bays, and they sped away from Four Winds at a brisk trot.

The brief stretch of sunshine disappeared behind rolling black thunderclouds as the three riders followed the tracks of the elusive grizzly. Gem knew they had come too far to make it back to their designated campground before nightfall, yet how could they give up now while the trail was so fresh?

As tiny shards of rain began stinging her cheeks and the wind picked up, bending the trees before it, Gem pulled the collar of her jacket up around her neck and bent her head forward. She kept her eyes moving from one side of the trail to another. Nothing seemed to move except as blown by the wind, but she had a nagging sense of dread. Something wasn't right.

Chase was some ways up the trail ahead of Ben when the younger rider stopped suddenly. Ben leaned over in his saddle and stared at the ground. "Hey, Gem," he called back to her. "Look at this."

She raised the brim of her hat just in time to see the giant bear rise up from the forest greenery. A mighty roar thundered from deep in its chest as it swung in Ben's direction. Even as Wichita reared and twisted, Gem could see with sickening detail the crushing blow that twisted Ben's head around on his neck. Her fingers barely clung to the butt of her rifle as her mare spun out from under her. She hit the trail with a breath-wrenching thud, and her Winchester landed in the brush several feet away. But her eyes weren't on her rifle or her runaway horse. They were riveted on Ben as the bear's mouth closed over his head, holding him in the air as his mount bolted into the forest in the opposite direction, eyes wild and nostrils flared. Twice the bear shook Ben as a dog would shake a rat.

A petrifying scream filled the air. Was it her own voice? It must be, for even in her terror she knew that Ben was already dead.

The grizzly threw Ben's lifeless body away as if he were nothing more than a rag doll. Then it turned its shaggy, silvered-brown head in her direction. It lifted its dipped nose toward the sky, shaking its head from side to side, and then roared once more.

She was going to die. Like Ben. The bear was going to drop to all fours and come lumbering down that path to strike her dead. She should reach for her rifle. She should move. She should run. She should do something. Anything. But panic kept her frozen to the ground.

Through the wind and rain, Chase heard her scream and turned in his saddle to witness Ben's quick but gory death. And in the blink of an eye, the grizzly was finished with Ben and turning its attention on Gem.

Chase's gelding quivered beneath the saddle, but he forced him mercilessly down the trail. He pulled the rifle from its sheath and raised his voice in a cry of warning, hoping to draw the bear's attention away from Gem. In a moment it would be too late. In a moment the grizzly would have her.

He vaulted from the saddle and began firing even as his feet hit the ground.

The grizzly spun in mid-stride and was upon him before he knew what had happened. He fired one more round before the rifle was knocked from his hands by a giant paw. Chase stumbled backward, blood already soaking his tattered sleeve. The giant animal rose to its full height. Chase knew he had shot it at least twice, but it showed no signs of being wounded except by its cries of rage. A wide-swinging paw, armed with long lethal claws, caught Chase from the side, knocking him to the ground, leaving behind a welter of blood and torn flesh. He rolled and tried to rise, only to find the bear already there. Through a stunned haze, he looked up into the face of the deadly silver-tip—into the face of death itself. He could feel the bear's hot, stinking breath on his skin. Great jaws were opened, exposing blood-flecked teeth, teeth prepared to clamp over his head just as they had done to Ben.

Desperate and unarmed, Chase swung with his clenched fist, jabbing the grizzly in the eye. It howled its surprise before clamping its teeth over his wrist. Bones crunched, and Chase cried out as pain shot through every inch of his body.

There had been that terrible moment when the bear was almost upon her, but it was nothing compared to the terror she felt as she watched the giant bear mauling Chase. She only knew one thing. She must save Chase.

She reached for her rifle and hurried down the path.

"God, help me!" she cried aloud as she planted her feet firmly and drew a bead on the bear. She couldn't afford to miss.

She fired. Once. And then again. She could hear the smack of lead balls striking flesh, giving proof that the bullets had found their mark.

The grizzly dropped its victim and turned slowly toward Gem. It rose on mighty legs, its body stiffened by an inner flood of strength, rising higher and higher until it posed majestically over her beloved Chase. Its wild, indomitable will refused to die, even as its lifeblood flowed from the wounds in its body.

She was crying now. "Fall, damn you! Fall!" She sobbed helplessly as she fired once more, hitting the silvered grizzly in the shoulder.

With one more outraged cry, it fell forward onto all fours before it began to gallop, tumble, and roll its way into the forest and down the hillside. She could still hear its retreat as she raced to Chase.

Gem fell to her knees beside him. His rain-spattered face was ghostly pale, and his blood mingled with the rain to make red mud beneath him.

"Chase," she sobbed. "Chase."

He opened pain-glazed eyes slowly. "It's gone?" he asked, his voice weak.

"It's gone, Chase. It won't be back." She put her arm beneath his head. "We need to get you out of the rain. Can you walk?" Her eyes traveled quickly over his body. His clothes all seemed to be in tatters. Blood was everywhere. It was impossible to tell just where and how badly he was injured. She looked back at his face, awaiting an answer, but he was unconscious once more.

Cold and afraid, she tried to gather her thoughts. She had to get him someplace dry so she could attend to his wounds. She was certain the grizzly had gone off to die—she knew it must be mortally wounded —but she couldn't take the chance of leaving Chase here alone while she went for help.

Putting her hands beneath his armpits, she dragged him off the trail and into the forest, finding some respite from the weather beneath the piney arms of the tall ponderosas. Then she removed her jacket and covered his bleeding chest. Her own blood was pounding in her temples, and she stopped a moment to press her fingertips against them.

Think. I've got to think.

She looked up at the sky. The black clouds roiled overhead, no end in sight, and the wind was whistling through the trees with a vengeance, bringing a winter chill to the late June afternoon. What was she to do?

Her roving glance fell on Ben's crumpled body. She grabbed her rifle from the ground where she'd dropped it and, clutching it at her side, walked resolutely down the trail. Swallowing the sudden bile that rose in her throat, she knelt beside him and touched his throat, seeking a sign of life, though she knew she would find none.

"I'm sorry, Ben," she whispered as tears returned to fall from her eyes.

She heard rustling and hopped up, her rifle poised instantly, her heart nearly stopped. She stayed her finger just in time as Chase's gelding stepped into the clearing. She'd never seen anything that looked more beautiful than that horse at that moment.

"Whoa, boy," she said gently, walking toward him. "It's all right. Come here, fella."

The horse whickered nervously and drew his head back.

"Easy there. We've got to get Chase off this mountain. Easy, boy."

She closed grateful fingers around the leather reins and breathed a quick prayer of thanks before leading the gelding back up the trail toward Chase.

The rain fell in sheets, nearly knocking her to her knees as she led the horse blindly down the mountainside. Several times her feet slipped out from under her. Her clothes were covered with mud and her hair clung to her cheeks and fell into her eyes.

Somehow—heaven only knew how—she had managed to get Chase across the saddle. He was still unconscious, lying on his stomach across the horse's back. Every now and then she would hear him moan, but he didn't come to. She didn't know where they were or which way they were headed. She just kept trying to go down hill. They had to get off the mountain.

It was dark as pitch when they stumbled into the small clearing and she discovered the tiny log cabin. Long since deserted by whomever had built it, it had become the abode of many a small forest creature, but at this moment it seemed a veritable haven.

Gem tied the gelding at the side of the shack and stepped cautiously inside. Striking a match, she held it high and surveyed the single room. A mouse skittered into hiding amid the leaves and pine needles scattered over the floor. There was a mattress lying in one corner of the room. A rickety chair and table with a single candle in its center stood in another corner. There were no windows, and although the door had been swinging open in the storm, it appeared that it would close tight and hold out the weather.

The match had burned down nearly to her fingers. She blew it out and was immediately encased in inky darkness once again. She felt her way to the table and struck another match, then lit the candle. The flickering light gave her a feeling of revived hope as she turned and hurried outside to the waiting horse.

"Chase? Chase, can you walk?" She touched his cheek. "Please wake up, Chase. I don't have the strength to lift you again. Chase?"

He groaned.

Gem raised her voice. "Chase, you have to wake up. You've got to get inside."

He looked at her then, but she doubted he knew

her. She hurried around to the other side of the horse and gripped the saddle in both hands, bracing her body against his as he slid from the saddle. His legs buckled beneath him, causing both of them to land in the mud.

"Chase, you've got to help me," she pleaded. "Get up."

"Aunt . . . Enid?"

"No, Chase. It's me. It's Gem. Please help me get you inside." She draped his arm over her shoulder and struggled to rise.

Miraculously he rose with her, and together they shuffled into the cabin, barely making it to the tick mattress before he collapsed in her arms and dragged her down with him once more. Her arms enfolding him against her breast, she gasped for breath. Her lips brushed his rain-and-mud-soaked hair, and she allowed her tears to fall freely.

"Oh, Chase. What am I going to do? Don't die. Please don't die. I love you. You mustn't die. Oh, God. I promise I won't covet him any more. Please let him live. Please, God, help me."

She sniffed back the tears and slipped her arm from beneath him. If she was going to help him, she had to do more than pray. She had to take action, and there was little time for the useless tears she was shedding.

She hurried out to the gelding and pulled the bedroll from behind the saddle. Back inside, she closed the door firmly behind her, then unrolled the tarp. Inside, the soogan was still dry, and she draped it over Chase to keep him warm while she prepared to cleanse his wounds. She poured water from his canteen into a tin cup, then brought the candle from the table and placed it on the floor beside the mattress.

Drawing back the soogan, she stifled the gasp that rose in her throat. Scraps of material were imbedded in his ragged wounds. His left wrist was mangled, perhaps beyond repair, and his upper arm was laced with angry welts and deep scratches. His left side lay open and exposed, as did the inner thigh of his right leg. The twin red lines that marked his face from his right temple to his jaw seemed minor in comparison to his mauled and mangled body.

Resolutely she began to strip away his shirt, hurrying to stanch the flow of blood from his side, the most dangerous and life-threatening of his injuries. At least it seemed so to her layman's eyes. If only she could get him to a doctor . . .

After washing the wound, she tore a clean shirt, taken from the bedroll, into wide strips and bound his chest and side as best she could. All the while she prayed that the bleeding would stop soon.

She needed her knife to remove the scraps of fabric embedded in his upper arm. She heated it in the candle flame, hoping it would sterilize it some to prevent infection. Several times while she dug out the offending material, Chase cried out, but he remained unconscious, much to her relief.

Gem cleaned the mangled flesh of his wrist as best she could. Then she broke off the leg of the chair and tightly bound his wrist to the wood with her neckerchief, hoping against hope that she wasn't making it worse.

Turning her attention to his thigh, she stripped

away his Levi's and longjohns. She gave no thought to his nakedness. She had no time to be concerned with proprieties or to be embarrassed. Muscle and sinew lay exposed, but the blood was drying. The water that remained in the cup was nearly as red as his leg, but she dabbed at the torn flesh, cleaning the wound as best she could before using the last of the torn shirt to bind his leg.

With a shudder of fatigue, she turned her gaze back upon his wan face. She knew that what she'd been able to accomplish was only temporary. He needed a doctor, and soon. The wounds needed to be sewn or they would heal into painful, angry scars. Perhaps he would be left crippled.

She poured a little more water onto a strip of cloth and touched it to the deep scratches on his face. "You'll be all right, Chase." She said it more to assure herself than the unconscious man before her. "But you've got to fight." Slowly she drew the quilt over his naked body, then leaned against the side of the cabin and closed her eyes.

Was it just minutes or had several hours passed when she heard him whisper her name?

"Gem—"

Instantly alert, she leaned forward. "I'm here, Chase."

He was shivering violently, his teeth chattering in his head. The cabin was cold as ice, and the candle had burned low. Quickly she extinguished it, simultaneously reaching for the tarp to draw over the soogan. Then she shucked off her own damp clothes and climbed onto the tick mattress beside him. She drew up close to his back, trying hard not to touch his wounded side as she wrapped her arm around him and shared the warmth of her body.

"Don't you dare die, Chase Dupre," she threatened softly. "You've got too much to live for. I won't let you die. Do you hear me? You fight, damn you. You left me once. You're not going to do it again."

12

He had never known such searing agony. His entire body seemed to be on fire. He opened his eyes, but the room was shrouded in darkness. Was he dead? No, he wouldn't have this much pain if he were dead. He tried to move. A groan slipped between gritted teeth.

"Be still, Chase."

The whispered words were spoken close to his ear. He stopped himself from trying to roll toward the voice, knowing that the pain would only increase with movement.

"I'll keep you warm, my love."

Slowly he became aware of the tender arm that draped over him and the warm length of flesh that curved along his back. Through the sharp edge of pain, he recognized his nakedness and the near nakedness of the body lying against him.

"Consuela?"

There was a long pause before the reply came. "No, Chase. It's me. Gem."

He sighed and closed his eyes. He tried to think where they were and how they'd gotten there, but the agony of his flesh was too great. It was too difficult to make his mind work.

He felt her slip from beneath the covers and heard her moving about. Then she was kneeling before him and saying softly, "I've got to find us some water, Chase, and some wood to build a fire. I won't be long."

Chase tried to open his eyes, tried to speak her name, but already he was descending into unconsciousness once more, driven there by the unrelenting pain.

The rain had slowed to a mere drizzle. The wind had died to a whisper in the treetops. Were it not for Chase's condition, Gem would have enjoyed the fresh scents of the mountain morning after a rain. As it was, she shrugged deep inside her jacket, ignoring the remaining dampness of her clothes, and hurried to find a stream to refill the canteen and some wood to build a fire. She hoped that the chimney in the cabin wasn't damaged or filled with leaves and pine needles like the floor. She had to get Chase warm before he died of exposure.

She was right about the stream. She had guessed the cabin would have been built close to one. It wasn't difficult to find. She scooped the canteen deep into the rushing water, then cupped her hands and drank her fill before splashing her face with the icy liquid, rinsing off the traces of dried mud that still clung stubbornly to her skin and hair.

Gem stood and turned back toward the cabin, her thoughts rushing on ahead of her. Her first job was to get him warm, but they couldn't remain here for long. Chase needed a doctor or he would surely die. Hopefully, the weather would hold. She would need to build a travois since he couldn't ride. Did she have the right materials? Could she do it?

"Oh, please let them find us soon," she prayed as her eyes scanned the forest surrounding them.

One unspoken prayer was answered when she found a stack of wood against the back wall of the cabin beneath a lean-to. She loaded her arms with several pieces of dry pine and scraps of kindling left next to the neatly stacked wood pile. Inside the cabin, she quickly laid the wood and kindling and was relieved when it took hold and the smoke snaked its way up the chimney instead of back into the cabin.

At last she could turn her attention back to Chase. She hurried to his bedside and knelt on the floor. The flickering firelight danced over the angry red welts on his face. She felt the urge to cry again but angrily swallowed it. She had no time for such foolishness.

"Chase . . . Chase, drink some of this water." She held the canteen against his lips. "Can you wake up, Chase?"

She watched the fluttering of his eyelids as he struggled to obey.

His sapphire eyes were dulled by the pain and seemed sunken in their sockets. "Is that . . . you, Gem?"

"It's me."

"How—"

"It's not important, Chase. What's important is getting you out of here. I'm going to lift your head so you can drink some of this water. It'll help." She slipped her arm beneath his head. "Easy now. Don't drink too fast."

He swallowed weakly, most of it dribbling back out the corner of his mouth. As she lay him down, he raised his eyes to meet hers. "I'm . . . so . . . cold."

She touched his forehead. It was hot with fever. "I've built a fire. It'll warm up soon."

"So . . . cold. . . . Hold me . . . Gem—" His eyelids drifted closed.

How could she deny him? How could she not hold him when he asked it of her? She would cut out her own heart if it would take away his pain or save his life. Lying next to him, holding him against her, was such an easy request to fill. Once again she discarded her damp clothing and slipped beneath the tarp and quilt to share her own warmth with him and, hopefully, impart the strength and the will to survive.

They found Wichita early in the morning, her bridle snagged in a fallen tree. Julio found Ben's body shortly before noon. Two men stayed behind to bury his remains; the others set out to find Gem and Chase. The tracks had all been washed away by the storm, so they spread wide and rode slowly, calling their names.

* * *

The pain was still with him when he awoke, but now his thoughts were a little clearer. He remembered asking her to lie down with him, to hold him and keep him warm. And there she was, her chin resting gently on his neck, an arm placed carefully across the abdomen.

It was a bad time to admit how much he cared for her, even to himself. There was a good chance he wouldn't live through this, and if he did, there was an even better chance that he would be crippled. He didn't have to be able to see his wounds to assess the damage the bear had done.

Little Gem. How had she managed to get him to this cabin? He was so much bigger than she. But she was strong on the inside. Feisty and indomitable, that was his Gem. *His Gem.* He let out a silent sigh. If only it were true. If only she really were his. But he was married to another woman. No matter what Consuela was, no matter what a disaster their marriage had become, he was still married. Admitting he felt anything other than friendship for Gem, even to himself, could only bring them both more heartache.

"Gem—"

She was instantly awake. Her breath was warm on his neck. "Yes, Chase?"

"You shouldn't . . . be in bed . . . with me—" He gritted his teeth. It hurt even to talk. "Like . . . that," he finished.

"I had to warm you, Chase. I couldn't do it with wet clothes on."

His injuries didn't allow him to desire her, but even his pain couldn't keep him from acknowledging how good she felt nestled against him, how warm and comforting the feeling. "How'd we get here?" he asked, just to hear her talk.

"Your horse came back. You were out, but I got you over the saddle and started down the mountain. We came on this place after dark. I got you inside and cleaned up your wounds best I could, but we've got to get you to a doctor soon, Chase. You need stitching, and that wrist of yours needs more doctoring than I can give it." She moved away from him. "My clothes should be dry now, and the cabin's warming up. I'm going to start work on a travois."

"Gem?"

She knelt beside him, her face close to his. "Yes?"

He opened his eyes. "Thanks." He wanted to keep looking at her, but his eyelids were too heavy, and they once again sank closed.

Gem waited a long while before she started to rise. He knew she was watching him and thought him asleep again. He wanted to talk to her, but his voice wouldn't obey.

"I love you, Chase Dupre," she whispered. "And the only way you can thank me is to get well."

I love you, Chase Dupre. He'd heard those words before from other lips. Lying lips. He had hardened his heart against them. Yet something cracked in his protective shell when Gem whispered them, and he drifted into slumber, taking comfort in her presence.

Julio rode into the clearing in mid-afternoon. Gem was dragging a lodge pole pine toward the cabin, grunting and muttering beneath her breath. Julio thought he'd never seen anything so wonderful. She was alive.

"Gem!"

She dropped the pine as she looked up. A smile burst upon her smudged face, and she came running toward him. "Julio. Thank God, you've found us."

"Where's Chase?" he asked as he leaned over in the saddle and grabbed her outstretched hand.

"He's inside, but he's hurt bad. We've got to get him a doctor. I was trying to build a travois, but I wasn't sure I could do it." She pulled on his hand, and tears glittered in her eyes. "Hurry, Julio."

He jumped out of the saddle and followed her inside. Chase was lying on a thin mattress in the corner of the small cabin. A fire warmed the room and cast its flickering glow over his pain-etched features. Julio knelt on the floor next to the bed and carefully lifted the tarp and quilt beneath it. The strips of bandages were stained red but appeared to be drying. At least he wasn't bleeding to death. Or at least he wasn't right now. He might before they got him off this mountain.

"*Amigo?*"

Gem knelt on the mattress behind Chase and gently touched his shoulder. "Chase? Julio found us. He's come to take you back to the ranch. You're going to be all right."

Julio's dark eyes lifted from his friend to the beautiful young woman. Mud was encrusted in the fine red-gold hair, which straggled over her shoulders and down her back. Her lovely aquamarine eyes, rimmed with dark circles, watched Chase with heart-piercing devotion.

She will die if he dies, he thought, *and I could not bear to lose either of them*.

His gaze returned to Chase. "*Amigo*, we must get you out of here."

"Julio, he's not answering." There was panic in her words. "What are we to do?"

"Stay with him. I will prepare the travois." He reached over Chase to gently caress her cheek. "Do not worry, *mi amiga*. We will get him back to Four Winds."

She nodded, but she didn't look up at him. Her eyes remained fastened on Chase, and Julio thought he would give anything if she would look at him that way.

"I don't like it, Frank. I've got me a bad feeling inside." Enid moved from the side of the bed to the window, pushing aside the lace curtains to stare out at the cloudy sky.

"You knew they'd be gone a few days, and Chase won't let anything happen to Gem once she catches up with them." He patted the bed at his side. "Now, come sit down beside me, woman, and quit your fussing. It's enough to drive a man crazy."

She turned from the window to meet his blue gaze. Her heart did a little dance beneath her breast. How very much she loved him. And how it hurt her to see him lying there, unable to get up, unable to ride, unable to do all the things he used to do with so much robust ambition. Now he had to be waited on and taken care of. Not that she minded for herself. She would love him no matter what. But she knew it was hard on him, not being able to get up and be out there with Chase.

She went over to sit beside him. With tender fingers, she brushed back the graying brown hair from his forehead. "You need a haircut, Mr. Dupre."

"Well, you're the best barber on the ranch, Mrs.

Dupre. If you say I need one, you'd better get to trimmin'."

But she only partially heard him. She was thinking about that morning, when Consuela returned in Powell's buggy. She wished she could talk to him about it. Oh, how she hoped what she suspected wasn't true. She thought she'd made her peace with that family, but if Consuela was . . . But it was too awful to even think about.

"What's really troubling you, Enid?" Frank asked, his forehead scrunched into a frown. "It's more than just that bear."

She patted his hand fondly and smiled. "No, it isn't. And you're right. I've got to quit this fussing. Chase is a grown man, and Gem is a good shot with that rifle of hers. They're as at home out there as they are in here. Maybe more so. Besides, the Good Book says not to be borrowing trouble. I suppose that means to quit imagining what could happen and wait till it does."

"I reckon that's what it means," Frank agreed with a chuckle, the wrinkles in his forehead changing from dour to amused.

"I'll go get my scissors."

"And I'll wait right here for you."

He said it with humor, but it brought another sting to her heart. Before she could let him see her threatening tears, she hurried out of their room.

Gem walked beside the travois all the way down the mountain, hanging onto Chase's hand most of the time. He only regained consciousness once, long enough to ask her, "Are you . . . trying . . . to kill me?" as they jostled over a rocky stretch of ground.

The smile he offered did little to improve her spirits as he slipped into the black slumber once again.

Before they'd reached the bottom, they were joined by all the men. Teddy arrived first, bringing news that they had found the grizzly. It was dead. Rodney rode on ahead to bring the doctor out to Four Winds. Zeke arrived with Wichita in tow. He led the mare beside his own horse until they were off the mountain, then brought the pinto over and told Gem to mount up. When Gem refused to leave Chase's side, Julio physically picked her up and set her onto the saddle.

"We can travel faster, *amiga*, with you on a horse."

"But—"

"Do not argue with me, senorita. He is my friend, too, and I mean to see that he lives through this."

Teddy and Pike rode up, one on each side of her.

"Julio's right," Teddy said. "We gotta move fast now that we're on flat ground."

"If'n you want," Pike offered, "you and me can git on up to the ranch and tell Miz Enid so's she can be ready for him."

Gem shook her head stubbornly. "I'm stayin' right here with him." Her eyes moved from man to man, challenging any of them to say differently.

"She is right, Pike," Julio said. "You ride on and let the senora know what has happened. Gem will stay with us." He nudged his horse forward, leading Chase's gelding, the travois strapped to the sorrel's sides.

Gem guided Wichita over close to Chase. Her gaze never left him. "You live, Chase Dupre," she whispered. "I'm not going to stand for anything less."

And I got to hold you. I got to lie next to you and hold you and touch you, and I won't ever forget it. You get well and you do what you have to do. I know you're another woman's husband, and I won't ask you to do what's wrong. But I won't ever have to forget what it was like, even if you don't remember it.

It didn't matter that he had called her Consuela when he awoke the first time. After that, he'd always called her by her name. He'd known it was Gem caring for him. He'd known it was Gem worrying about him and nursing him.

And it was Gem he'd asked to lie down with him and keep him warm. She would have that to think about later . . . in the loneliness of her room.

He heard the voice. A muffled voice. As if it were coming from miles and miles away. Darkness surrounded him, sucked at him, trying to pull him ever deeper. But there was that voice, a gentle yet strong voice that called him in another direction.

"Chase. Chase, you're home now. You're safe. Don't die, my love. I won't let you. Wake up, Chase. We're home."

Even through the pain, it called to him. Sweet as honey. Warm as the morning sun.

And then more voices, strident voices.

"¡*Madre de Dios*! You cannot take him to my room. I cannot take care of him. He will not live."

"You! You . . . you . . . *witch*! He's your husband. How can you say that?"

"How dare you call me names. I am Consuela Valdez, daughter of Manuel Valdez of Casa de Oro,

and you . . . you are nothing but the penniless orphan of a—"

"Say it and I'll rip your heart out. Put him in the
room next to mine, Julio. I'll take care of him till the
doctor comes."

Soft, gentle again. "Stay with me, Chase.
Please—"

Sweet as honey. Warm as the morning sun. Her
gentle call was stronger than the beckoning darkness.

13

The doctor came. Gem stayed with him while he sewed up Chase's wounds and set the mangled wrist.

"Don't put much store in what I've done there, gal," he told her, raising his eyes to look at her above the rim of his glasses. "That bear chewed it up real good. If we can keep the infection out of it, he won't lose it, but more'n likely it'll stiffen up on him and be as good as lost."

"Then we'll just have to do all we can to see that doesn't happen." Gem clenched her hands, and her eyes dared the doctor to say she couldn't do it.

He patted her shoulder on his way to the door. "I'll be back tomorrow to look in on him." His gaze shifted to Enid, standing at the foot of the bed. "He's a strong lad, Mrs. Dupre. It'll take some time 'fore he feels himself, but he'll make it."

"Thanks, doc." Enid followed him from the room, leaving Gem alone with the patient.

"Darn right you'll make it," Gem said to Chase, even though he couldn't hear her.

He had awakened when the doctor first arrived and started prodding and poking him. But Doc Bailey had given him a dose of laudanum, and now he slept deeply, the drug removing him temporarily from the pain.

Gem curled her fingers around his right hand and laid her head on his shoulder ever so briefly. "I'll take care of you, Chase," she whispered. "We'll get you well, and we'll make that wrist of yours strong again. I'll help you."

"Gem."

She looked up to meet Aunt Enid's understanding gaze.

"Gem, he's married to Consuela." It was a gently spoken rebuke.

She felt the sting of anger. "But she doesn't love him. She won't even look after him now when he needs her."

Enid came around the bed and drew Gem to her feet. For a long moment she stared down into Gem's defiant eyes. Then she pulled her close, nestling her against her breast. "Oh, my dear Gem. Don't try fooling yourself. Chase married her, and for better or worse they're married. It's not Christian to come between a man and his wife, no matter what the reason, no matter who's at fault. You think Chase didn't know that before he came back home? There was already a terrible wrong between them, something that's hurt this boy real deep, but he didn't leave her. He's a good man, Gem McBride, and he won't be leaving his wife, no matter what he might feel . . . or what *you* might feel either." With tender fingertips she lifted Gem's chin so that their eyes would meet again. "Don't go tempting him to do something you'll both regret."

Gem's vision blurred behind her tears. Her heart was breaking all over again. "I can't stop loving him, Aunt Enid."

"I know that, dear, but just don't let him see that it's a woman's love. You've been his little cousin for a long time. Let him keep thinking of you that way."

"I'll try." Gem sniffed back the persistent tears.

"I knew you would." Enid kissed her forehead, then patted her back. "Now you go get yourself some sleep. You've had a terrible ordeal yourself, and Chase'll be needing lots of care. You get some rest so you can spell me with him."

There was no point in arguing with Aunt Enid. Gem could see it in her eyes and the set of her shoulders. With a sagging spirit she left the spare bedroom and entered her own.

He would watch her when she didn't know he was awake. She would sit by the side of his bed, reading to him from a book of sonnets or talking about a new litter of puppies found in the barn. He would awaken from slumber to the sound of her voice, and rather than open his eyes immediately, he would observe her from under shrouded lids, seeing her through the veil of his own eyelashes.

Her pretty pale strawberry hair usually lay in two braids over her shoulders. Her aquamarine eyes would move quickly over the pages if she were reading, and when she was just talking they darted around the room, always returning to gaze down at him. Then she would see that he was awake, and her rosy mouth would break into a smile that outdid the sun in its brightness.

These were special times, just for the two of them. As the hours and days passed, he coaxed her to tell him more about her childhood before she'd lived at Four Winds and then about the years when he'd been away. And as he improved, she likewise drew from him the stories he had never shared with her before.

With each passing hour, they drew closer in spirit. But propriety would never allow Gem to confess her feelings to Chase, and Chase would never admit his feelings to himself.

At last the time came when Gem felt free enough to ask the question she had avoided for so long. "Tell me about Consuela. Why are you so unhappy?"

He was sitting up that day, braced in a chair by the window, allowing the morning sun to warm his face. Gem was seated on the windowsill, her eyes turned toward the mountains that jutted skyward not far away. It surprised Chase how easily the words came, how easy it was to open up and share what he'd thought he could never share with anyone.

"I met Julio not long after I got to Texas. He told me that Casa de Oro had one of the finest herds of longhorns in Texas, and he took me home with him. I already liked him, and when I met his parents and his brothers, I felt like I'd found another family."

"And Consuela?"

"She was away at school. I was planning to leave

in early spring, and then Consuela came home for a visit. She seemed so sheltered, so protected, so fragile. Dark and pretty—" His voice drifted into silence as he remembered her that first night.

She had watched him over the rim of her fan, her black eyes sparkling before she coyly lowered those long lashes of hers. Dona del Gado had sat between them, ever protecting her beautiful charge. But it was already too late for Chase. Like a spider weaving her web, she used her subtle charms to win his devotion, and he never knew that for her it was just a game.

Chase looked up at Gem. Her face was still turned toward the mountains. She didn't want to look at him while he was talking about Consuela. He understood that. What he couldn't understand was what a fool he had been. How could he have ever thought a girl like Consuela was what he wanted? Even before he knew the darkest of her deeds, she had never offered anything close to what was there before him at this very moment. Gem. Fresh, joyful, stubborn, earthy, feisty, gentle. All these and so much more, and she'd been waiting here at Four Winds for him while he'd been . . . while he had been proving himself a fool.

"I guess I was green out of the mountains," he said with a humorless chuckle as he continued. "I fell for her flirtations from the first bat of her eyelashes. Julio tried to warn me, but—" He shrugged. "She told me that her father would choose a husband for her before another year was gone, and that she hoped I would be around when he did. Then she went back to school."

He shook his head and closed his eyes. "I was sure she meant she wanted him to choose me, and I thought I wanted it too. So I stayed on at the Valdez ranch, growing closer to the family and waiting for her to come back. The day she returned, I asked Senor Valdez if I could court his daughter, and he gave me his permission. I was one happy fellow."

How was he to have known that the fragile, protected Latin flower he was pining for just liked to flirt with and conquer anyone in pants. It was a game with her, and he was just another player.

"When I asked her to marry me later that summer, she accepted. Senor Valdez told me he'd be happy to have me for a son. He said there was plenty of room at Casa de Oro for us and our children. When I told him I meant to bring Consuela back to Montana with me, he wasn't very happy. Still, he gave his permission for us to marry, but the marriage couldn't take place until spring."

Gem finally turned to look at him. "You must have loved her very much," she said softly.

He returned her gaze. "I suppose I did. I *thought* I did. I really don't know any more."

"And she must have loved you."

"No," he denied vehemently, suddenly angry. "Consuela has never loved anyone but Consuela. I don't know why she agreed to marry me except that her father approved of me as a husband. I suppose she thought she could control me. I was far from my home and my family. She thought we would go on living at Casa de Oro, and she could continue to be everyone's spoiled little darling."

His outburst was followed by a long, embarrassed pause. He felt drained. He could have stopped, but he didn't want to. He wanted to tell her. He wanted her to know everything.

"I was eager to get home to Four Winds, but I couldn't leave without my bride so I wrote to Uncle Frank and Aunt Enid and told them why I wasn't coming yet. It was my second letter."

"We never got it."

"The wedding was planned for March. Five days before the wedding, Consuela's mother became ill and died. The whole ranch went into mourning. The wedding was postponed for six months. We got married in September. I was ready to leave right then, but Consuela pleaded and cried and begged me not to take her away so soon. Then Julio said that the weather would be better in the spring and why not wait. And Senor Valdez told me he had lost his wife such a short time before, could I wait to take away his daughter just a few more months. So we stayed."

He didn't tell Gem that he'd suspected Consuela wasn't the innocent virgin he'd thought he was marrying. He didn't tell her that almost from the first she had used her body to punish or reward him, depending upon her moods. He didn't tell her how quickly love based only on desire can die when there's nothing more substantial to back it up, no sharing of hopes and dreams, no gentle moments of laughter, no times of understanding.

"I had all the plans made to leave Texas come March, and nothing was going to stop me. Then Consuela told me she was going to have a baby, and the doctor said he wasn't sure she'd be able to carry it if I took her off on such a trip. What could I do but stay?"

A baby. A son. How he'd wanted that child. Someone that was his. Someone that would love him. Someone that would bring laughter and sunshine back into his life. Someone he could teach to ride and to rope. A son to . . .

Gem reached out and touched his shoulder. Her voice broke as she asked, "What happened, Chase?"

"Consuela never did plan to leave Casa de Oro. I guess she thought she'd change my mind somehow. The baby was merely a delay. And when she saw I wasn't going to change my mind, she . . . she made other plans."

He balled his right hand into a fist in his lap and squeezed his lips together as he swallowed hard. There was a lump in his throat, but he forced himself to speak around it.

"She was about seven months along when she ran off with one . . . with one of her lovers—"

Gem breathed a soft, "Oh, no!"

"We didn't know he was her lover, of course. Not then. The buggy hit a rut and overturned. She was thrown down a ravine. The man was . . . killed. Broke his neck. We found them and brought her home. Her labor started that night. It was long and hard. The baby was born dead."

"Oh, Chase."

Tears streaked both her cheeks, but Chase was expressionless, hardened long ago against revealing the depths of this sorrow.

In a stilted voice, he said, "He never had a chance, Gem. He was so tiny but so perfect."

"I . . . I didn't know."

Chase swallowed hard before he could continue. "I named him Jean after my father. Jean Valdez Dupre. We buried him, and we thought for a while we'd be burying his mother too. She lost a lot of blood and was tore up inside. Doctor said he didn't know how she ever lived through it. He said she would never have another baby." He paused again, drawing a deep breath, seeking to restore his control.

"It was weeks before I talked to her of leaving. I told her it would be better for us. We'd have a fresh start. We could begin again, make our marriage strong, make it better. We could fall in love again. She laughed at me. She said she'd never loved me and never would. Then she told me about her different lovers, and said she wondered if the baby had even been mine. She told me she'd been running away rather than go to Montana with me. She said a lot of things. Ugly things. Things she was sorry for when she learned her father had been waiting outside to speak to her and heard everything."

"Oh, Chase," Gem repeated so softly he could scarcely hear her. "It's worse than I could have imagined."

He continued without acknowledging her interruption. "He waited a week before he called her in to see him. He told her Casa de Oro was no longer her home and he was no longer her father. He banished her from the ranch and forced her to come to Montana with me. We left the ranch then, but it was a few more months before we actually left Texas." He sighed heavily. "It was a long trip home."

They both turned their eyes out the window toward the tall mountains that framed the eastern edge of this valley. They sat in silence as the minutes ticked painfully away.

14

Powell laughed as he buried his face in her generous breasts, then flopped back on the disheveled bed. "You're a witch. I can't think of anything but you."

Consuela ignored him as she reached for her chemise. She was bored. There was no excitement in sneaking out to meet Powell any more. No one seemed to notice. They were all too preoccupied with Chase.

Suddenly Powell was leaning over her, his bare chest pressed against her back as his lips nibbled at her throat. "I'll meet you here tomorrow. Same time."

"I cannot come tomorrow. I will be busy." She pushed him away and continued to dress.

A hand on her shoulder spun her around. Hazel eyes peered at her from a face dark with anger. "You'll meet me when I say."

"Who do you think you are to order me about, Senor Daniels?" She tossed her ebony hair behind her shoulder in a show of defiance.

Powell's voice was low. "And who do you think you're playin' games with, Senora Dupre?" Sarcastic. Venomous. His fingers slipped around the back of her neck. "Did you think I was just another fool like that husband of yours? I know what you are, Consuela. You haven't fooled me."

A shiver ran up her spine despite the infernal heat that already baked the grasslands. "It was never my intention to try to fool you."

"Ha!" He laughed again as he swatted her bare buttocks and turned to find his own clothes.

Her fingers shook as she fastened the button of her blouse. What was she afraid of? He could do nothing to her. Her husband's family was an important one in this valley. People looked up to the Dupres. Powell Daniels wouldn't dare do her any harm. She turned to find him watching her and again felt the chill of fear icing her veins.

He rolled a cigarette, never taking his eyes from her, and lit it. He held the match out in front of him as she had seen him do many times before and let it burn down to his fingertips. It wasn't until the flame touched his skin that he dropped the match and stepped on it.

"Do you know what I'd do with you if I found you with another man?" he asked softly. "I'd step on you and break you like I did that match. There wouldn't be no hidin' from me. Not on Four Winds. Not in Montana. Not anywhere. Do you hear me, Consuela? You're my woman. Mine."

"You *are* a fool, Powell Daniels," she snapped as she brushed past him.

Her horse was tied in the shade of a cottonwood that stood by the dry creek bed. She hurried to it and stepped up into the saddle. She straightened her skirts, threw her loose hair over her shoulders, and picked up the reins.

"I'll be waitin' for you tomorrow, Consuela."

"Wait if you like, senor."

He was upon her before she could kick her horse into action. In an instant he had dragged her from the saddle and was crushing her in his arms, his mouth pressed harshly against hers. The fingers of one hand closed slowly around her throat. "Don't toy with me, Consuela Dupre. I'll be waitin'." Then it was he who pushed away and went for his own horse.

Consuela stood rooted to the ground, her breasts heaving as she gasped for air, rage and terror warring inside her. The game was not just a game any more. The rules had been changed, and she was no longer in control. She knew he meant what he said. He would find her and snap her like a match.

She touched her fingers to her throat and knew she would be there tomorrow. Unless . . .

"Well, boy, you're healin' up fine. Don't see why you can't get up and move about some. That is, if you'll keep that wrist there in a sling. Don't want to risk jarrin' it. There's a chance, if it heals right, that it'll pull through this better'n I thought."

"I promise, doc. I'll keep it in a sling whenever I set foot out of this room."

Doc Bailey glanced over his spectacles at Gem.

"I bet he's been a lousy patient." His eyes twinkled as he shook his head in mock seriousness.

"Lousy," she agreed with a frown and a stern nod of her head.

The doctor chuckled, his gaze returning to Chase. "At least your cousin here's a pretty nurse."

Gem blushed, the color beginning at the collar of her cotton blouse and rising steadily to the roots of her strawberry-gold hair. Both men laughed, making her color deepen.

Gads, how he enjoyed looking at her. She didn't have to be doing anything. Just standing there was enough to make his blood quicken in his veins. He almost hated to get well. Their special times together would soon be over. He would miss them. He would miss having her all to himself. But soon he would have to return to reality—and to Consuela.

Aunt Enid entered the room carrying a tray with glasses of lemonade. Her eyes swept over the three people in the room, lingering on Chase. Then she set the tray on the table near the window. "Doc, you'd better have something to drink before you head back out in that heat."

"Don't mind if I do, Enid. Can't say as I recall a hotter summer. Haven't had a drop of rain since the night I came out to tend to Chase here. Grass is dryin' up and so's the creeks."

They shared a few more words of gossip as they drank the lemonade, then Enid asked Gem to show the doctor to his buggy. Chase knew right away that there was something on her mind.

"What's bothering you, Aunt Enid?" he asked as she closed the door behind Gem and Doc Bailey.

She drew a deep breath as she turned concerned

gray eyes in his direction. "Chase, I haven't ever minced words with you. I don't mean to start now. I'm going to say my piece and then I won't mention it again. You were plenty sick for a while, or I would've said it sooner."

He waited.

"You're a married man, Chase Dupre. You've got a wife right here on Four Winds. Now, a person could be stone-cold blind and still see you've got plenty of problems with that girl, but she's your wife all the same, and you've got no right to be thinking otherwise. Gem's a fine girl. A good girl. I've brought her up these past few years to know right from wrong, and I won't have you taking it back. You always called her your cousin. Other folks still think of her that way. You'd better start thinkin' that way again, too. There. I've said it. I won't say nothing about it again."

She turned and left quickly, leaving Chase to ponder her words, over and over again.

"Gem, I could use your help with the washing today. Chase is well enough to fend for himself, I think."

"Of course, Aunt Enid. I'll be glad to help." She felt a twinge of guilt, thinking how little she'd done around the place since Chase was hurt. She'd been so happy up in his room, having him all to herself so much of the time.

Gem was standing in the shade of the box elder, an apron tied around her middle as she bent over the tub. She heard the cantering hooves and looked up as Consuela rode into the yard. Consuela's head was bare, and her hair flowed loosely down her back. It was the first time Gem had ever seen her less than perfectly coifed.

Consuela saw her watching and cast an indignant glare in her direction, one that spoke volumes about the common girl and her washtub. Gem felt her temper rising as she returned to her task, nearly wearing a hole in one of Uncle Frank's shirts before she cooled off.

Consuela washed herself carefully with the tepid water in the pitcher in her room. Then she splashed her favorite toilet water on her wrists and throat and between her breasts before dressing in a bright yellow day gown made from the finest linen. She artfully arranged her hair high on her head, allowing soft wisps to fall free to caress her neck. The final touch was to clasp on the locket Chase had given her on their wedding day.

The house was quiet as she stepped into the hallway and approached Chase's room. She paused, her fingers on the doorknob, then quickly rapped with her other hand and opened the door.

Chase was seated by the window. His head turned around, and she could read easily the surprise that registered when he saw her.

She, too, was surprised. The last time she had laid eyes on him was when they'd brought him back on the travois. She'd been certain he would die. But there he sat, looking nearly as good as new. His tan had faded, and he'd lost weight, but he looked as handsome as he'd ever been.

It had been fun once to toy with him. He had been so earnest in his pursuit. She had been convinced she could twist him around her finger and get whatever she desired. But she had been wrong. He had a will of iron, and he had seen through her charade all too quickly. But he was also a man of honor, which bound him to her no matter what she did. That was one thing she could always count on. His honor.

"May I come in, Chase?"

He frowned but nodded.

Consuela folded her hands in front of her as she approached him. "My husband," she began softly, "I have done much thinking these past weeks."

"Really?" An eyebrow raised.

"I know you will find this difficult to believe, but I have been very much afraid that you would die." She dropped her gaze to her hands. "I have made so many mistakes, Chase. I have been cruel and hateful to you, but it is because . . . because I was a foolish little girl, and I was afraid to be a proper wife. What if I did not please you?"

She allowed a single tear to fall from each eye as she lifted her chin and met his stare through blurred vision. "While you were in here fighting for your life, senor, I have been fighting for words that would save you and me, the two of us."

Chase sighed and turned his head toward the window. "Spare me, Consuela."

"Chase, I swear on the grave of my blessed *madre*, I know now that I love you. I've always loved you." She dropped to her knees and grasped his right hand, pulling it close until it nestled between the valley of her breasts. "Give me a chance, my husband. I will show you. *Por favor*." She leaned her cheek against his knee, whispering, "*Por favor*, my love."

She felt his hesitation and knew a great sense of

elation. He was going to fall for it. She would win his love again, and then she would be safe from Powell's threats.

"You're wasting your tears, Consuela."

Surprised, she looked up at him.

"If you were afraid I was going to send you away, you can forget it. You're my wife, and come what may, we're married." He spoke in a flat voice, a voice devoid of emotion. "But you don't need to lie to me any more."

Here was a new challenge. The game was on again.

Still on her knees, she drew close to him, her hands on his chest. "I am not lying, my husband. I swear I am not. And I will prove it to you." Her fingers snaked behind his neck and she leaned into him, her mouth seeking his in a long, luxurious kiss. When he didn't respond, she hid her irritation and pressed her body closer to his.

"Chase, I—"

Consuela released his mouth but moved not an inch away from him as their heads turned in unison toward the door.

Gem stood there, her mouth open in surprise, then the color started rising. "I . . . I'm sorry. I didn't . . . I—" she stammered before backing quickly out of the room.

Consuela felt Chase stiffen as if he'd been struck. She expected many things from him. She expected he might jump up and run after Gem. She expected he might fling her away from him. She even expected he might hit her. But she never expected him to say, "I'll move back into our room tonight."

Consuela, caught by surprise, could only whisper a soft, "*Gracias*, Chase."

Slowly, Chase started to rise, giving Consuela a chance to move back from him before he got to his feet. "I need some fresh air," he said without looking at her as he headed for the door.

Julio was in the barn, doctoring the leg of an injured saddle horse. The sweat was rolling down his back and his sides and dripping from his forehead and the end of his nose. He set the hoof down and straightened, reaching with one hand for his discarded shirt to use as a towel while his other hand rubbed the small of his back.

Maldito! Was it only hot or cold in this Montana and nothing in-between?

Leaving the horse for a moment, he walked to the south end of the barn and leaned against the open doorway as his eyes moved slowly across the baking earth. He had seen this happen before. The wet spring, the long grass, the drought-stricken summer. The valley had turned into a tinderbox. A lightning storm. A careless cowboy tossing away a match or a cigarette. The tiniest spark and this valley would become a range fire befitting of hell itself.

"Julio."

He turned from his dour thoughts, a grin returning to his mouth. "*Amigo*!" he exclaimed as he watched Chase walking through the barn door at the opposite end. He favored his right leg, and his left arm was in a sling, but it was good to see his friend up and about. "I did not think the doctor would have you out so soon."

"Long as I take care with this hand, I'm free to do whatever I feel good enough to do. And I felt the need of some fresh air and a good stretch. What say we saddle up and take a look at the cattle?"

"Will your nurses allow so much the first time out?" Julio jested.

Chase's face darkened. "I didn't figure on asking them."

"Oh?" Julio chuckled. "You have fought with Gem and lost, I see."

"No, I haven't fought with Gem."

Julio heard the defeat in his friend's voice and saw the weariness etched on his face. "What is wrong, *amigo*?"

Chase sat on a bench, leaned back against the slats of the barn wall, and closed his eyes. "Julio, are you still in love with Gem?"

"*Amigo*?"

"You heard me. Are you still in love with her?"

Softly, he answered, "Who wouldn't be." It was a statement, not a question.

"Then I hope you'll do all you can to make her happy."

"But she—"

Chase opened his eyes. There was pain written in their brilliant blue depths. "I've got no right to try to make her happy, Julio. I've got a wife of my own, in case you've forgotten. And even if I weren't married, I couldn't love her. There's no love left in me, Julio. It's all dried up." He paused, then added, "Take care of her."

"We have had this conversation before, *amigo*. It is not up to me but up to Gem."

"Damn it, Julio! It *can't* be up to her. *You* must

make it happen. Understand me? Make it happen."
He got to his feet and stepped up close to Julio, his
eyes impaling his friend. "For my sake, Julio," he
whispered hoarsely. "Make it happen for my sake, if
not for your own . . . And hers."

Gem stayed against the side of the barn until she
heard him say, "I've got no right to try to make her
happy, Julio. I've got a wife of my own." Then she
took off at a run for the corral, tears continuing to
streak her face. The little dream world she'd been
living in had been shattered up in his room when
she'd seen him kissing Consuela. This was just
adding insult to injury, hearing him forcing a friend
to court her.

She didn't take time to saddle and bridle Kansas.
The mare didn't need those trappings. Still wearing
her dress and apron, her sleeves rolled up from doing
the laundry, and her feet bare, she swung up onto the
mare's back and, with only a halter and rope to guide
the horse, galloped toward the mountains and the
old clearing where she used to do her target practice.

Once there, she slipped from Kansas's back and
dropped to the ground beneath the quaking aspen. "I
wish you were dead, Consuela Dupre," she spat out
angrily, venting all her pain and hurt and frustration
on the woman who had spoiled her dreams. She
pounded her fist against the ground. "I wish you
were dead."

Three days. Three days Powell had come to the
line shack and waited. Three days and she hadn't
come. The rage boiled within him, as hot and as
deadly as the drought that singed the range.

On the fourth day, he arrived and found she was already there before him. Her horse was tethered to the tree. A man possessed, he raced inside to find her sitting on the bed, her clothes already discarded, the blanket pulled up to cover her breasts. Her black hair tumbled over her shoulders in enticing disarray. She looked pleasantly sleepy.

"You are late," she said, a pout drawing up her full mouth. "I began to think you would not come."

Powell threw off his shirt as he walked across the shack. "This isn't a game, Consuela."

"You think not, *hombracho*?" She let the blanket fall from her fingers, exposing herself to him. "I think it is a wonderful game."

Blood pounded in his head and his loins.

A wicked gleam glinted in her black eyes. "Did I tell you my husband is so improved he has moved back into our room?"

Rage exploded before his eyes, blinding him in a flash to anything around him except Consuela. He gripped her bare shoulders and hauled her up from the bed. "You are mine, Consuela. I won't let him have you."

"How can you stop him?" she asked breathlessly.

"I'll stop him, Consuela."

And then he took her.

Gem did anything she could to avoid being with Chase. Her emotions swung violently and rapidly from deep heartbreak and depression to an anger so great she felt she could commit murder. And now her anger wasn't directed only at Consuela. She was angry with Chase too. How dare he barter her away!

His poor little kissin' cousin. Lovesick over a married man. Needs help to find herself a proper beau. Ha!

It was in just such a mood that Julio found her as she sat beneath the box elder. She was soaping a bridle, working the soft leather between her fingers, while her thoughts whirled in her head, dark and forbidding. She had braided her hair in one long braid and wound it on top of her head, trying to keep cool, a hopeless task in the hot breeze that blew out of the south that summer morning. Her blouse was open at the throat. Her feet, bare once again, were curled beneath her riding skirt.

"*Buenos dias, amiga*," he greeted her.

"Morning," she replied, the word sounding nothing like a greeting.

Julio hunkered down beside her, still grinning. "Is it the heat that makes you growl at your friend?"

A sharp reply flew to her lips, but as she looked up at him, she caught sight of Chase on the porch. So he wanted his good friend to take care of the kid, was that it? Okay. So she'd give him what he wanted. She dropped the bridle and rose on her knees, facing Julio. Her hands rested on his shoulders as she leaned close to him.

"I'm sorry, Julio. It *is* the heat. Let's ride down to the river and cool off."

"I have much work—"

"Oh, Julio, it's too hot to do anything. Nobody's going to miss you for an hour or two."

He smiled again. "Perhaps Chase would like to join us." He started to turn toward the porch to call out an invitation.

Gem's fingers tightened on his shoulders and she pulled herself even closer to him. "We don't want anybody else with us, Julio. Just you and me. Come on." She took his hand as she jumped to her feet, drawing him with her. She turned a triumphant glare in the direction of the house, but Chase was no longer there. Her fingers loosened their hold on Julio's hand. The anger was gone. The sorrow returned.

Oh, Chase. I love you so.

15

The very air seemed to crackle as the hot wind blew the dark clouds up from the south. Chase heard the thunder while the storm was still a long way off. The hair on the back of his neck stood on end. He sauntered out on the porch and watched as the dark thunderclouds raced across the sky, swallowing the late morning sun.

The horses in the corrals tossed their heads and galloped around their enclosures, stopping to trumpet their fright before bucking and bolting once again. Dust devils swirled across the dry fields.

"I've been praying this wouldn't happen," Enid said softly as she stepped up beside him, leaning her hands on the porch rail.

"Rain would be a blessing." But Chase knew rain wasn't likely to come, at least not in time.

Enid didn't dispute him. Both of them were

aware there was more lightning in the dark clouds than rain. The range was dry, drier than they'd seen it in all the years since the Four Winds began with two tiny cabins and two families filled with dreams for the future. Now, one bolt of lightning touching the parched grassland, and everything they'd built could be taken from them.

A brilliant flash of silver split a jagged line from heaven to earth, and within seconds the sky and ground shook as the thunder rolled, the boom reverberating across the valley and echoing off the mountaintops. A hot wind rolled with it, like a breath out of hell itself.

"Julio and Gem rode over to the river. They shouldn't be out there in this."

Enid frowned but didn't look up at him. "Neither should your wife."

He had forgotten all about Consuela. She'd told him she found the solitary rides restful. She'd said she began riding during the weeks of his recuperation, going each morning while the heat was held at bay, and she wanted to resume them. She'd ridden out this morning while the shadows of the mountains were still long.

"I'd better go after them," he said, already stepping down from the porch.

"A man's in a lot of danger sitting on a horse in a storm like this. Julio's got enough sense to stay out of the open. You should too."

Chase glanced back at his aunt. She was right, of course. It would be foolish to go out in this. "I'll feel better once I've found them," he answered and kept walking.

His horse was quickly saddled, and he left at a gallop. He told himself the reason he headed toward the river first was because he had no idea where Consuela might have ridden. In truth, it was because his first thoughts were always of Gem. Damn! How it had hurt to see her flirting with Julio. Could he have misunderstood her? Was it merely friendship, or was she as fickle as . . . as other women?

The storm grew in intensity. The heavy clouds cloaked the valley in the darkness of night, then shattered it with sudden flashes of lightning. Again and again the heavens exploded with thunder.

Julio and Gem took refuge from the storm under a rocky ledge. They didn't speak as they watched the frightening display of nature's wrath. The sudden flash of light was so bright, so white, that for a moment they were both blinded. The loud boom rang in their ears, and the ground shook beneath their feet. Diablo and Wichita reared simultaneously, pulling on their reins as they whinnied in terror.

Across the river, the cottonwood broke in two, its trunk left black and charred. Flames crackled to life around its base.

Julio handed his stallion's reins to Gem. "Hang on to him." Then he slid down the rocky embankment and slipped and splashed his way across the low flowing river. He pulled his shirt over his head and began beating at the fire as the wind whipped the flames to life.

Gem spoke soothingly to the frightened horses, even though she felt anything but calm. She was as frightened as they were. The acrid smell of the lightning and charred tree filled her nostrils. Despite the heat, she shivered.

The storm mirrored their violent lovemaking. Consuela had returned to the line shack, feeling once again in control. She needn't fear Powell any longer, for her husband had returned in defeat. But she hadn't been prepared for the intensity of his passion, and as the morning passed, so had her sense of control. Now she was growing frightened.

"Please, Powell. I must get back before the rain begins," she protested as the thunder rolled overhead.

"You don't have to go back, Consuela. You can come to the Big Pine with me." His eyes burned into her with the glow of hot coals.

"Senor, do you think me a fool? I cannot leave my husband. There would be a scandal. My father would never forgive me." She pulled away from him and reached for her clothes. She dressed hastily, her eyes darting toward the ceiling with each thunderclap.

"I don't want you to go, Consuela," Powell said from behind her. His voice was low and threatening.

Consuela drew herself up in haughty disdain. She threw her heavy black hair over her shoulder as she turned to look at him. "I do not care what you want, Powell. I do as I please." She turned her back to him once again and finished buttoning her blouse.

She heard the door of the line shack open and Powell go out. She smiled to herself. The fool. Who did he think he was? Was she not the daughter of Manuel Valdez? She was not a servant to be ordered around like a peon. She would come and go as she pleased. She would tell him when she wanted to see him, when she wanted to make love, and when she chose to discard him.

A ferocious crack of thunder rattled the interior of the shack. Consuela squealed in fright as she turned to hurry toward the door, carrying her shoes in her hand. She raced outside, then stopped abruptly as her eyes spied the fleeing horses. Powell stood near the copse of cottonwood where the horses had been tethered. Without asking, she knew he had turned them loose. But he wasn't watching as they ran away. His eyes were turned in another direction.

The icy finger of premonition slid up her spine as she turned to follow his gaze. In the distance she saw what appeared to be a piece of black cloud, torn off the sky and rolling along the ground. And then she saw the orange fingers that raced before it, consuming the tinder dry range.

Fire!

Gem led the horses across the river to the place where Julio stood, his brown skin glowing with sweat, his face smudged with soot. The fire was out. He had beaten it before it had a chance to spread.

"Julio!" Her voice was laced with relief as she called his name.

He glanced in her direction. Weary brown eyes looked down at her as she hurried closer. "Gem, we must get back to the ranch. Even now more fires must be starting." He raised his voice to be heard above the wind.

"How will we fight them, Julio?"

"The best way we can."

"Julio?"

He looked down at her.

"I'm frightened."

He put a tired arm around her shoulders and hugged her against him, wishing he could do more.

As if she read his thoughts, she stepped back and raised her eyes. "It wasn't right of me to bring you out here thinking . . . Well, thinking there might be something between us."

"You do not need to tell me, *amiga*. I know where your heart is."

There was a glitter of tears in her blue-green eyes. She placed her hands on his shoulders, stood on tiptoe, and planted a kiss on his cheek. "Thanks, Julio. You're just about the best friend I've ever had. Thanks for understanding."

Chase pulled his lathered mount in just as he crested the rim. Just in time to see Gem kissing Julio. His friend had one arm around her shoulders, and his chest was bare. Chase felt a hollow thumping beneath his ribs, but he pushed the feeling aside. He hadn't the time to deal with it now.

"Julio!" he shouted.

The wind whipped his cry away even as it left his lips. Pressing his spurs against his horse's ribs, they clattered down the river bank and galloped toward the pair.

"Julio! Gem!"

Gem turned around. Seeing him, she raised her arm and waved.

Chase looked beyond them to the charred tree. "You two all right?" he asked as he reined in.

"*Si, amigo*. We are fine, but I think we had better

get back and round up the men." He jerked his head toward the tree. "I feel we are in for more trouble than this."

"You're right, Julio. I thought I could see smoke south of here." He looked up at the sky. The clouds were still black and roiling, but the lightning had passed on. "We'd better pray there's some rain in them."

Without further comment, Gem and Julio swung into their saddles, and the three riders galloped toward the ranch house.

And to the south, the fire grew in strength as it consumed the parched grasslands of the Four Winds range.

16

Fire! It swept before the wind on fleet feet of orange and red.

Powell watched it coming. Fascination held him where he was. His breath quickened. A strange excitement flowed through him as he watched glittering sparks flying against the dark smoke. The sight aroused him as nothing else could. Desire surged in his loins.

"Powell, we must go!" Consuela shouted at him, tugging on his arm.

His fingers closed quickly over her wrist. "Look, Consuela. Look at it. It's beautiful."

"Are you mad?" she screamed. "Let go of me. We must get out of here now." She tried to pull away from him, but his grip merely tightened.

"We're not goin' anywhere yet, Consuela. Not

till you look at it. Look at it, Consuela. It's darn near
as pretty as you."

Sweat streamed down her face. Gem brushed her
hair from her forehead and raised red-rimmed eyes
upon the hungry fire that traveled toward the house
of Four Winds at a frightening pace. Hot air stifled
her lungs, and soot stung her nostrils.

"Gem!"

She turned toward the voice.

Chase was hurrying toward her from the house.
"We've got Uncle Frank in the wagon, and Wichita is
saddled and ready."

"I'm not going." She started pulling on the well
rope, drawing up the bucket of water.

"Don't argue with me, Gem."

She grunted as she lifted the bucket from the
edge of the well, then looked up at Chase again.
Quietly she said, "I'm not arguing. I'm just not
going."

"Gem—" His hand closed tightly on her shoulder.

She shook him off. Blue-green eyes flashed a
challenge. "This is my home, and if you think I'm
running away from this, you've got another think
coming. You tell Aunt Enid to get Uncle Frank out of
here, but I'm staying." With another grunt she
hoisted the bucket down in front of her and started
walking toward the house, throwing over her shoulder, "If I have to douse every board of this place
myself, I'm going to do it."

Chase ran after her, jumping around and stopping before her, bringing her to a sudden halt.

"Gem," he shouted above the noise of the wind, "I can't stay here. I've got to find Consuela. She's out in this somewhere."

"Then quit wasting time. Julio and me and the others can take care of the place here."

A deep frown worried his forehead. His dark eyebrows drew together as his mouth worked silently. Whatever he wanted to say, he was finding it difficult.

She moved to step around him.

"Gem . . . I want to know you're somewhere safe from this."

She looked deep into his sapphire eyes, now reddened from the smoke and soot that filled the air. Why should she care what he wanted? He had bartered her away to his friend. He had returned to Consuela's room after Gem had nursed him back to health. Why should it matter to her that he looked so sad, so beaten?

"I'll be all right, Chase," she said, her voice gentle, sweetened by the love she couldn't deny him. "You get out and do what you must. Consuela must be awful scared, wherever she is. Julio'll take care of me if things get out of hand."

"Yeah. Julio."

She nearly didn't hear him as he muttered his response and spun from her on the heel of his boot.

"Up here, Gem."

Resolutely, she turned to the task at hand, hurrying to pass the bucket to Teddy, then rushing back to fill another one at the well.

Bandanna over his nose, Chase rode through the broiling smoke, following what he hoped to be the tracks of Consuela's horse until he could no longer make them out. His eyes watered and his throat burned. He stopped his horse long enough to take a swig from his canteen, rolling the warm water around in his mouth before allowing it to trickle down his parched throat. His horse danced nervously beneath him.

He tightened the top of the canteen, then turned the animal toward the mountainside and galloped across the grassland, away from the onrushing flames. He had no idea where to look. She could have ridden in any direction. Was she safe even now, far from this blazing inferno? Or was she in the very midst of it? He quelled a shudder. Even Consuela didn't deserve such a fate.

His spurs rolled across the gelding's sides, and they began their search once more.

How could it be that the fire approached with such speed, yet time crawled so slowly?

Gem dragged another bucket from the well. She paused briefly to splash a little water on her face, then hauled the bucket toward the house with complaining arms and hands.

Above the wind and the increasing din of the fire, the men shouted at one another. The livestock had been turned loose long before, all except the saddle horses, their last means of escape. Aunt Enid had left with her invalid husband, hurrying the sturdy animals in harness toward Virginia City and the promise of safety.

Gem passed the bucket into someone's hands. She was too tired to look up and see whose. Automatically she grabbed an empty one from the ground and headed back toward the well. Her gaze alighted on the barn. Were they to lose this one to fire too? she wondered. It seemed hopeless. If only the wind would change directions. If only the clouds would release the rain.

Then her eyes moved to the south, in the direction of Chase's departure. If only he would return . . .

Pike Matthews jogged toward her from the barn. "Time t'get out o'here, Gem. Get on that mare o' yours and ride."

"But, Pike, we can't—"

"Matthews is right." Rodney stepped up behind her. "It's time we left. There's nothing more we can do here."

She whirled around, her eyes wide as she gazed upon the only home she could remember. If it burned . . . If she lost it . . .

"We can't go," she protested. "We've got to save it." Panic rose in her voice. She shook her head, her long braid sweeping across her back. "I'm not going." Tears glittered against her lower lashes.

The men were all there now. From somewhere Julio appeared, Wichita in tow.

"Oh, Julio. I can't go. I can't let the fire have it. And what about Chase? I need to be here when he gets back. He isn't well yet. He shouldn't even be out there alone."

"Hush, *nina del ojo*," Julio replied tenderly. "The house can be rebuilt. *You* cannot be replaced." With that, he lifted her into the saddle.

The men swung onto their horses, and immediately the riders galloped away from the approaching doom.

Chase had begun to think he'd stepped off the edge of the world and fallen into the pits of hell. As a boy he'd heard Reverend Sharply telling about it when they'd gone on Sundays to church in Virginia City. It certainly seemed that this was the hell the white-haired old preacher had been talking about.

He skirted the edge of the fire, forcing his stinging, watering eyes to stay alert for some sign of Consuela. There was nothing. He knew the fire must be nearing Four Winds. He longed to turn his gelding toward home. He wanted to assure himself of Gem's safety. He wanted to help save his ranch from the ravaging fire that licked at the dry range and swallowed everything into its orange belly, spitting up the remains in a smoldering black ash. But he pressed on, calling her name, his voice cracking in his parched throat.

The wind shifted, then stilled. And then came the rain. In a torrent, as if the gates of heaven had been opened and the flood waters turned loose. It struck the retreating band of men and lone woman with a force that nearly unseated them, but it also brought a whoop of joy to their lips. They spun their horses and galloped back in the direction they had come. Their prayers had been answered.

Dawn came with a clearing sky and the arch of a rainbow. Beneath it, a ravaged valley still smoldered in blackened ruins. The carcasses of cattle lay in hideous mounds across the rolling range.

Chase's gelding picked his way through the devastation, snorting in complaint as the burnt scent pierced his nostrils. Chase's face was grim as he surveyed the range. Each time he spied a fallen animal he feared the worst, and finally his fears seemed to prove true. He found Consuela's horse in a ravine.

He stepped wearily from the saddle and squatted beside the charred remains. His head drooped forward. He hadn't wanted this. He swore he hadn't wanted this. Freedom from her, yes, but not this.

He drew in a deep breath as he stood up, turning to lean against his horse. He laid his head against the gelding's neck, allowing his weariness of body and spirit to sweep freely through him. Guilt assailed him. Had he searched as hard as he could have? Had he intentionally missed some sign of her direction? If he'd turned one way rather than the other, could he have found her in time?

He would never know.

Chase straightened and put the toe of his boot into the stirrup, hauling himself up into the saddle. His shoulder and side throbbed, and pain like tiny needles shot up his arm from his wrist. He longed for a drink of fresh, cool water. But there was nothing to do but go on looking for Consuela. There would be no rest until he'd found her. He nudged his horse forward, and the animal lunged up the side of the ravine.

Half an hour later, perhaps more, Chase spied a movement in the distance. He pulled in on the reins and peered through the haze drifting up from the earth. The apparition walked toward him on shuffling feet, stumbling occasionally but never falling. It was a man, and in his arms he carried another, much smaller body.

He'd waited too long. Caught in the web of fascination, Powell had stood watching the fire, and suddenly it was all around him. When had Consuela slipped from his grasp? When had she run to escape the flames? He hadn't been aware that he stood alone until reason returned, and he'd known he must flee or die. But first he had to find Consuela.

Chase jerked his galloping mount to a sliding stop and jumped to the ground. His stomach churned as he stared at the sight before him. He recognized the man as Powell Daniels, although the left side of his face was swollen and red, painful white blisters distorting the damaged skin. His hair was singed completely from his head.

Chase had no difficulty recognizing the woman in Powell's burn-damaged arms. Her luxurious black hair fell in a heavy wave toward the ground; her head hung limply over Powell's forearm. Her eyes were closed, as if in sleep, and her face was blackened with soot.

"Consuela?" he whispered, stepping forward.

Powell made no effort to speak or to stop. He turned and moved around Chase and kept walking.

"Daniels!"

It was as if he couldn't hear. Powell just kept walking, his eyes set in the distance.

Chase hurried to catch up with him, in desperation grabbing Powell's arm and forcing him to stop. "Is she alive?"

Powell flinched at his touch but didn't turn his

head toward Chase, didn't answer his question. He continued to stare straight ahead with glazed eyes.

"Is she alive?" Chase asked again, releasing his grip on the blistered flesh.

At last Powell turned toward him. There was little energy in his movements as he motioned Chase away. And all the while, his tortured gaze never left Consuela's face.

Chase held out his arms. "Give her to me, Powell. I've got to get her back to Four Winds. I'll send someone for you."

Once again Powell stepped mutely around Chase and began walking. The fire and pain had driven him mad. It was the only explanation.

Uncertain what he should do next, Chase started after Powell. If Consuela was still alive, she needed a doctor. So did Powell, for that matter. He was about to speak again when he heard his name called in the distance. Several men galloped toward them on horseback, followed by someone driving a buckboard.

Julio was the first to reach them. His dark eyes swept from his sister to Powell to Chase.

"She might be alive," Chase said, answering his unspoken question, "but he won't answer me. I just found them. He won't let me take her. I'm not sure he even knows what I'm saying."

Julio dismounted. "Consuela?"

Powell started around him, just as he had Chase.

"Senor Daniels—" Julio's hand landed lightly on Powell's shoulder. "You must let us take her," he said softly. "Please, senor. Get into the wagon. Let us get you a doctor." He reached forward.

Powell shook his head, but woodenly allowed Julio to slip his arms beneath Consuela's still form.

"Rod," Julio called over his shoulder, "take care of your brother."

Chase had already swung into his saddle. He nudged his horse forward, stopping beside Julio as Powell was led toward the buckboard. "I'll take her, Julio. We'll get there faster than in the wagon."

Julio looked up at Chase. "There's no hurry, Chase. She's already gone."

For once, Gem had done as she was told. She waited at the ranch house. Julio and Rod, Zeke and Teddy had ridden out before first light to look for Chase and Consuela. Pike had followed them in the buckboard, a grim reminder of what they could find. Gem had stayed behind to await Aunt Enid's and Uncle Frank's return. Corky McGinnis remained with her when the other cowpokes went in search of the livestock.

Countless times she walked to the corner of the barn and gazed across the valley, searching for some sign of them returning. Countless times she was disappointed. But finally, as the golden summer sun approached its zenith, she saw their approach. She held her breath as her eyes strained to catch a glimpse of their faces. Was Chase among them?

She counted the riders. Five had ridden out. Only four returned. The buckboard was nowhere in sight. She fought the sickening swirl of panic that swelled in her belly.

"He'll be all right," Gem whispered. "He's got to be all right."

She leaned against the barn and closed her eyes for a moment, then drew a deep breath and looked again. They were nearly upon her before she recognized Chase in the lead. He was holding something —no, someone—in his arms.

He'd found Consuela.

There was that terrible split second when she recognized the truth. She hadn't *wanted* him to find her! Only days before, she had whispered those ugly words in a moment of hurt and anger. *I wish you were dead, Consuela Dupre*. Now they had come back to haunt her.

Horrified by her own cruel thoughts, Gem turned and raced toward the house. It wasn't true. She was glad he had found her. If Consuela was hurt, she would help care for her. She would nurse her as carefully as she had Chase. Somehow she would make up for her terrible thoughts. She would offer penance for her sin of coveting another woman's husband. Reaching the porch, she turned and waited.

Chase jogged his horse into the yard and reined in at the steps. His eyes met Gem's only briefly, but she read the agony in their sapphire depths and her guilt increased. As he dismounted, her gaze dropped to Consuela. Her clothes were gray with soot as was her ashen face. Gem had an ominous feeling in her breast.

Wordlessly Chase moved by her and carried Consuela's lifeless body into the house.

Julio's hand cupped her elbow. "Come, *amiga*. He will need our help."

"Is she . . . is she alive?"

"No."

She heard the pain in Julio's voice and belatedly

remembered that Consuela was his sister. "I'm so sorry, Julio."

"Come," he repeated.

Chase laid Consuela carefully on the bed, then washed her face with water from the bedroom pitcher. He tenderly straightened her torn, rumpled blouse. His mind refused to acknowledge that it was too late to make a difference.

Unbidden, the memory of the first time he'd seen her flashed in his head. Flirtatious black eyes flashing beneath dark lashes. A perfect, oval-shaped face. Smooth olive skin stretched over high cheekbones, and a full, temptable mouth, begging to be kissed. A woman's figure with full bosom and narrow waist. Tiny feet made for dancing. What had happened to her, that girl she had been, so full of beauty, so full of self?

Had he loved her? He supposed he had once. But even when the love was gone, even when their marriage soured, even in their worst moments, he wouldn't have wanted this for her. She had died, far from her father and home. If Consuela had ever loved anyone other than herself, it was Manuel Valdez. Had Chase been at fault to take her away from her beloved *padre*, away from Casa de Oro and all she held dear? Had he brought this tragedy upon Consuela?

The door opened, admitting Julio and Gem. They moved silently across the room. Julio knelt beside the bed opposite Chase and picked up his sister's hand. He gazed at her still face for a long time before closing his eyes and breathing a prayer. When he looked up again, he turned his eyes on Chase. "*Amigo*, what can I—"

"Just leave me alone with her, Julio. Please."

Julio glanced at Gem, standing behind Chase. "If that is what you wish." He rose from his knees, then walked around the bed and took Gem by the arm. "Come, *nina*." He led Gem away. At the door, he added, "Gem and I will be right outside, *amigo*."

The door closed, leaving Chase in silence.

He stared at her for the longest time. Scenes from the past flickered through his head until he saw again that moment of discovery, the moment he'd seen Powell carrying Consuela across the smoldering range. He saw again Powell's tortured gaze. And he knew in that instant that his wife had been with Powell. His wife had been Powell's lover.

"Why, Consuela?" he asked aloud. "Why would you do it?"

He closed his eyes, trying to squeeze out the memory. But instead, he could see her even more clearly, as she had been. Alive and vibrant. Alive and beautiful.

You were always such a fool, my husband. It was a game I played. Just a game. You could not keep a woman such as I happy. So much honor. Always so much honor. Why did you not leave me in Texas where I could be happy? Why did you bring me here?

"But why Powell?" he whispered, laying his forehead against the counterpane.

Because he is your enemy, Chase. Why else?

Of course. Why else.

My husband?

Her voice seemed to be fading in his head, growing more faint with each word.

You can never trust a woman, my husband. Love is just a game we play. Look at my brother and Gem. They are lovers, Chase. Gem and Julio . . . lovers. Do not trust a woman's love. It is just a game we play.

The voice was gone. The room was silent. Even in death, Consuela had defeated him.

The game was over.

17

They buried her the next day as the sun crested the mountaintops. Only the family and ranch hands were there. From his cot Frank Dupre spoke words of comfort and benediction as the young widower stood in stony silence at the foot of the grave.

Gem's eyes seldom left him. Since the moment he had closed himself in his room with his wife's body, Gem had been filled with a sense of dread. More had died in that room than just a woman. She could see it in the set of his shoulders, the glazed coolness in his eyes, the emptiness of his voice. Gem knew he didn't grieve for Consuela as a husband in love would have done. This was different. It was cold, devoid of emotion, and it frightened her.

Julio's arm encircled her shoulders and he squeezed lightly. He could read the fear in her eyes as she stared across the grave at Chase. He had no real comfort to offer her, nor did he seem able to help his friend.

His gaze shifted to the casket. *Nina*, he thought, *what have you done to this family?*

Always the prettiest flower in every bouquet, his sister. Even when she was a tiny girl in bright dresses and petticoats, the men in her family had showered her with compliments and catered to her every whim. She had only to drop one little tear and Pedro would take her riding or Juan and Iago would play hide-and-seek with her. Fidel would sneak into the kitchen and steal some of their mother's pastries for her. And Julio? She had only to ask and he would sit up half the night reading to her or telling her extravagant tales made up in his head.

It was hard to believe that delightful, whimsical child of his memories had become the woman who had caused so much heartache to those he loved. Why couldn't she have stayed sweet and innocent? Was it his fault? The fault of his father and brothers? Had they spoiled her beyond repair? Or would she have been the same no matter what they'd done?

His gaze shifted to Chase. His friend. His *amigo*. Consuela had taken much from this man and given nothing in return. Would that easy grin ever return to Chase's mouth, or the spark to his eyes?

Finally Julio's gaze returned to Gem. Pretty little Gem. If Chase would let her, she would help heal the scars Consuela had left. Julio couldn't stop the selfish wish that Gem would turn to him instead. But she wouldn't. He knew the kind of woman she was. She would love Chase until the day she died, whether or not he loved her in return.

From the corner of his eye Chase saw Julio's

arm around Gem's shoulders, and a taunting echo filled his head. *Gem and Julio . . . lovers . . . Gem and Julio . . . lovers . . . Gem and Julio . . . lovers.* His fists clenched at his sides. He ignored the shooting pains in his left wrist. Pain was almost welcome.

As his uncle said a final "Amen," Chase turned and walked swiftly away from the family cemetery. He went straight to the corral and brought out a pinto gelding, a four-year-old offspring of Kansas called Dodge. Despite his stiff left hand, he saddled the horse quickly and rode out before anyone could ask where he was headed. Besides, he didn't know himself.

He rode north, avoiding the charred grasslands of the Four Winds. Tomorrow or the next day he would look the land over and figure their losses, then make plans for their future. What cattle hadn't been run down by the sweeping fire would be scattered over miles. It would be hard work rounding them up, but hard work was just what he needed. Hard work to take his mind off Consuela. Hard work to take his mind off Gem.

Dodge carried him at a swift gallop across the range. It wasn't until Big Pine Ranch came into view that he realized it had been his destination all along. Hatred festered up inside of him, twisting his gut and leaving a red haze before his eyes. Powell Daniels. She'd lain with Powell. Powell. Of all the men in the world, why Powell?

Chase drew the pinto back to a walk and slowly approached the silent yard. When he reached the front of the house he stopped, but he didn't dismount. He just sat there, staring at the two-story log house. Waiting. Allowing the rage to grow in strength. Nurturing the desire for revenge.

How long did he sit there before the door opened? It could have been minutes. It could have been hours. Time meant nothing to Chase. His thoughts were churning, playing scenes over and over again in his mind.

Consuela had been right, of course. He was a fool. But so was Powell. She had used them both in an evil game, pitting enemies one against the other. No, it wasn't because Consuela had bedded another man that he had come here. It was because Powell had sought out his wife to try to bring injury to the Dupres.

Josh stepped onto the porch. "Howdy, Chase," he said, his face lined with weariness.

"Is Powell alive?"

"He's alive." He stepped to the edge of the porch. "My thanks for sendin' him home in your wagon."

"You tell him Consuela is dead." Chase spoke with cold exactness.

Josh shook his head. "I'm sorry. I didn't know. Was it the fire?"

"Doc says it was the smoke that killed her." He paused. "They were together. Consuela and Powell were together."

A heavy silence separated the two men, stretching out interminably. Finally Chase picked up the reins from Dodge's neck. The gelding's ears perked forward, and he snorted.

"Daniels, you tell Powell I'll wait till he's well, and then I'm coming gunning for him."

"Chase—"

"You tell him I'll be waiting." He turned his horse abruptly and cantered away from the house at Big Pine.

By nightfall Chase's riding had brought him into Virginia City. He stopped the pinto in front of the first saloon and slid from the saddle. He wanted a drink. A long drink.

Dawn kissed the sky, leaving a pink stain upon the fluffy clouds that dotted the azure sky. Seated on the corral fence, the heels of her boots hooked over a rail, Gem watched the coming of day with melancholy eyes.

Two days. Two days since the funeral and no sign of Chase. If only they knew where he'd gone. What if it would be another five years before he returned?

Gem gave a short whistle, and Wichita nickered in return, then trotted over to the rail. The mare pressed her velvety muzzle against the palm of Gem's hand.

"No treats today, girl. You'll have to settle for this." She scratched the pinto behind the ears for a few moments before letting out a deep sigh. She laid her head against Wichita's neck as she whispered, "Oh, girl, where do you suppose he's taken himself to?"

The mare whickered and shook her head.

"If you were askin' me instead of that horse, I'd say he's holed up some place where he can forget."

Gem started. "Aunt Enid!" she exclaimed in surprise, twisting to look at the woman standing behind her. Startled by her mistress's sudden movement, Wichita shied away.

"Sorry, child. Didn't mean to come sneaking up

on you." Enid leaned across the top rail and clucked to Wichita. "Come back here, you ornery filly. You haven't any call to be so skittish."

The mare twitched her ears and eyed Enid warily.

"Gem, I think I've spoke my mind too often as it is, and I probably should just keep my thoughts to myself." She turned her head to look up at Gem, perched on the fence rail. Enid's face was care-worn and her cheeks were hollow, but there was still a special frontier strength in her voice. "That boy wants to love you. Fact is, I'm believin' he does already, but it appears to me he's going to have to get over a few fences before he's ready to admit to loving a woman again. Any woman. Even you. You give him time and lots of care, and I'd be willing to wager he'll come around."

Gem's heart thrilled as Enid spoke. How she wanted to believe he loved her! Ever since he'd looked at her in the old barn and told her she could have Kansas's filly, she'd been loving him. Sure, it had been a girl's love, but it had grown into something deeper. She loved as a woman now, and she wanted him to love her as a man. If only he'd never gone away . . . if only he'd never married Consuela.

Renewed guilt assailed her. Gem turned her face away from the older woman, her eyes locked on the mountaintops in the distance. "Aunt Enid?" she began in a small voice.

"Yes, child?"

"I . . . I wished she was dead. Not more than a few days ago I sat up in that meadow I always liked to ride to, and I wished to God she was dead." Her guilt hung like a heavy chain around her neck.

Enid's wrinkled hand covered one of Gem's. "You think you've got enough pull with the Almighty that He'd strike a woman down just for your wishing?"

Gem's eyes widened as she glanced down at her aunt.

"Girl, Consuela died cause she couldn't get away from a range fire. Your angry wishing had nothin' to do with it. I'm not saying you shouldn't get down on your knees and ask the Lord to forgive you for those mean thoughts. They're wrong and no way around it. But don't be taking on a load of guilt that's not yours. We've all got enough troubles of our own to worry about." She squeezed Gem's hand, then started to turn. "You might try riding into Virginia. Chances are, that's where he is by this time."

As Enid walked away, Gem brought her legs around and hopped to the ground. She ran after the older woman. Jumping in front of her, she threw her arms around Enid's waist and gave her a tight hug. "Thanks, Aunt Enid. Thanks for understanding."

Enid's hand cradled the side of Gem's face in a gentle caress. "I love you two children as if you were my own. Only want what'll make you both happy." She kissed Gem's forehead, then left her standing in the yard as she went to prepare breakfast for the hungry men of the Four Winds.

Her hair in a long braid down her back, a wide-brimmed felt hat shading her eyes, and wearing her favorite attire of split skirt and soft leather boots, Gem trotted Wichita down Wallace Street. Her eyes scanned the street for any sign of Dodge at a hitching rail. Her search continued on Jackson Street. Outside of Con Orem's Champion saloon, she stopped her mare.

"Silva," she called to the grizzled old miner standing on the boardwalk. "I'm looking for Chase. Have you seen him?"

Silva scratched his gray beard and frowned. "Well, miss. Seems I seen him a time or two."

"Do you know where I can find him?"

"Well—" He glanced up and down the board-walk.

"It's important, Silva. I *really* need to find him."

The old man squinted one eye closed as he looked up at her. She could read his thoughts as they played over his face. He was remembering the first time he'd seen her, the day Chase hauled her out of a saloon and carried her kicking and screaming out of town, and he was thinking she sure had grown up a mite. He grinned, exposing a dark gap between his front teeth. "Last I seen him, he was walkin' with two of Miss O'Grady's girls."

Not any too pleased with the information, Gem muttered, "Thanks," then turned her horse back toward the far edge of town.

Mary O'Grady ran a hurdy-gurdy house, a place for the miners and cowpokes to kick up their heels and dance a jig or two with a pretty girl. Next door she had a few rooms for those men who chose not to go home at night. Her girls were known for their attractive gowns, clean bodies, and affectionate natures.

Gem had seen Mary O'Grady just once since she first came to Virginia City, and she wasn't likely to ever forget her. She was what Aunt Enid liked to call a "robust" woman with a more than ample bosom, a narrow waist, and generous hips. She accentuated these assets in gowns with low-cut bodices and tight skirts. She had riotous orange hair which she wore piled high on her head in a spectacular bouffant. She painted her cheeks with bright orange splotches, the lids of her eyes a deep verdant shade, and her lips the color of cherries.

Gem remembered how the ladies of Virginia City had stepped aside, whispering behind their hands, as Mary O'Grady walked down the boardwalk toward the mercantile. Gem and her aunt had just been coming out of Mrs. Culverson's Restaurant. Mary O'Grady had nodded and greeted her aunt, and instead of ignoring her as the other women had, Aunt Enid had returned the greeting.

When Gem had asked Aunt Enid why, she'd answered, "I don't hold with how she makes her living, Gem, but there's not a one in this territory that doesn't have something of their own to be ashamed of, the fine ladies of Virginia City included. False pride instead of Christian charity. That's what makes them behave that way. A kind word can only do another some good, and it wouldn't do them any harm to speak it, neither."

Gem stopped Wichita outside Miss O'Grady's "boarding" house. There were a couple of horses hitched to the rail outside, neither of them Chase's gelding. The hurdy-gurdy house was quiet this early in the day.

Taking a deep breath, Gem swung out of the saddle and wrapped the reins around the post next to the other two horses, then started for the front door. Not knowing what else to do, she knocked several times and waited.

Mary O'Grady herself opened the door. She was wearing a long, flowing peignoir, the same green color of her eyes, and matching mules on her feet. Upon seeing Gem, her eyebrow cocked above one eye.

"Miss O'Grady? I'm Gem McBride. I . . . I'm looking for Chase Dupre and heard he might be . . . here."

Mary lounged against the door, a smile beginning to play on her mouth. "So you're bein' Gem. I've heard o' you." A heavy brogue laced her words. She furtively glanced up and down the street. "I think you're safe from spyin' eyes this time o' day. Come in, Miss McBride."

"He's here then?"

"Aye, he's here, and in not too good o' shape, either. It's time you come t'take him off my hands."

The parlor into which she stepped was like nothing Gem had ever seen before. Red. Everything was red. Red velvet covered the settees and the walls. The lamps were made of red glass with tiny red tassels hanging around the edges. Even the carpet and the drapes were red. A bouquet of red roses filled a red glass vase which stood on a red table near the window. If Gem hadn't already felt entirely intimidated by the voluptuous Miss O'Grady, this room would have completed the job.

Mary closed the door. "So? And you've come for Chase, have you? As I was saying, you'll not find him in very good spirits." The woman continued to smile.

Gem straightened her spine. "Miss O'Grady, I thank you for lookin' after Chase, but—"

"Here now. Don't go gettin' your back up,

lassie. He's had himself a wee too much liquor these past few days. I had my girls bring him here 'fore he got himself in a ruckus he was too drunk t'handle. You'll find him in that first room to the top o' the stairs."

Gem felt the blush rising from her neck.

"If you're worried that your man's been a triflin' where he naught have been, miss, you can lay it t'rest." There was kindness and warmth in the painted woman's voice. "He's quite alone."

"He's not my—" Gem began, the flush deepening.

"Go on with you," Mary interrupted, pointing toward the door on the second floor. "An' good luck t'you, lassie. He's a fine lad, he is, and proud I am t'call him my friend."

Suddenly Gem smiled. She couldn't help herself. She liked Mary O'Grady.

Mary watched the little slip of a girl climbing the stairs. She shook her head, grinning all the while. She was a lucky lass, that one. What Mary wouldn't give to have a man like Chase loving her. Aye, and love Gem he did, though he was too wounded at heart to know it himself just yet. From the moment he'd walked through those doors, Ruth on one arm and Laura on the other, he'd done nothing but talk about Gem McBride. It wasn't just the drink that had kept him from delighting in one of Mary's girls. Mary was glad she'd had a chance to see for herself the leprechaun that had charmed him with her magic.

She remembered when he'd first come to her place. Just a lad and barely shaving yet. Had she been a wee bit younger or he a touch older, things might have been different between them. But there was something about the boy that made Mary O'Grady want to know him in a different way than most of her male companions, and an unexpected friendship had blossomed. Now that he'd grown into such a fine, strapping man, she sometimes regretted that things had stayed platonic between them.

Suddenly she chuckled. She'd bet a month's wages that Gem McBride would give him a merry chase, and glad she was about it, too. When he'd visited her after his return from Texas, she had seen more of his unhappiness than he would have wanted her to see. Now that Consuela was gone—God rest her soul; she wouldn't think ill of the dead now—Mary was certain he would find his old carefree spirit. Those two would probably be raising up sons in no time to inherit the Four Winds Ranch.

Well, she had no time to dawdle with such musings. With a yawn and a stretch, Mary headed for the back of the house. It was time she was getting dressed and waking her girls. The days started late at Mary O'Grady's but they lasted long after the darkness came.

18

The door squeaked as Gem pushed it open. The curtains were closed tight against the light of day, but she could make out Chase's form on the bed. Thankfully, Mary O'Grady was right. He was alone.

"Chase?" She stepped cautiously into the room. He didn't move.

Gem closed the door. "Chase?" She moved closer to the bed.

He groaned and rolled onto his side, facing her.

She bent over. Two days' stubble darkened his chin, and his breath reeked of whiskey. His dark hair curled around his temples. She wanted to reach out and brush it back from his forehead. He lay on his side, clutching the sheet against his bare chest. At this moment he seemed so very vulnerable. Gem wavered between feeling furious at him for choosing whiskey as a means of escape and feeling sorry for him for all he was suffering.

"Ah, Mary, is that you?" he said without opening his eyes. "Where have you been? I've missed you."

Fury won over pity.

"No, it's not Mary O'Grady," she snapped at him, then marched to the window and threw open the curtains. "But you'll wish it were before I'm through with you, Chase Dupre." To think she'd been worrying about him for two days. And here he lay, in his cups, telling Mary O'Grady he missed her. Why, the no-good, flea-bitten mongrel.

Chase shot up in bed, dragging the sheet along with him. One hand flew to his head in an attempt to still the pounding of a thousand tiny hammers on a thousand tiny anvils. "Gem," he croaked, closing his eyes once again. "What're you doing here?"

"I could ask you the same."

He shook his head slowly, then opened bloodshot eyes. "What are you doing in a place like this? Go home."

"I'm not leaving here without you. Chase Dupre, you ought to be ashamed of yourself. Worrying your aunt and uncle." It was only a tiny lie. Aunt Enid *would* have been worried if she didn't have so much faith in his ability to take care of himself.

Still cringing beneath his hangover, Chase scowled at her. "What I do is none of your business."

Gem marched back over to the side of the bed. "You don't think so? Well, maybe not, but the Four Winds *is* my business. It's my home, and there's work to be done there. It's not gonna get done with you layin' on your back in a . . . in a—" She groped for an acceptable word amid the dozens of unacceptable ones that filled her head.

"In a what?" he baited her.

"In a . . . in a house for soiled doves."

He laughed sharply, then grabbed his head again and moaned. "You got along without me pretty well while I was in Texas."

"Well, of all the selfish thinkin' I've ever run across," she shouted, poking him in the chest with her index finger, "that's gotta be the worst excuse I've ever heard for doin' nothin'. Now you get your pants on and come back to Four Winds with me."

Chase's face darkened with an anger to match her own. "If you think I need a little wet-nosed kid telling me what to do, you've got another thing coming, *Miss* McBride." He swung his legs over the bed and stood up, wrapping the sheet around his waist. "When I need your advice, I'll ask for it."

"Well, *Mr.* Dupre, do you see anybody else taking charge and getting things done?" she retorted sarcastically. Then, with a toss of her head, she turned for the door. "Come to think of it, I could run things just as well as you. Probably better. Stay here and wallow in your whiskey and . . . and whatever. I've got a ranch to run."

She pulled open the door, stepped into the hall, and slammed it behind her. Still seeing red—and not because of the decor—Gem raced down the stairs, pausing only when she saw Mary O'Grady once again lounging against the archway between parlor and dining room.

Mary winked at her. "That should do the trick, lass," she said with a nod of her head.

Gem was still too angry to acknowledge the woman's wry compliment. She stormed out of the house, leaving the door wide open as she hurried toward Wichita.

Chase had stumbled over the sheet as he grabbed for Gem's arm. He hit the floor just before the door slammed. His oath was muffled by the resounding crash of the closing door. Rolling onto his back, he cradled his head in both hands and moaned.

What had he done to get her so riled up? Wasn't a man entitled to a few drinks?

The door opened again, and Mary poked her head around it. "You still alive, cowboy?"

"Go away, Mary," he groaned.

"And isn't that a fine welcome." She let out a hearty laugh. "Laddie, you'd be well advised t'get back to that ranch o' yours and take that girl in hand." She motioned toward a chair in the corner. "You'll find your clothes over there. Come see me again some time, Chase. I'd love t'hear how you work things out." She threw him a saucy wink before closing the door.

Chase tried to sort things out in his mind as he got to his feet and went for his clothes. The past day or two had become a blur. Only bits and pieces could be recalled until the moment he awoke to the blinding light pouring through the window and Gem's angry voice biting his ears. How had Gem ever found him here? And, come to think of it, what right did she have to come in here and tell him what to do? He was a grown man. In fact, he was a free man. He didn't owe any explanation to her if he wanted to spend a night or two with Mary or one of her girls. Wasn't

Julio enough for her? Did she want to play games with him just like Consuela had? Well, he wasn't going to play. And he darn well wasn't going to let her tell him what to do.

He sat on the chair and pulled on his pants, then slipped his feet into his dusty boots. He stood, dropping his shirt over his head as he walked toward the door, combing his hair with his fingers as he went. He glanced quickly around the room, wondering if he was forgetting something. He wasn't even sure what he'd had with him when he got there. No matter. If he forgot something, Mary would see that it was returned. She might run a house of ill repute, but she was an honest woman all the same. With a shrug of his shoulders, he set his hat over his rumpled hair and opened the door.

As his boot touched the bottom step, Mary's voice called to him from the back of the house. "You'll find your horse stabled in the back."

"Thanks, Mary."

Still cringing beneath the wretched pounding in his head, he headed for the barn behind the hurdy-gurdy house. He picked up his saddle just inside the door.

"Dodge, old boy," he said softly as he approached the big gelding, "I think I'll swear off whiskey for a long time to come. The forgetting just isn't worth the headache."

It was a long, slow ride back to Four Winds.

"You did not find him, *amiga?*"

"I found him." Gem dismounted and led her mare into the barn for a rubdown.

Julio followed her inside. His presence was a silent question.

"I don't know if he's coming or not," she answered. She pulled the saddle from Wichita's back and laid it on the floor. Eyes flashed as she glanced quickly at Julio and then began brushing the heated mare. "And I don't care, one way or the other."

So that was how it was. They had exchanged words, those two. And it had done her good. There was more color in her face than he had seen in weeks. "Perhaps I should go and talk to him," he suggested.

Gem whirled around, shaking the brush in his face. "Don't you *dare* set foot in that woman's place, Julio Valdez. Chase can rot there for all I care. We've got work to do."

Woman? This grew even more interesting. "What woman?" he asked, although he was sure he knew.

Gem pressed her lips together and turned back to her horse, brushing her hide so briskly that Wichita snorted and stomped a hoof in complaint.

"*Si*, I think I understand, *amiga*." Julio spun on his heel and walked outside, letting the smile steal onto his mouth. She must have found Chase at Mary O'Grady's. Julio had suspected that was where he would be, but he couldn't tell Gem that. A gentleman didn't speak of such things to a lady. His grin widened. But then again, Gem wasn't the usual lady. It wasn't likely that Gem would let the man she loved wallow in self-pity, let alone take his comfort in the company of the town's irrepressible madam.

These two, his friends Gem and Chase, they

would be good for each other once time had healed old wounds.

By the time his horse was nearing Four Winds, Chase had convinced himself he was a thousand times a fool.

What right did he have to be upset if Gem and Julio were lovers? Hadn't he told his friend—more than once—to love her and take care of her? Did he have any claim on her? Or any right to a claim, for that matter? No, he had turned his back on her love each time she had offered it. Besides, what kind of a man would he have been to have accepted it when he had nothing to give her in return? Even now. Even now that Consuela was dead, and he was a free man, he still had nothing to offer her. There was no love left in him. He was wrung dry.

He walked Dodge slowly toward the barn, pulling up on the reins when Julio came out of the bunkhouse and waved for him to stop.

"You look weary, *mi amigo*."

Chase nodded. "Gem back?"

"She is still in the barn. She was plenty angry when she got back." His hand fell on Chase's thigh. "She found you at Mary's?"

Again he nodded.

Julio grinned. "She is very jealous, our Gem. Those she loves and this ranch. She fights hard for them."

"Yeah." Chase turned the gelding's head. "I'd better talk to her."

He rode away from Julio, dismounting when he arrived at the barn door. He squinted as he encountered the darkness of the barn.

"Gem?"

As his eyes adjusted, he stepped inside. He didn't see her anywhere. Wichita was in one of the stalls munching on a flake of hay, but Gem wasn't with her.

"Gem?" he called again, a little louder.

A slight rustle in the loft gave her presence away. Chase glanced up and waited, but she still didn't acknowledge his call, so he led his horse into an empty stall and unsaddled him quickly. Then he headed for the ladder leading to the hayloft.

She was sitting in a dim corner, her knees tucked up against her chest, her hands clasped around her shins. As he drew closer, he could see that she watched his approach with still-sparking eyes.

"Mind if I set a spell?" he asked before squatting on his heels.

Gem shrugged and turned her gaze down at her toes.

Chase drew a deep breath and plunged forward. "Gem, I'm sorry for saying the things I did. You were right. There's too much to be done around here for me to go off and drink myself stupid."

She met his eyes again.

"One more thing. I expect you *could* run this ranch as well as me. Maybe better." He offered his hand. "Forgive and forget?"

The corners of her mouth twitched. "I never was much good at stayin' mad at you, Chase," she said softly, letting the smile take over as she took his hand.

It was as if her fingers were squeezing his heart. His own hand tightened, and for a moment he treasured their aloneness and the gentle air of forgiveness and understanding that surrounded them.

"Chase?"

"Yeah?"

"I'm sorry, too. I guess if I'd . . . if I'd been through all you've been through lately, I'd have gone drinkin' myself. I'm just glad you're home again."

From some forgotten corner of his brain came the memory of the morning he'd returned from Texas. She had come racing from the house in her nightgown and thrown herself into his arms and kissed him. Looking at her now, he felt a sudden hunger for another of her kisses, for another impassioned welcome. His palm grew sweaty and he suddenly let go of her hand.

"Thanks, kid," he replied, his voice grown husky. "I'm glad I'm home too." He stood and turned. "Guess I'd better let Aunt Enid and Uncle Frank know I'm back."

It was insane. He had already come to the conclusion that he had nothing to offer Gem. He couldn't love her. He couldn't love any woman. But suddenly he wanted her more than he'd ever wanted a woman before in his life.

They had a conference in Uncle Frank's bedroom. The older Dupre rolled around the room in his newly acquired wheelchair while Enid sat on a chair near the window, her eyes never leaving her husband as he enjoyed his refound freedom. Gem sat on the bed with her legs tucked beneath her, and Chase and Julio and Rodney leaned against various places on the wall, out of the way of Frank Dupre's wheels.

"I'd say we lost a couple hundred head to the fire," Rodney was saying. "Hard to tell how many we'll lose in the hills. They're spread all over creation. It'll take us another week or two to finish roundin' 'em up. We're short-handed but so's everybody in the valley. Four Winds wasn't the only ranch to suffer from the storm."

"Well, I see only one thing to do, boys. We'd better get those cattle to Grogan in Cheyenne a bit early this year. The best of the grass is gone, and there's not much for water neither. We'll sell off some of the heifers too. Might make it easier to get the rest of them through the winter here." He swiveled his chair around, looking at his nephew. "You see what you can round up for trail hands. See if any of the other ranchers want to join us in the drive. We'll try to hit the trail in two weeks."

Enid spoke from her place by the window. "We'll only need a few hands to stay behind and mind the place. Most of them can go on the drive."

"We'll leave Zeke to mind things, Aunt Enid," Gem offered. "He's good with the men and can handle anything that might come up while we're gone."

"Whoa!" Chase turned brilliant, questioning eyes her way. "You don't think you're going on the drive, do you?"

"Of course I'm going. I've been going on them for years, and I don't see any reason to change now."

"But this year's a little different, Gem. Water's low and the feed'll be scarce. We'll be pushing hard. This won't be an easy drive."

Gem felt herself bristling. Not two hours ago he

was telling her she probably could run this ranch as well as he could, and already he was trying to make her stay behind. Rather than start an argument here with everyone watching, she looked at Uncle Frank. "I'm going, Uncle Frank. You know I carry my own weight on the drives, and I'm needed as much this year as I ever was, maybe more."

"She's right, Chase. She's a good hand, and you'll need her more on the drive than we'll need her here at the ranch."

Triumphant, she glanced back at Chase. His sapphire eyes smoldered, and she couldn't suppress a smile which only made his responding glower grow even darker.

"Thanks, Uncle Frank," she said as she unfolded her legs and hopped off the bed to give him a tight hug. "I knew you'd see it my way."

Frank chuckled and patted her back.

"Now that that's settled," Chase interrupted abruptly, "can we get on with more important things?"

As the men continued to discuss the details of the roundup and cattle drive, Gem settled once more on the bed. She allowed her gaze to move slowly from Uncle Frank to Julio to Chase, and there it remained. She felt the same flutter of butterfly wings in her stomach that she had felt during their brief interlude in the barn loft. She hadn't been mistaken about the feelings that had passed between them. Desire had been etched on his bronzed face. She wasn't about to let a cattle drive separate them again. Not now. She was going with him whether he liked it or not.

"I'll call on a few of the neighbors, then head into town in the morning," Chase said, his hand on the door. "Besides, I've got some business along the way to take care of before we go."

Enid rose to her feet and walked across the room. She placed a hand on Chase's arm. "If you're thinking what I know you are, don't do it, Chase. It's not worth it."

"There's some things a man's gotta do, Aunt Enid," he replied softly.

Enid shook her head but loosened her hold on his arm. Chase kissed her troubled brow, then pulled the door open and left the bedroom, followed by Julio and Rodney.

Gem moved from the bed and stepped to Enid's side. "What's he gotta do?"

"I reckon he's aiming to settle a score with Powell Daniels."

Chase lay awake in the dark hours of the night, something gnawing at the pit of his stomach. He meant to settle with Powell in the morning. It had to be done. It had to be finished. It had been coming for a long time, ever since they were small boys. Powell Daniels had been born hating the Dupres and wanting what was theirs. It was time an end was put to it. But would killing Powell really help stop the bitterness that ate at him? He didn't know. All he knew was that he wanted to get even with someone for playing havoc with his life. Powell was the best choice.

He rolled onto his side and punched his pillow several times, then tested it with his head again, but sleep was a stranger to him. He got up and walked to the window. A light spilled into the night from the room next to his own. Gem must be awake.

He felt a flicker of anger at the way she had outmaneuvered him with Uncle Frank. He hadn't wanted her on the drive, not after the way he'd responded to her in the barn. He couldn't guarantee how he would behave after weeks on the trail. Even now, just thinking about her, and it was all he could do to keep from going to her room and . . .

Damn! What a mess he'd made of things!

Josh Daniels sat on the porch, waiting. He had awakened this morning and known that Chase would come calling.

He saw the man, riding tall in the saddle, when he was still far off. Josh got up from his chair and walked to the edge of the porch, squinting into the morning sun. It seemed ages before Chase jogged his big pinto gelding into the yard of Big Pine Ranch. Josh felt a hundred years older than he had just a week ago.

"Daniels."

"Mornin', Chase."

"I've come to see Powell."

"You won't see him here."

"Where is he?"

"Buried up next to his ma. Just yesterday." Josh turned his back toward young Dupre and returned to his chair. He sank into it with a weariness of both body and soul.

Chase sat there looking at him for a long time, thrumming the fingers of his right hand on his thigh near his gun belt. Finally he lifted the reins and turned the pinto's head.

"Chase," Josh said, stopping his departure. "It's done with now, the hate between our families."

Chase didn't look back. "It's done with, Daniels."

Josh nodded and watched Chase ride slowly away.

Perhaps, if Enid had married me, we would have had a boy like that, he thought.

Then he closed his eyes and slept for the first time in several days.

19

After two weeks of riding from one end of the valley to the other, days and nights of scouting mountainsides and creek bottoms, the surviving Four Winds herd was rounded up, and those bound for Cheyenne had been separated. The trail branding was finished. The remuda had been selected from the trustiest cow ponies on Four Winds. The cowboys were eager to hit the trail. Even Corky McGinnis was ready.

As the cook for the Four Winds drive, Corky had filled the wagon bed with the bulk foodstuffs—plenty of coffee beans, flour, pinto beans, sugar, salt, dried apples, onions, potatoes, and salt pork, even some grain for the work horses pulling the wagon. The bedrolls and slickers, guns and ammunition were all stored in the chuckwagon too, along with lanterns and kerosene and supplies to repair the wagon should it break down. The honeycombed drawers and cubby-holes in the chuck at the rear of the wagon were filled with whatever food might be needed during the day, plus the cutlery with which to eat it. Tucked away in extra nooks and crannies were plenty of bandages, needles and thread, chewing and rolling tobacco, and a drop or two of whiskey. The boot held the skillets and coffeepot and dutch ovens.

First light on that August morning found Gem swinging lightly into the saddle after bidding her farewells to Enid and Frank. She pulled the brim of her hat down low on her forehead, then tugged at her gloves before picking up the reins.

"We'll drive them as slow as we can to keep their weight up." Chase shook his uncle's hand. "Grogan will get us whatever's top dollar." Then he turned to his aunt. "If the weather holds, look for us before November, but even with early snows we'll be back before Thanksgiving."

"Just get back safely. That's all we ask." Enid patted Chase's cheek. "Take care of my girl there."

Chase nodded and stepped off the porch.

"Same goes for you, Gem," Enid called. "You take care of my boy."

"I'll do it, Aunt Enid, but he won't like it." Gem's gamine grin was sure to set Chase's teeth on edge.

"Let's go," Chase grumbled in her direction.

He'd hardly spoken more than a dozen words to her in the past two weeks, yet she wasn't deterred in the slightest. In fact, her spirits were brighter than ever. For some strange reason she felt that his protests to her presence on the drive were a good sign and not a bad one. She had caught him watching her more than once during the roundup, watching her with an intense stare that made her shiver with unnamed emotions. And now she would be with him every single day for over two months.

Gem followed Chase's cantering horse as they rode toward the waiting herd. The cowpokes had been watching for them, and as soon as the drovers saw their approach, they began to throw the cattle onto the trail with a cry of "Ho cattle ho ho ho." The cowboys riding in the rear and on the sides held firm, pressing the herd forward and chasing after stubborn strays. The point riders opened up the trail for the lead steers as cows called mournfully for their calves.

"Tell Rod to move up to swing," Chase called to her. "You ride drag." Then he spurred his mount ahead, circling wide so he wouldn't spook the herd.

Gem eased back on the reins and glared at Chase's back. She knew his game. He thought if she had to ride at the back of the herd the first day out she might turn around and go home. Well, it wasn't going to work. She'd eat dust and harass lame cattle and orphaned yearlings the whole trip if she had to, but she was here and she was going to stay.

She turned Wichita to the left and loped toward the stragglers. Just as she approached, a steer doubled back from the herd, and without hesitation Gem kneed Wichita after it. The coils of the grass rope slid easily into her left hand while her right held the main line and loop.

"Ho there," she called, gripping Wichita with her legs as the mare cut quickly to block the steer's escape.

Gem twirled the rope, using its whirring sound to turn the cow. With surprising agility in an animal so awkward-looking, the longhorn changed direction and headed back toward the herd. Gem followed after him more slowly, turning off when she caught sight of Rodney.

"Chase says for you to ride swing," she told him as she fell in beside him. "I'll take your spot here."

Even Rod understood Chase's motives. "Doesn't aim t'make it easy on you, is that it?"

"That's it," she answered.

"Maybe I should tell him about the past few years and what a good hand you are."

"Don't bother, Rod. He's not in a listening mood when it comes to me and this drive. Now get on up there before he thinks I'm causing you to shirk your work."

Rodney laughed and touched the brim of his hat in a mock salute. "See you when we noon."

Gem watched him ride away before pulling up the bandanna over her mouth and turning her attention back to the stragglers. "Ho cattle ho ho ho," she crooned and swung her rope.

The noon rendezvous found them just outside the northern most boundary of Four Winds. Corky had stirred up a mess of cowboy beans made from salt pork, pinto beans, and onions. Pike and a new man, Sam Rivers, rode loose herd over the cattle, allowing them to rest and graze while the drovers ate their dinner.

Chase took his plate and sat on his heels in the shade of the chuckwagon as he ate. His gaze moved slowly over the herd of 2,500 cattle, alert for any signs of trouble. Moving at about twelve miles per day, they should have the cattle to Cheyenne in just under two months. That was assuming they didn't have any trouble with stampedes or weather or Indians.

Gem's laughter drew his attention away from the herd. She was seated on the ground. Julio and Teddy sat on either side of her, while several of the other hands stood or squatted nearby. She had pushed the hat from her head, letting it hang against her back, and a line of dust could be clearly seen across her forehead. It would be even worse by nightfall.

Chase felt a twinge of guilt. He could have made it a little easier on her. There wasn't a worse job on a cattle drive than riding drag. Still, if she had stayed at home where she belonged . . .

Again she laughed, and again he looked at her. Splashes of pink dotted her cheeks, and her blue-green eyes sparkled merrily. Pecos Pete, the young wrangler who had signed on for the drive, turned bright red under her teasing, which only made the other cowpokes laugh harder. Chase felt left out. No, if he was honest with himself, he would admit he just wanted her all to himself; that's what really troubled him.

"All right, men," Chase said gruffly, getting quickly to his feet. "Let's hit the trail. We've got a long day ahead of us." He plunked his plate down on the end of the chuckwagon and lit out for his fresh mount.

For four days they headed north, following the Madison River. Chase had ridden ahead and chosen a grassy bedding ground near the river. Corky set up his wagon, made a fire, and began preparing supper for the hungry trail hands. As twilight fell, the men of the first watch began circling the herd in a diminishing spiral, drawing the herd in close together. Finally one of them changed direction, and the two men began riding the opposite circles of the night guard.

Gem turned her saddle horse loose with the others of the remuda, then walked slowly toward the campfire. She stopped when she saw Chase riding in. Her heart squeezed, and she felt a terrible emptiness in her stomach.

Even after four days he continued to put distance between them, even to the point of ignoring her. She had begun to wonder if she'd been wrong about coming. Maybe she should have stayed at Four Winds. Maybe two months on the trail wouldn't bring them together as she'd hoped it would. Maybe Aunt Enid was wrong too. Maybe Chase never would love her.

"*Amiga?*" Julio stepped silently up beside her. "You are worried?"

She turned to glance up at her friend in the gathering darkness. "Not worried, Julio. I was just . . . just thinking."

"He will come around, senorita."

She was silent for a long time before she asked, "Does it bother you, Julio? I mean, me loving him when he was . . . when he was married to your sister and all?"

"No, Gem," he replied, "it does not bother me. I am only troubled to see you so sad." With that, he left her, walking quickly toward the chuckwagon and his supper.

Gem wasn't hungry. She was tired and dusty and sore of heart. She turned away from the friendly chatter of the trail hands and walked toward the river.

Tomorrow they would leave the Madison and cut through the mountain pass, heading east toward Fort Ellis and Livingston.

She sat on a rock near the bank and pulled off her boots. A half-moon showered the low-running river with glitters of pale moonlight. Barefooted, she squatted near the water and cupped her hands, drawing the cool liquid up to splash her face. She repeated the motion several times before drawing her bandanna from around her neck and using it to dry her face.

She sighed as she settled back on her heels, but the corresponding intake of breath froze in her throat. She suddenly had an overwhelming feeling that someone—or something—was watching her. She glanced around her. Nothing moved. Nothing rustled in the still summer night air. But she was certain she was not alone. She reached quickly for her boots and pulled them on, then started hastily back toward the night camp. Several times she glanced back over her shoulder.

As she turned her eyes back on the trail, a dark figure stepped in front of her. A frightened scream rose in her throat and was strangled there as strong fingers gripped her arms.

"Gem, what are you doing out here by yourself?"

Of their own volition, her arms wound around his neck and her head pressed against his chest. "Oh, Chase!" she gasped. "I thought I saw something."

"What?" His hand moved to hold the back of her head.

Her galloping heart began to slow. "I . . . I don't know." She looked up at him.

With the moonlight bathing his rugged face, his eyes looked black and seemed able to see clear through her. Once again her heart raced, but no longer from fear.

"I'd better get you back to camp," Chase said softly, "then I'll take a look around."

She nodded, keenly aware of the feel of his arms around her, the echo of his heartbeat so close to her ear. She wished they could stay that way just a little while longer, but already he was loosening his hold on her and stepping backward.

"Come on," he said, and started walking.

Wordlessly she followed after him.

20

Day followed day with unbroken sameness. The dust, the flies, the heat. Hours in the saddle were followed by quick snatches of sleep on the hard ground. The food was basically the same—bacon, beans, and biscuits for breakfast, cowboy beans for dinner, son-ofabitch stew for supper, all meals served with black coffee and often times ill humor from the cook.

They had bedded the cattle on high ground that night. Gem crawled between the blankets of her bedroll beneath the chuckwagon and drifted immediately into a weary slumber. It seemed she had hardly closed her eyes before a voice was saying, "Your watch, Gem."

"Thanks, Pike," she groaned, pulling on her boots and scrambling from beneath the wagon before her eyes were even open. She buckled on her batwing chaps and pulled her hat over her hair as she headed for the remuda.

She and Teddy Hubbs were sharing the third watch that night. A glance at the big dipper told her it was almost precisely two a.m. She moved quietly toward her night horse and pulled her complaining body into the saddle. Teddy threw back a cup of boiled-down coffee before joining her.

"Julio says it's been quiet," he whispered to her, then started off in a counterclockwise circle around the sleeping herd.

Gem rode clockwise, singing gentle lullabies in a clear voice. She made up the songs as she went along. The words weren't important to the cows.

Only a sliver of moon still shone overhead, but Flap Jack, Gem's favorite night horse, picked his way safely along the gullied land in the inky shadows of the night. Flap Jack was a big sorrel gelding with an ugly jug of a head and a wide white blaze running from between his eyes down to the pink and black splotches of his muzzle, but he was as calm as they came. He never shied at sudden noises, and his sharp eyes could carry him at a full gallop in the blackest night without putting his hoof in a gopher hole. Most importantly, he was fearless in the midst of a night stampede.

As she sang, Gem thought about Chase. Something had happened that night on the riverbank. Something invisible, something intangible, yet something very real. A new bond had formed between them. It was just a tiny thread, but it was there. She knew it.

It didn't make any sense that she should feel that

way. He still didn't speak to her any more often than before, nor did he seek her out to spend time with her. She rode her position on the drive, sometimes drag, sometimes point or swing or flank. She took her two-hour turn of night watch right along with the others. She didn't ask any favors and he didn't give any. Yet somehow they had drawn just a little closer than before.

Flap Jack's big head raised and his ears cocked forward. Gem was instantly alert. She felt it again. Something was out there.

Chase couldn't sleep. His body was tired, but his mind wouldn't let him rest. He kept imagining Gem out in the darkness, riding watch. He wanted to be with her.

He tossed aside his quilt and got up. He scanned the sleeping herd, just slightly darker shadows than the ground around them, then he drew a deep, pine-scented breath and headed for the coffeepot, still sitting over the coals of last night's fire. The coffee would be cool and bitter, but he poured himself a cup anyway.

"Could not sleep, *amigo*?"

Chase didn't show his surprise as he turned toward the voice.

Julio was leaning against the wheel of the chuck-wagon, quietly smoking a cigarillo.

"Nope. Couldn't sleep. What about you?"

"I just finished watch."

"I know. You oughta be catching some shut-eye." Chase sipped the bitter brew as he stepped closer to the wagon.

"It is a strange night, *amigo*."

Chase turned his head once more toward the herd. "Maybe I should check on things." Checking on Gem was what he meant.

"My friend, you would do well to love such a woman," Julio said softly, seeming to read Chase's mind.

"What do you plan to do, Julio?" The sting of jealousy revealed itself in his sharp question. "Give her back to me?"

"*Amigo*, she was never mine to give. She has always loved you."

Then why did you and she . . .

Again Julio seemed to read his thoughts. "We have been only friends. I will not lie to you, Chase. I would wish it could be more. But she will love only you."

"It's too late," he protested stubbornly.

"No, *amigo*." Julio's hand fell on his shoulder. "It is just in time. Do not let my sister shrivel your heart even in death."

Chase was about to reply when he heard the noise every cowboy dreads.

It was amazing how quickly it could happen. Suddenly the bedded cattle jumped to their feet and took off in a rumbling stampede. The ground trembled beneath their feet.

"All hands and the cook!" Chase bellowed, tossing the cup aside as he bolted for his horse.

Julio was right beside him, and together they made a blind dash toward the point. The high mountains on either side of them formed a natural barrier which would keep the herd from spreading out too far. There was no other sound in the night air except the pounding of hooves and clatter of horns.

Stampeding cattle, oddly enough, didn't bawl but became a whirling dervish, a tempest of horns and tails.

The two riders galloped past the lead steers. "Ho ho!" they shouted, beginning the turn that would rotate the herd into a spinning wheel. In the darkness they could only trust their mounts and hope they wouldn't find themselves beneath the crushing hooves of the wild-eyed cattle.

The herd began to circle. Gradually their pace slowed until at last they milled. The hands remained alert. This was a dangerous time, with the cattle all jammed together, ready to spook again at the slightest provocation. Slowly they urged the herd to drift back toward their bed-ground.

Chase walked his horse around the edge of the herd. As he neared Julio, he asked in a near whisper, "Have you seen Gem?"

"No."

"I'll find her." He moved on, quickening his mount's pace ever so slightly.

She stopped Flap Jack near a lone pine tree at the edge of the bedded herd. She rode a wide circle around the tall pine's thick trunk. Leaning forward, she peered intently into the surrounding night.

"What is it, boy?" she whispered to the horse. "What did you see?" She pulled her rifle from its scabbard and dismounted.

Turning her head from side to side, straining to hear anything unusual, she stepped cautiously forward. She circled the tree once again, then dropped down to rest on her heels as she ran her fingers over the ground as if searching for a sign she could feel if not see.

It was at that moment she felt the sudden thunder of the earth beneath her fingertips. She straightened quickly, but it was already too late. The terrified cattle were almost upon her. She flattened herself against the back side of the tree trunk, her arms stretched above her head as her fingers gripped a flimsy, moss-covered limb. She closed her eyes. She could feel the near-blistering heat put off by the stampeding cattle as they divided around the pine, passing so closely their long horns raked the bark from the tree. She held her breath and wished herself smaller.

It seemed like hours before they were passed her. She could still feel the quaking ground beneath her boots. Slowly she loosed her death-grip on the tree and slipped to the earth. Her eyes still closed, she hugged her arms over her chest and gave in to the shaking that threatened to rattle her teeth.

That was how he found her.

"Gem!"

She tried to open her eyes but couldn't.

His arms were around her, and he was lifting her up from the ground. "Gem, are you hurt?"

She pressed herself against the safety of his chest just as she had against the safety of the tree.

"It's okay, Gem. It's okay. I've got you now."

He held her, whispering comforting nothings into her hair, and little by little she began to stop shaking. But she didn't want to tell him she was all right. Not yet. She just wanted to stay there in the circle of his arms.

Finally his finger moved to her chin and he lifted her face. She felt the same scorching heat as when the cattle passed, but this time she had the insane desire to become a part of the heat instead of hiding from it.

"I'd better get you back to camp," he said, but didn't move.

She nodded, her cheek brushing his shirt. "I . . . I don't know where Flap Jack is."

"He's too smart a brute to get caught in a stampede," he assured her gently. "We'll find him in the morning."

"Chase?" She spoke his name softly, savoring it on her tongue.

"Mmmm?" His hand slid across her back.

For a moment she couldn't remember what she had wanted to say. She stood mesmerized by his nearness, aching for his caresses, for his kisses. Her knees felt too weak to hold her up, and her heart beat erratically in her chest.

The hoof beats forewarned them just before Julio's voice called, "*Amigo*."

He set her back from him. "Over here. I found her."

The fragile moment was broken.

Julio rounded the tree and jumped from the saddle. "Is she hurt?"

"I'm okay," Gem answered for herself.

"Her horse is gone, Julio. Give her a ride back to camp, will you? I want to circle the herd, check with the men."

"Of course, *amigo*."

Gem raised a tentative hand to his chest and touched him lightly. "Chase? What caused the stampede?"

"I don't know. Everything was quiet. I don't know what brought them to their feet."

"I think there was someone here," she told him. "A stranger."

Julio stepped closer as she spoke. Both men's heads turned to survey the landscape bathed in starlight.

"I was riding watch. Flap Jack acted like he heard something, so I rode over to take a look for myself. I never saw anything, but—" She paused and felt a shudder pass over her. "It was the same feeling I had the other night. Like I was being watched. I got down and was looking around. That's when they bolted. I didn't have time to remount."

"Well, we won't find any trace of him tonight if there was a stranger around. You go on with Julio. Get some sleep. You'll need it tomorrow."

It was a dismissal, but she heard the tenderness in his voice and was comforted yet again.

Before dawn the trail hands were all mounted, searching out strays. Pecos Pete had found all the remuda, including an unharmed Flap Jack, and had them roped off in a makeshift corral. Breakfast that morning was a quick cup of black coffee, a couple of slices of bacon, and hastily consumed biscuits smothered in thick gravy before they broke camp and threw the cattle back on the trail.

Chase went over the area near the pine tree several times, but if there had once been any signs of an intruder, they had been erased by the thundering hooves of the previous night. Giving up, he went to tell Gem what he had found. She was riding flank when he brought her the news.

His eyes scanned the mountains around them, and he frowned. "I hope you were wrong. If we've got Indians dogging us, we wouldn't be in much of a position to protect ourselves."

"I don't think it was Indians." She was utterly serious.

He grinned as he turned his sapphire gaze upon her. "Maybe you were just seeing things. Spooks maybe."

"I wasn't *seeing things*," she protested, but she couldn't resist his smile. Good humor lifted the corners of her mouth.

"I've gotta ride on ahead and find a spot to noon." He glanced at the clear blue of the sky. "Looks like it'll be another hot one."

"You'll find water about five or six miles down."

He glanced her way again. She looked no worse for wear after her scare last night. In fact, she didn't look a whole lot different from the rest of the trail hands, clad as she was in loose shirt and vest, chaps over her denim trousers, spurs buckled around her boots. Her wide-brimmed hat covered her braided strawberry-blonde hair. Experienced fingers encased in leather gloves held the grass rope lightly. The only thing missing was some stubble on her chin or a mustache beneath her pert, upturned nose.

"You know this trail pretty good," he told her.

"I've ridden it a time or two."

He wished he'd been with her on those other rides.

"See you at dinner," she said, then trotted after a steer veering away from the herd. "Ho there," she called after it.

Chase sat his horse and watched her work, at the same time remembering the feel of her last night as he cradled her shivering body in his arms. Rough-and-tumble cowboy and vulnerable little child, all rolled into one tiny package. An odd combination to twist his heart and make his body hot with desire.

Chase was about two hours ahead of the herd when he spied the wagon near a slow-running creek in the shade of a grove of cottonwoods. A team of horses were tied to the side of the wagon, their eyes half closed as they dozed in the morning heat. A ribbon of smoke trailed up from a dying campfire. A coffeepot was turned over on the ground, and a tin plate rested on the wagon wheel, the remains of breakfast drying to its surface.

"Hello," Chase called, alert eyes searching for some sign of movement. His right hand reached slowly for his Colt. "Hello."

He dismounted and walked cautiously toward the camp. Except for the occasional swish of the big work horses' tails, the splash and gurgle of the creek were the only sounds that greeted his ears.

"Hello," he repeated.

He pushed aside the canvas opening and peeked inside the wagon. A trunk in one corner was open, and clothes were scattered over the floor. The covers were pulled back from the cot. Flour and sugar and other supplies spilled out of the little storage bins near the back of the wagon. It wasn't a very neat sight.

Chase turned away from the wagon, scanning the area once more for signs of life, again in vain. Yet he knew that someone had been there that morning. Instinct told him that trouble had arrived here before he had.

He began walking again, slowly, making no sound as he moved along the creek bank. He was about to holster his revolver and return to his horse when a big yellow dog burst onto the path in front of him. It snarled a warning, showing its fangs. Its back was hunched and its hackles were raised.

Startled, Chase jumped backward and pointed his gun at the truculent dog. Then he saw the bleeding wound in its side. It looked like a bullet wound.

"Easy there," he said gently.

The dog was having none of it. A threat rumbled in its throat.

"Hey, I just want to help." He knelt in the path. "Easy there, fella."

"Gretchen."

The male voice that called was weak, but the dog heard and turned quickly from the path, darting into the brush. Chase stood and waited. When no one showed himself, he moved forward once again.

"She'll tear your throat out if ya come any closer," a voice warned.

Chase stopped. "I mean you no harm. I want to help if I can."

"Who are ya?"

"Chase Dupre. I'm the trail boss of a herd headed for Cheyenne."

There was a long pause before the hidden man said, "Come ahead." Then softly, "Stay, Gretchen."

Chase pushed the brush aside.

The old man was leaning against a tree. Gnarled fingers gripped his bleeding side. One leg was braced at an angle, a rifle resting against his thigh. His grizzled face was pale, pain etched clearly in every line. Red-rimmed, faded blue eyes watched Chase's approach. The yellow mongrel lay beside him, her muzzle on her master's hip. The man's free hand stroked her head.

Chase holstered his gun, then held his hands up in the air, showing he carried no other weapon, before walking over to the injured man. He hunkered down beside him.

"There's no helpin' me, young fella. It's a mortal wound." He lifted his fingers, revealing the injury.

The old man was right. It didn't look like much could be done. Still, Chase tried to convince him otherwise. "Our chuckwagon shouldn't be too far behind me. Corky's only a fair cook, but he's pretty good at doctoring. We'll get you fixed up in no time. And your dog too."

"Good ol' Gretchen," the old man whispered. "I'm thinkin' she won't make it either."

Again Chase had to agree. "What's your name, mister, and what happened here?"

"Name's Chester Brine. I was on my way north. Got a brother in Spokane up in Washington." He gasped sharply and squeezed his eyes shut.

Chase started to reach out to touch Chester's shoulder. Gretchen immediately lifted her head and snarled a warning. Chase pulled back his hand.

Chester opened his eyes. "Man rode into camp . . . early this mornin'. He was wearin' a black hood . . . over his face. He just . . . started shootin'.

Never said a . . . word. No . . . reason for it. I lit for cover, but . . . but Gretchen went after him. He shot her . . . then me."

The old man was failing quickly, and Chase couldn't do anything but watch.

"Young . . . fella?"

"Yeah."

Chester coughed, then dragged in a ragged breath. "Gretchen won't . . . leave me. Don't . . . let her . . . suffer. Just bury . . . us . . . together."

"Sure, old timer," Chase whispered.

"Young fella," he said again, even softer this time.

"What, Chester?"

"Gretchen's . . . pup. Take care o' . . . her."

Chase looked around. "What pup, old timer?"

Chester Brine lifted his hand from Gretchen's head, then reached beneath his bent knee, pulling out a yellow ball of fur by the scruff of its neck. "Name's Sunny . . . She'll need . . . some . . . lookin' after."

Gretchen whined as her dying master passed her pup to Chase, but she raised no other protest.

"Thanks—" the old man sighed.

Gem's body ached all over. There had been little sleep after last night's stampede, and the day was turning into a hot one. Dust seemed to be imbedded in every pore of her body. Her eyes felt as if her eyelids were made of sandpaper. She longed for nothing so much as a long bath and a night in a nice, soft bed. She was glad to see the chuckwagon come into sight. She was hungry, and it meant at least a short reprieve from the saddle and the dust.

She helped bring the herd to a halt, then rode toward Corky's noon camp. Dismounting, she shook out her legs and lifted her hands above her head, clasping her fingers as she stretched, popping the little kinks in her spine.

"Gem!"

She turned toward Teddy's voice.

"Chase wants to see you." He jerked his head toward the creek. "Down that way."

Gem nodded, wondering if she'd done something wrong to earn a tongue lashing from the trail boss. She hoped not. She'd been secretly basking in the memory of his smile all morning. With quick strides she headed for the creek.

Chase was waiting for her near a tall cottonwood, its branches spreading a green canopy over the clear water of the stream. His hands were clasped behind his back, and his face looked grim.

"You wanted to see me, Chase?"

"Yeah."

She stopped a few feet away from him. Her thumbs slipped beneath her gunbelt at her sides, arms akimbo.

"We're going to stay here tonight. It'll be a long day tomorrow to reach water. The grass is good here, too. We'll let the herd rest early and get their bellies full, then push them a little harder tomorrow."

"Sure. It's a good place to bed." Her eyes revealed her puzzlement.

Chase glanced toward the creek and stared silently into the distance. "I buried a man back a ways this morning. Murdered."

"Indians?"

"No." He returned his gaze to her. "Before he died, he asked me to take care of somethin' for him. I'm going to need your help."

"Sure, Chase. What is it?"

From behind his back he drew a yellow puppy, not much bigger than his hands. "Her name's Sunny. Her bitch was killed too. Think you can take care of her?"

"Oh, Chase." She reached forward. "Of course I can."

He placed the orphaned puppy in her hands.

Gem raised Sunny to her cheek. "What a sad day for you," she said. "Are you hungry? Let's see what we can find for you to eat." She glanced at Chase again. "I'll take good care of her, Chase. I promise."

"I know you will." He tossed her a warm smile.

Gem hurried back to the chuckwagon. "Corky, what's for dinner?" she called to the cook.

"Why?" he growled without turning around. "You got a special request?"

"I sure do. We've got a new trail hand, and she's a mighty picky eater."

"Well, I'll be hanged if I'm going to—" He swung around, ready to let the "picky eater" have a piece of his mind, then stopped when he saw what Gem was holding. "Well, I'll be. Where'd you find her?"

"Chase found her. Says her ma and master were killed down the creek a ways. Can we fix up something to eat for her?"

"I reckon we can at that."

The whole crew became involved with the feeding of Sunny before dinner was finished. She wasn't more than five weeks old, if that. Gem doubted she'd been weaned before her bitch was shot, but Sunny was hungry and dug into the mashed beans and pork with the first signs of enthusiasm she'd shown since she was placed in Chase's hands.

"We could rope us a cow and get her some milk," Pike suggested. "Johnny Blue'd be happy to do it for you, Gem."

Johnny laughed. "I'm 'fraid my ropin' arm's just a bit weak, Pike. Junior, didn't you say your pa raised a milk cow or two? You'd be just the man for it."

Junior Stewart shook his head. "Naw. Ain't never been no milk cows on our place. 'Sides, pup that age oughta be off milk anyways. Shoot. If she was my dog, I'd have her out scoutin' her own supper 'fore she was more'n a month older."

Sunny had finished her meal by this time and was pushing the plate around with her nose. Her yellow tale was wagging fiercely, shaking her entire backside. Gem picked her up and snuggled her against her chest.

"Sunny, I don't think these fellas know what they're yammerin' about." She got to her feet. "Thanks for a good meal, Corky. Sunny and I appreciate it."

"Gem?" Chase had been standing near the chuckwagon, listening to the banter of the crew.

She stopped and looked at him expectantly.

He stepped forward and said in a low voice, "There's a pool just up the creek a bit. I'll keep the men away if you want to take a bath."

"A bath." What a wonderful idea! It sounded like paradise. She sighed deeply. "Would I ever!"

"I'll keep the pup for you."

Gem passed Sunny into his hands once again.

"Thanks, Chase." She hurried to the wagon to find a change of clothes.

White clouds scudded across the warm blue of the sky. A hot breeze rustled the leaves of the cottonwoods that surrounded the clear mountain pool. The tall pines that climbed the nearby hillsides swayed in gentle circles as they reached needled branches toward heaven. A crow complained loudly in the distance.

Gem dove beneath the cool surface and swam the width of the pool. Touching the bank, she came up, gasping for air. Sitting on a submerged rock, she uncoiled her braid and let her red-gold hair float out around her. She reached onto the bank and grabbed the bar of soap, then began scrubbing her arms and throat and face. Next she worked up a lather in her hair, rubbing her scalp vigorously with her fingertips. Finally she sank once again beneath the surface, rinsing away the soap before swimming the length of the pool again.

It felt so good she didn't want to get out, but she knew the rest of the crew would want to put the pool to use too. It wouldn't be fair to hog it any longer.

With a reluctant sigh she reached for the clothes she had peeled off so hastily and pulled them into the water where she scrubbed them with the same bar of soap. She knew that by tomorrow night she would feel as if she hadn't bathed in weeks and no one would be able to tell she had washed her clothes, but at least she would sleep clean tonight.

Gem tossed the shirt and trousers up onto some brush on the bank to dry before reaching for the blanket she'd brought with her. She wrapped it around her as she stepped out of the pool, then sat down in the shade and began to work a comb through her tangled hair.

Through slits in his black hood, he watched her from his hiding place in the shadows of the pine grove. Her blanket had slipped to one side, revealing a trim calf and shapely thigh. Her hair, the color of sunset in a wheat field, lay spread over her shoulders and down her back. The swell of her breasts pressed firmly against the wrapped blanket.

A smile lifted one side of his mouth. One day he would remove that blanket himself. But the time was not yet right.

21

She wasn't assigned a watch that night. It seemed everyone had taken it into their heads that her role was to mother Sunny. Gem was certain the special treatment wouldn't last more than one day. She told herself she probably shouldn't allow them to show her any favors even this once, but tonight she gave into it.

Across the camp, Teddy was playing a mournful tune on his mouth organ. Three other men were involved in a game of poker. She had been invited to play but had declined, choosing instead to sit cross-legged near the chuckwagon at the far reaches of flickering firelight with her new friend asleep within the circle of her legs.

She heard his horse trotting into camp. He spoke a few words to Pecos Pete, then the crunch of his boots brought him closer. He stopped, rolled a cigarette, and lit it with a twig from the fire. As he drew on the rolled tobacco, the red glow of light played across his bronzed features.

Gem watched him intently, studying the rugged planes of his face, the strong jaw, the broad brow. He had shaved earlier in the day, but already there was a dark shadow on his chin. It would feel rough against her skin.

He turned and caught her watching him. He tossed the twig back into the fire and walked over to her. "Care for some company?"

She'd been waiting for him. All afternoon. All evening. Actually, ever since he'd held her in his arms last night under that lone pine. She'd been waiting for him.

"Please," she whispered.

He sat beside her, removing his hat and setting it on the ground. He raked his fingers through his shaggy hair, then leaned against the wheel at his back and drew on his cigarette. As he released a string of pale blue smoke, he asked, "How's Sunny?"

"Tired. It's been a long day for her."

"You've got a gentle way with animals. They like you."

For some crazy reason her heart was pattering in her chest as if she'd just run a foot race. "I like them. They can feel it."

He still hadn't looked at her. He sat in thoughtful silence, smoking his cigarette.

"I remember the last time you gave me an animal of my very own."

"Wichita," he replied.

"I've treasured her 'cause she came from you."

"Good cowpony. You did a good job training her."

"I had the best teacher. Uncle Frank helped me every step of the way."

At last he turned his eyes upon her. "Wish I'd been there to help too."

She swallowed. "I thought about you lots." *I love you, you big galoot*, she thought and leaned toward him. *Why don't you just put your arms around me and kiss me?*

But he turned his head away and stared out toward the bedded herd. "Julio's a fine man. Ought to make some lucky girl a good husband."

A flash of anger, a touch of humor, a sting of sorrow. She felt them all, understanding what he was doing. Softly she replied, "You're right. Someday he's going to find the right woman. One who's going to love him as he deserves. He's going to make a wonderful husband for her. I hope I get to be there to see them get married."

"Yeah. Me too." He got to his feet. "Maybe we can both be there."

"I hope so."

"Night, Gem."

"Night, Chase."

She crawled beneath the wagon and settled beneath her quilt, cuddling Sunny against her breast. She couldn't help believing he understood at last. She allowed her joy to wrap her in a glowing warmth, and she slept.

Chase lay beneath his blanket, an arm behind his head, listening to the occasional lowing of the cattle. He stared up at the broad expanse of heaven. A star shot across the sky in a burst of glory, then disappeared into oblivion.

He had tried for hours to fall asleep, but it just wouldn't come. Every time he closed his eyes he saw her. In a million different ways he saw her. And he wanted her. He ached with wanting her. He wanted to hold her, mold her body against his. He wanted to kiss her, taste the sweetness of her lips. He wanted to listen to her laughter and smooth away her tears. He wanted to see her eyes light up when he brought her a gift. He wanted to watch her comb out her long, silky tresses at night.

Chase clenched his fist, stifling a groan. Never in his memory had he been so tortured by desire. If she were any other woman than Gem . . . But he couldn't tell Gem he loved her when he didn't. He couldn't lie to her and use her as he wanted. And if he couldn't tell her he loved her, what could he offer her?

She didn't want Julio. She'd made that clear. And Julio had said himself that she was in love with Chase.

But Consuela had said she loved him too.

But Gem wasn't Consuela. Two women couldn't have been more different.

But he'd thought Consuela was different when he'd met her.

But he knew Gem better. He'd known her when she was still a child. She'd cared for him when he was sick. They'd shared something special, so many private moments.

But . . .

But he could never love her. He had no love left inside him. Consuela had seen to that.

Chase rolled onto his side. He had no love to give, but it didn't change the fact that he was a man and he wanted Gem McBride. He wanted her as a woman. He'd known when Uncle Frank agreed that Gem could come on the drive that it would be hard. He just hadn't imagined *how* hard.

When they threw the cattle on the trail that morning, they knew they were in for a long, hard day in the saddle. They would be forced to cover more miles that day at a faster pace in order to reach water by nightfall. They would be leaving the protection of the mountains, and the cattle would have a tendency to spread out more, keeping the drovers busy with obstinate strays and renegades. At least this herd didn't seem to have any perpetual troublemakers.

Before breaking camp, Julio helped Gem rig a special saddle bag for Sunny so the pup could ride with Gem for a while each day. The rest of the time, Sunny would share the chuckwagon with Corky. Several times during the morning one of the men cantered up to her position at point to inquire on Sunny's enjoyment of the ride. The yellow puppy and her new mistress seemed to have captured all of their hearts.

The day passed with hypnotizing sameness. Dust rose in choking clouds. The land undulated before them in a sea of drying grasses beneath the scorching August sun, making the men wonder how it could be as hot as Hades in the daytime and colder than the dickens at night. The only sounds were the muffled crack-crack of the cows' ankle joints as they pushed forward, the rhythmic thudding of hooves, the occasional whistle or shout of a cowpoke, and the clatter

of horns, one against another. They watered on the
Stillwater River that night.

In the following days their pace slowed once
again, but little else distinguished one day from
another. The trail drive was progressing much better
than Chase could have hoped. The cattle weren't
losing weight; if anything, they were fattening. There
had been no foul weather, no repeat of the stampede
early in the drive. But something was troubling him.
He couldn't put his finger on it, but something
wasn't right.

As he rode far ahead of the herd, seeking out
bedding grounds, watering holes, places to noon, he
was nagged by a sense of impending disaster. He
looked everywhere for signs of trouble but found
none. Perhaps it was his sleepless nights.

He was bone-tired every night, and still he
couldn't sleep. He would crawl beneath his soogan,
close his eyes, and immediately be assaulted with
thoughts of Gem. It was enough to drive him crazy.
It would have been better if he could just stay away
from her, yet like a bear to honey he kept going back
each night, sitting beside her as he smoked, listening
to her as she chatted about all sorts of things,
watching her as she played with Sunny, reveling in
her smiles and her laughter.

And then he couldn't sleep. No wonder he
thought something was about to go wrong. He was
probably hallucinating half the time.

The Indians appeared in the path of the herd late
in the afternoon. There were about ten of them. They
sat their ponies quietly, waiting as Chase cantered
toward them. Knowing the herd was now crossing
the Crow Agency, he assumed they were Crow

Indians and friendly to the whites. But one could never be sure. Although the Sioux wars had ended several years before, a man stayed wary in Indian country. Through sign language and a few shared words, he was able to understand that they were demanding two cows to let them pass. It was little enough payment, and Chase ordered a couple of cows cut out of the herd.

As he watched the Indians riding off with the cattle, Chase sighed a sigh of relief. That must have been what had been troubling him. He'd probably been worried about running into some hostile Indians and losing many valuable cattle to their night raids. Now he could relax a little. Maybe he would even get some sleep.

Gem snuggled deep beneath her quilt. She was dreaming and she was frightened. She struggled to wake up, to escape the unseen fear that pursued her in sleep. Breaking suddenly into consciousness, she sat up and cracked her head against the underside of the wagon. She swore angrily under her breath while still fighting the racing beat of her heart and the lingering terror of her nightmare. She touched her fingers gingerly to her forehead, wincing at the lump quickly forming.

Sunny cuddled against her thigh, unaware of her mistress's distress. Gem allowed a tight grin to lift her mouth as she tucked the blanket carefully around the sleeping puppy. Then she reached for her coat and boots and slipped from beneath the wagon. She shivered, noting the cloudy sky and the wind that whistled across the land. The night was ink-black. The air smelled like rain.

Gem could hear the horses milling in their rope corral. She stepped out in their direction, sensing her way in the dark more than seeing. Then she stopped. She had a terrible feeling that someone else was nearby. Her heart doubled its beat as her ears strained to hear.

You're being silly, she told herself. *It's just 'cause of your nightmare.*

She started walking again, then froze.

There it was again. A sound. A footstep. She was sure of it. Someone was there. Someone moving very carefully. Someone who must not belong.

She turned—and walked right into a broad chest and a pair of strong arms. She gasped.

"Gem?"

Her heart still thundered in her ears.

"What're you doing, sneaking around out here. You trying to get yourself shot?" Chase's arms closed around her. "Don't you ever stay where you're supposed to be?"

"I . . . I couldn't sleep. I was taking a walk."

His hand touched the side of her face, lightly tracing her cheekbone, then her jaw. She was drawn closer to him, just as to a magnet. Her hands pressed against his chest as she leaned into him.

"Ah, Gem," he whispered.

And then his mouth was covering hers, lightly at first, carefully tasting her lips from corner to corner. His fingers locked behind her head, supporting her neck as he drew her up on tiptoe. She gave herself over to the kaleidoscope of crazy feelings that raced through her veins. She felt turned upside down. Tingles ran the length of her.

His exploring lips moved on, to her eyelids, then

her brow, her hairline, her earlobe. A breathless moan escaped her, stolen away on the wind before it could be heard.

Then he was kissing her full on the mouth again, this time without tenderness. His kiss demanded more, much more, from her. His arms drew her ever closer against his muscular body. She sensed the heat, the desire, emanating from him, but before she could respond, his hands were suddenly withdrawn from behind her head as he stepped away. She staggered, nearly losing her balance.

"Damn!" he swore. "Go back to bed, Gem."

"Chase, I—"

"Do you hear me? Leave me alone. Go back to bed." Anger and loathing laced each word.

She didn't understand what she had done. Tears welled and spilled over. "Chase," she pleaded.

"Don't you understand? I don't have anything for you."

She choked on a sob as she turned and stumbled back toward the chuckwagon.

He'd never in his life come so close to taking a woman right where she stood. He was sweating beneath his jacket. And he was angry. Angry at his lack of self-control. Angry at Gem for almost making him do what he knew he would later regret.

"Damn!" he swore again, louder this time.

Chase jammed his hands into his coat pockets and stalked off into the darkness.

22

The sky rumbled and flickered with the approaching storm. The trail hands, fearful of being struck by lightning, removed their metal spurs and put their knives and six-shooters into the chuckwagon. In the distance they could see the brilliant forks of light as they streaked from clouds to earth. Tension was palpable around the restless cattle.

Feeling about as grim as Mother Nature's current condition, Gem turned the big piebald gelding she had chosen from the remuda that morning and galloped off to the chuckwagon, depositing the puppy into Corky's waiting hands.

"I don't think I'd better have Sunny with me this morning, Corky. Take good care of her for me."

"I'll do it." The cook frowned up at the sky. "You just take care o' yourself."

"I will," she mumbled as she spun the horse and hurried off again.

In truth, she didn't much care about herself today. She hadn't slept a wink all night long. Her eyes were puffy and they hurt from crying. She couldn't imagine feeling any worse about anything. Besides, why should she care about herself when Chase so obviously didn't care at all?

She hadn't even seen him this morning. He'd been gone before anyone was up and about except the men riding night watch. Gem wondered if any of them would see him at all today.

A bolt of lightning exploded against the ground about a mile away, followed by a crack of thunder that nearly rattled her teeth. With frightening quickness, the cattle became a mass of pounding hooves and clattering horns racing across the countryside.

Instinctively Gem dug her spurs into the piebald's sides and leaned forward over his neck. They galloped alongside the panicked herd, inching their way toward the leaders. En masse, the cattle made a sudden swerve toward her. She jerked the piebald's head to the side to stay with them. She knew that others would be trying to gain the front to help her turn the herd, but she didn't know how far back they would be. She didn't have the opportunity to look behind to see for herself.

The morning sky was as dark as night, black clouds rolling overhead. Wind whipped at her hat and shirt, and flying dust stung her cheeks and made her eyes smart. Another crash of lightning split the heavens, causing the herd to make another sudden turn, this time away from her. She turned the big gelding's head once again. His stride never changed from his all-out gallop as he strove for the front of the herd.

Gem leaned even lower over the pommel. "Git up there, fella," she shouted at the horse.

Each minute that passed seemed an eternity. Gem knew the damage that could be done to the cattle and to the Four Winds profits. In as little as four miles a stampeding cow could drop fifty pounds. As they ran, their horns gored each other. If one stumbled and fell, it could mean that many of them would be crushed under the trampling hooves of those following. Time was of the essence.

Alone, she reached the point of the herd. She eased back on the reins, trying to slow the charge. In front of a stampeding herd of cattle, a cowboy depended upon his mount's surefootedness to keep him from a grisly demise. It was here that the piebald stumbled over the uneven ground.

It all happened so quickly she had no time to prepare for it. She was thrown forward into the air, and when there should have been ground beneath her, it wasn't there. A sudden gulch split the grass-lands, and she dropped into it with a bone-jarring thud. The air whooshed from her lungs. Even as she rolled close to the upthrusting earth forming the sides of the narrow gully, the space above her became a mass of flying hooves as the cattle jumped the break in the land. Gem covered her head with her arms and pressed herself against the shuddering ground.

Chase turned Dodge back toward the herd as soon as the lightning started. He chastised himself for getting so far ahead of them. He'd been so lost in thought he hadn't even noticed the worsening of the storm. Any fool could have seen they were in for a royal squall.

He could hear the stampede before he could see it. The earth trembled, the vibrations moving right up through his horse and into his heart. He pressed the animal into a gallop, mounting a ridge just as three cowboys were reaching the front of the herd. Even as he galloped toward them, the leaders were slowing and beginning to turn as the cowboys flailed slickers in their faces. Other cowboys were pressing the turn from one side. Chase joined them near the back of the herd.

It took several miles before the turn was successful. Finally, after what seemed like hours, the cattle were circling, then milling. It was a dangerous time. A cowboy could get trapped among the closely jammed cows and get jostled from his mount. If that happened, there was little hope of survival.

Just when a semblance of order was returning, the rain began to fall in soaking sheets. As after the first stampede, Chase gave little thought to the loss or injuries of the cattle. He had only one goal—to find Gem. He rode around the circumference of the herd, eyes peering through the rain and gloom. It took him some time before he met up with Julio. Julio's hat was missing, and his black hair was plastered to his head by the drencher.

"Julio!"

His friend twisted in his saddle, his shoulders hunched forward against the rain. "*Amigo*," he answered, squinting as the water ran into his eyes, "we are in for a long day."

"Have you seen Gem?"

"No, *amigo*. I have not seen her since just after breakfast."

"What was she riding?"

"The piebald. We saddled at the same time." He looked deep into Chase's eyes. "Do not worry, my friend. She is a good hand. Even now she is probably riding the herd looking for you."

Chase nodded and moved on. It was several more minutes before he spotted Rodney Daniels. "Seen Gem?" he asked without preamble.

"Nope."

He received the same reply from Teddy and from Junior when he reached them.

It was Pike that gave him his first shred of information. "Saw her givin' that yeller pup to Corky jus' 'fore they stampeded. She lit out fer the point. Last I seen her."

They weren't words to calm his rising concern. Chase thanked him and headed back along the trail toward that morning's camp, his hat pulled low over his forehead as the rain poured off the brim in a steady stream. It was nearly a half hour before he met up with Corky in the chuckwagon.

"Sorry, Chase. She was gallopin' after that herd, just like all the men. I had my hands full with the team here and didn't see her again." He shook his head morosely. "You don't suppose—"

Chase jerked Dodge around. "Follow the trail till you reach the herd. We'll bed 'em down right where they are. Tell the men I'm lookin' for Gem."

The rain kept up through the morning and into the afternoon, hampering the search for Gem. Rodney and Julio and Pike all left the herd to help with the search, each man privately dreading the worst but refusing to speak their thoughts aloud.

It was Julio who discovered the piebald. The big gelding stood on three legs, the fourth held gingerly off the ground, the knee grossly misshapen. His head hung forward until his muzzle nearly touched the ground. His sides were bloodied, gashed by the long horns of the cattle. One stirrup was missing from the saddle. Julio checked the area nearby, then went to find Chase.

It seemed an eternity before the cattle had passed over. Even after they were gone, even after the ground quit shaking, Gem didn't try to rise. A terrible nausea twisted her stomach. She squeezed her eyes shut against it.

Rain began to pelt her face, and rivulets of muddy water surrounded her as the clouds loosed their torrent. Slowly she pushed herself upright, wincing at the bruised muscles in her shoulder and side. The world seemed to spin crazily, and she took a moment to draw a slow, deep breath, waiting until everything righted itself again.

Gem wondered how long she had lain there without daring to move. She drew another deep breath and tried to stand. Like hot forks of lightning, the pain shot up her leg from her ankle, and she crumpled back to the ground. Her hands shot out to lightly hold the injury as she gritted her teeth. Tears sprang to her eyes, and she moaned softly. Biting her lower lip, she began probing her ankle with careful fingers; she guessed it wasn't broken, just a bad sprain. Still, she couldn't walk on it. She would have to wait for someone to find her. That could be quite some time, depending upon how long it had taken them to stop the cattle. In the meantime, she was being drowned by the downpour.

Cautiously Gem dragged herself along the ground, following the twists and curves of the gulch until she found a rocky ledge forming a natural umbrella. Exhausted, she pulled herself underneath it and lay down to wait out the storm. Drenched clear through, her muscles bruised and battered, and her ankle throbbing incessantly, Gem drifted in and out of a restless sleep.

Chase refused to quit looking, even after night began to fall. The rain had slowed to a drizzle by this time.

"*Amigo*, come back to camp with me," Julio suggested gently. "We will look again in the morning."

"No! If she's out here, she needs to be found. What if she's hurt?" Chase nudged his weary pinto forward. "You go on back. See that everything is all right there."

Julio sighed. "I will stay."

Chase turned his head to look at his friend in the failing light. "I'd rather do this alone," he replied, sadness weighing heavily in his voice.

They both knew what he expected to find.

Chase walked his big pinto gelding slowly through the inky darkness. "Gem!" he called, then waited, praying he would hear her echoing cry, yet fearing he wouldn't. "Gem!"

He couldn't bear it if she had died under the crushing hooves of the cattle. To never again hear her lyrical laughter. To never again see the flash of her greenish-blue cat's eyes. To not feel the heat of her anger and the lash of her tongue when he'd crossed her. To never again see her riding Wichita across the range, red-gold braid flapping against her back.

Please, God, not that, he prayed.

"Gem," he called, even more urgently than before.

Suddenly Dodge halted. His ears perked forward, then one cocked back. He snorted.

"What is it, fella?" Chase peered ahead into the darkness. Seeing nothing, he pressed his spurs against the pinto's sides.

Dodge took two short steps forward, then stopped again and refused to go on.

Chase dismounted, wondering what the horse could see that he couldn't. He nearly stumbled face first into the gully. Leaning forward, he could see that it was about three or four feet wide. Instead of trying to force his horse across it in the dark, he began walking alongside it, leading Dodge behind him. The gulch meandered across the rangeland with little change in width or depth, and he followed it, continuing to call Gem's name.

Because he called without much hope, he couldn't believe his own ears when he heard a distant, "Here. Over here."

Chase swung into the saddle and hurried Dodge forward. "Gem! Where are you?"

"Here." Her voice sounded so weak. "I'm over here."

"Where?"

"In the gully."

He was dismounted and slipping his way into

the gully before she had finished speaking. His feet carried him swiftly in the direction of her voice, his hands held out as he felt his way in the darkness.

"Gem?"

"I'm here, Chase." There was a tiny sob tacked on to the end of her response.

And then he found her. He was on his knees in the mud, gathering her shivering, small body into his arms and pressing her tightly against him, heedless of the gasp of pain that slipped between her lips as her arms circled his neck.

"Doggone it, Gem," he whispered. "Can't you stay on your horse when there's a stampede going on?"

"I'm sorry, Chase."

"Do you know how worried I was? Do you know how long we've been looking for you?" Fear made his words sound harsh.

"I'm sorry, Chase," she repeated.

His arms tightened, and he rocked her as he would a child, pressing his cheek against her wet hair. He stayed like that for a long time, hunkered beneath the ledge out of the drizzling rain, feeling the birdlike racing of her heart against his chest. She seemed so fragile, not at all like the girl he'd seen roping an obstinate steer or playing poker with the men.

He loosened his hand behind her neck, drawing back so he could look down at her even though he couldn't see her. "Are you hurt?" he asked gently.

"Mostly just bruised. But my ankle's sprained. I can't walk on it. That's why I didn't try to catch up with you." She turned her face up toward him. He could feel her breath on his chin as she spoke. "I'm okay now that you're here."

He felt a tender agony as his head dropped toward hers. He couldn't help himself. He had to feel for himself that she was all right. He had to taste her lips and know that warmth and life surged through her. She responded with a surprising fury. Her arms tightened behind his neck. Her mouth opened to accept his probing tongue. Her firm, rounded breasts were pressed hard against him.

When their mouths parted, his lips moved over her face and stopped in her hair. "Oh, Gem . . . Gem . . ." he whispered. "Why do you do this to me?"

"I thought I'd never see again. The cattle were jumping over me and the earth shook and I knew I was going to die and I'd never see you again. Chase—"

They kissed again, an odd combination of white heat and tenderness. He wanted to protect her, cherish her. And he wanted to take her. Here. Now. This very moment.

"Ah, Gem," he groaned, "you're like a fire in my veins. I want you."

Her words came in tiny, breathless gasps. "I want you too, Chase. I want to always be yours. I love you."

Those three little words were like a bucket of ice water, cooling his desire. "Nothing's for always," he said stiffly. He could feel her surprise at his sudden withdrawal. He knew she didn't understand.

"Chase?"

Frustration made him cruel. "Don't you understand, Gem? I want to make love to you. I want to share your bed and your body. Nothing more. I don't have any more to give you."

There was a long, pregnant pause before her arms slid from around his neck, and she pushed herself from his grasp until she sat alone on the cold, hard ground. "I see," she finally responded.

"No, you don't see! No one sees! I need you, Gem. I want you till it's about to drive me crazy. But I can't love you. I can't love anybody."

She remained stoically silent.

He grabbed her shoulders and gave her a shake. "Do you hear me, Gem McBride? I *can't* love you. Don't you think I would if I could? But that's what you want from me. You want me to say I love you and we'll get married. But I can't say it. I don't *want* to say it. Not ever again. You know what it is *I* want? I want to take you to bed. *Just* to bed, Gem." His voice grew in intensity along with his frustration and rage. "But you want marriage, isn't that it? Aren't I right?"

"Don't shout any more, Chase," Gem said in a soft voice, each syllable an indictment of the hurt he was hurling against her. "Just get me back to the wagon."

It was as if he didn't hear her. "Aren't I right? Isn't marriage what you want?"

She choked on a sob. "Yes," she shouted in defense, sudden anger mingling with her tears. "Yes, I wanted marriage. Marriage to the man I love. Is that so terrible? Do you know how long I've loved you? How long I've waited so we could get married? You promised to marry me years ago, and I waited. I waited and I went on waiting and loving you. Even when you returned with a wife, I went on loving you." She hit his chest with a balled fist, crying as she added, "I was always waiting to marry you."

"All right, damn it! All right! You want to be

married to me? I'll marry you." He picked her up roughly from the ground and carried her out of the gully. "And if you're not happy, it'll be your own fault. I warned you I've got nothin' more to give." He shoved her into the saddle, unmindful of her gasp of pain, then swung up behind her. "As soon as we get to Cheyenne, we'll get married."

He dug his spurs into Dodge's sides, and the pinto jumped forward into a gallop, carrying two equally miserable people toward their camp.

All right, damn it! I'll marry you.

Gem lay in the back of the chuckwagon, biting back the groan that tried to suface as the wagon jerked and swayed. Her body was a mass of bruises, but as bruised as the outside was, her spirit was even more so. Her heart ached. Again and again, Chase's angry proposal echoed in her mind.

No. It hadn't been a proposal. It had been an annoucement. A sentence. He was going to marry her without love. She should tell him she wouldn't marry him. She should tell him to go be hanged. She should tell him she had a little pride left, that she wasn't so desperate for a husband that she would marry him, feeling as he did.

But she must not have any pride left, for she had every intention of marrying him, love her or not. If she didn't, she would have to stay behind in Cheyenne. She couldn't bear to return to Four Winds with him, she couldn't bear to live in the same house with him and not be able to love him. And, after a long sleepless night, she knew that she wouldn't want to live if she couldn't see him ever again.

The canvas flap moved aside at the front of the wagon.

"How are you feeling, *mi amiga?*" Julio queried as he poked his head through the opening.

Gem braced herself on her elbows, grimacing as the wagon jostled her once again. "I'm okay, Julio." She wanted to ask how Chase was, but she didn't.

Julio crawled past Corky and into the wagon, letting the canvas fall back in place to give them a modicum of privacy. He shook his head, flinging tiny drops of water over her. "I believe the rain will never stop now that it has started." His black eyes peered at her in silent study. "*¡Valgame Dios!* You are a sight, senorita."

"Thanks." She frowned at him, adding with a touch of sarcasm, "Any more good news?"

"*Si.* We will soon arrive at the Little Big Horn River. Tomorrow we will cross into Wyoming." Julio settled on a sack of flour as he spoke. He cocked an eyebrow and leaned close. "Do you care to tell me what has happened between you and *mi amigo?*"

She shook her head.

"I have never seen him in such a state. When he left this morning, he said he was riding into Sheridan for a few supplies and would join up with us by the end of the week. This is not like him."

Gem couldn't meet his gaze any longer. Her eyes fell away, locking onto the back side of the chuck.

"Gem?" Julio's hand touched her shoulder lightly, then dropped away. "Do not give up on him. He cares for you more than even he knows. When he thought you were lost yesterday—" His voice faded off in a verbal shrug.

"I haven't given up on him," Gem responded, stiffening her back a fraction and looking at Julio again. Her eyes dared him to ask any questions. "We're getting married in Cheyenne. He told me so last night."

He was puzzled but obeyed her silent command. "It is good news, *amiga*. I am happy for you both."

"Yes, it's good news." She sighed as she sank back onto her bed on the floor of the wagon. She closed her eyes and turned her face away from Julio. "Wonderful news."

23

After a week of rest, Gem had improved both in body and spirit. Although she still couldn't sit a horse because of her weak ankle, she was able to join Corky on the seat of the chuckwagon. The cattle moved slowly south and east toward Cheyenne, stirring up dust clouds as soon as the rainy weather had passed over.

In Chase's absence, Gem had done a lot of soul searching. She hadn't changed her mind. She was still going to marry him. What had changed was her attitude. She wasn't a quitter. She wasn't going to just sit back and let the cards fall where they may. Chase didn't think he could love her. He didn't think he could love any woman. Well, Gem thought differently. Maybe today or this week he couldn't love her, but with time, with patience, all that would change. She meant to see that it did.

He was due back soon. She was certain it would be today. It had been a full week since he'd left for Sheridan. Gem found herself glancing behind the chuckwagon often, hoping she would see him galloping toward the spread-out herd. They had paused one extra day near the site of Fort McKinney, allowing the cattle to graze and rest, but this morning they had thrown the herd on the trail at the break of dawn. It seemed to Gem they were moving too quickly for Chase to ever catch up with them. Of course she knew better. A lone horse could cover five times more ground in a day than a herd of cattle. Still, she wished they could lay over another day or two, just in case he had been delayed.

At the noon stop, she crawled inside the wagon and washed herself from a bowl of water, then changed into a fresh blouse and skirt. Just in case he arrived, she wanted to look her very best. She brushed out her hair, working the strawberry-blonde locks until they fairly gleamed, then she rebraided it, tying a pretty yellow bow at the end of the long braid. She drew a deep breath and hoped against hope that he would arrive soon while her courage still ran high.

She climbed down from the wagon and gingerly limped toward the chuck at the back. Corky slopped some beans and pork onto a plate and shoved it into her hands. Gem was hungry, but she eyed the mixture with something less than enthusiasm. Corky was a pretty fair cook when he set his mind to it, but after weeks on the trail, everything tasted pretty much the same. She had a longing for a sizzling steak and a big slice of Aunt Enid's famous apple pie. She sat down on the ground, curling her feet beneath her, and took a forkful of the beans.

Suddenly her appetite was gone. She had spied the lone rider, cantering along the trail. It was Chase. It had to be Chase. She set her plate on the ground and got to her feet, her stomach filled with butterflies.

Chase cantered into the noon camp, then slid his big pinto to a sudden stop, sending up a choking cloud of dust. His eyes flicked over Gem and on toward the men without a moment's hesitation. His face was covered with a week's growth of beard, and his eyes were red-rimmed as if he'd been without sleep the entire time he was away. She wanted to go to him. She wanted to hug him and tell him once again that she loved him and all would be right. But there was something in the set of his shoulders that warned her to stay back, and so she waited.

He dismounted and tossed his reins to Pecos Pete. The young wrangler scurried off with the lathered gelding while Chase strode toward the chuckwagon.

"What's for dinner, Corky? I'm starved."

"If you're starvin', what difference does it make?" the cook snapped. "Eat what's there and keep your peace." He filled a plate and handed it to Chase.

Chase squatted right where he was, balancing his plate on his knee, and began to eat. After several quick bites he glanced toward the other men seated on the ground near the end of the chuckwagon. "You've made good time."

Rodney nodded. "Rested near old Fort McKinney. Grass was good."

"The cows don't look much the worse for the stampede." Chase took a swig of coffee. "How many'd we lose?"

Julio had arrived in time to hear Chase's question. "About twenty, twenty-five head." He took his plate from Corky and sat on a boulder near Gem. "Any news from Sheridan, *amigo?*"

"Nothing special. We seem to be the first of the herds pushin' through. Ought to help with the prices Grogan can get us. The ranchers'll be selling off more cattle than usual this year. Water's been short just about everywhere." He continued to stare at his plate as he spoke.

Gem sat down once again, pushing her food around her plate with her fork, her eyes never wavering from Chase. Her emotions swung from relief that he was back to disappointment that he hadn't shown any sign of being happy to see her to anger at the way he continued to ignore her. Well, she might as well take the bull by the horns right now.

"Chase?"

"Mmmm?"

"They know we're getting married in Cheyenne. I told them."

His head came up, his sapphire eyes meeting her pair of aquamarine. A strange haunting seemed to swirl in their troubled blue depths, and Gem felt it all the way to the pit of her stomach.

Julio cut the emotion-laden moment short by rising and walking over to Chase. "You have my congratulations, Chase," he said, holding out his hand.

Chase took it, then stood up.

"You are a lucky man."

Chase wished he felt lucky. He knew he *should* feel that way. It wasn't that he didn't want to love Gem. It wasn't even that he didn't believe she loved him at this moment. But how long would she love him when he couldn't love her in return? Would her love die a long, slow death, or would it end quickly?

He looked at Gem again. Her face was so pale, except for the fading bruise on her cheek near her temple. She must have gotten that the night of the stampede. He wished he could kiss it away. Her eyes were large and luminous; she watched him with a mixture of apprehension and longing. She was wearing a yellow blouse and a skirt instead of her usual trail attire. Her hat was missing, and her honey-red hair gleamed in the sunlight. He was keenly reminded of just how beautiful she was.

Chase wasn't aware of Julio's jerk of his head, motioning the other cowpokes away. It just seemed that suddenly he was alone with Gem. He set his plate on the end of the chuckwagon and walked over to where she sat on the ground. He reached out his hand to her. She took it and allowed him to draw her to her feet.

"You sure you want to do this?" he asked, not certain what he wanted her to say.

She blinked away the tears that quickly filled her lovely eyes. "I'm sure."

"I didn't mean to be . . . to be so harsh the other night."

"I know."

"Gem, I . . . I don't ever want to hurt you. It's just . . ." He struggled for the right words. "It's just I don't know if I can make you happy." He couldn't admit to the emptiness that remained where his heart had once been.

He didn't have to. She already understood. "I love you, Chase," she said, so softly he nearly couldn't hear. Her free hand tentatively touched his chest. "I know she hurt you bad. But I'm not Consuela. I'm Gem McBride. Give me a chance. Give *us* a chance."

It was like a knife in his belly, hearing her speak those words aloud. He didn't think he wanted anyone knowing him so well. His voice hardened once again. "Don't pretend you can change things, Gem. We're getting married because I want you in my bed. I like you well enough, but don't go wanting more than I can give."

He'd expected to see tears again, but there weren't any. Instead she just nodded, saying, "I won't, Chase. If liking's the best you can do, then I'll settle for it."

His mood seemed to get more foul the more understanding and patient she was. Exasperating woman! Why didn't she just admit that marrying him would be a terrible mistake?

Chase had spent the better part of the past week at a poker table, getting little sleep, forgetting to eat. He'd even tried taking one of the local soiled doves to his room, hoping to relieve the tension that tortured him, but it hadn't done him any good. He hadn't wanted her, so he sent her away. She wasn't Gem. He had wanted Gem.

Chase had thought about her constantly, wondering how she was feeling, wondering if she missed him, wondering if she had decided that as long as he couldn't love her, she was better off without him. He'd driven Dodge hard to get back here as soon as he did, fearing what he would find.

But there she stood, just a wisp of a girl, as resolute as ever. She was going to marry him. She still said she loved him. But could he trust her to go on loving him? She was so different from Consuela. He'd known that all along. So why couldn't he believe she loved him and would keep on loving him? And even if he did believe it, what difference would it make? He still wasn't capable of loving her back, as much as he might want to.

"I don't have time to stand jawing with you, Gem. I'd better get this herd moving." He spun on his heel and went after a fresh horse.

24

Back home the cottonwoods and aspens would be changing from greens to golds and oranges. There was the crisp sting of fall in the air each morning as they broke camp. It was more than just colder nights. There was something one could feel when one season was giving reluctantly over to the next.

Sunny felt it. She awakened early each morning and began to frisk around Gem's head, grabbing her hair and tugging until her mistress paid her some heed.

Gem felt it too. Her spirits seemed to lift with the passing of August's oppressive heat. She was riding again, although she had to wrap her ankle each morning before pulling on her boot. The sore muscles had faded along with the nightmarish memory of the stampede. Each day carried her closer to Cheyenne. Cheyenne meant her wedding, and despite her taciturn bridegroom, Gem was filled with excitement and joy—and more determination than ever to prove to him her love.

No matter how early she rose, Chase always seemed to be up earlier. She saw him only briefly each morning before he was riding out ahead of the herd, finding the place to noon, looking for water and good bedding grounds. She missed him throughout the day and was glad for the work that kept her occupied until they saw each other again at day's end. She knew he purposely kept his distance from her, using his trail boss's duties as an excuse to avoid her, yet each evening he returned to sit beside her before turning in. He never tried to hold her hand. He never tried to kiss her, although she longed for him to do so. Still, she was filled with quiet confidence that there was a bond between them greater than he was willing to admit or recognize. All she needed was the time to help him see it for himself.

They had been on the trail over five weeks. There had been little trouble with the herd, discounting the two stampedes. River crossings had been made smoothly. Most of the cattle had gained weight on the drive. In two weeks or so they would be in Cheyenne. The cowboys were as eager to reach their destination as Gem, although not for the same reason. To them, Cheyenne meant an opportunity to cut loose, to drink a little whiskey, play a little cards, dance with a pretty woman and . . . well, whatever else that pretty woman wanted to do.

It was mid-morning and the sun was bright in the powder-blue sky when Rodney loped his horse up to Gem's position. "Hey, Gem! How'd you like some fresh meat for supper?"

Her eyes lit up. "Would I ever."

"I think I spotted some antelope back that way." He pointed over his shoulder. "I'm goin' after one. If you see Chase at noon, let him know where I've gone. I'll catch up with you in time for Corky to serve up something other than stew for supper."

"I'll tell him." As Rodney turned to gallop back the way he'd come, she shouted, "Good luck."

He waved his hand without glancing back at her.

Gem's stomach growled, and she chuckled to herself. Fresh meat. What a treat that would be. She couldn't wait for supper.

Rodney left his horse tethered in some brush and set out on foot, moving cautiously toward the herd. At the top of a ridge he knelt down and drew his rifle to his shoulder. He had a big buck in his sights. He slowly squeezed the trigger.

A sudden movement to his left caused him to jerk. The antelope were off in a flash, the big buck leading the way. He turned his head in anger at the stranger's approach.

"What the hell—" he began.

Dressed in black, his face hidden behind a fitted hood, the man slammed the rifle butt down in a crushing blow against Rodney's skull. Josh Daniels' youngest son was dead before his bloodied head hit the ground.

Stew again, and everyone seemed to be angry at her. It wasn't Gem's fault Rodney hadn't returned with his antelope yet. She was just as disappointed as they were. Her only mistake was in telling them where he'd gone and that he'd promised them something different for supper.

Gem took her plate of stew and stalked away from the grumbling crew. If they couldn't be civil, she'd rather eat with the cows and horses. She stopped near the remuda and sat in the shade of the tall brush that lined the creek. Her stomach complained as she took her first bite, and she chewed without tasting her food.

Her eyes roamed slowly over the stark, rolling countryside. The range grass was pale brown. The landscape was barren of sage. The only trees or brush that boasted a varying shade of green grew in the creek bottoms that meandered through the draws. The wind blew without respite, never stopping, only changing in intensity. Days were hot, nights were cold, and the dust was endless.

She suddenly longed for a glimpse of the majestic mountains that surrounded the Four Winds. She longed to see the patches of golden aspen mingling with the dark greens of the mighty ponderosa. She wanted to hear Aunt Enid calling her to supper and listen to Uncle Frank as he instructed her on the training of a troublesome colt.

Her heart fluttered erratically. She had a sudden and very terrible premonition of things gone wrong. She set her supper plate on the ground and jumped to her feet, her hand lifting to shade her eyes as she searched the herd for a sign of Chase who was riding first watch. Spying the big pinto, she relaxed a little but still couldn't shake the worrisome feeling that something wasn't right. Could something be wrong with Enid or Frank? She had been thinking of them when the terrible fear gripped her. No, she was being needlessly worrisome. That was all.

Darkness fell before the first watch was over. Gem was sitting on a keg beside the chuckwagon, mending a tear in one of her shirts—anything to keep her hands busy while her thoughts churned— when Chase turned his horse over to the wrangler and came over to the chuck for the last of the stew. A mournful tune from a mouth organ drifted across the campfire, mingled with the steady hum of voices as the men talked and joked with one another.

Gem laid her mending aside, watching as Chase filled his plate and turned toward the campfire. Long strides carried him into the midst of the relaxing cowpunchers, and he lowered himself with ease onto the hard Wyoming earth. The golden firelight flickered across his face as he pushed his hat back on his head and began to eat. She was tempted to go to him now to tell him that something wasn't quite right. But things were so tenuous between them; she didn't want to ruin what little time they had together with silly, unfounded fears.

Chase glanced up and met her gaze. He didn't smile, but she felt a tenderness in his expression all the same. A warmth spread from the pit of her stomach through her veins, and the rhythm of her heart quickened. In that moment she forgot all about her troubled thoughts of impending doom. There was only the two of them. She was alone with the man she loved. No one else existed.

"Boss?"

Their private moment was broken. Chase turned his head, glancing toward the sound of Pecos Pete's voice. "Yeah?"

"Junior thinks you'd better come look at somethin'."

Gem didn't know why, but she knew that this was the something she had dreaded all evening.

"Be right there," Chase replied before taking one more quick bite, then pushing up from the ground.

Gem hurried after him, close on Chase's heels as he followed Pecos Pete past the remuda and around the south edge of the sleeping herd. As the moon crested the earth's surface, she could see two horses, their reins gathered in the hands of a cowboy, in the pale silver light. It wasn't until they were nearly upon them that she saw the body lying on the ground in front of the man's boots.

Chase approached the still form, his gaze flickering up to Junior's pinched expression, then returning to the body as he knelt down. He turned his head to the side. "Go back to camp, Gem," he ordered.

But it was too late. The rising moon had cast its glow onto the dead man's face.

"Rodney." His name was painful in her throat.

Blood covered his forehead where his skull was cracked.

"Where'd you find him?" Chase asked Junior, his eyes still on Rodney's face.

"Slumped over his saddle down in the draw back there." Junior jerked his head to indicate the direction. "Looks like he musta fell while he was huntin' and hurt himself pretty bad, then climbed back onto his horse and tried to make it back to the herd. Died 'fore he got here."

Gem dropped to her knees beside Chase and took hold of Rodney's hand as tears welled up and fell down her cheeks, leaving streaks on her dusty face. "Poor Katie. Oh, how will we ever tell her?" Sweet Katie with her mousy brown hair and laughing brown eyes. Plump and merry and so in love with her husband. And little Maggie. Just two years old, and she would never see her daddy again.

Chase's arm went around her shoulders. "Take care of him," he told Junior as he drew Gem to her feet. "Come on back to camp, Gem."

"It's not fair, Chase. Why should this happen to Rodney? What will happen to Katie and Maggie?" She clung to him as she sobbed brokenly. "Oh, Chase, it's just not fair."

"I know," he whispered against her hair, pulling her tight against his chest. His own voice sounded choked. "I know."

Fear welled up in her chest. "I *knew* something was wrong. I *knew* something terrible was going to happen."

"Shhh." He patted her head.

She pushed at his chest. "Really!" she insisted. "I knew it." Her heart thundered in her ears as she looked up at him, and a cold terror washed over her. "It's not over, Chase. Something else is going to happen. I know it." She glanced toward Junior and Pecos Pete. "Can't you feel it?"

"Gem!" Chase shook her, drawing her gaze back to him. "It was an accident. That's all."

"But it wasn't! It wasn't an accident!" Her eyes rounded as her voice rose hysterically.

Chase scooped her up from the ground and started back toward the campfire, calling back over his shoulder, "Bring him into camp. We'll bury him at daybreak."

She was sobbing uncontrollably now, her arms fastened around his neck. Something else was going to happen, next time to Chase, and he wouldn't listen to her. She would get that cold feeling again, and then it would be his body they would find. She would never know his love. She would never experience his embrace or watch him shave in the morning or fix his breakfast or bear his children. She would be like Katie, alone without the man she loved.

"Don't leave me, Chase," she cried. "Don't leave me alone."

"I won't leave you," he promised.

She wasn't aware of the alert silence of the crew as Chase carried her toward the chuckwagon, nor was she aware of the men as one by one they slipped away from the camp. She clung desperately to Chase as would a drowning man to a life raft. Even when he knelt to place her on her bed beneath the wagon, she didn't release her hold. It would be too frightening without him.

"Don't leave me," she sobbed again.

Chase lay beside her beneath the wagon, cradling her against his chest as her sobs lessened to tiny hiccups. His calloused hands caressed her back and his lips moved lightly over her hair. His shirt grew wet between her cheek and his chest.

How long before the terror left her? How long before she forgot the sight of Rodney's smashed and bloodied face? How long before the tragic events of the evening gave way to her awareness of those precious moments in the night?

The ground surrounding the wagon was awash with the silvered light of the full moon, but beneath the wagon the couple was swathed in darkness. All was silent except for the occasional lowing of a cow. The campfire had burned low, leaving only the red glimmer of coals to mark its place.

She drew her face from his chest. She knew he was awake and watching her, though all she could see were shadows. It was the most natural thing in the world when his mouth lowered to capture hers. It began as lightly as the flutter of butterfly wings. It made her breath catch in her throat. Her arms tightened around his neck once more, her fingers spreading through his hair.

Chase's lips left hers, flicking across her cheek to her ear, nibbling lightly on her earlobe before moving up along her hairline to her forehead, then back along the bridge of her nose to return once again to her mouth. She shivered and pressed herself closer against him, learning the pleasant feel of his rock-hard body against her own.

A strange longing burned within, and somehow she knew that only Chase could fulfill it. Her breathing quickened as if she'd been running. She felt both hot and cold at the same time.

When his fingers lightly touched her breast through the fabric of her blouse, she gasped but didn't pull away. It was a delightful feeling, sending tiny pulses up and down her side. A sigh escaped through parted lips. Instinct and love mingled into a scorching desire to become a part of him.

He whispered her name.

"Chase," she responded breathlessly.

"Not here," he said softly in her ear. "Not this way."

"Chase," she repeated.

"We'll wait until Cheyenne." His hand withdrew from her breast. His lips departed from her own. "Just like you wanted."

She didn't know what she felt at that moment. Gratitude for his control? Frustration?

"Don't leave me," she begged as she had earlier in the night.

Chase nestled her cheek against his chest once more. "I won't leave you, Gem."

She closed her eyes and drew in a deep breath. "Chase?"

"Hmmm?"

"I love you."

A long silence, and then his whispered, "I know you do."

Somehow it was enough for now.

They buried Rodney early in the morning. Dry-eyed, Gem listened to Chase's words of blessing and comfort. In the light of day, her premonitions of the previous night seemed groundless. Rodney's death was an accident—a tragic accident, to be sure, but still just an accident. There was no reason to believe that more tragedy would follow.

Her aquamarine gaze shifted from the mound of dirt to Chase. Strange how one evening could hold equal memories of sadness and joy. The sorrow she felt over Rodney's death wasn't diminished by her night in Chase's arms. She had sought comfort within his embrace and had found a growing passion. If he had pressed, she would have given herself to him, marriage or no. They both knew it. It was his voluntary denial that proved his love for her, whether or not he would admit it to himself or speak it to her.

Chase spoke a final prayer over the grave, then

fell silent. After a moment the cowboys began filing away until only Chase and Gem were left.

"He loved Montana," Chase said, his eyes locked on the mound of brown Wyoming soil. "I wish he could've been buried there."

Gem nodded, the lump in her throat too big to speak.

"We'll wait till we get back to Four Winds to tell Katie. I don't want her finding out in a letter." Chase looked at her, and she saw the mist of tears in his sapphire eyes. "He was a darn good friend, Gem. Only good thing that ever came out of the Big Pine."

Again she nodded.

Chase shoved his hat onto his head and turned abruptly from Rodney's final resting place. "Let's get this herd to Cheyenne."

25

A mere thirteen years before, Cheyenne had been nothing more than an area of rippling, windswept prairie grass. Now it was a thriving city of several thousand, a major shipping and travel center for the new mines in the Black Hills with daily stages running between Cheyenne and Deadwood, and a railhead for the shipment of cattle and sheep back East.

Shane Grogan had been buying and selling cattle in Cheyenne for ten of those thirteen years, and Frank Dupre had been bringing his herd to him for the past eight. The two men had first met in California. Once Frank heard that Grogan was doing business in Cheyenne, he wouldn't consider selling his cattle to anyone else. Even now there were rails being laid in Idaho, almost in Frank's own backyard. Soon tracks would reach Miles City with a quicker link to

Chicago. But Frank knew that Shane Grogan would give him the best dollar available for his cattle, and so he continued to drive them to Cheyenne.

While the drovers guided the herd into the holding pens, Chase turned his horse toward Grogan's office at the edge of town. The sign over the doorway of the single story building read simply "Grogan's, Cattle Buyer." The red lettering had faded since Chase's last visit. There were curtains in the window, which, he recalled, had stood stark and bare six years before. Otherwise everything looked the same.

He eased down from the saddle and looped the reins over the hitching post. His spurs jingled as he stepped onto the boardwalk. He opened the door and entered the compact front office. A tiny bell rang above his head. The office was empty, but he could hear voices coming from the living quarters in the back.

"Hello," he called.

"Keep your shirt on! I'll be with you in a minute."

Chase recognized the gruff voice and smiled. Shane Grogan had never been known for his manners.

The curtain was pushed aside and a barrel-chested man in his late fifties stepped into the office. The thick, bushy mustache had grayed, and the black hair was sparser on top the rounded head, but he was definitely the Grogan that Chase remembered.

"Well?" Grogan questioned. "State yer business."

Chase grinned and remained silent.

Suddenly Grogan's green eyes narrowed and he stepped closer. Recognition came slowly. "Well, I'll be a—" His hands slapped down on Chase's shoulders. "You'd be Chase Dupre. How you been, boy? I was thinkin' we wouldn't see you in these parts again." He turned his head to the side and hollered, "Molly! Molly, get out here and meet an old friend o' mine."

Chase quirked an eyebrow and waited.

The curtains moved aside again, this time revealing a short, plump woman with gray hair, rosy cheeks in a wrinkled face, and a sparkle in her umber eyes. She wiped floury hands on her apron as she hurried closer to Grogan.

"Chase, meet Molly Grogan, my wife. Molly, this here is Frank Dupre's nephew."

"Your wife!" Chase exclaimed. "Why, you old buzzard. You told me you'd never get married."

Grogan removed his hands from Chase's shoulders and dropped one arm around Molly's back. "Wouldn't have if I'd never met my Molly here. Did you ever see such a pretty face?" And he kissed her cheek with a noisy smack.

"Go on, you," Molly sputtered, pushing at his ample stomach. Deep crinkles appeared around her eyes as she tried to stifle a pleased grin. The pink in her cheeks grew more radiant.

Chase pulled off his hat. "I'm pleased to meet you, Mrs. Grogan."

"Just call me Molly." Her voice was high pitched and soft. "Everyone else does." She held out her hand to him. "So you're Frank's boy? I've heard a lot about you. Glad I could meet you at last." She brushed at the flour on her apron. "I was just making an apple pie. Come on back to the kitchen and set a spell."

"What brings you to Cheyenne, boy?" Grogan asked as the men followed Molly toward the home behind the office. "You on your way to Four Winds?"

"We just drove the cattle down from there."

"Frank down at the corrals?"

Chase sat down at the kitchen table before he answered. "He's not with us this trip. I guess you haven't heard."

"Heard what?"

"Uncle Frank took a fall last spring during roundup. Lost the use of his legs. He's in a wheelchair."

Grogan raked thick fingers through his thinning hair, his face somber. "Sorry to hear that, Chase. Can't say as I've ever known a man I liked more than Frank Dupre."

"He feels the same about you."

"Well!" Grogan's hand banged down on the table, causing it to shimmy. "You said you've got cattle for me? Let's have us a piece of Molly's pie and go have a look see."

Gem slipped from the saddle and flexed her legs a few times, trying to work out the kinks. A cool autumn wind swept dust devils across the cattle pens, and flecks of dirt stung her cheeks before she could turn her back. Johnny Blue's voice carried on the wind to her as he closed another gate. He and Junior were in agreement about a drink and a juicy steak dinner. The first thing she wanted was a bath.

She hunched her shoulders deeper into her coat

and swung around to gaze in the direction of Shane Grogan's office. Chase and Grogan were walking toward her now. She lifted an arm and waved at them.

Grogan's face burst into a grin as he marched up and swung her high above his shoulders. "Well, look at the little tadpole. If you don't get prettier each time I see you. I'd thought for certain you'd've given up this trail business and settled down with some lucky cowpoke since last year."

"It's good to see you, Mr. Grogan." She darted a hesitant gaze toward Chase. Should she tell Grogan about them?

"As a matter of fact, Grogan," Chase answered for her, "she's about to do just that."

"What? Get married? Is that right, Gem? Who's the lucky fella?"

Again it was Chase who answered. "Me."

Gem dared to look at him again and was surprised to find him smiling tenderly, his gaze caressing her. She felt her insides turn to mush as her heart beat a crazy pattern beneath her breast.

"Wait till I tell my Molly!" Once again Grogan's hands gripped Gem's waist and lifted her off the ground. "A weddin'."

She discovered herself laughing merrily. It sounded so wonderful the way he said it.

"And just when is this weddin' taking place?" Grogan set Gem back on her feet.

She felt herself growing warm as she replied, "Soon, I hope."

Grogan bellowed a great laugh and slapped Chase on the back. "You'll have your hands full with this one, Chase, but she'll be worth it." He started walking. "Now, let's get this business over with so we can start celebrating."

"Rent us a few rooms at the hotel, Gem. When I'm through with Grogan, I'll get the men's pay from the bank and then join you there." He lightly touched her under her chin. "We'll have supper together."

Gem watched him amble after Grogan. She wanted to sing for joy. She wanted to shout her happiness to the whole of Cheyenne. Something wonderful had happened between them in the past two weeks. He *wanted* to marry her. Even he might not know it yet, but it was true. And she was in love with him. More every day. Could life ever be more wonderful than this?

Her heart still filled with joy, she made one stop before heading for the hotel.

She paid extra for a private bath in her room, but it was worth it. She sank into the hot water with a sigh, holding her breath as she dropped beneath the surface. She stayed under until her lungs couldn't bear it another second, then she slid her head above the water and took great gulps of air. She kept her eyes closed, enjoying the sound of lapping water against the sides of the tub and the feel of droplets as they trickled down her forehead from her hair. It seemed an eternity since she'd had a bath. A *real* bath with warm water and fragrant soap.

Finally she roused from her pleasant state of inactivity and picked up the bar of soap. She lathered her body from top to toe, scrubbing her scalp until it tingled. She felt pounds lighter as the grime of the trail was washed away. When she was finished, she sank into the water one last time to rinse off the suds, then stood and reached for a towel.

She dried her long hair with a brisk rubbing before twisting it up on top of her head and fastening it with a comb. Then she toweled herself dry, reveling in the clean feel of her skin. It was difficult to believe at the end of the trail drive why she always wanted to go along at the start. Yet every year was the same. She wouldn't think of staying home, even for frequent baths and clean changes of clothing.

Thinking of clean clothing, she turned her eyes on the new items that were laid out on her bed. She fingered the eyelet trim on the chemise before slipping it over her head, then donned the foulard petticoat with its many tiers of ruffles down the back. Feeling suddenly nervous, she turned her back on the new gown and walked over to the dresser.

Gem pulled the comb from her hair and let the tangled, damp mass of strawberry-gold tresses fall down her back. With careful strokes she began to brush away the snarls. She wondered how long she had before Chase would knock on her door. Would he think she was pretty in her new dress?

She sank onto a stool, her hands continuing to work her hair while her thoughts drifted. She thought of Consuela and the dark Latin beauty she had possessed. Never a hair out of place. Always clad in something pretty and feminine. Her olive skin flawless and her black eyes filled with mystery. Then she thought of Mary O'Grady with her pale white skin and riotous orange hair and the ample bosom revealed by low-cut gowns, not to mention eyes the color of emeralds and just as sparkling too.

In comparison, Gem considered her own common appearance. Too little bust and what she had hidden beneath the blowsy work shirts she wore; split riding skirts of brown; dusty, floppy-brimmed hats; boots and spurs. That was how he'd seen her for too long a time. She didn't have any intention of giving up her comfortable dress nor did she mean to quit riding the range and driving cattle, but for the first time in her life she wanted him to see her as a woman.

With uncertain fingers she coiled her hair into a chignon, then rose from the dressing table and returned to the bed.

The dress was a warm rose batiste polonaise, the draped overskirt gathered to reveal the delicate ruffles of the underskirt. She'd never before dreamed of wearing a dress like this, and she whispered a quick prayer that Chase would like it before she quickly slipped it over her head. She hooked the tiny buttons up the front of the bodice, then turned to survey her appearance in the looking glass.

The narrow waist and bustled back of the gown gave her figure a whole new look, accentuating her firm breasts and the gentle swell of her hips. The color of the gown brought out the pink in Gem's cheeks, and the ruffles and lace lent an air of femininity which she wouldn't have believed possible. She could hardly believe the girl in the mirror was her own reflection.

Reaching for the matching bonnet, she hoped that Chase would come soon before she lost her courage.

Like the rest of his drovers, Chase was scarcely recognizable as the same fellow who had ridden into town. He'd taken advantage of the bath house and the barber and bought himself a new suit of clothes. He had even splurged for a new hat. Now he was headed for the hotel and a hot meal.

He found himself whistling a tune as he walked. Uncle Frank would be pleased with the fine purse the cattle had brought. Perhaps it would make up for all the troubles that had plagued the ranch this past year. But for now Chase was going to put thoughts of trouble behind him. Gem was waiting for him at the hotel. And in a few days she would be his bride.

Chase didn't know what had come over him. Had the change been gradual or sudden? He wasn't sure, but he knew the thought of marrying Gem made him feel happier than he'd ever been before in his life.

He stopped at the desk and asked about Miss McBride's room, then took the stairs two at a time. Pausing before her door, he adjusted his collar and tie and tugged at the front of his fawn-colored coat. Still feeling buoyant, he tapped out a quick tune on her door.

Chase wasn't prepared for what he saw when the door swung open. There she stood in a frothy rose-pink gown, pink slippers peeking from beneath the rounded hem, a pretty bonnet perched over her coiled tresses, her cheeks blushing and her blue-green, tip-tilted eyes shining, her heart-shaped mouth curved in a smile. Was this the girl he'd always called "kid"? Was this the boisterous cowhand that roped cattle and played poker with him and the other men? Was this even the same girl who had nursed him after the grizzly attack and sat talking with him for hours during his convalescence?

"Do you like it?" she asked softly, the smile disappearing as he continued to stare at her.

He shook himself mentally and reached for both her hands. "You look like an angel on a pink cloud." He kissed the backs of her hands.

He watched the color heighten in her cheeks. He could sense her uncertainty and knew that this was all very new to Gem. She didn't know how to flirt with a man. She was guileless and honest, everything she felt written in her eyes for anyone who would look to see.

"Would you be kind enough to join me for supper in the dining room, Miss McBride?" He offered her his arm.

The awkwardness vanished. Gem giggled as she placed her hand in the crook of his elbow. "I'd be most pleased to join you, Mr. Dupre."

They walked along the hall and descended the stairs. Again and again, his eyes drifted to the top of her bonnet. She was so petite. She seemed so fragile. He had the sudden urge to protect her from all of life's hardships. Then she looked up at him, eyes filled with adoration and a vivid excitement, and he knew she didn't want to be sheltered and protected from life. She wanted to live it right alongside of him.

A surge of wanting shot through him, and he wished that he'd taken her straight to the Justice of the Peace the moment they'd entered town.

Gem stretched her arms above her head, groaning contentedly while grinning like a cat who has just finished the cream. The air in her room was cold, and she quickly brought her arms back beneath the quilt, snuggling deep within its warmth. She refused to open her eyes to see if it was morning. She would rather just lie still and revel in the memory of last evening.

They had taken a table in a far corner of the dining room. Chase had ordered for them, and while they'd waited for supper, he had observed her with glowing eyes that set her heart to skipping. She couldn't remember a single word they had said. She was certain it was nothing important. Words were meaningless; it was the sense of belonging that had been important. Oh, and she did belong to him.

How handsome he'd looked last night, his wavy brown hair trimmed and his strong jaw free of whiskers. His startling sapphire eyes had seemed even brighter than usual. She had been acutely aware of his broad shoulders and narrow waist beneath the cut of his new suit coat. She'd felt flushed with a strange need to draw closer to him. And soon . . . soon she would know what it meant to be his wife. She understood well enough the principals of mating; she'd seen too much in her younger days not to know. And yet she felt terribly ignorant. Ignorant and perhaps just a little frightened by the intense urges that flowed through her veins.

Her eyes opened. Two days! He'd told her at supper. Just two days and she would be Mrs. Chase Dupre. With joy she noticed the sunlight pouring into her room through the window, mirroring the warmth in her heart and the sunshine in her soul.

All right, damn it! I'll marry you.

She could laugh at the memory now. He might have proposed in anger, but the anger was gone. He loved her, and if it took her all her life, one day she would hear him speak those words aloud.

She tossed aside the quilt and threw her legs over

the edge of the bed, her feet sinking into the Brussels carpet. She couldn't lie in bed and waste away the day. She had too many things to do. And she didn't know where to start. She wished they were back home at Four Winds. Aunt Enid would know just what needed to be done and in just what order.

"Molly Grogan," she said aloud, thinking of the cattle buyer's wife of two years. "She'll help me."

Quickly she poured water into the bowl on a nearby table and performed her morning ablutions. With nimble fingers she braided her hair into one heavy strand and left it to hang loose down her back. Then she donned a white blouse and her favorite split riding skirt before tugging on her boots and reaching for her coat. She hoped it wasn't too early to go calling.

Molly Grogan couldn't have accepted her request for help with more enthusiasm. She bustled Gem into her warm kitchen and poured them each a hot cup of coffee before starting a list.

"The Reverend Snyder. We'll send Chase to talk to him. There'll be none of this Justice o' the Peace business, my dear. I'll send you back to Frank and Enid properly wed or not at all. Now, there's Mrs. Wilkens. She's got the fastest needle in town. We'll have you the prettiest wedding dress in two shakes of a lamb's tail, or my name isn't Molly Grogan." She continued to scribble notes on the slip of p per, her brow wrinkled in concentration. Suddenly her eyes grew very round as she looked up at Gem. "Oh my. Oh my goodness."

"What is it? What's wrong?"

"Oh my dear." Molly's voice was breathless.

Gem grew alarmed and started to rise from the table.

Molly waved her hand at Gem. "No, no. Sit down, dear. I'm fine. It's just that I've had the most wonderful idea. You mustn't plan on leaving Cheyenne right after your wedding. Oh my goodness. It's perfect."

"What is?" Gem was almost crazy with curiosity by this time.

"Oh, I couldn't tell you. It must be a surprise." She jumped up from the table and hurried toward the cloak hook near the door. "Put on your wrapper, dear. We'll pay a call on Mrs. Wilkens and get her started on your dress. My, my. There's so very much to do."

"Pete, cut out the piebald and the buckskin there and put them into the other corral with the others going back to Four Winds. The rest of these we'll sell." Satisfied that he had kept the best of the remuda to return to the ranch, Chase hopped down from the fence rail and turned toward Julio who was standing nearby. "Well, that about finishes our business in Cheyenne. Looks like the Four Winds won't do so bad this year after all." He grinned as they started walking, side by side. "Now all that's left to do is get married. Then we'll head back to Montana."

Julio's black brows pulled together as he grimly shook his head. "No, *amigo*, I will not be going with you this trip. I have decided to return to Casa de Oro and my family."

Chase stopped and placed a hand on Julio's shoulder. "Why now, Julio? I need your help."

"You do not need me at the Four Winds, Chase.

You have your family. You will have your bride. Gem will help you with the Four Winds."

"I can't make you stay, Julio, but I wish you would."

"No, my friend. It is best that I go."

Chase stared intently at Julio, who met his gaze with a steady one of his own. "It's because of Gem, isn't it? You're still in love with her."

"*Amigo*," Julio answered seriously, "I was given no encouragement to love her. She has always been yours for the taking. But now there is no room in your life for a third person. You must give all of yourself to her." He paused before adding, "You must love her, *amigo*."

Chase almost said he did love her. The words nearly slipped out before he could snatch them back. "I'll be good to her, Julio. She'll never want for anything."

"You are my friend, Chase Dupre. I will give you some advice. Forget what Consuela did to you. My sister was selfish and concerned only with her own pleasures and desires. You told me once you had had enough of love and could do just as well without it. You are wrong, my friend. You can do nothing worthwhile without love." He started to turn away, then looked back. "I will tell you one thing more, Chase. I think you already love her. You are just afraid to admit it. You will do well to think about it, *mi amigo*." With that, he spun on his heel and walked off in the direction of the cattle pens.

Chase stood rooted to the ground, his friend's words echoing in his head. Wasn't it enough that he wanted to be with her? Wasn't it enough that he could make her smile, make her laugh? Wasn't it enough that he held her with tenderness and could bring a flush to her cheeks? Wasn't it enough that he would promise to be faithful and to support and care for her? Must he risk everything again?

Hardening his heart, he turned away from Julio and his wise advice. He couldn't do it. He couldn't love her. He would do all in his power to make her happy. He would be a faithful husband and a good father to their children. Together they would make Four Winds the best ranch in the valley. But he couldn't love her. He had no love left to give.

Gem saw very little of anyone except Molly Grogan and Mrs. Wilkens for the next two days. Molly hustled her from one shop to another, buying this, buying that, then rushed her back for another fitting. Molly wouldn't even let her see Chase, insisting, "It's not good luck for him to see the bride."

"But, Mrs. Grogan," Gem protested, "that's just when the bride's in her wedding dress on her wedding day."

"We'll not take any chances with the two of you. He can just take his meals with the drovers, and you can eat in your room."

26

In the still crepuscule just before dawn, Gem stood at the window of her hotel room, gazing over the silent town. At the end of the street she could see the church steeple, the white spire reaching in elegant simplicity toward heaven. This was her wedding day.

Her waist-length strawberry-blonde tresses cascaded over her shoulders and down her back, obscuring the high-necked nightgown she wore. Her feet were bare, but she didn't notice the cold that made them appear almost blue. Her complexion was pale, and butterflies tormented her stomach.

In just a few hours she would leave for the church. Would he be there or would he change his mind? She'd been so sure after their supper together the day they'd arrived, but she hadn't seen him in the two days since. How did she know what he might be thinking? Perhaps she had only imagined he loved her. Maybe he had left her here and returned to Four Winds without even telling her.

She pressed her forehead against the cool glass window and closed her eyes. "Oh, please," she prayed, "let me be the wife he needs. Let me make him happy. Let me love him. I won't ask anything in return. Just let me love him."

Opening her eyes, she witnessed the coming of the morning. The sky turned from slate to blue. The street turned from gray to brown. The board buildings, some whitewashed, some not, were equally bathed in the bright yellow light of dawn. Day renewed. It promised a new beginning, another opportunity. Gem smiled softly, her earlier fears fleeing before the light and warmth. They were going to be all right. She wasn't afraid any more.

The town began to stir. A wagon bumped its way down the street. A lone rider entered town near the church. A storekeeper raised the blinds to reveal his wares. It was all so normal. So everyday. Didn't they know that this was her wedding day? Didn't they know that it was the best day in the world?

A soft rapping sounded at her door, and she knew it must be Molly with her breakfast.

"My, my!" the plump woman exclaimed as she bustled into the room, tray in hand. "I've never seen a prettier day." She set the breakfast tray on the small round table near the bed, then turned toward Gem as she pushed back her bonnet. "Good heavens, child. You've not even begun to get ready."

"But it's still early, Mrs. Grogan."

"You've no idea how much there's still to be done, Gem McBride. Now you sit down and eat while I lay out your things. Tsk, tsk. So much to do."

Gem obeyed, although she didn't think she could swallow even one bite. The butterflies were back again. Happy butterflies, but butterflies nonetheless.

Another knock brought her gaze toward Molly.

"Must be that impatient bridegroom of yours," Molly huffed. "I'll get rid of him in short shrift." She opened the door just a crack.

"Please, senora. May I see the senorita?"

"You most certainly may not! You get away from here this minute or I'll call the sheriff."

Gem got to her feet. "Mrs. Grogan, it's okay. I know him. Let me get my wrap and then let him in." She hurried to the side of her bed and slipped into her robe. "All right. Open the door."

Looking scandalized, Molly obeyed.

Julio was clad in a handsome black suit and stark white shirt. His boots had been shined to a high gloss, and he held his black sombrero in his hands. His dark brown eyes perused her in silence.

"What is it, Julio? Is something wrong? Chase—"

Julio shook his head and offered a somber smile. "Nothing is wrong, Gem. This will be a busy day for you, and I wanted to say my good-byes before the wedding. I am going back to Casa de Oro."

"Back to Texas?" Gem stepped forward. "But why, Julio?"

"It is better that way, *amiga*." Again his eyes caressed her face.

Tears swelled as she said softly, "I'll miss you. You've been my dearest friend."

"*Si*, and I will miss you." He reached out and stopped a tear midway down her cheek, lifting it onto his fingertip where he held it for a long time. "Senorita—"he began, then shook his head as if he'd thought better about what he was going to say. "You will take care of my *amigo*? He needs you."

"I love Chase more than anything in the world, Julio. I'll take care of him."

"One day he will tell you he loves you. You must be patient. *Amore conquista todo*."

Softly she asked, "What does that mean, Julio?"

His brown eyes searched her face. And then he answered in a voice rich with checked emotion. "Love conquers all."

For a long time they stood looking at each other. She understood what was left unsaid, what he wanted to say but couldn't, and it saddened her. *You'll find the right woman one day*, she wanted to tell him. *You'll find someone better than me, someone who'll love you just as much as I love Chase*.

"You must make me a promise, *nina*."

"What is it?"

"You must give me your word you will send for me if you or Chase ever need me."

"I promise, Julio."

He covered his slicked-back hair with his black sombrero. There was no sadness in his smile when he offered it this time. "I will see you at the wedding, senorita. *Que Dios guarde*. May God keep you." He turned toward the door, nodding to Molly. "*Gracias*, senora." And then he was gone.

Gem wiped away the lingering tears on her cheeks. She sorely wished her own joy hadn't caused someone else's sorrow.

* * *

The Reverend Snyder was a short, bespectacled man in his late twenties or early thirties. His countenance was one of warmth and friendliness, but he was a man of few words when it came to idle conversation. And there was nothing Chase would have liked more than some idle conversation at the moment.

He was standing at the front of the church, awaiting the appearance of his bride. His shirt collar felt too tight, and he longed to reach up and loosen it with a jerk of his finger. His palms were sweaty. His new boots suddenly seemed to be pinching his toes. Internally he chastised himself for his nervousness. He would have thought he'd never been a bridegroom before.

His gaze passed over the gathering in the pews. All the drovers from the cattle drive were there, plus Shane Grogan. Molly Grogan was somewhere in the church, helping Gem with her last-minute preparations.

Blasted women, he thought. Couldn't they just put on a dress and get this over with without so much fuss and bother?

The reverend's wife struck a chord on the organ, bringing Chase's thoughts up short. He turned his eyes toward the back of the church and drew in a deep breath. This was it.

She came through the door in a creation of white satin and lace. He supposed it was something quite beautiful with all its drapes and gathers and its long train that spread out behind her, but he really didn't see the gown over which Mrs. Wilkens had labored so hard for two days. He had eyes only for the face of his bride.

A pretty splash of color accentuated her cheekbones in an otherwise flawless, ivory complexion. Her champagne hair with its strawberry highlights was gathered in a mass of curls atop her head. Her eyes, that unique shade of bluish-green that was all her own, glittered with anticipation. A timorous smile curved the corners of her mouth.

His heart beat erratically. He discovered with delight and some surprise that he had no wish to escape this union at the last moment. In fact, he hoped the preacher would hurry up and speak his words before *she* could change *her* mind. He felt his chest swelling with pride, knowing she would soon be his wife.

She stood before him, looking up with shimmering eyes. Only a fool couldn't have seen the inestimable love swirling in their aquamarine depths. He took her small hand into his own larger one, noting with a hidden smile the calluses on her palm. She was special, his Gem. There was no other woman like her on this earth.

They turned in unison to face Reverend Snyder.

Later she would wonder about the wedding ceremony itself. She assumed she made the correct responses when asked, but she couldn't recall them. The reverend's voice seemed only a hum in the background, the church and everyone in it a blur. Everyone except Chase. She had eyes only for Chase.

"In conclusion, my children, remember . . ."

For some reason Reverend Snyder's voice at this time brought her out of her fog.

". . . charity suffereth long, and is kind; charity envieth not; charity is not rash, is not puffed up, doth not behave itself unseemly, seeketh not her own, is not easily provoked, thinketh no evil; rejoiceth not in iniquity, but rejoiceth in the truth; beareth all things, believeth all things, hopeth all things, endureth all things. Charity never faileth."

Reverend Snyder paused and gave them both a long, serious gaze that seemed to ask, *Do you understand?*

Yes, she understood. This was the kind of love she had for Chase. It was the kind of love she would always have for him. She smiled, her heart in her eyes.

With a satisfied nod of his head, the reverend completed the ceremony. "By the power vested in me by the Territory of Wyoming, I pronounce you man and wife."

Gem turned to look up into the blue eyes she adored. The fingers of his right hand tipped her chin upward as his head came down. The touch of his lips against hers was tentative, undemanding, yet it sent a bolt of heat coursing through her veins. Her knees quivered. Her arms reached up to circle his neck, and her lips parted as her eyes fluttered closed.

A sudden cheer resounded in the church as the cowboys tossed their hats in the air. She loosened her embrace, feeling the flush spreading up from her neck and into her cheeks. And then they were besieged by laughing, back-slapping cowpokes, all of them talking at once.

Pike Matthews was the first to hug her. His blue eyes looked suspiciously misty as he brushed her cheek with his weathered lips. "Can't say I ever taught anyone to crack the old bullwhip as good as you, 'cept maybe your husband here."

"And to lasso too," she reminded him fondly.

Tall, skinny, red-haired Teddy Hubbs was next,

pushing the older Pike out of the way with mock roughness. "Quit hoggin' the bride, you old bushwhacker." He grinned at Gem, a twinkle in his green eyes. "Just 'cause you're married now, I don't want you forgettin' how t'play the mouth organ. You come down to the bunkhouse anytime you feel like another lesson. Ya hear?"

"I hear."

It was Corky's turn now. He shouldered Teddy aside and winked at her, saying, "Just 'cause you married the trail boss, don't think I'll be cookin' you anything special next drive. It's beans, biscuits, and stew. Same as always. No expectin' special treatment."

She laughed. "I won't. I promise."

"And don't give a thought to Sunny. I'll get her back to Four Winds safe and sound for you. Her and me've become good friends."

"Thanks, Corky."

One by one the others all kissed her, heartily shook Chase's hand, and wished them both well. Carried on a cloud of euphoria, Gem thanked them all and waited for the moment when Chase would lead her away so they could be alone together.

Then Julio stood before her. "Much happiness, Senora Dupre," he said softly as he took her hands in his before kissing her cheek.

She felt the sting of his bittersweet farewell and knew she would miss him always.

He looked at Chase, standing at her side. "You are a very lucky man, my friend."

Chase's arm, placed casually around her back only moments before, tightened as he replied, "I know, Julio. Thanks."

"Little tadpole." She was engulfed in Grogan's mighty embrace. "I haven't seen me anything so pretty since I married my Molly here."

Molly leaned over and kissed Gem on her cheek, then dabbed at her eyes with a handkerchief as she said, "Beautiful. Just beautiful."

"I can't thank you enough, Mrs. Grogan, for all you've done."

"Think nothing of it, dear. I was pleased to do it." She turned umber eyes upon her husband. "Well, Mr. Grogan. Don't you think we should be showing them our wedding gift?"

They followed the Grogans out of town in their rented buggy. Gem sat stiffly beside Chase, wanting to touch him, to snuggle up close, but feeling incredibly shy and uncertain. She was almost afraid to look over at him. And he didn't help any. Not a word from him since he'd helped her into the buggy. They seemed to ride on forever, leaving behind any semblance of civilization. Nothing to be seen but grass— miles and miles of undulating grass.

Out of nowhere it appeared, a white, three-story manse with shutters framing every window, even in the attic, and a yard surrounded by a black iron fence. Trees had been planted, and there was a smattering of green shrubs and flowers blooming in well-tended beds. The whitewashed outbuildings all looked brand-new. As they drew near, they could see a bay stallion trotting back and forth in his corral, his nostrils flared and tail flying. He needed no papers to prove his good blood.

"Whose place can this be?" Gem wondered in a hushed voice.

"I've no idea." Chase was frowning in puzzlement as his eyes swept over the house and outbuildings again and again.

Grogan stopped his wagon in front of the gate leading to the house. He jumped down and held his arms out for Molly, swinging her to the ground before turning with a self-pleased grin toward the newlyweds.

"Well? What do you think?" he asked, throwing his arm in an expansive gesture toward the mansion.

Chase eased back on the reins. He leaned his forearms on his knees, the reins held lightly in his hands, and stared hard at Grogan. "It's nice. What are we doing here, Grogan?"

"Nice! Is that all you can say? Nice? Fine way to talk about where you'll be spendin' your honeymoon."

The expression on Chase's face said plainly that he thought Grogan was daft.

Molly nudged her husband's side with her elbow. "Help down the bride, Mr. Grogan, and let's take them inside."

With three swift strides the big man was beside the buggy and lifting Gem from the leather-covered seat. She glanced back over her shoulder, feeling as if she'd just found herself in someone else's dream. She didn't know what to do or say. Shane Grogan placed a firm hand beneath her elbow and ushered her quickly along the walkway leading to the porch. Before they reached it, the front door opened and a man and two women stepped outside. The man, wearing a shiny black suit complete with vest, was middle-aged with carefully groomed light brown hair and a trimmed mustache. The women, one about the same age as the smartly dressed man and the other probably no older than Gem, were attired in long black dresses with crisp white aprons and white caps.

"Mrs. Dupre, meet Thompson, your butler."

Thompson executed a smart bow. "Your servant, madam."

"And this is Clara . . ."

The older woman curtsied primly. "How do, mum."

". . . and Bernice."

Bernice copied Clara's curtsy, but the younger woman added a smile, saying, "We're glad to 'ave you at the Lucky W, mum. If you need anythin' at all, you just call me."

Chase arrived at the bottom of the porch just as the introductions were concluding. "Grogan, what is all this?"

Grogan's round face was flushed with pleasure. "As luck would have it, my good friend Charles Weatherspoon, owner of the Lucky W and this magnificent home, has left me the use of his place while he's on an extended visit back home to England. 'Grogan,' he said when he left, 'you use this place as you see fit. I trust no one as I trust you.' So this is how I see fit. It's yours for as long as you want to stay."

Thompson bowed toward Chase. "Sir, if you and your lady would care to come inside, Clara has prepared tea for you in the parlor."

Chase glanced at Gem. She looked as if she would burst if she couldn't see the inside. He had to admit it would probably be better than the hotel in town. And it would definitely be more private.

"Come along, Mr. Grogan." Molly tugged at

her husband's sleeve. "Let's leave these two children to themselves. They don't need our company."

Gem turned her face up toward Chase. "May we stay?" she asked breathlessly.

How could he deny her anything? Her cheeks were flushed and her eyes glittered with excitement. The buggy ride had blown fine wisps of red-gold hair free to curl around her temples, making her look wild and free, like a wood nymph perhaps.

"We can stay if that's what you wish," he said, a slow smile turning the corners of his mouth.

"Oh, yes!"

"Follow me, sir." Thompson turned and led the way into the house.

The entry hall was nearly as large as Gem's bedroom at Four Winds. A curved stairway was directly before them, the railing of hand-carved walnut. Doorways on both sides opened into large, airy rooms with high ceilings. A crystal chandelier hung from the ceiling, which had been hand-painted with scenes of the West—antelope and cattle, buffalo and bear, snow-capped mountains and wind-swept prairies.

"The parlor is this way."

Thompson guided them to the left. The parlor was an enormous room with a fireplace at each end. The mantels were made of cherrywood and were adorned with Dresden porcelain figures. A deep burgundy carpet covered the shiny hardwood floor. A grand piano filled a far corner of the room, but it was to the grouping of chairs near the front fireplace that Thompson led them. With a hand he indicated they should sit. They did.

Clara entered the room with a silver tray. She

walked swiftly, her back straight and her face unreadable. Her neat black hair was swept up in a bun at the nape, nary a strand out of place. She set the tray on the low table and immediately filled two china cups with tea from a silver teapot. She poured a generous helping of cream into each cup, then set them before the silent pair. Next she set a large plate of hot scones, smothered in honey, onto the table, then backed away to wait unobstrusively near the far wall.

"Just call, sir, if you or your lady need anything. Bernice will see to your luggage." With a curt nod Thompson spun on his heel and left the parlor, ever so stern and proper.

Their heads turned toward each other at the same time. In silence they met the other's gaze, surprise mirrored in their eyes. And then in unison they began to laugh, muffled giggles at first, growing louder while they both fought tears of mirth.

Gem placed a hand on Chase's arm. "Shh," she demanded, wiping away a tear with her free hand. "You'll hurt their feelings."

Which only made it harder for Chase to control his laughter. It was all too preposterous. Here he was, fresh off the range from a cattle drive, sitting down for high tea in an English mansion in the middle of the Wyoming plains. As if he were some lord or something. Then he looked at Gem again as she picked up a teacup with dainty fingers, and it suddenly didn't seem so preposterous. The sheen of her satin wedding gown seemed perfect for this setting. Her clustered curls kissed the back of her neck, her bare shoulders white and enticing. She *could* be the wife of an English lord. But she wasn't. She was his wife. She was his.

She lifted heavy-lashed eyelids, and her cup stopped midway to her lips. Her mouth parted in a silent *Oh*. The laughter faded between them. Her eyes grew wider, swirling blue-green filled with wonder, fear, tenderness, trust, love.

He took the cup from her hand and set it back on the table, never taking his eyes from hers. He leaned forward until their lips were almost but not quite touching. He could feel her quickened breathing. Her lips parted; she moistened them with her tongue.

"Are you hungry?" he asked, his voice husky.

She shook her head.

"Neither am I."

Blood pounded in his ears. The urge was to crush her against him and kiss her like she'd never been kissed, but he forced himself to go slow. He meant to make this a day and night to remember, for himself, but most of all for Gem.

"Let's find our room, Mrs. Dupre," he whispered as he took her hand.

27

Golden sunlight spilled through the white lace curtains that framed the high plate windows of the bedroom suite. Tiny panes of colored glass formed a pyramid above the window, throwing a pattern of purples, greens, and blues onto the white counterpane of the four-postered, canopied bed.

Chase carried Gem into the room, her head nestled on his chest beneath his chin. She could feel the beat of his heart against her cheek, and it made her feel warm clear down to her toes. He closed the door with his heel, then carried her across the bedroom toward the bed. Tenderly, he set her on her feet.

She didn't know what to do, where to look, so she stared at the floor. The lightheartedness they had shared downstairs had been replaced by something too strong for words, too intense for laughter.

"Mrs. Dupre?"

Slowly she looked up at him. He towered over her, so handsome, so strong. She wanted to remember him always just as he was at this moment, his chiseled jaw softened by a tenderness she could sense beneath the emotion-laden surface, his eyes smoldering with a feral yet comforting fire. She trembled, but she felt no fear. The dark irises of his sapphire eyes seemed bigger, more black than she remembered. She wondered what he saw.

He cupped her face between his hands, gently bending her head backward. She could feel the calluses and scars that marked his palms and fingers, but somehow the work-roughened skin felt all the more tender against her own smooth flesh. Her breathing stilled as his mouth began its slow descent toward hers. Anticipation made her stomach quiver, her heart flutter. Could she stand much more than this? Her eyes drifted closed, and she waited for her heart to stop beating altogether.

She stood as still as a statue as he kissed her, so light at first that it could have been merely a feather brushed over her lips, and then deepening, sending tiny shock waves down each of her limbs. His hands slipped slowly—ever so slowly—from her cheeks and began a lazy slide down her throat, to her shoulders, along her arms, then back again. When each hand cupped a breast through the satin fabric, she gasped into his mouth, but she didn't pull away. She couldn't have even if she had wanted to. She had no will of her own. But it didn't matter, for she didn't want to pull away.

Chase released her lips, his mouth hovering only a hairsbreadth from her own. She sensed he was watching her and opened her eyes. His gaze was strangely warm. His eyelids were at half-mast, as if they couldn't open any further. She felt mesmerized. She was being drawn into their startling blue depths. Soon she would be swimming in a sapphire sea.

She moaned, but she didn't know that the sound came from her own throat, so strange did it sound.

His hands began their slow journey of discovery, moving from her breasts to encircle her tiny waist, then sliding over her hips, all the while holding her eyes and her heart captive by his gaze. Her skin tingled, burned, everywhere he touched. She wanted to pull away. She wanted to pull closer. It was paradise. It was torture.

His hands moved to the back of her dress and began the slow process of unhooking each tiny pearl button. It took her a moment to even realize what he was doing.

"Shouldn't we . . . shouldn't we close the shutters?" she asked weakly. "It's so . . . bright in here."

He kissed her throat near her shoulder, then nibbled his way up to her ear. "Never," he whispered. "Never hide yourself from me. You're too beautiful to be hidden in the dark."

Then with hands on her shoulders he turned her back toward him. Each button was freed from its hook, and after each one he kissed the nape of her neck, sending chills skittering down her spine. Sweet agony. She closed her eyes to better experience his touch. His fingers stilled, and she waited, every nerve alive with a fevered desire. She wanted to swirl around. She wanted to throw her arms around his neck and meld against him. Instinct made her want what she'd never tasted, what she'd never experienced.

Warm hands touched the cool flesh of her back. She sucked in her breath as they slid languorously toward her shoulders, taking the bodice of her gown and her thin chemise with them. The fabric clung precariously to her taut breasts, then dropped to her waist. Her knees turned to jelly as his hands pulled the pins from her hair until her tresses fell into a red-gold cloud around her shoulders, wispy strands tickling her bare breasts and naked back.

Chase stepped around her. "Look at me, Gem," he said huskily.

She obeyed.

He watched her with a gaze so intense it was almost frightening. She knew him, but she didn't. She loved him, yet they were strangers.

Although her eyes were held captive by his, she was acutely aware as he removed his coat, his tie, his collar. When the white shirt was tossed aside, her hands drifted up of their own choosing, reaching out to tentatively touch the hard, muscled wall of his chest. She had seen him many times bare-chested, his skin glistening with sweat as he worked. She had nursed his wounds when he was injured. But never had she felt the intimacy of this moment.

She allowed her gaze to drift to his chest and then to his left side. She caressed the angry wound that remained as testimony of the grizzly's strength and the miracle of life. She might have lost him, but she hadn't. He was here. He was hers. Tears blinded her momentarily.

"Chase," she whispered in a voice choked with emotion.

He gathered her to him. For the first time, her breasts touched another's flesh. It should have startled her, yet it seemed the most natural thing in the world. Warm and safe. His lips returned to claim hers, and her arms rose to circle his neck. With a single hand he pushed off her recalcitrant wedding gown and layer of petticoats, then gently rolled away her cotton undergarment, lifting her off the floor with one arm until all she had worn lay in a pool of white beneath her feet. Then he swept his other arm beneath her knees and placed her gently on the bed.

She didn't open her eyes when he left her suddenly alone. She knew he was shedding the remainder of his clothes. She wanted to look, yet couldn't. She wanted to see him in all his splendid nakedness, but she hadn't the courage at this moment.

The bed gave beneath his weight. His body stretched out beside hers.

"Ah, Gem," he murmured against her throat. "I've wanted you for so long."

His lips continued their path of discovery, trailing lightly across her skin until they reached the taut peak of her breast. A startled breath sucked through her teeth as his tongue traced a lazy circle around the dark areola. Her hands shot to his head, her fingers tangling in his dark, shaggy locks. Did she seek to hold him there or move him away? Even she didn't know.

She whispered his name.

His face returned to the pillow beside hers. She could feel his hot breath on her cheek as his hands began to explore, slow, gentle, teaching hands. Everything in her cried out for more, for release. Instinctively she moved closer to him.

"Chase . . . I love you so."

And then he was poised above her. Her arms reached to encompass his chest. Inexperienced but willing, she drew him to herself.

Muscles tensing.

Bodies rising and falling.

Hands stroking.

Murmured endearments.

It was a primitive act, but love turned it into a dance of joy.

Replete, they lay on their sides, arms and legs still entwined, waiting for their breathing to slow.

Nothing in her past had prepared Gem for what she had just experienced. She thought she must be like a flower just blooming, opening its petals and coming to life, and Chase was her sunshine, giving her light and warmth and a reason for living. She heard his sigh of satisfaction and smiled to herself.

"What are you thinking?" he asked softly.

She opened her eyes to look at him then. His sapphire gaze was still warm from their loving. She reached up to caress one thick, dark eyebrow, enjoying the freedom and the right to such a tender and intimate gesture. "I was wondering. Is it always like this?"

"No," he replied, his arms tightening around her back. "It will always get better." He placed a whispery soft kiss on her temple.

She lay her cheek against his damp chest. "I love you, Chase." Her heart quickened, then stopped in anticipation. He had given her so much already, but there was still more she wanted, more she needed from him. Would he give it to her now?

"I know." His fingers stroked her hair, then

stilled, his hand lying against her head. "I know you love me, Gem, but don't ask me to give what's not there. Don't expect it. Take what I can offer. We can be happy. We can have a good marriage. Just don't . . ." He let his words die away.

She didn't dare look up. There was too much emotion in his voice for her to meet it in his eyes. She nodded her head, her cheek rubbing the skin of his chest. She would be patient. She had a lifetime to teach him how to love and trust again.

And then, still wrapped in each others arms, they drifted into sleep.

28

Dusk was laying its gray mantle over the bedroom when Gem awoke. Her head rested on Chase's shoulder and an arm was flung over his chest. She opened her eyes slowly and tried not to move, wanting to relish the sensation of waking up with her beloved.

Her stomach growled loudly, protesting its neglect.

Chase chuckled. "I thought you'd never wake up. I'm starving."

She tilted her head back. His blue eyes caressed her face with a tender gaze, and a satisfied smile curved the corners of his strong mouth. A warm tingle emanated through her as she thought of what his mouth could do when he made love to her.

Again her stomach growled.

"Either we get up and eat," he warned in a low voice, "or I find my satisfaction here." His arm slipped around to her back and he pulled her quickly against him. His eyes had the hooded look of a predator as he stared at her, their noses nearly touching. "Your choice."

She felt that wonderful flowering sensation low and deep inside her. She was hungry, but was she hungrier for food or for Chase? "That's hardly a fair choice, Mr. Dupre." She felt herself blushing. "Can't I have both?"

"Greedy little kid, aren't you?" he teased, then smacked her bare behind before rolling away from her.

Gem watched as he rose from the bed and padded across the floor to the wardrobe. She discovered she felt no embarrassment in watching him. She noted the dark tan of his muscled upper body, comparing it to the stark whiteness of the skin of his buttocks and legs. A smattering of dark, curly hairs spread across his upper chest, then narrowed slowly as it descended to his navel. She liked the way he moved as he walked and as he pulled on his trousers. Smooth, strong, perhaps even dangerous. Like a mountain lion.

He glanced over her way. "Aren't you coming?"

Emboldened, she shoved aside the sheet and hopped from the bed, hurrying toward him and her clothing. Chase paused in his dressing as she approached, his gaze as admiring as hers had been only moments before. She reached to pull a teal cambric dressing sacque from the wardrobe, but his hands stopped her, pulling her up off the floor and into his embrace.

The humor was gone from his eyes, and in the dying light, she thought she could almost see into his soul. She wished she could understand what she saw there.

"I'll always treasure this day," he said somberly. "You've given me a great gift. You'll never know . . ."

She had no reply. She could only gaze back at him and will all her love to show in her eyes.

Softly he said, "Get dressed." He set her back on her feet.

She slipped quickly into her dressing gown, tossing her tangled tresses over her shoulder to flow in wild disarray down her back. Then like two children they slipped from the bedroom, holding hands, sneaking down the stairway in search of something to eat.

After two incorrect turns, they found the kitchen in the back right corner of the mansion. The immense, white-tiled room was filled with glass cupboards and two huge stoves.

Chase struck a match and lit the lamp on the wall, turning it low. Then, while Gem looked for a loaf of bread, he headed for the icebox. He was just turning away from it, his hands clutching a hunk of cheese and some cold beef, when a side door suddenly flew open.

"What's this?" a voice demanded.

In unison, guilty expressions on their faces, Chase and Gem whirled to meet their inquisitor.

Thompson held a lamp above his head, allowing its bright light to spill onto the intruders. "I say!" he exclaimed as he recognized them. "Sir, you should have called for me." He was obviously appalled to find the guests of the manse raiding the kitchen, Gem clad in her nightclothes with tumbled hair hanging about her shoulders and Chase wearing only a pair of trousers.

Chase set the food he'd found onto the counter. "We're sorry if we woke you, Thompson."

The butler looked highly insulted. "You most certainly did not waken me, sir. I was merely awaiting your summons in my quarters." He looked over his shoulder. "Bernice," he snapped smartly, "we do *not* have prowlers. It is Lord Weatherspoon's guests. They are hungry. Get them some supper."

Bernice bustled into the kitchen, straightening her cap as she came. Her face was flushed. She was obviously upset.

"Please," Gem said quickly. "Don't go to any bother for us. We don't want anything fancy." Indicating the bread, cheese and cold meat they had found, she added, "This is plenty."

Thompson raised an eyebrow. "Sir?" he inquired of Chase.

"My wife is right, Thompson. We *want* to fix it ourselves, if it wouldn't be too much trouble for you."

The butler's expression clearly stated it was highly irregular, but he was merely a servant and must obey. "If that is what you wish, sir," he agreed with a resigned sigh. "Come, Bernice."

The young maid started to turn, then glanced shyly toward Gem. "I'm sorry, mum. I 'eard a noise an' I was fright'ned, I was."

"There's nothing to apologize for." Gem offered a smile to the embarrassed girl. "Good night, Bernice."

"'Night, mum, sir." She curtsied and fled the kitchen.

Gem's gaze followed her through the door, then turned upon her husband.

"Thompson must rule with an iron hand," Chase said, a glint of humor in his swirling blue eyes.

"I don't think they quite know what to do with us."

"I know what to do with us." He pulled a knife from a rack on the wall and stuck it into the cheese. "First we satisfy one hunger . . ."—he looked at her suggestively—". . . and then we satisfy another."

When Gem awoke, the new day was well on its way toward noon and the sunshine was spreading its golden rays over the thick carpet. She couldn't remember another morning when she'd slept so late.

For some reason she wasn't surprised to discover herself alone in the bed, alone in the room. Even though she didn't know where he was or when he'd left, she knew Chase would return soon. She snuggled down beneath the bedcovers, flopping her arms above her head and groaning in pure delight, a Cheshire-cat smile curving her rose-pink mouth. She could almost purr, she was so contented.

The bedroom door swung open, admitting Chase. He carried a silver serving tray. "Your breakfast, mum," he announced, mimicking Clara and Bernice.

With surprise she discovered she was famished once again. She pushed herself up, drawing the quilt with her as she held it to her breasts. "You didn't raid the icebox again, did you?"

"Are you calling me a thief, ma'am?" His eyes twinkled as he pretended to be insulted. "I'll have you know Clara fixed this breakfast just for the blushing bride." He set the tray on the bed and leaned forward to claim a languid kiss, saying in a low voice as he released her lips, "Blush for me, Mrs. Dupre."

She obliged as his gaze slid from her mouth to the valley between her breasts.

Chase grinned. "Thanks, ma'am." He picked up the tray and set it on her lap, then sat on the edge of the bed beside her. "Hurry and eat, honey. I'd like to have a look around this place. Our visit won't last forever."

"How long can we stay, Chase?" she asked before taking a bite of scrambled eggs. When he didn't answer, she looked up and found him still watching her.

Blue eyes should be cold, she thought, *but his aren't*. He looked at her with immeasurable warmth and tenderness. *Oh, Chase, don't you realize yet that you love me?*

"You'd like to stay awhile, wouldn't you?"

"Only if you would, Chase."

His fingertips pushed away some wispy tendrils from her cheek. "You won't get all spoiled on me, will you? You're my best cowhand. I don't want you turnin' into some hothouse flower."

"Chase Dupre! You know darn good and well that I—"

He laughed at her outburst. "Yes, I know darn good and well." He kissed her with a loud smack on the cheek, then moved off the bed and walked over to the tall window, tossing over his shoulder, "Eat." He stared out the window in silence for quite some time before finally answering her earlier question. "We can stay two weeks, Gem. No more. We need to get back to Four Winds before much longer. Aunt Enid will be wondering about us."

She didn't argue with him. Two weeks in this English mansion would be enough. It was wonderful. A kind of fairy tale. But she would be ready to go home too.

Home. Not just because some kind folks took in a scruffy little orphan. But home because it was *home*. Her home. Hers and Chase's. *Mrs. Dupre*. She played with the sound of it in her head as she finished her breakfast. *My wife*, he had called her in the kitchen. *Greedy little kid*, he had teased last night. *Honey*.

Yes, she was going to be ready to go home with him. She would go anywhere with Chase Dupre.

Bundled against the cold westerly wind that blew across the range that morning, Chase and Gem began their exploration of the Lucky W in the stables. As with the three-story mansion, Lord Weatherspoon had pinched no pennies here. Chase had never seen better bloodlines in his life, nor a finer stable.

The bay thoroughbred stallion they had seen upon their arrival the previous day was inside the massive horse barn instead of in the corral. As soon as the stable door opened, he threw his regal head over his stall door and whinnied, the shrill sound echoing throughout the building. Hand in hand, Chase and Gem hurried toward him.

"Hello, fella," Chase said as he carefully placed a hand on his neck.

The bay suddenly backed into his stall and turned a profile in their direction, as if he were offering his best side to a photographer. His red-brown coat gleamed. His black mane and tail had been carefully groomed free of snarls. The stallion arched his neck and snorted, then stomped a black-stockinged leg three times.

"He's showing off for you, Gem. Look at the way he's acting. You know a pretty lady when you see one, don't you, fella?"

The horse turned his head, observing them with black, wide-set eyes, nostrils flaring.

"Right nice piece of horse flesh, ain't he?"

Gem and Chase turned at the voice.

Not much taller than Gem, the man approached from an open stall across the breezeway. He was wearing a tatty wool suit and a derby hat that had seen better days. His jaw was covered with sparse gray whiskers. Alert slate-gray eyes studied the couple.

"M'name's Smith. Hezekiah Smith." His English attire was at odds with his Western twang. When he grinned, he displayed a gap where a tooth should have been, giving him an even more rustic appearance. He held out his hand toward Chase. "I'm the groom here at the Lucky W. You must be Grogan's kin."

"Just friends," Chase replied, returning the handshake.

Hezekiah shrugged his answer away. "Kin. Friends. All the same out here." He looked at Gem. "You like horses, little lady?"

She nodded.

"Come have a look see at this'n." He spun around on his boot heel and headed for the opposite end of the barn, pausing before the last stall door on the left. He opened the top half and motioned for Gem to hurry closer.

Inside the stall, lying in the clean bed of straw,

was a silver-gray mare and her matching foal. The slight dip in their sculptured heads spoke of their Arabian breeding.

"This here's Sheba, and the little one is Jericho. Whatcha think of 'em?"

"They're beautiful," Gem answered in a hushed tone. "May I go in?"

"Sure thing." Hezekiah opened the stall door.

Chase, watching Gem over the half-door as she knelt down in the straw, suddenly remembered the night that Wichita was born. Gem had been just a little waif then, an orphan with no folks and no place to go. He remembered her close cap of strawberry-gold curls and the freckles that had bedecked her nose and cheeks. And here she was, once again kneeling in the straw of a stall, her hands stroking the coat of the gangly young colt, only this time she was a woman. Her hair was long now, reaching clear to her hips, finely textured, the color of champagne with misty red highlights, her complexion as pale as milk.

His heart caught in his throat. If he should ever lose her . . .

"Look at him, Chase," she called to him, her voice like the nectar of roses.

He wanted to harden his heart to the fetching picture she made, but he couldn't. It had happened. Against his will and better judgment, it had happened. He had fallen in love with his wife.

But did he ever dare tell her so?

29

Pike, Teddy, and Corky stopped by the Lucky W at the end of the couple's first week of marriage. The three cowboys were on their way north, returning to Four Winds with the remainder of the remuda.

"You and Gem take your time comin' home," Pike told Chase with a solemn nod while they all stood on the veranda. "Me'n the boys can handle the ranch. Done it for a long time. We can do it again."

Corky winked at Gem. "He treatin' you right? If he ain't, you just tell me and I'll give him a set to."

A becoming pink rushed to her cheeks. "He's treatin' me just fine, Corky." Her eyes flickered to Chase as she added softly, "Just fine."

The cowpokes chuckled, trying to hide their own sudden embarrassment.

"Well, we'd best be off," Pike said as he turned toward his waiting horse. "Like I said. You two stay here till spring if you want. We'll take care of the ranch."

Arms around the other's back, they watched as the three men cantered away from the Weatherspoon manse.

"I guess we could stay longer if you want," Chase offered.

She stared out at the rolling rangeland, the long grasses bending in the autumn wind. She was enjoying this special time in their honeymoon hideaway. She knew that never again would they have as much privacy as they'd enjoyed here. Once back to the ranch, their lives would become embroiled in the busy activity of running the Four Winds. They would be surrounded by others. How often would they be able to slip to their room in the middle of the day to spend hours wrapped in each other's arms?

But although Chase was offering her a chance to remain, she knew he longed to get back home to Four Winds. It was as it should be. She knew with confidence that it wasn't because he didn't want to be with her. He belonged at Four Winds. And so did she.

"No. I'll be ready to leave when you are."

There was a look of pride in the sapphire gaze he turned upon her. He pushed aside a renegade curl from her cheek, then leaned down to kiss her neck below her ear. "Well . . . I'm not in too big a hurry to leave." His mood shifted from serious to merry as he asked, "How 'bout a ride into town to see Molly and Shane?"

She brightened. "I'd love it."

"You change and I'll get the horses."

Within the half hour they were cantering along

the trail toward Cheyenne. The cold spell had lifted, and the Wyoming plains were being blessed with a warm reprieve from the promised winter. The horses that Hezekiah had provided were frisky and ready for a good run. Gem and Chase didn't disappoint them.

Laughing, faces flushed from the wind and pure delight, they arrived at Shane Grogan's office. Gem jumped from the saddle and flipped her long braid over her shoulder as she stepped onto the boardwalk. Chase wrapped the reins of the two saddle horses around a hitching rail and followed Gem toward the office door.

"Hello!" Chase called out as the bell jingled overhead.

No answer followed.

"Hello?" He stepped toward the curtain separating office from living quarters.

"Perhaps they're at the cattle pens," Gem suggested.

"Let's try there."

They had just stepped outside when they saw Molly's short, plump form hurrying in their direction. Her head was bent forward, her calico bonnet shading her eyes. It wasn't until she was stepping onto the boardwalk that she looked up and saw them.

"Oh!" she cried, grabbing at her heart. "My, how you startled me." Then she smiled. "Let me look at you. Yes. I can see it. You're happy as two jaybirds. What brings you to town so soon?"

"You and Grogan," Chase replied with a grin. "To tell the truth, I just needed to see your pretty face."

"Don't you go teasing me, Chase Dupre," she spluttered, pleased by his compliment.

"Where's Grogan?"

"Did you go inside?"

Chase nodded.

"Then he must be sleeping. Come on in."

"Sleeping?" Gem echoed, surprised. "It's the middle of the day."

"Oh, that man of mine went and got himself hurt. Doctor says he'll be up and about in a month or so, but it's driving Mr. Grogan crazy." Molly opened the door as she talked and led them through the office and into her small kitchen. Motioning for them to sit at the table, she said, "I'll just check and see how he's doing." She was gone and already returning before they had time to pull out the chairs from the table. "He wants to see you, Chase. You can come too, Gem."

The Grogans' bedroom was barely large enough for the bed and armoire, let alone three people standing at bedside. Still, they crowded in.

Shane Grogan was a sight. His massive chest was wrapped round and round with bandages, and his right leg was propped with pillows and set with splints. His skin had the pasty pallor of a very sick man, except where it was black and blue with bruises.

"What happened to you, Grogan?" Chase asked, his eyes running the length of his friend.

"Had an argument with a crusty old longhorn. He won."

"So I see. Care to tell me about it?"

"Not much to tell. Steer got a bit upset and I was in the way of his horns. I tried to get out of the pen 'fore he could take another swipe at me, but my leg was too slow. Doc says I got myself a serious puncture, a few broken ribs, and a broken leg. Other than that, I'm fit as a fiddle." Grogan grinned as he finished, then shifted his gaze to Gem. "You're lookin' as pretty as I ever seen you, little tadpole." He tried to change his position, then winced and settled back on the bed. "Chase, I need to ask a favor."

"Sure. Anything, Grogan. You know that."

"The Gypsy Creek herd will be in in another week, and I hear tell that the Davis Bar ain't far behind. I need someone to act for me. If I'm not there to buy, they just might load them cattle into the box cars and take 'em east to sell themselves. I'd lose my business that way." He took a deep breath, wincing once again. "Can you stay around a few more weeks and help me out?"

Chase glanced over at Gem. She nodded slightly.

"Sure, Grogan," he answered as his fingers closed around her hand. "I'll be glad to stay and help out."

"Thanks." Grogan sighed and closed his eyes.

Chase rode into Cheyenne every day. Sometimes Gem went along and spent the day with Molly, sometimes she remained at the Lucky W, talking with Hezekiah Smith while he groomed the horses or reading a book in the library of the mansion. Clara served them supper when Chase returned late in the evening.

Gem thought sometimes that she loved these moments best, the two of them sitting across from one another at the table, the soft glow of candlelight flickering on the tablecloth, Chase sharing with her what had happened that day and she doing the same. They had been married just over two weeks, but it seemed to Gem they had always been together. Sometimes she even knew what he would say before he said it. It was a wonderful feeling to be so much a part of another person, almost as if they shared the same heartbeat, the same thoughts, an extension of each other.

And so the days drifted, one into another.

A chilling wind whistled around the corners of the mansion. Gem wandered from one room to another, feeling lost and adrift. Chase had sent a rider late in the afternoon with a message. He wouldn't be able to return until late the next morning. The Gypsy Creek cattle had arrived, and he didn't think he'd be finished in time to return.

Suddenly the enormous mansion was too enormous. The rooms that had been so much fun to explore with Chase became too many and too empty. The warmth of their honeymoon hideaway was forgotten in the lonely, chilling wind of autumn. Gem wished she had ridden into Cheyenne that morning with Chase, but there was nothing she could do about it now.

She crawled into bed alone. Several times she pounded on the pillows, trying to make them more comfortable, but try as she might, they couldn't comfort her as Chase could. It wasn't just the passion which she'd discovered in his arms that she missed; it was the warmth, the safety of his embrace, the sense of belonging.

She lay in the dark, listening to the rising wind

rattle the windowpanes, and hoped that sleep would come to hurry the night away.

She sat up with a start, her heart galloping in fear. The nightmare left her feeling afraid to move, afraid to get out of bed. She couldn't quite recall what the dream had been about. She only knew the lingering terror. She hugged a pillow to her breast and tried to calm her breathing.

Then her breath stopped altogether. She wasn't alone.

Her eyes peered into the inky darkness of the bedroom, searching for a shadow that was out of place. There was nothing, and yet she knew she wasn't alone.

"Who's there?" she demanded with a voice much more self-assured than she felt.

There was no reply. Nothing moved.

Gem drew another deep breath. She was being silly. She was allowing a nightmare to frighten her even once she was awake. Perhaps if she turned her mind on pleasant thoughts, she could shake off the lingering effects of the nightmare.

She lay back, drawing the warm comforter tight beneath her chin. Well, if she meant to think of pleasant things, she could think of nothing better than her husband. She began by conjuring up the image of his face. Strangely, it wasn't the more mature Chase whom she'd married that Gem pictured in her mind, but a younger Chase, the Chase in the saloon the day she'd first seen him. A confident young man with deep-set blue eyes, dark eyebrows, shaggy brown hair, and chiseled features. The Chase with the quick, easy smile. The Chase she had known before he returned from Texas. The Chase she had first fallen in love with. And then she pictured him as he was upon his return—troubled, angry, hurt, the easy smile hidden away, even the confidence wavering.

She could smile as that image faded, replaced by the man she had known as her husband these past weeks. The gentle hands, the loving embraces, the tender lover, the jester. He was like the old Chase but even better.

She had loved him against all odds, and love had not failed her.

The man's silhouette moved from the darkness of the wall to stand before the window. The moonless night cast no real light into the bedroom; yet his shadow was distinct.

The gasp rose in her throat.

"One by one . . ." The raspy voice seemed as eerie as the howling wind. "One by one, the Dupres will pay."

He pushed the window open and was out onto the veranda roof before she could find her voice. Then she screamed. It was a fear that went deep into her soul and was torn from her lips in a cry of terror.

Before the echo had died in the room, the door crashed open and Thompson raced in, followed quickly by Hezekiah.

"What is it, madam?" Thompson inquired as he lit a lamp.

She pointed. "The . . . the window."

Hezekiah hurried toward the window, looking outside before he closed it against the frigid wind. "It's just the storm."

"No . . . no. A . . . a man. He was here in my room."

The two men exchanged glances just as Clara and Bernice arrived, their faces as white as sheets.

"Take care of the missus," Hezekiah ordered gruffly. "Me'n Thompson'll have a look 'round."

Bernice went quickly to the bed, sitting on the counterpane and placing a protective arm around Gem. "What is it, mum?" she inquired.

Gem drew a deep breath, calming the panic that threatened to rob her of reason. "Something woke me. A bad dream or the wind. There was . . . there was a man in my room."

"Sounds like your bad dream made you see things, mum," Clara said stoically. "I'll get you some warm milk."

"You just lie back, mum, an' I'll tuck you in." Bernice began to plump the pillows behind Gem as she spoke.

"Bernice, please quit fussing. I'm quite all right." She tossed off the bedcovers, refusing to be relegated to the role of the foolish little woman frightened by a storm when her husband's away. "I'm getting dressed."

"Mrs. Dupre, mum. If there's someone out there, wouldn't it be better t'stay inside? Thompson an' Mr. Smith will 'ave a look round an' tell you if they find anythin'."

Gem caught the quiver in the maid's voice and glanced over at her. Her skin was the color of her carefully starched white nightgown, and her pale green eyes were as round as saucers. Gem could almost believe it was Bernice who had had the nightmare and then seen a man in her room. Despite her own eagerness to find the intruder, Gem pulled the blankets back over her legs.

"All right, Bernice. Perhaps you're right. I'll let the men take care of things."

"That's better, mum. You just lie still an' don't give it another thought. Clara'll be 'ere with the 'ot milk in no time at all. I'll just sit 'ere with you an' keep you company."

She spent a restless night tossing and turning in the big bed, hearing again the sandpaper voice . . . *one by one, the Dupres will pay . . . one by one, the Dupres will pay . . . one by one, the Dupres will pay . . .* An old sense of foreboding returned, a twin to the one she'd felt just before Rodney's accident. She racked her brain for a reason for the intruder's threats, but failed to find one.

Questions filled her mind. Who was he? What could he have meant? Why had he come? How did he mean to make them pay?

Thompson and Hezekiah were unable to find any signs of the intruder, either that night or the next morning. Without saying it aloud, Thompson managed to convey that he thought she had dreamed the whole thing.

Well, Gem knew she hadn't, and she meant to find out the truth. She dressed hastily the next morning and began a search of the grounds beneath the bedroom window. There had to be a sign left there someplace. She would just have to look until she found it.

She was down on her knees running her fingers over the ground when Chase cantered into the yard. Before she could rise, she saw Thompson come out of the house to hold Chase's horse. As the butler spoke, Chase frowned and glanced toward Gem, then returned his gaze to the other man. Finally he nodded grimly and began walking in her direction.

Gem brushed the dirt from her hands as she straightened and met his quizzical look with a firm one of her own.

Chase stopped, his hands coming up immediately to grasp her shoulders. "Thompson said there was some sort of trouble here last night?" It was a question, waiting for her explanation.

"You mean Thompson said I had a nightmare and caused a ruckus for the whole place. Chase, I'm not crazy and it wasn't a dream. There *was* a man in my room." Unconsciously she had placed her knuckles on her hips and thrown her head back in a gesture of challenge.

"Whoa, honey," he responded with a chuckle and a quick smile. "I wasn't saying you're crazy." The smile vanished. "If you say there was somebody in your room, I believe you."

She sighed, her tense body relaxing. "Really?"

"Really. Now, you tell me what happened."

Gem glanced up at the veranda and the window of the bedroom. "I don't know what woke me. I'd been having a bad dream, but I don't remember what it was about. I thought right away there was someone in there with me. But I could hear the wind blowing and there was still the nightmare bothering me, so I decided I was just imagining it." She shuddered as she remembered the eerie way he'd appeared before the window and the rasp of his voice. Her eyes flickered back to Chase. She wasn't aware of the paleness of her cheeks where usually there was a splash of color. "It was so dark in our room," she said softly, "I'm surprised I ever saw him. He was just a shadow. He just stood there. And then he said, 'One by one, the Dupres will pay.' Just whispered it, and then he went out the window." She reached up to her shoulder and covered one of her husband's hands with her own. "Chase? What do you suppose he means to do? Who is he?"

Chase frowned as he pulled her close against him. "I don't know, Gem, but I don't want you going out alone anywhere. From now on you're to stay in the house when I'm away. Keep Bernice with you until we find out what's going on. I'm not letting anyone harm the prettiest Dupre we've got. His last sentence was meant as a jest, an effort to dismiss the dark thoughts of danger.

She didn't hear the joking tone of his voice. All she heard was that she was to be kept prisoner in the house. Her eyes sparked dangerously. "Chase Dupre, do you honestly think I'm going to sit in that house while some crazy man is running around out there, threatening Dupres? It's me he scared half witless in the night, and I mean to help find him."

"Yes, it was you he threatened and scared, and that's all the more reason why you're going to do just as I say." Chase's own mouth hardened stubbornly.

"You just try and keep me locked up in that house." She spun around and stalked toward the horse barn, her stomach balled into a tight knot. She didn't know why she'd lost her temper with Chase. She should have been pleased he wanted to protect her. But Gem McBride had never hidden from a fight in her life, and just because she was married, she wasn't about to start now.

A strong hand grabbed her arm and swung her around. "Listen to me, Gem Dupre. When I said I wasn't going to let anything happen to you, I meant it." His sapphire eyes were stormy with anger.

"And I meant it when I said I wasn't going to be locked up in that house. If you want to look out for me, then you'll have to take me with you when you're looking."

Chase was silent, his jaw clenched and his eyes flashing. Slowly the anger began to disappear. He sighed. "I wonder why I thought you'd be any different about this than you were about hunting grizzlies or driving cattle?"

Gem's anger faded just as quickly. "Stubborn, aren't I?"

"As always." He offered a wry smile.

She put her hands on his shoulders, frowning as she said in all seriousness, "It isn't just 'cause I want to find whoever it was that was in our room. He wasn't just threatening *me*. You're a Dupre, too. Somebody's got to look out for you."

"I'm not about to let anything happen to me either, kid," he answered lightly, ruffling her hair as he'd done when she was younger. "I've got too much to live for."

His words were almost an *I love you*, and they made Gem forget for a brief moment, while she stood there in the safety of his embrace, the terror of last night and the stranger's promise of more terror to come.

* * *

They searched the area. They watched for any sign of a threat. Everyone on the Lucky W was on the alert for a stranger, for anything out of the ordinary. One uneventful day followed another until even Gem began to believe that the mysterious intruder had merely been an extension of a nightmare.

30

Gem wasn't feeling well. She hadn't felt quite right for the past week. But tonight they were celebrating, and she wasn't about to say anything to Chase. He would probably put her to bed, and she would miss out on the evening of fun.

Much to everyone's surprise, Shane Grogan was out of bed. He was still hobbling on crutches, but you could hardly say it slowed him down any. Even his cracked ribs didn't seem to bother him.

So tonight, in honor of his miraculous recovery —not to mention that Mr. and Mrs. Chase Dupre had now been married one full month—the Grogans and the Dupres were going to the opera house in Cheyenne to see a performance of *La Traviata*. Gem had never seen an opera before; she didn't have any idea what to expect. But she wasn't about to miss it because of a little nausea and dizziness.

Gem had spent the better part of the week in Cheyenne with the dressmaker. She could hardly wait to see Chase's expression when he saw her in the new creation. In truth, she couldn't believe it herself. Never in her wildest dreams would Gem have thought she would find herself willingly wearing fancy dress clothes to an opera.

She leaned close to the mirror, saying to her reflection, "Being in love must change a girl a lot."

A light tap on the door announced Bernice. "I'd better 'elp you dress, mum. It'll soon be time for you to leave."

Gem turned from the mirror. The yellow and amber dress was draped across Bernice's arms, yards and yards of silk and satin. The maid was grinning in anticipation of helping her visiting mistress. Gem couldn't help but return her smile. It was infectious.

The evening gown had a tight-fitting jacketlike bodice with a full frill of white point duchess lace around the square neckline, a neckline cut low to reveal the gentle swell of firm, white breasts. The three-quarter sleeves were gracefully caught up on the inside of each arm, revealing more lace. The basque was long-waisted, ending in a long, draped apron of Isabelle yellow brocaded satin, the lower edge trimmed with a fringe of amber beads on crimped silk. The apron was caught at the back of her waist, forming a gentle cascade of yellow fabric down to the floor, spilling into a flowing train. Beneath the apron front and under the train, darker golden brown plush was laid in pleats, and a full pleated muslin balayeause was used in the train instead of a separate trained petticoat.

"I've never seen anything so lovely," Bernice

whispered in a reverent tone as she stepped back to survey Gem in her new gown. Then she motioned toward the dressing table. "Sit down, mum, an' I'll do your 'air."

Bernice wove Gem's strawberry and champagne tresses into a coiled chignon, twining two yellow ribbons across the crown of her head. While Gem surveyed the results, the maid fastened another satin ribbon around her throat, catching it with an amber clasp.

"It's nearly as lovely as your wedding gown, mum. An' you've grown even more beautiful since I first saw you."

"Oh, Bernice," Gem said as she rose and turned before the mirror. "I can't believe it's me."

"It's you, all right, mum. 'Ere's your gloves."

Gem obediently slipped her fingers into the soft yellow gloves.

"An' 'ere's your fan." Bernice stepped back from her, beaming from ear to ear. "You 'ave a lovely time, mum."

Gem began to smile, but it faded as she swayed with a sudden dizziness. She groped quickly for the bedpost and clung to it.

"Mum?"

She waved her hand. "I'm all right, Bernice. It's just the excitement." She drew a deep breath, and the world began to right itself. She opened her eyes. She sighed and straightened her shoulders, then tossed the maid a brilliant smile. "I'm going to have a wonderful time, Bernice. Don't worry about me. Good night."

"'Night, mum." The worry was still in Bernice's voice as Gem moved past her and into the hall.

But Gem forgot the moment of faintness as soon as she reached the top of the stairs. Chase was waiting for her, her long coat draped over his arm. Her hand on the railing, she basked in his approving gaze. Then, her yellow satin slippers carried her slowly down the staircase until she paused on the last step.

"I didn't think you could get prettier," he said, his glance running the length of her one more time, "but you do. Every time I see you."

She smiled her thanks.

Chase drew a hand from behind his back. "I hope you'll forgive Molly. She told me the color of your gown. I wanted you to have this." He gave her the small box.

Gem accepted it in silence, her gaze questioning him about the contents before lifting the top to reveal what was inside. A tiny topaz pendant lay on a throne of yellow silk fabric.

"Oh, Chase. It's lovely."

She lifted it from the box, the gold chain draping over her fingers as she admired the sparkling gem.

"I wanted to give you something that would say . . . how special you are to me."

She looked up at him again, hoping that at last he would speak those precious words.

"You've . . . added beauty to my life, Gem. I'll always be grateful." He took the necklace from her hand.

Oh, Chase. I don't want your gratitude, she thought sadly. But this wasn't a night for sadness, and so she smiled at him again, hiding her disappointment.

Chase fastened the clasp of the pendant around her neck, then held out her wrap. She turned her back to him so he could slip it over her shoulders. Then he offered his arm and escorted her out to the waiting carriage. Holding her arm, he assisted her inside, then covered her lap with warm furs before climbing in beside her and taking up the reins.

The three-story opera house was made of pressed brick with stone trimmings. It occupied a prominent place in Cheyenne at the corner of Seventeenth and Hill.

As the two couples entered the auditorium, Gem's eyes were drawn immediately to the grand chandelier hanging thirty-eight feet above the floor. The floor inclined slowly down toward the stage. The velvet curtains were pulled closed, and Gem could only imagine what lay beyond. She was so excited her stomach was a mass of butterflies.

There were four small but elegant boxes in the theater, but the Grogans and Dupres held tickets toward the front and center of the main floor. An usher guided them to their seats. Gem and Chase sat side by side, while Shane Grogan sat on Chase's left and Molly Grogan on Gem's right. Gem was too busy looking around to pay much attention to the conversation of the men, and Molly remained silent, allowing her time for discovery. Her eyes swept up to the gallery, then back to the main floor, then once again to the hidden stage. One by one the seats were occupied as the minutes ticked closer to curtain time.

All of a sudden a violent wave of nausea swept through her. She clenched her hands in her lap and fought down the bitter taste of bile that rose in her throat. She closed her eyes and drew a steadying breath.

"Gem," Molly whispered in her ear, "is something wrong?"

She cast a covert glance in the older woman's direction. "I'm not feeling well. Could we . . ." She swallowed again. ". . . go to the lounge?"

"Of course, dear. I'll just tell the men—"

Gem grasped Molly's forearm and shook her head. "No," she hissed. "I don't want to spoil things. I just need a little air and something to drink."

"Well," Molly agreed doubtfully. "You know best."

Gem turned to her left. "Excuse us, Chase. We're going to step out for a moment."

"Would you like me to come with you?"

"No, dear," she replied with a smile as she rose from her seat.

She held herself erect, her chin high, as she walked down the aisle, unaware of the many admiring glances that came her way. It was enough to concentrate on keeping her balance as dizziness blurred her vision.

She reached the private lounge and sank into a chair with a sigh of relief. A strange ringing filled her ears.

"Gem," she heard Molly begin in a worried tone.

She tried to look at her friend, but Molly's plump face was merely a blur. And then everything went black.

She was riding Wichita across the Montana range, leaning low over the mare's neck, the wind whipping her braid against her back. What wonderful freedom! What joy! And at her side rode Chase. He was laughing and his eyes crinkled up with mirth. They were racing one another like children, carefree and irrepressible. And, oh, so very happy . . .

"Oh my. Oh dear. Gem, dear. Please wake up."

Gem felt quite angry at whoever it was that was drawing her away from her delightful dream. She lifted a hand to wave them away. She wanted to go back to her dream.

"Gem, please, dear. Wake up."

She opened her eyes. Molly was leaning over her, frantically waving her fan above Gem's face. Several other women's faces could be seen crowding around Molly's shoulders.

"What happened?" she asked weakly.

"You fainted, dear," Molly answered, then turned her head to look at the other women. "She's all right. She's fine. Thank you so much for your concern." As the strangers moved away, talking among themselves, Molly handed Gem a glass of water. "Drink this, Gem."

Obediently Gem sipped from the glass. "I've never fainted in my life." She straightened and took a deep breath. Feeling stronger, she was embarrassed by her "case of the vapors." She'd always felt a disdain for fluttery females.

Molly took the glass, then sat down beside Gem. "Are you feeling better now?"

"Yes, Mrs. Grogan. Thanks." She offered a sheepish smile. "I don't know what's been wrong with me lately. I'm never sick. I'm usually as hardy as a horse."

Molly leaned closer. "Are you feeling dizzy often, and no matter what you eat, it just doesn't sit right on your stomach?" Her voice was hushed, giving her words an ominous tone.

Gem nodded, suddenly worried.

"You certainly haven't wasted any time, dear." Molly grinned as she patted Gem's knee.

"Mrs. Grogan, what is it? I don't understand."

"Well, I could be wrong, Gem, but my guess is you're going to present Chase with a little Dupre in about another eight months."

"A baby?" She was stunned. "Are you sure?"

"I'm no doctor, my dear, but it sure sounds like it to me."

"A baby—" This time she said it with wonder, trying out the sound on her tongue. It had a pleasant ring.

She was surprised by the surge of maternal longing that gripped her. She hadn't had any idea she would feel this way. Oh, certainly she had hoped she and Chase would have children one day, but it had only been a thought about something somewhere in the future.

"Chase's baby." She glanced once again at Molly. "He had a son once. Did you know?"

Molly shook her head.

Tears sprang to Gem's eyes. "With his first wife, Consuela. He was born dead. Chase named him Jean after his father." Her fingers tentatively touched her abdomen. "Oh, Mrs. Grogan," she whispered, "I would so like to give him his son."

Molly placed her hand over Gem's, pressing it tightly against Gem's flat stomach. "It looks like you've got a good chance of doing just that, my dear. Now, do you feel good enough to go enjoy the show or should we call it a night?"

"Oh, no! I want to see the opera. And, Mrs. Grogan?" She rose from the chair. "Please don't say anything to Chase. I want to surprise him."

"Don't worry. If I know men, he'll be good and surprised, no matter when you tell him."

The night was a dazzling blur to Gem. With one part of her brain she watched and enjoyed the opera, but with the other she played with her joyous secret, turning the words over again and again in her mind. *Chase's baby. Chase's baby. Chase's baby.* It was so utterly glorious.

After the performance they had a late supper at the Inter Ocean Hotel where Molly and Grogan toasted the newlyweds several times, then Chase and Gem climbed into their carriage and began the long ride back to the Lucky W Ranch.

The night was clear and cold. Stars studded the black sky like tiny jewels on a velvet cloth. A silvery crescent moon hung over the distant horizon. Gem thought how beautiful everything looked, and wondered if it was really so lovely or if it was just her mood.

"You've been awfully quiet all evening, honey. Are you feeling all right?"

She snuggled up against him, hooking her arm through his as she laid her head on his shoulder. "I feel wonderful."

She felt his small shrug, as if he were saying there was no figuring women, and she grinned to herself.

"Hey, giddup there," Chase called to the horse as he slapped the reins lightly against its rump.

Should she tell him now? No, Gem wanted it to be sometime special. Perhaps she should wait until she'd seen a doctor. Mrs. Grogan could be wrong. But Mrs. Grogan wasn't wrong. Gem was sure of it. She should have realized she was late with her monthly flow. It was silly of her not to have put that together with the way she'd been feeling and surmise her own condition.

No, Mrs. Grogan wasn't wrong. She knew Chase's seed was growing inside her, slowly being shaped into a tiny human being. It made her feel so very special, knowing it was her body that would shelter and nurture it until it was ready to enter this world.

She lifted her head from his shoulder. "Chase—"

The carriage lurched suddenly. She grabbed for the side, but her hand caught only air as she was thrown from the carriage into the darkness.

The baby, she thought, clutching her abdomen as she flew toward the ground.

31

Chase grabbed for her, but it was too late. After that, things happened quickly. He heard the startled cry of the horse and felt the carriage flipping onto its side. Pushing off with his feet, he jumped free. He hit the ground with force, knocking the wind from him, then rolled over several times. Once he stopped, he lay still for a moment, dragging oxygen into his lungs, his head spinning. He staggered to his feet.

"Gem!" He tried to call, but the sound was hollow.

Another deep breath and his head began to clear. Peering into the darkness, he hurried back along the road.

"Gem!"

Gem lay still, testing her body for pain. Her first anxious thoughts were for the baby, just as they had been when she felt herself being thrown from the carriage, but she seemed to be all right. She sat up and pushed her tangled hair away from her face, wincing as she found a tiny cut above her eyebrow. She heard Chase's breathless cry and tried to stand, then tripped and fell back to the earth.

"Dad-blamed dress," she muttered, kicking to free her feet from the voluminous yards of satin. "I'm over here," she answered sharply as his voice carried through the night, stronger this time.

She heard his footsteps approaching as she continued the fight to untangle herself from her gown.

"Gem, are you hurt?" Chase asked, kneeling beside her.

"I'd be better if I was wearing something other than this darn thing," she grumbled. "Just get me up out of this mess."

He clasped strong hands onto her arms and pulled her to her feet. "Well, I'm glad to see our little accident hasn't affected your good humor." He chuckled.

Gem tossed him a scathing glance. But the laughter in his voice worked its charm despite her annoyance. It was impossible for her to stay angry. After all, they could have been hurt, even killed, but they hadn't been. They were both all right . . . and so was Chase's baby. She mirrored the grin she knew he wore. "Sorry. Didn't mean to bark at you. What happened anyway?"

"I'm not sure. Let's have a look." Chase placed his hand beneath her elbow and drew her along with him.

They found the carriage on its side, one wheel missing and the axle twisted. The shaft had broken free, and the horse stood nearby, traces dragging the ground. The animal was holding a front leg gamely off the ground. Looking at the leg, Gem realized just how lucky they had been, and whispered a prayer of thanks.

Chase freed the horse from the harness, then tied him to the overturned carriage. "We'll send someone for him in the morning," he said as he turned toward his wife. "Care for a late night stroll, Mrs. Dupre?"

He sat on his horse in the darkness, a pleased grin creasing his grotesque features beneath his black hood. He had hoped the wheel would give when they were a little farther from the ranch, when they were traveling a little faster. Still, the results were satisfactory. He hadn't meant for either of them to be killed. Not yet. No, he was saving that for later.

After the long walk back to the ranch, the couple climbed into bed and fell instantly asleep, but Gem came slowly awake before the dawn, her body snuggled close against Chase's back. She nestled her cheek against the nape of his neck and allowed her thoughts to drift once more to the discovery made last evening.

Chase's baby. His son. Their son. The heir to Four Winds. He would be tall like his father. In fact, he would be just like his father in every way. She wouldn't stand for anything different. Chase was perfect, and so would their son be.

When should she tell him? When they got back to the ranch? Before they left the Lucky W? She had been about to tell him last night. Perhaps right now would be a good time.

Her fingers began to run lightly over his chest,

tangling in the light mat of dark hair, then trailing to the hard plane of his belly. Without realizing she was doing so, she moved her lips lightly over his neck, pressing herself closer to him.

"Good morning, Mrs. Dupre," Chase said in a sleepy-husky voice. "I like the way you wake a man up." He rolled over quickly and drew her into his tight embrace. He looked at her from beneath heavy eyelids, a pleased curve turning his mouth. His hand stroked her back as moments before hers had stroked his chest.

She felt the delightful tingles begin to race up her spine and the familiar warmth spreading through her veins. How she loved the way he made her feel. Gem had always known she wanted to be his woman, that she wanted to belong to him, love him, unite with him, bear his children. But she had never imagined what a total, eclipsing experience the coupling of man and woman could be. Instinctively she knew that it could only be this way for her with the man she loved, with Chase.

Now. Now was the moment to tell him about the baby.

She tried to pull back from him. "Chase, darling. I have something—"

His kiss cut her words short, and soon she'd forgotten what it was she had wanted to tell him.

"Chase?"
"Hmmm?"

His dark locks tickled her chin as he lay with his head nestled above her breasts, their bodies languid as the morning light began to fill the bedroom.

"Chase, I want to go home to Four Winds."

His hand began to trace lazy circles around her navel. "Right now?"

"I'm serious, Chase." Her fingers raked through his hair, then dropped to his shoulders. "I want to go home."

Chase shifted his body, drawing his head up onto the pillow so he could look into her eyes. "I'm serious too. Grogan told me last night he could handle things. I'm free to leave whenever you're ready."

Her heart quickened when he looked at her that way. She could see the tenderness so clearly, read the love written in their blue depths. How she longed to hear him say the words aloud. She didn't want it to matter so much that he say them, but it did. She wanted him to confess his love with those three precious little words. She was suddenly afraid that if he didn't tell her before he found out about the baby he never would speak of his love. All his devotion, all his care, all his love would go to their son.

Her decision was made. She wouldn't tell him yet about the baby. She would wait a little longer, try a little harder, show him how easy it was to speak the words aloud. Once they were home at Four Winds, it would happen. She was certain it would happen there.

"I want to go home, Chase," she told him softly. "Let's say good-bye to the Grogans and leave right away."

He nibbled her ear. "As you wish, ma'am."

"Chase?" Her eyes drifted closed once more.

"Hmmm?"

She had been going to tell him she loved him, but she couldn't. She couldn't bear to hear him say one more time that he knew she loved him instead of telling her he loved her too.

"Nothing," she whispered.

And then his hands began moving across her smooth flesh once more, and she could forget, if only temporarily, the small ache in her heart.

"We'll miss 'avin' you 'ere, we will," Bernice said, dabbing her eyes with a handkerchief.

Even Clara's eyes were suspiciously misty.

"It's been a pleasure serving you, sir." Thompson bowed his head stiffly and shook Chase's hand.

Gem impulsively leaned forward and kissed first Bernice's cheek and then Clara's. "You've been very good to us," she said. "Thank you so much."

Clara looked askance at the show of affection. "You must come again when the master is here."

"We'll try," Gem promised, then turned with Chase and left the veranda.

Feeling comfortable once again in her riding skirt and boots, Gem swung easily into the saddle, knowing that if she looked up she would see Thompson and Clara watching her with disapproving gazes. After all, a proper lady would never ride astride, let alone be seen in such deplorable clothing.

The day was overcast and cold as they cantered their horses toward Cheyenne from the Lucky W for the last time. They paused briefly beside the site of the previous night's accident. The men from the ranch had already pushed the remains of the carriage off the road and taken the injured horse back to the stables, and Chase could find no more reason for the accident in the daylight than he'd been able to surmise the night before.

Their eyes met, each of them silently acknowledging how much worse it could have been.

"We'd better get a move on," Chase said at last. "We've got a lot of ground to cover in the next few weeks. We'll be lucky as it is to beat the snows."

They arrived in Cheyenne just before noon. Chase stopped at the mercantile to replenish their supplies for the journey home, and Gem rode on to the Grogans'. Molly was in her kitchen.

"Oh, look at you, my dear," she exclaimed when she saw Gem. "There's color back in your cheeks."

"I'm feeling wonderful this morning, Mrs. Grogan. Just wonderful. We're headed home today."

"Today! But you never said a word last night."

Gem sat down at the table. "I didn't know I was pregnant until last night. I want to be at Four Winds before I tell Chase."

"Oh my," Molly said in a sigh. She sank into a chair across from Gem, wiping flour onto her apron. "You haven't told Chase?"

"No."

"But surely you're going to take that terrible trip by coach instead of on horseback?"

Gem leaned across the table and patted Molly's hand. "I'll be all right, Mrs. Grogan. Really I will. I'm young and I'm strong. And I promise I'll be careful. I've been riding horses all my life . . . Well, nearly all my life."

"But you've never been carrying a chi d before while you were doing it," Molly protested with a frown. She shook her head solemnly. "I think you're wrong not to tell him."

"I can't. I just can't tell him yet."

Molly rose once again from the table, returning

to her baking. "Well, I suppose you know what's best, dear. I don't know. I just don't know . . ." She continued to shake her head as her voice drifted away.

The tinkle of the office bell intruded on Gem's response, followed by Grogan's boisterous voice.

"Molly! Is the little tadpole in there?"

"I'm here, Mr. Grogan," Gem called back as she stood.

Grogan pushed aside the curtain and hobbled into the kitchen, making it seem smaller just by his presence. Chase followed after him.

"Chase here tells me you're leavin' us. Is that right, tadpole?"

"It's time we went home," she answered.

He gave her a tight bear hug. "We're going to miss you. Kinda got used to having the two of you around."

"We'll be back, Mr. Grogan."

"I'm not so sure." Grogan looked over Gem's head at Chase. "The way the cattle and cattlemen are pourin' into the territory, it's not gonna pay you to bring your herd down this way. You'll be puttin' 'em right on the train in your own backyard and shippin' 'em to Chicago."

"But we—" Gem began, but something in Chase's face told her Grogan was telling the truth. Things were changing, and changing very quickly. It had never occurred to her that they wouldn't return to Cheyenne at the end of every season.

"We'd better go, Gem," Chase urged gently.

She nodded, then stood on tiptoe and kissed Grogan's cheek. "I'll miss you, Mr. Grogan. But we'll be back someday. I promise."

"You do that, tadpole."

Gem went over to Molly and gave her a warm hug, whispering in her ear, "I'll write you about the baby."

Molly returned the hug. "You'd better, my dear. You'd better." She patted Gem's cheek with a floury hand, then turned back to her dough, sniffling.

Gem hurried on out of the kitchen, fighting her own tears, wondering how you could be so glad to be going home and yet so sad to be leaving where you were. She didn't hear Molly's farewell to Chase.

"You take it slow goin' home, Chase Dupre," Molly hastened to say as she hugged him. "Gem's not said anything to you, but she's . . . she's not feelin' well."

Chase raised an eyebrow. "She's not? But . . ."

"I don't care about your buts. You just make it an easy trip back to your ranch. And don't you dare tell her I said so."

"Maybe we shouldn't leave until she's better. Maybe she should see a doctor."

Molly looked shocked. "Heavens, no! She'll be madder than a wet hen if she finds out I said a word. Now you listen to me. I've taken care of my share of sick folk. Isn't anything wrong with her that time and a little tender care won't cure. She doesn't need a doctor and she doesn't need to stay here. You just take her on home without pushin' her too hard."

Chase was confused but could do little else than promise he would do just that. He walked on out to the boardwalk, his eyes quickly lighting on Gem. She was already in the saddle, her wide-brimmed hat pulled low on her forehead, her coat fastened up high against the wind. She looked as hale and hardy as he'd ever seen her. But if Molly said . . .

He stepped down from the boardwalk, pausing beside Gem's horse. He placed a hand on her thigh and looked up at her. "Maybe we should wait and get an early start tomorrow. We could stay at the hotel."

Gem shook her head. "No. Let's go now. If we ride hard, maybe we can beat the snows and be home before the middle of November."

Chase nodded and grinned. Molly must be wrong. Gem never looked better to him, and together they were going home.

32

They had been on the trail for nearly two weeks. They should have been almost back to the ranch by now, but for some reason Gem couldn't figure, Chase was taking his time. If the weather was warmer or if there were a few more places to stay along the way, perhaps she wouldn't have minded his dawdling, but as it was, she awoke in the mornings chilled clear to the bones. She felt grumpy and irritable. She was managing to hide her nausea and dizzy spells from him, but it wasn't easy and she would like it a whole lot better if they were home.

Low clouds hung in a gray mist over the nearby mountains as the day neared its end. An icy wind whistled across the high mountain valley, carrying with it the smell of snow. Like a turtle, Gem pulled her head deeper inside her coat collar and wished for someplace warm to spend the night.

As if in answer to her silent wishing, Chase pulled back on Dodge's reins and pointed. "Over there. A cabin. Come on. We'll see if we can sleep in their shed or something."

Her fingers were too cold to do much to guide Wichita. She nudged the mare with her boots and counted on her to follow after Dodge.

Chase stopped once again as they neared the homestead. They could see smoke curling from the chimney. There were no windows in the tiny log cabin, but it looked tight. A small shed and corral were off to one side.

"Hello!" Chase called, giving those inside warning of their presence. He waited a moment, then pressed his mount forward. "Hello inside."

The door opened a fraction. A rifle barrel protruded through the opening. Chase stopped abruptly, and Gem nearly ran into him.

"Please," Chase said above the wind. "We're cold and need a place to stay for the night. We don't want to put you out any. Can we just stay in your shed?"

The rifle disappeared. Chase and Gem waited. Even as they sat there, the temperature seemed to drop another five degrees. Then the door opened a little more. Finally it opened far enough for a woman to step outside. It was an Indian woman, wrapped in several blankets. With a hand she motioned for them to come inside.

Gem grasped the saddle horn and clung to it as her legs slid to the earth. She was afraid they wouldn't hold her after so many freezing hours on horseback. Chase grasped her elbow and hurried her toward the door.

"Wel . . . come," the Indian woman said in a deep voice as she waved them inside.

As soon as she stepped through the door, Gem's nostrils were assaulted with the pungent smell of frying pork, mixed with dense smoke from the fire. Her stomach protested quickly and violently. With a hand to her mouth, Gem wheeled and raced back outdoors. She fell to her knees on the frigid ground and promptly lost all she had eaten that day.

"Gem?" Chase's hand touched her back.

She hated for him to see her this way. "I'm all right, Chase. Go back inside. I'll be in in a minute."

"No, I'll . . ."

"Go back inside," she snapped as perspiration beaded her forehead and her stomach wrenched her insides a second time.

Chase remained.

Tears ran down her cheeks as she sat back on her haunches, drawing a deep breath. "If you must stay," she whispered hoarsely, "make yourself useful. I need a drink of water."

She waited, shivering in the cold, yet feeling sweaty inside her coat. With shaking hands she accepted the tin cup he returned with and raised it to her lips, sipping slowly, washing away the vile taste that lingered in her mouth. Then she started to rise. His hands were immediately there to aid her. She glanced up at him, her eyes still watering.

"I'm okay. Really."

Chase was frowning ferociously.

Once more they stepped into the cabin. She braced herself for the smell, and this time curbed her initial response to the unpleasant odors that filled the room.

A man, probably no older than Chase, was lying on a pallet, braced against the wall near the fire. Beneath the blanket they could see the shape of only one leg. His face was bearded, his black hair hanging past his shoulders. "Welcome. I'm Parker Evans. This here's my wife, Deer Woman."

Chase removed his hat. "Chase Dupre. My wife, Gem. We appreciate your hospitality, Mr. Evans."

"Never no mind. Glad t'have some company. Been a while since we seen any white folk here. Deer Woman, fix 'em some vittles."

Gem felt herself growing pale. "Nothing for me, thanks," she mumbled.

Parker pointed toward a chair opposite him. "Your wife don't look too good, Dupre. You'd better set her down."

"Gem?"

"I'm fine, Chase. Really—" The floor rolled beneath her feet, then rose suddenly toward her face.

Chase barely caught her in time. He scooped her into his arms. Her head fell back. Her hat dropped to the floor, freeing her long braid.

"Put her on them blankets there," Parker ordered from his pallet. "Deer Woman, get her some more water."

Chase laid her carefully on the blankets against the wall. He brushed aside the stray tendrils of hair. He held her cold fingers between the palms of his hands, rubbing them gently. He'd never seen anyone look so pale. What was wrong with her? Molly had warned him she wasn't well, and he had gone easy on her. Any normal year they would've almost been home by now. But had he not gone slow enough?

"Gem?"

What would he do if he lost her? He could never bear it. She'd brought a ray of sunshine into his dark and dreary world. She'd given him back laughter. She was life itself to him.

When had she come to mean everything to him? Today? Last week? Their wedding day? During the cattle drive? When she nursed him back to health? Or much, much before? Perhaps the day he'd won her in that poker game and she'd looked at him with those lovely, angry cat's eyes of hers and swore at him for packing her out of town over his shoulders.

"Gem?"

He loved her. He'd known he loved her for weeks now, but he'd never told her so. It was dangerous to love a woman. He'd learned that. And the more you loved, the more hurt you risked. It would be better if he didn't love. But it was too late now. He loved her more than life itself. Would she die without knowing he returned her love? He would never forgive himself if that happened. He would rather die with her.

"Gem, honey?"

Sooty lashes flickered on pale cheeks, then fluttered open to reveal dazed blue-green eyes. "What happened?"

"You fainted."

"Again?" she sighed, her eyelids closing.

What did she mean, *again*?

"Water." The squaw handed him the tin cup, filled to the brim.

Chase slid his hand beneath Gem's neck and lifted her head. "Drink this," he commanded gruffly.

She opened her eyes once more, her gaze still glazed and blank. But she drank, and by the time he laid her down again, she seemed to be coherent.

"Please don't look so worried," she told him softly.

He leaned down close to her face. "What's wrong with you, Gem?"

Gem's eyes looked beyond him to the watching Indian woman, then returned to her husband. "I'd really hoped to get home before telling you."

"Molly told me you were sick. I should've kept you in Cheyenne. I should've made you see a doctor. I'll never forgive myself if—"

"Chase." Her fingers lifted to cover his lips, silencing his self-recriminations. "There's not a thing a doctor could do for me. Not for several months anyway."

There was a pain in his heart. Nothing a doctor could do . . .

Gem smiled. It was a smile that brought warmth into her blue-green eyes. "Chase, darling, you're going to be a father."

He stared at her as if she'd lost her mind. "A father?" he echoed stupidly.

She laughed, and color returned to her pale cheeks. "Yes. A father. You know, Chase. A baby. Yours and mine."

A grin spread slowly across his mouth. "A father!" He pulled her into his arms as he began to laugh with her. He held her there and held her there, rocking back and forth and letting the joy spread through him. She wasn't sick and dying. She was pregnant with his child. Suddenly he sobered and lowered her gently back onto the blankets. "We've got to get you home to Four Winds right away."

"That's what I've been trying to do."

"We should have left Cheyenne right after the wedding."

"I wasn't expecting right after the wedding," she reminded him, and then blushed.

Chase cupped her cheek with his hand. His blue eyes darkened with emotion. "There's something I should've told you before, too."

He glanced over his shoulder at Parker Evans and his wife, wondering if now was the time. But when he looked at Gem again, he knew that any time was a good time to tell her what he had to say.

"Gem, I—" His voice caught as he gazed down at her. Her love shone brightly in twin orbs of aquamarine, guileless, without reservation, trusting. How had he ever won such love from this woman? How had he ever been so lucky to have earned her for his wife? "Gem, I . . ."

Gem waited breathlessly, knowing that at last he was ready to speak aloud the words she'd longed to hear.

The cabin door burst open in the midst of that breathless waiting. Gem's startled cry was whipped away by the rush of wind swirling through the open doorway. Chase twisted, his hand moving toward his gun, but it was already too late. The two men, bundled in furs, were already inside, their rifles aimed and ready, one of them pointed at Chase's head.

"Looky what we got here." The taller of the two men stepped toward the pallet where Deer Woman stood protectively before her husband. "We got us a squaw man an' his woman. I always did like me . . ."

But Gem wasn't listening. She was staring at the black hood over the other man's face. Her fingers tightened on Chase's arm. "It's him," she whispered.

"Get away from the squaw, Brown," the hooded man's raspy voice commanded. "You can have time for that later. Get rid of his gun. And that rifle over there, too. Tie their hands, then take 'em out to the shed." Eyes peered at Gem from behind the slits in the hood. "All but the little gal there."

Chase tensed, but there was nothing he could do. The man called Brown was upon him, wrapping a rope around his wrists and jerking it tight. Brown hauled Chase to his feet, then pulled him across the room.

"Hey! The squaw man's only got but one leg," Brown informed his leader. "How'm I supposed to get him out to the barn?"

"Drag him if you have to."

Gem sat up straight, her back pressed against the cabin wall. She could feel the hooded man's eyes upon her, but she refused to look at him. She kept her gaze fastened upon Chase, praying that he wouldn't do anything foolish.

Deer Woman shook off Brown's attempts to tie her wrists together. "I will help my husband," she said in stilted English. She lifted Parker Evans from his pallet, supporting his right side while he stood on his left leg.

"All right. Let's go." Brown led his three captives toward the open door.

Chase stopped beside the hooded man, jerking back on the rope that pulled him forward. "If you harm her, I'll hunt you down if it takes all my life."

A mocking laughter rose from the stranger's

throat. "I'm countin' on it, Dupre." Then he put the barrel of his rifle between Chase's shoulder blades and shoved him out the door, saying before he closed it, "Keep a close eye on 'em, Brown. And leave that Injun alone. You can get your fill of that some other time."

Gem watched with wary eyes as he slowly turned around. With measured steps he approached her.

"Are you frightened, Gem?" he asked.

His rasping voice grated on her nerves like fingernails on a chalkboard. She cringed internally but refused to let her fear show on her face. She lifted her chin and stared at him, half-wishing she could see his eyes behind the mask and half-thankful that she couldn't. "How do you know my name?" she demanded, surprising even herself that her voice didn't quiver.

"I know a lot about you. You'd be surprised." Gloved fingers stretched out to touch her throat.

Gem gasped and pressed herself harder against the wall at her back.

"Take off your coat, Gem. It's warm in here."

"I'm fine, thanks."

Chuckling once again, he backed away from her, leaving his rifle against the wall as he shucked his fur coat. He was clad all in black from his hood to his boots. Gem studied him, trying to find some clue to his identity. He wasn't tall like Chase, but he was big, broad-shouldered, and bulky in build. But that wasn't enough. There could be any number of men like that. Without being able to see his face or his eyes or his hair, she had no hope of learning who he was or why he held them captive.

"You can't guess who I am, can you?" he asked in his sandpaper voice.

Ignoring his question, she asked one of her own. "Why do you want to hurt us?"

"I have my reasons." He leveled the rifle at her forehead. "Take off your coat."

Would it be better to die than to submit? she wondered. But there was Chase's baby to think about, and there was Chase himself. There was still hope the stranger wouldn't defile her. She did as she was told.

"I watched you bathin' in the river."

Her eyes widened. "When?"

"During the drive."

A cold feeling washed over her. "You've been following us for so long?"

"You've got the prettiest white skin. Unbutton your blouse there, Gem, and let me see some of that pretty white skin."

"Why are you doing this?" she asked, swallowing the tears that threatened to swell in her eyes.

Again he laughed as he motioned with the rifle for her to obey.

Her fingers shook as she fought the buttons of her blouse. Her blurred gaze fell to the floor. Her breathing seemed labored. When her blouse was open down the front, she let her hands fall limply to her lap. She waited.

Suddenly his hand was beneath her chin, forcing her head back and her eyes to return to his ominous black hood. "That's enough for now, Mrs. Dupre. I don't aim to taste your pleasures in a smoky cabin smellin' of pork and squaw. You just remember that there'll be more. I'll see you as naked as I seen you before, but next time I'll be naked too."

"Chase'll kill you," she said breathlessly.

He chuckled.

Anger and humiliation sparked, overruling her fear. She pulled her blouse closed with white-knuckled fingers. "And if he doesn't kill you, I will."

He stepped backward toward the door. "You'll have to know who I am first. Do you wonder who I am, Gem?"

"I won't have to know," she replied, her voice low, her eyes flashing. "I can follow the smell of a skunk anywhere."

He stopped his retreat. His throaty whisper was laced with anger. "That's only one of the things you'll regret when it's your turn to pay, Gem Dupre." He opened the door. "Brown!" he yelled above the wind.

"Yeah?"

"Make sure they can't follow us, then get the horses."

Gem shivered as the frigid November air filled the cabin once again. She longed to reach for her coat but refused to allow her hands to do so. Not as long as he was standing there watching her. She would continue to return his gaze with eyes filled with loathing.

It seemed to take forever before Brown led the saddle horses up to the cabin, but at last the hooded stranger turned to leave. Then he looked back at her, saying, "You'll never know when I'll be there. But I'll be there. When something happens to a Dupre, you'll know it was me. It may be next week or next year, but your turn will come." He paused. "One by one, the Dupres will pay."

What did we do? she wanted to demand. How did the Dupres harm you? she wanted to ask. But she couldn't. In a mind so filled with hate, the reasons could be nonexistent.

"Good evenin', Miz Dupre."

The door slammed shut. She stared at it, gulping in deep breaths of air, feeling the fear flooding through her. Tremors shook her body as tears ran down her cheeks. With quivering hands she pulled on her coat and hurried toward the door. She opened it cautiously, but there was no one to be seen, so she let it fly wide and raced toward the shed.

"Chase!" she cried. "Chase!"

She pushed the door open before her. She stopped, letting her eyes become accustomed to the dim light of the shed. And then she was almost sorry when she could see.

Chase lay unconscious on the floor, a smear of blood on the side of his head. Deer Woman was kneeling beside him. Parker Evans, his hands tied behind his back, was seated in some straw in an empty stall.

"No!" Gem gasped. "Chase!" Could her worst nightmare have come true?

Deer Woman looked up as Gem rushed toward them. "He is not dead."

Gem fell to her knees beside Chase's inert form. She touched the bloody wound near his temple.

"That Brown fella hit him with his rifle butt." Parker Evans said. "He was goin' after my woman, an' your man tried to stop him. Weren't much he coulda done with his hands all tied up, but he tried." He shifted in the straw. "Deer Woman, git over here and untie me."

Gem cradled Chase's head in her lap, only half-listening to Parker Evans' explanation. "I knew you'd do somethin' foolish," she said softly.

His eyelids moved. She heard his sharp intake of breath, then his hand came slowly up from his side to touch his head. He winced. One eye opened very carefully. "Gem—" he said, then closed his eye again.

"I'm all right, Chase. He didn't hurt me."

"I thought he—"

"He didn't."

He winced again as he moved his fingers over the side of his head. "Are they gone?"

"They're gone."

Parker Evans hopped toward them, leaning on Deer Woman's shoulders. "You stay here while I get up to the house. Deer Woman'll come back and help you get him inside."

Gem nodded, her eyes not leaving Chase's face. "I knew you'd do something foolish," she repeated, bending down to kiss his forehead.

A wan grin curved his mouth as his brows drew together in a frown. "Couldn't help myself." He groaned and opened both eyes. "You sure you're okay?"

She nodded. "He didn't do anything except threaten."

He sat up, shaking his head as if to clear it.

"Sit still, Chase. Deer Woman will be right back." She put her arm around him.

Chase looked at her, their faces only inches apart. "I don't know who he is, but I'm going to kill him," he said with quiet determination.

"Shh. Don't talk about that now. We're both all right. That's all that matters."

"Gem?"

"Yes?"

"I love you."

It came so simply. She had pictured his declaration of love in many ways and in many places, but she'd never imagined hearing the words in a place like this or at a time like this. She sought for something special to say, something to let him know what his words meant to her.

"And I love you, Chase Dupre," she returned softly.

It was enough for now.

They lay in each other's arms throughout the long night that followed. Neither slept much. Both were very much aware of how lucky they were. Things could have turned out so differently. Gem could have been raped. Chase could have been killed. And so each held onto the other, grateful they would be together in the morning.

Gem listened to the wind howling around the corner of the log cabin. She knew it must be snowing. Tomorrow they must begin an arduous journey home, pushing themselves hard to reach Four Winds as quickly as possible. Chase would be reluctant to move as quickly as they should, now that he knew she was pregnant, but they had to get home. The man in the black hood hadn't threatened only them; he had also threatened the rest of the Dupres. They had to get home.

Chase's arm tightened around her, drawing her closer to him. She wondered if he was awake, but she didn't speak. She wished they were alone in the cabin. She wished she could shed the rest of her clothes and feel the warmth of his skin against hers. She wished they could make love.

She pressed her cheek against his chest and closed her eyes, breathing a silent prayer of thanks that he was alive, that she was his wife, and that he loved her. Knowing she had his love, without reservation, would make it easier to face whatever difficulties life brought in the days to come.

Chase listened to her breathing, felt her move willingly into his embrace, and knew she was awake. But he didn't speak. He preferred to lay in silence, enjoying the simple beauty, the simple miracle, of having her in his arms.

The time he had spent in the shed last evening had been the worst of his life. He had imagined so many terrible things. He had wanted to strike out, to maim, to kill. He had blamed himself for being careless. He had blamed himself for not doing more to find the man who had invaded Gem's room while he was in Cheyenne. And when there was nothing he could do to help her, to save her, he had felt an agony beyond description.

He didn't know why the stranger had spared them, but he thanked God that he had. Now, it was up to Chase to make certain nothing could ever happen to Gem. She must be kept safe from such threats. If he should ever lose her . . .

His lips brushed the top of her head. *I love you*, he mouthed silently and smiled at the new freedom he enjoyed in saying so.

The snows came with fury. The snows came and remained.

Through the high Montana passes and rolling Montana valleys, they pushed toward home. During the day the big pinto gelding and the smaller pinto mare lunged through the deep drifts and slid down slick hillsides and gullies. Chase never relaxed, always on the alert for trouble from the man in the black hood, always wondering if he was asking too much from Gem. At night he found whatever shelter he could, wrapping Gem in his arms to share his warmth and hoping the next day would see them closer to Four Winds.

Time seemed to stand still. Each mile was gained with agonizing slowness. The temperatures continued to drop. The snow continued to fall. And they continued to push toward home.

33

As if from a bad dream, Enid awoke with a start, her heart racing. Outside, a sharp wind howled through the pines and shook the eaves of the house. It was snowing again. She could hear the snowflakes stinging the windowpanes.

She lay in the dark listening to these sounds, mingled with the gentle snoring of her husband, and sought to draw comfort from them. But comfort wouldn't come. Something unusual had awakened her. Some sound not in keeping with the usual night sounds.

She reached for her robe as she slid her legs over the side of the bed. On bare feet she padded across the bedroom and opened the door, listening. Nothing. Only the wind.

Enid began to turn away, ready to close the door and return to her bed, when she heard it again. A creaking sound, like the sound of a rocking chair. She stepped into the hall and closed the bedroom door, straining even harder to trace the sound. It was coming from Chase's room. Had a window been left open?

She hurried down the hall, not needing a lamp to light her way. She had walked this hallway in darkness for many years. As she neared the bedroom, the sound grew louder. It was indeed the rocking chair. Had she aired the room and forgotten to close the window? Oh, she must be getting old if she was forgetting such things. She opened the door and stepped in, her feet carrying her almost to the window before she realized it was closed.

"Evenin', Miz Dupre."

Enid gasped and whirled around as the whispery voice carried across the room. "Who's there?"

"Sit down, Miz Dupre."

She clutched her robe in front of her as she edged toward the bedroom door.

The intruder was there before her, closing it softly. "I said sit down, ma'am." A match flickered to life. He held it in his gloved fingers, lifting it so the light fell briefly upon his black hood. Then he put it to the lamp near the door.

Enid sat on the edge of Chase's bed, her hands clenched in her lap. There was no one in the house except she and Frank. Katie no longer lived in the little house out back; she and Maggie had left Four Winds two weeks before to go live with her parents in Missouri. The men had all retired to the bunkhouse hours ago. With the wind blowing as it was, no one would hear her even if she screamed. There was little she could do but hear him out and hope for the best.

"Who are you, mister, and what do you want here?" She was pleased with the calm tone of her voice.

"I never had much use for you Dupres. Always more uppity than other folks. Always thinkin' you was better." He picked up the lamp and carried it toward the bed. "Never saw much to look at in you neither. Tall and wiry. No meat on you. I like more substance to my women." He turned away, returning to the rocking chair. He set the lamp on a table, then settled his large body into the chair and began to rock. It creaked a steady rhythm against the floor.

Enid quelled the shiver his perusal had sent through her. There was something familiar about him despite his disguise. Enid stared hard, trying to figure out his identity.

"You're wonderin' who I am, ain't you, Miz Dupre? In time. You'll know in time."

"Why do you hide behind that mask if you don't care if I know who you are?"

Again he ignored her. "Four Winds is gonna be mine. Some day soon. It was meant to be mine."

"You're very wrong there, mister. Four Winds will always belong to the Dupres."

The rocking stilled. "Look at the lamp, Miz Dupre. See how pretty it is. Fire's a right pretty thing. I've always liked a fire. All yellow and orange and red and white. And real hot, too."

The fear returned to flow through Enid's veins in an icy torrent.

His rasping voice continued. "You know, my pa never did have the gumption to get what he wanted here. Like I said, I don't know why he wanted it. You ain't nothin' to look at, and this here house ain't

nothing special. But this land . . . this land and the
cattle. Look at the flame in the lamp, Miz Dupre. It's
pretty, ain't it. I told her that when the fire came. I
told her to look at it, to watch it. If she hadn't run
off . . . She was my woman, you know. All hot-
blooded and mine. Like a fire. Just like a fire."

Enid stood and stepped toward him. "May
I . . . may I get something for you? A drink, perhaps?"

"Sit down, Miz Dupre." The voice was deeper,
harsher this time.

She couldn't see any gun. If she moved quickly,
perhaps she could make it to her bedroom. Frank
always kept his gun beside the bed. She backed away
from him, but not toward the bed. She heard the click
as the revolver hammer was drawn back before she
saw the silvery gleam in the lamplight.

"Sit down," he warned once again.

He was crazy. Whoever he was, he was stark
raving mad. There had to be some way to get away
from him. All those men in the bunkhouse. If she
could only make enough noise to draw someone's
attention.

"He's got himself a new wife now. But you
know that, don't you. Always thought she was kinda
cute, but not much to her. He'll get to see what I do
to her. I want him to see. I want him to pay. If he'd
let her come to me, she wouldn't be dead now."

It was all a jumble. Nothing made any sense to
Enid. Her nerves were screaming. "Please. What is it
you want?"

He seemed to hear her this time. He stood and
walked over to her.

Enid felt dwarfed beside his enormous girth. She

bent her head back, her gray hair falling over her shoulders. She suddenly felt very old and very tired. She couldn't fight this man. He was insane, and there was nothing she could do.

"Fire, Miz Dupre. You remember the fire. The barn was the first. There was gonna be others, but then he came back with her. I didn't have time for no fires when I was with her. And then there was the storm. That was a fire to be proud of. It was like it was mine. It's his fault she died. She shoulda stayed with me."

"Oh, dear Lord above," Enid whispered. "Powell."

He laughed, a low, guttural sound. "Powell's dead, Miz Dupre. Burned in the fire. Breathed so much smoke, couldn't even talk at the last. He's dead, ma'am. Powell's dead. Just like Consuela."

"It was a terrible thing that happened, Powell. Terrible. But it wasn't anyone's fault." Panic made her voice sound shrill, but she had to keep talking, she had to do something. "Chase tried to find Consuela. He wanted to save her. And you tried to save her, too. Chase told me you brought her out. Consuela—"

His backhand caught her by surprise, knocking her sideways onto the bed. She cried out and touched her stinging cheek.

Powell leaned low over the bed, his black hood only inches from her face. "Don't speak her name to me. Don't ever speak her name to me." Then he jerked her upright and stuffed a gag in her mouth.

She tried to pull away as he reached for her hands, but there was little she could do against his superior strength. He caught her wrists and bound them together in front of her. Then, roughly, he dragged her to her feet. He grabbed the lamp from the table and pulled her from the room and down the hallway toward her own bedroom.

"Nothing like a good fire, is there, Miz Dupre," Powell said as he turned the lock in the door.

She stared at him in horror as he removed the lamp shade and calmly turned the lamp on its side, spilling the kerosene and watching as the flame flickered and spread. A gagged protest fought to be heard but died in her throat. He shoved her before him. She looked over her shoulder, and her frantic eyes watched the flames licking at her bedroom door.

Frank! her mind screamed.

She stumbled down the stairs, only Powell's harsh grip on her upper arm keeping her from falling headlong to the bottom. On the last step he suddenly threw her over his shoulder. He turned toward the kitchen and carried her to the back of the house and out the door. She kicked with her feet and struck his back with her hands, but she was no more trouble to him than a pesky fly. He paid her no heed.

Two horses stood waiting outside the kitchen. He threw Enid onto one of them and bound her tied wrists to the saddle horn, then mounted his own horse and headed away from the burning house, leading her horse after him. Enid twisted to look behind her, jerking hard at the bindings that held her captive. Already she could see flames from an upper window.

Frank!

"Don't worry, Miz Dupre," Powell's voice carried back to her. "Soon as we're out of sight, we'll stop and watch. Nothin' like a good fire."

She slumped forward, a coldness seeping through her that had nothing to do with the frigid temperatures.

Frank . . .

It had taken them nearly two weeks. Two weeks of blinding snow and icy winds. But at last they were on Dupre land. Although temperatures still dipped into the teens, the wind had stilled and the sun was shining in a clear blue sky on the day they would arrive home.

Chase glanced at his wife. She was huddled inside her heavy winter coat, her legs protected by fur-covered chaps known as "woollies." Her hands were shoved inside her pockets and her shoulders were hunched forward. A wool scarf was tied over her hat and wrapped around her neck and lower half of her face, revealing only her eyes and the bridge of her nose.

"We'll be there in an hour or so," he told her.

She nodded silently.

Chase knew she was exhausted, but she'd never complained. Not once. They had shared an urgency to reach Four Winds, and today they would see it at last. They had reached Dupre land yesterday and spent the night in one of their own line shacks. They had already seen cattle with the Four Winds brand. Chase expected any moment to run into one of the hands riding line. This was his land, *their* land. This was home.

His thoughts ran on ahead of him to the ranch house. Aunt Enid's gray eyes would sparkle with greeting, and she would enfold Gem in her mother-hen manner. Pike and the others would have arrived home more than a month before, so Uncle Frank and Aunt Enid would already know about Chase and Gem getting married. And, on a sadder note, Katie would already know about Rodney's accident. But the baby would be a surprise to all.

Beneath his scarf, he grinned. He'd be a father come June. Gem insisted it would be a dark-haired boy with bright blue eyes. He'd like that. Four Winds needed an heir, a son to inherit everything his parents and his aunt and uncle had worked for and everything he and Gem would work for in the future. But then, a daughter would be nice too. A tiny vixen with greenish-blue eyes and red-gold hair. A daughter who would be the same mixture of tomboy and lady as her mother. He glanced at Gem once again, thinking, *One of each would be nice*.

Gem straightened in her saddle, her eyes peering from beneath her hat brim. "Look," she said, pointing into the distance.

He followed the direction of her finger. Against the white earth and the blue sky a gray cloud hung in the still air. He didn't know what had happened, but he knew in that instant they hadn't arrived soon enough. He slapped his reins in front of his saddle and spurred Dodge forward, driving the weary animal to the peak of its endurance.

Chase had a feeling of *déjà vu* as he rode into the yard toward the smoldering remains of his home. Less than six months before, he had ridden into a similar scene, only that time it had been the barn. He stopped his mount not far from the front porch—or what used to be the front porch—and just sat looking at the rubble. He wasn't aware of Gem drawing up beside him. He wasn't aware of the appearance of the ranch hands. He just sat looking and feeling a terrible numbness spreading through him.

Pike was the first to step close. He peered up at Chase, frowning into the sun, his face lined and haggard. "Chase. Thank God you're back."

"What happened?"

"Fire started sometime in the night. It was pretty far gone by the time we knew it was burnin'." Pike halted, then added, "Looks like it was set."

"The folks?" he asked, never taking his eyes off the charred remains.

Pike cleared his throat and looked down at the ground. The lengthy pause was a painful one. "We found Frank in his bedroom. Looked like he tried to get to the window." Another long pause. "He's dead, Chase."

A muscle in Chase's jaw jerked. His voice was strained. "Aunt Enid?"

"We . . . haven't found her yet."

Slowly Chase dismounted. He handed the reins to Pike and approached the still-smoking ruins. His eyes stung and tears welled up, but he blinked them away as he leaned his forehead against a still-standing porch post. His palm struck the railing, once . . . and then again and again.

"Chase—" Gem's voice broke as she laid a hand on his shoulder.

"Why, damn it? Why would he do this?"

"I don't know."

He turned on her quickly, almost violently. "I won't rest until I find him. If it takes all my life, I'll find him and kill him."

* * *

Through the afternoon they sought through the rubble. Gem refused to be relegated to the sidelines. She worked beside Chase, tears blinding her eyes more often than not. But they found no trace of Enid's body. In the morning they would bury Frank's remains, but Enid's grave would be empty.

Night came early, wrapping the mourning ranch in a black cloak to match the misery they each felt. Gem and Chase moved into the little house that had been Katie's and Rodney's. Gem fixed something to eat, but neither of them did more than shove the food around on their plates.

Gem watched Chase with a growing dread. His face was set in hard, forbidding lines, his eyes icy cold. He hadn't spoken since they entered the house. A barrier had arisen between them, a barrier she didn't know how to break down. Her own heart was breaking, as she knew his had; she wanted to share and receive comfort, yet they were kept apart by the misery that should have brought them together.

Chase rose from the table and walked to the window. He moved aside the calico curtains, gazing into the blackness, the rigid set of his shoulders speaking volumes of his hurt, his rage, his impotence in finding revenge.

Gem's eyes followed him there. *This should have been a joyous evening*, she thought. They should have been sitting in the parlor telling Aunt Enid about the baby, about how happy they were, about how much they loved each other. They should have been laughing at Uncle Frank's bedside, detailing the cattle drive and all the news from Shane Grogan and Cheyenne.

Soul-weary, Gem stood and crossed the room,

pausing beside him and gazing out the window as he was doing. "Chase, let's go to bed."

"I couldn't sleep."

"I know," she answered, looking up at him, "but let's try." She took hold of his arm and tugged gently. "Come on, Chase."

He dropped his gaze to meet hers. "How do I find him?" His voice was so low she could scarcely hear him. "How do I find him, Gem?"

She had thought her tears were spent, but they welled up instantly. "Come to bed." It was all she could say. She had no advice, no words of wisdom.

His shoulders sagged in defeat, and he went with her into the bedroom.

They undressed in the dark, climbing between the cool sheets from opposites sides of the bed. Chase lay on his back, one arm behind his head.

Gem waited, hoping he would pull her into his arms, but when he didn't, she made the first move. She slid up against him, throwing an arm over his bare chest and laying her head upon his shoulder. She listened to his breathing, feeling the ache in each beat of his heart. Her tears flowed silently.

She had no idea how much time had passed— was it minutes or hours?—when he began to speak.

"Frank Dupre never hurt anyone in his life. He was strong and gentle and good. You know how much he loved Aunt Enid? Sometimes he'd bring her flowers in the middle of the day, picked off the range while he was riding herd. He would just pick a bunch and ride back to the house and give them to her."

His arm pulled from behind his head and he placed it around her back, drawing her closer against him.

"When my folks died, they were both there for me. I don't know how they did it, but they eased the pain."

Gem sniffed. "I know . . . They did the same for me. I'd never been loved by anyone before them."

"There wasn't any reason for this, Gem."

"No."

"I'll find him if it takes me all my life." His voice was deadly cold.

"I want him found too, Chase. I loved Enid and Frank as much as you did. But we can't live with hate. It'll kill us."

"I don't want to feel any pain now, Gem. I want to smash and to kill. I want to tear that man apart with my bare hands. I don't want to hurt. I want to feel nothing except hate."

She tightened her arm. "Chase—" She was frightened. Frightened of what such hatred might do. To Chase. To them. To their child.

There was a long, aching silence. Then a choked sob shook his chest. Chase pulled Gem into a tight embrace. "God in heaven, I hurt," he whispered into her ear. And then the tears came, torn from him with great, racking sobs.

Gem had never seen or heard a man cry before. But with wisdom beyond her years, she knew that his tears didn't make him less of a man. They made him more of a man. They would make him stronger. The pain would heal. The hate would lessen.

Together, they would survive even this.

34

Pounding on the door awakened them in the morning.

"Chase! Chase, get out here. Quick!"

He jumped from the bed, pulling on his Levi's even as he raced for the door. Gem was a few seconds behind him, holding her robe closed with her hands and entering the kitchen just as Chase jerked open the door to reveal Teddy's excited face.

"Get out here, Chase. It's about your aunt."

Chase glanced over his shoulder, exchanging a glance with Gem, then looked back at Teddy. "I'll get dressed and be right out."

Gem beat him to the bedroom. She dressed quickly, not bothering to rebraid her hair. She didn't dare speculate what it was Teddy had found. She was afraid to be hopeful, yet . . .

She pulled on her coat just as Chase was heading

for the door, and side by side they raced from the small house. The cowboys were gathered near the barn, their voices muffled and somber. The men parted as Chase and Gem reached them.

Tacked to the corral fence was Enid's dark blue robe. Against the fabric fluttered a white piece of paper. Chase tore it from the nail, his eyes scanning the scrawled writing.

"What is it?" Gem demanded, the air freezing in a white cloud as she spoke. "What does it say?"

Chase frowned, reading the missive aloud, "It says, 'A fire takes mine. A fire takes yours. One Dupre has paid a little. The next Dupre will pay a little more. Perhaps tomorrow. When Enid is gone, Gem will be next. Beware, Chase. One by one, the Dupres will pay.'"

Gem pulled the robe from the nail. She rubbed it lovingly against her cheek, hope shining in her eyes, no longer denied. "Chase, that means Aunt Enid's still alive."

"'A fire takes mine. A fire takes yours . . .'" Chase turned to look at the burned out house. "'A fire takes mine. A fire takes yours . . .'" He began to walk toward the rubble, still mumbling the words from the note.

Gem's gaze touched each man around her before she followed after Chase.

He stopped near the porch post. "It's someone we know," he told her when she reached him. "Someone that knows our family, knows us well. Someone that's been hurt by fire and thinks it's our fault."

"But, Chase, that doesn't make any—"

"Daniels." He said the name beneath his breath.

"Josh Daniels? But he's too old. He—"

"Powell Daniels."

The way he said Powell's name made her flesh crawl. "But Powell's dead," she reminded him, voice quivering.

"So we were told."

Gem grabbed his arm, forcing him to look down at her. "Chase, be reasonable. Consuela and Powell both died—" And then she interrupted her own protest. Consuela and Powell. Her eyes widened. "Oh, Chase . . . he's crazy."

"I'm going over to the Big Pine."

"You don't think he's got Aunt Enid there? Surely Josh wouldn't—"

"I don't know what Josh would do. But Powell knew I'd figure out his riddle eventually. He'll think I'll come storming in with a lot of men, but I won't."

Gem turned away from him, her feet ready to carry her to the barn. "I'll saddle our horses."

His hand stopped her flight. "I'm going alone." He spoke with deadly earnest. "You're going to listen to me this time, Gem. He's after you next. I'm not taking any chances. You're staying here."

"He's after you too," she argued unconvincingly.

"Do I have to lock you up in the house?"

She could see in his face there was no point in arguing with him. She shook her head. "No. I'll stay here." She pressed her hands against his chest. "Promise me you'll be careful. Take some of the boys with you. They can hang back out of sight. Please, Chase."

"Okay." He hugged her to him, kissing her

morning-mussed hair. "Don't fret. I'll be back soon. And I'll bring Aunt Enid with me."

Chase took a back route to Big Pine, hugging the mountains as much as possible. Teddy and Pike rode with him. Red and Corky stayed behind, with orders to keep a close watch over Gem.

It was late morning when Chase stopped his horse and peered down at the house at Big Pine. "You men stay here. I'm going in alone."

"Don't you think one of us should go with you?" Teddy asked.

"No. I'll go alone. But if you don't see me in the next hour, come a running." He spurred his mount forward.

As he neared the ranch house Chase slipped his coat behind his holster, feeling the butt of the Peacemaker with his fingertips as if testing it, making sure it would be ready when he was. Then he pulled his Winchester from the saddle scabbard. He was ready.

"Daniels!" he called as he drew to a halt. "I'm here, Daniels." His sharp eyes watched the windows. His ears were tuned for any sound. He expected anything and everything.

The door opened. A middle-aged woman wearing a drab brown dress and a crisp white apron stepped onto the porch. "Mr. Daniels says for you to come inside, sir."

Cautiously he dismounted, his rifle still ready, his eyes still watchful.

"Mr. Daniels is in his study," the woman said as Chase stepped inside.

Chase glanced up the stairs, then turned in the direction the woman was walking and followed her.

She glanced back at him before opening the door. "Please don't stay long, sir. Mr. Daniels has not been well of late." Then she lifted the latch and pushed open the door before him.

Chase hadn't seen Josh Daniels in four months. He wouldn't have believed that four months could age a man so completely. In fact, he wouldn't have recognized Josh if he'd seen him on the street instead of in his own home.

Josh was seated in a chair near the roaring fireplace. A blanket was tucked tightly over his lap and beneath his legs, and a shawl warmed his hunched shoulders. His light brown hair and bushy eyebrows had turned completely white. His ruddy complexion had turned sallow. He looked up as Chase entered, turning faded, lifeless eyes on his guest.

"Hello, Chase."

Chase shook off his initial shock. "Where's Powell?" he asked sharply.

"Powell is dead." Josh turned his face back toward the fire.

"He's not dead, Josh, and you know it. I've come for him. Where is he?"

"Powell is dead. Both my sons are dead." His voice was as lifeless as his eyes.

Chase moved farther into the room, stopping on the edge of the braided rug that covered the study floor. He was angry, yet he could see that anger would get him nowhere with Josh. Something had snapped inside of the man in recent months. There was an air of defeat clinging about him more tightly than the shawl about his shoulders. Chase felt a twinge of pity for the man he had once known. He'd never liked Josh, but he couldn't help feeling sorry for him now.

"You knew about Rod." Josh spoke in a monotone as he stared into the flames. "He died on the drive. Buried in Wyoming. I always thought he'd come back home. Always thought he'd bring that little wife of his and the baby and come home. Never knew why he turned away from us. I loved that boy, but I guess he never knew it. Always thought he was so different from his brother and me. He was a good boy. He was a good boy—" His voice drifted away.

"Where is Powell? I know he isn't dead."

Josh didn't seem to have even heard him.

Chase stepped closer and leaned forward, asking in a quiet but firm voice, "Where is he, Josh? I've got to find him."

Again no reply.

"Josh . . . he's got Aunt Enid."

The older man closed his eyes.

"He killed Uncle Frank. He burned the house down with him in it. He left a note saying he was going to kill Aunt Enid, too. Josh, I've got to find him."

Gem paced back and forth from the kitchen to the tiny parlor and back again. How much time had passed? Would he be at the Big Pine yet? Was Powell there? Was Aunt Enid there? Was it an ambush? Was Chase all right?

She went to the door and looked out. Zeke was

just heading out to relieve one of the line riders. Red was pitching the horses in the corrals some hay. Smoke curled from the chimney of the bunkhouse. Everything looked so peaceful, so normal.

She began pacing again.

Why had she promised Chase she would stay home? She should be with him. She could shoot as good as any man and better than some. She could have stayed out of sight and protected herself and the baby and still been with him, still known what was happening. Oh, why had she promised him she would stay at Four Winds?

Once more she walked to the door. This time she opened it. The barn door was swung wide. Red must have gone inside. Perhaps if she just spent some time talking to someone besides herself, the hours would pass quickly instead of dragging out. She pulled on her coat and hat and wrapped a scarf around her neck, then headed across the crusty snow toward the barn.

The building was quiet. No sign of Red. She closed the door behind her, then walked to the first stall. Wichita was lying in the straw, her legs tucked beneath her belly. Gem slipped inside and sat in the straw near the mare's head.

"How're you doing, girl?" Gem murmured, scratching the pinto behind an ear. "Tired, huh? Me, too."

She ran a hand over the young mare's side. She had mated the mare to Julio's stallion before he left Cheyenne, and now she wondered if the hard riding they had done and the scant rations had harmed Wichita's first colt.

That thought too dour, she made a stab at levity.

"What do you think, girl? Is that colt of yours going to be black like Diablo or will it be another pinto as pretty as you?"

The mare snorted and nodded her head.

"I sure hate the waiting, Wichita." She patted the mare one more time, then pushed to her feet mumbling, "I sure hate the waiting."

As she left the barn she considered going to the bunkhouse, then decided against it. The men didn't want to be bothered by her today. They had enough troubles. She knew that everyone was still reeling from Uncle Frank's tragic death. They were all worried about Aunt Enid and wondering if Chase would be safe. They didn't need an anxious wife wringing her hands in the middle of their private domain.

Shoulders hunched forward, she headed back toward the little house behind the blackened rubble that was once the big house at Four Winds. She didn't look at the ruins; it hurt too much.

"So now what?" she asked herself aloud as she closed the door behind her. More pacing? More worrying? More waiting?

She removed her coat and tossed it across a chair, dropping her hat and scarf on top of it. Then she headed toward the bedroom. Perhaps if she could make herself fall asleep, Chase would be there when she awoke. She lay down on the bed still wearing her clothes and pulled a blanket up from the foot of the bed, resolutely closing her eyes. She forced herself to draw long, slow breaths.

"It won't help." The raspy words were whispered right next to her ear.

A scream rose in her throat before her eyes could

open, but it died on her lips as something heavy struck her brow. She could feel herself falling into a deep, black pit. She struggled to return to daylight, to consciousness, but to no avail. The darkness swallowed her up.

35

"Josh? Help me find him."

At last Powell's father turned his face from the fire, opening his eyes to look up at Chase. "He killed Frank?"

Chase nodded.

"There was a time I wanted to kill him. But he was a good man. Enid loved him." His eyes seemed to clear. "He's got Enid?"

"Yes. Where has he taken her?"

Josh shook his head slowly. "I don't know. Not here. He came back. Two, maybe three days ago, maybe more. I don't know. He took some food and blankets. I asked where he was going. He didn't answer." Once again his face turned to the fire. Once again he spoke in a monotone. "I told him once he was too full of hate. I told him it'd eat him alive. He's got no soul left. It was burnt up in the range fire."

Chase could feel the old man's mind slipping away from him. Frustrated, he dropped to his knees, laying down his rifle, then gripping Josh by his shoulders. He gave him a light shake. "Josh, you've got to help me. There must be some place he's keeping Aunt Enid. Some place he's hiding out. Where would he go, Josh? Where would he take Aunt Enid?"

"Enid was the prettiest girl in all of Clearfield County. Well, maybe Denise was prettier, but I always liked Enid best. We were gonna be married. Everybody knew it. Everybody knew we were supposed to get married. And then Frank came along and stole her away from me. Took her all the way to California. But I found 'em. It took me a lotta years, but I finally found 'em right here in Montana. I was gonna take her away from Frank, just like he'd done to me. But I couldn't. She loved him, and I couldn't do it. Powell always hated me for that. He likes to take what he wants, no matter what he has to do to get it."

Josh fell silent, then looked at Chase. "He's got an old cabin up in the mountains where he liked to go when he and Rod were boys. I ain't been there in years. Don't even know if it's still standin'."

"Where is it? Tell me how to get there."

Gem felt a terrible ringing in her head. She tried to lift a hand to her pounding skull but found that she couldn't move her arms. Her wrists were bound together, the harsh rope cutting into her flesh. She realized then that she was sitting up with her back braced against a wall. She was cold, but she could hear a fire burning not far away. She kept her eyes closed and concentrated on things around her.

She heard a chair scraping against the floor, then footsteps. She knew it had to be Powell, and fear jumped to her throat. The door opened, then closed. She waited tensely, but the footsteps didn't return. She opened her eyes. The cabin was small with a wood floor and only one small window. There was a cot in one corner, farthest from the fireplace, and a table and one chair closest to the hearth.

The door burst open. Before she could feign sleep again, Enid came tumbling into the room, landing in a heap near Gem's feet.

"Try that again, old woman, and I won't wait till Chase gets here," Powell snarled from the doorway.

"Aunt Enid," Gem whispered, frightened by the stillness of the woman before her.

"So . . . you're awake at last." Powell closed the door.

How she hated that black hood. She'd like to see his eyes—just before she scratched them out!

He returned to his chair near the fire, pushing Enid roughly out of the way with the toe of his boot. He picked up some food from the plate on the table. His back toward her, he lifted the hood and began to eat.

Gem turned her attention to Enid. Her hair spread around her like a gray cloud. Her white nightgown was soiled and torn. There was an ugly bruise on her cheek.

"Aunt Enid?"

The woman's eyelids shifted.

"Aunt Enid, it's Gem," she encouraged softly.

Enid opened her eyes. She looked at Gem for a long time before pushing herself upright. Dismay was written in her weary features. Dark circles rimmed her eyes.

"What has he done to you, Aunt Enid?"

"Nothin' she hasn't deserved," Powell answered.

Enid glanced toward the table, then crawled over to sit beside Gem. "It's Powell," she whispered. "He killed Frank."

"I know." Gem's eyes watered.

"Chase?"

"He's all right. He's looking for you right now."

"I tried to get away. I told him I needed to relieve myself. But he found me." Enid looked old and defeated. "It wasn't so bad when it was just me, but I wanted to get help for you. I'm so sorry he found you, Gem."

That look of defeat frightened Gem more than anything else. Enid had always been such a strong woman. Gem mustn't let her lose hope. She glanced quickly at Powell's back, then mouthed silently, *Try to untie my hands*.

Enid's gaze also flickered toward their captor before furtively working at the tight ropes binding Gem's wrists. When Powell pulled the mask back over his face, she jerked her hands away from Gem, letting them lie idle in her lap. Gem saw Enid shiver with the cold and noted the near translucence of her skin. Her lips looked almost blue.

"Powell," Gem pleaded, "at least give Aunt Enid a blanket. She's freezing."

"She ain't got much longer to live anyway." He

pushed up from the table and, without giving them more than a glance, left the cabin.

Gem sawed furiously at the ropes. "Help me, Aunt Enid."

But just as the older woman reached out, Gem pulled a wrist free of its binding, rubbing her flesh raw on the rough rope. She shook her other hand free as she jumped to her feet. Her head throbbed and the room danced and swayed. She steadied herself with a hand against the wall while she sucked her bleeding wrist and silently cursed the pain.

Enid stood beside Gem. "He'll be back soon."

"Throw some water on the fire," Gem ordered, moving even as she spoke. She picked up the chair and carried it toward the door. She heard the splash and sizzle as the fire was doused. The cabin quickly filled with choking smoke from the wet coals. "Tip over the table and get behind it. Don't come out, no matter what happens."

Gem positioned herself behind the door, her ear pressed against the wall as she listened for sounds of his return. Once before, she had coldcocked Powell Daniels with a chair. Perhaps, with the luck of surprise, she just might be able to do it again.

She hadn't long to wait. The door rattled, then opened. He stepped through the doorway.

"What—"

She swung with all the strength she had in her, but the chair was deflected by a raised arm. It was wrenched from her hands and thrown across the room with force. Instinctively she jumped to one side, hoping to avoid his swing in her direction, but he caught her by the hair and hauled her back toward him. Arms flailing, she struck him with every blow she could muster. She heard his laughter as he pulled her outside into the daylight.

She was nearly crazed with anger. "You dirty no good—"

He backhanded her, but his other hand kept her from falling.

Gem saw only red as she leaped toward him, nails bared. She grabbed the ominous black hood with one hand, tearing it from his head, even as her other hand gouged his neck.

It was an inhuman growl that tore from his throat. With a mighty thrust he knocked her to the ground.

Gem stared up at him, stunned into inactivity. The face that looked back at her was grotesque and frightening. The entire left side was a mass of scar tissue, the eye little more than a slit in the twisted features. There was no left ear, and only sparse splotches of hair grew on his head.

"You think I'm ugly?" He reached down for her, pulling her roughly to her feet once again. "Do I frighten you, Gem?" He laughed hoarsely. "Look at me close. Will you cringe from me when I make you my whore? I was going to kill you, but that'd be a better revenge. Don't you think so, Miz Dupre?"

"No—" She tried to pull free, but it was hopeless.

"But first we got your aunt to take care of. How do you think she oughta go, Gem? Should we make it fast, or should we make it slow? Maybe I should make her face look like mine."

"Powell, you're crazy. You'll never get away with this. Let Aunt Enid go. You've got no reason to hurt her. I'll go with you if that's what you want. Just let me get her back to Four Winds."

His face contorted. "Four Winds. Always Four Winds and the Dupres. You thought I'd let you go back to them, Consuela. You thought you'd just use me for fun and then go back to them. Well, it's not so easy, is it, Consuela? I found you, and this time you won't get away."

He was mad. Gem felt a sinking feeling, a sweeping of the despair she had seen in Enid's face. Powell was stark raving mad.

Josh stopped his horse. Frowning, he looked first to his left, then to his right. "I'm just not sure. I think it was . . . No, it's this way."

Chase felt the impatience ready to explode inside him. The day was quickly slipping away from them. They had to find Aunt Enid soon. Even now, she could be . . . "Which way, Josh. You've got to be sure."

"I am sure. It's this way."

Chase pondered each trail, feeling the weight of his decision. His aunt's life could hang on his choice. He would have preferred to have more men, but . . . "Pike, you and Teddy try up that way. If you find them, one of you come for me. I'll go with Josh."

For another half hour they continued to climb, the sounds of the horses' hooves muffled in the snow. Chase was beginning to lose hope of finding them before nightfall, if they found them at all. Perhaps Josh was leading him on a wild goose chase. Perhaps he knew where Powell was and wasn't telling Chase the truth. Perhaps Powell and Aunt Enid were at the Big Pine even now.

Josh stopped on the trail in front of him. "I think my horse is lame," he said as he dismounted. He lifted the animal's front left leg, testing it for swelling, then checking his hoof. "Sure 'nough. A rock."

Chase nudged his horse forward. "You get it out. I'm going on ahead. Catch up if you can." He wondered if Josh was just playing a game of delays, but it was too late now. He had to trust him. Josh was his only hope.

Perhaps another ten minutes up the trail a sound carried through the dense trees. Chase pulled back on the reins and listened. Voices. He was sure of it. He dismounted, pulling his rifle from its scabbard. He wrapped the reins around a bush and started off on foot, following the muted sounds.

As the voices grew louder, Chase paused, his heart seeming to skip a beat as he recognized her voice. It was Gem. Gem was there with Powell. He moved on, more cautious than before, stifling his urge to race ahead into whatever he would find. There were two lives depending on him now.

The scene that met his eyes as he carefully pushed aside a bush made a cold sweat break out. Powell, his face hardly recognizable, was holding Enid in front of him, her back against his chest. In one hand he held a knife. In the other he held a flaming piece of wood, waving it dangerously close to her face. Gem, bound hand and foot, was on the ground at their feet.

"You always were ugly, old woman," Powell said with a harsh laugh.

Gem struggled to rise. "Let her go, Powell."

"I never knew what my old man saw in you.

Always hankerin' after you. Always thinkin' you were better than my ma. Wonder what he'll think when I'm through with you."

Chase tried to get a clear shot at him, but Powell kept moving, always holding Enid in front of him as if he knew Chase was out there. Chase glanced around the clearing. Perhaps if he moved to the right . . .

Gem didn't know what happened. One moment Powell was standing above her, Aunt Enid in his grasp. The next he had pushed the older woman away, discarding the burning wood as he did so, and pulled Gem up from the ground, twisting her around until her back was to him. The sharp knife touched the tender flesh of her throat. He backed up, dragging her with him, until his back was against the cabin.

"Come out, Dupre. Come out quick, or she dies."

Gem drew a startled gasp. Chase was here.

"Now, Dupre!"

The knife cut her, and she cried out.

He stepped into the clearing. His face was set in a hard mask, but when his eyes met hers she felt his message of love. He was here. He would take care of her.

"Throw that rifle back into them trees," Powell ordered in his rasping voice, "and drop your gun."

Chase's gaze shifted to Powell. He did as he was told. "Let the women go, Powell. This is between you and me."

Powell laughed sharply. "Miz Dupre, get that rope and tie him up." His grip on Gem tightened. He flicked the knife, drawing more blood. An involuntary cry escaped her once again. "Don't try anythin' stupid, old woman. Just do as you're told."

Close to complete exhaustion, Enid stumbled to her feet, picked up the rope, and moved across the clearing to Chase.

"Do a good job. I'm gonna check your knots."

Gem watched as Enid tied Chase's hands behind his back. Then with an anguished sigh Enid dropped to the ground at Chase's feet, her head sagging forward.

Hope was quickly dying in Gem's heart. They would probably all die now. She wished she'd had just a little longer to be his wife. Just a little longer to enjoy hearing him say he loved her. She wished she could have seen their child and held him to her breast as he suckled. She wished . . .

"Now kick that gun over here."

The Peacemaker skidded across the snow-covered ground. Taking Gem with him, he bent to pick it up. He kept the knife pressed against her throat while he pointed the revolver at Chase.

"Why are you doing this, Powell?" Chase asked, his jaw clenched, his thick dark brows drawn together.

"Why?" Powell hissed. "Don't you know, Dupre? Don't you know how it's been, growin' up in your shadow? My pa always hankerin' after the old woman there. Folks always talkin' about the fine Dupre family and what a great ranch the Four Winds was. My brother preferrin' to live there than with his own family. Well, I showed you, Chase. I took one wife from you and I mean to take another. And when I'm all done, I mean to take that ranch of yours, too. I mean to have it all."

"You'll never get away with it. My men know what you've done. You may kill us, but you'll never get the ranch."

"You want to hear how I had your wife? She'd meet me just about any place. I had her in the line shacks and at the Big Pine and anywhere I chose. She'd tell me how much she hated you. You were nothing, she said. Not man enough to keep her happy. She was a hot-blooded woman, and she was mine. And then you killed her in that fire."

"She was with you, Powell. She was with you in that fire."

Powell's voice lowered and he pulled Gem with him as he sidled toward the nearby shed. "You killed her, Chase, 'cause you wouldn't let her come to me. And now I'm gonna kill Gem. But I'm gonna keep her as my whore first. When you die, you'll die knowin' what I'm gonna do to her."

Chase took a sudden step forward, a growl rising in his throat.

Powell raised the blade toward Gem's eye. "You want her blind, Dupre? I don't care if I've got a one-eyed whore."

Chase checked his advance. His face went white. His eyes locked onto Gem. Impotence held him in a cruel vice. He couldn't help her, and she could read the agony in his gaze.

"I love you, Chase. Don't ever forget it," she called to him in desperation.

"Shut up," Powell snarled.

I love you, too, his gaze told her before it shifted once more to Powell. "Think of your father. What will this do to him, knowing you've killed Enid and me?"

"My pa." Powell spit at his feet. "My pa don't care what I do any more. He's been comparin' me and you for years. He thought I didn't know it, but I did. He even took to sayin' he understood Rod after a while. Rod. Can you beat that? That no-good brother of mine. Well, I took care of him too. Crushed his skull just as easy as pie." He laughed at Chase's expression. "You thought it was an accident, didn't you? Proves what a fool you are, Dupre. Of course I killed him. I'd kill anyone who gets in my way."

For a moment all was silent in the little clearing by the cabin. Gem wondered if it could all be just a bad dream. Maybe if she closed her eyes she would wake up all safe and sound in bed with Chase, and he would hold her and comfort her and make the nightmare go away.

"You know what, Dupre?" Powell asked, cutting into her wishful thinking. "I'm tired of talkin' to you. I think it's time I quit talkin'."

The gun came up quickly. The hammer cocked. Gem heard a scream without realizing it was torn from her own lips. Disregarding the knife, she threw her shoulder against his arm. She heard a shot. And then another. Even as she watched Chase falling, she waited for the knife to plunge into her and end her nightmare.

It didn't come.

Gem turned to look behind her, realizing suddenly that she stood alone with no one at her back. Her gaze dropped. Powell lay prone on the ground, his one good eye staring at the sky. Staring but seeing nothing. Blood trickled from a small hole in his left temple.

She looked up as a white-haired Josh Daniels

emerged from the edge of the forest. He walked slowly toward her, his right arm hanging rigidly at his side, his gun clenched in his hand. He came steadily forward until he stood at Powell's side. His eyes studied the body before him, his expression as dead as his son.

"He killed his own brother," Josh said in a low monotone. "His own brother."

His voice awakened her from her shock. She turned, already calling Chase's name, expecting to see him lying as cold and as dead as Powell. But he was racing toward her. She tried to hobble toward him on bound feet, but he was there before she'd moved scarcely an inch, his right arm encircling her and pulling her against him. His left arm hung limply at his side, his coat stained red with blood.

"Thank God," he whispered into her hair. "Thank God."

"Oh, Chase. Your arm—" She was sobbing.

"It's nothing. Just a graze."

"Aunt Enid? She—"

"I'm here, dear."

Gem lifted her face from Chase's chest long enough to meet Enid's gray gaze. "We must get you home, Aunt Enid. Chase, take us home."

36

"You're sure you don't mind, Aunt Enid? I don't have to go."

"For land's sake, Gem. You act as if you're going miles away. You've hardly stepped a foot outside this house these past weeks. Now go on with Chase and enjoy yourself. If I need you, I'll send for you and you can come running."

Gem smiled sheepishly as she leaned over to kiss Enid's pale cheek. "Well . . . if you're sure—"

Enid had lost weight in the months since Frank's death, her gray hair had thinned, and there were a few more lines on her face. But this summer had brought the smile back to her lips and the twinkle to her eyes. Gem supposed her aunt would never completely recover from the loss of her husband or the ordeal that had followed. They had feared they would lose Enid to the pneumonia that laid her low in the days and weeks following her rescue. Perhaps it was knowing that new life was coming to Four Winds that had pulled her through.

Gem turned from Enid and bent over the cradle. Frank Jean Dupre, five weeks old—and an incredibly beautiful child, Gem thought—stared up at her with dark blue eyes. "Hello, little man," she crooned as she lifted him into her arms.

"Gem Dupre, you hand that baby to me and get on out to your husband. Little Frank and me'll be just fine."

"All right. But you call if you need me." She kissed her son's downy head before placing him in his great-aunt's waiting arms, then left Enid's room.

She stopped at her own bedroom to grab her hat. Then she turned and took a quick peek in the mirror. She was pleased to see how quickly her figure had returned after little Frank's birth. Actually, it had more than returned. Her breasts were fuller, her hips more shapely. She was the same, yet different. She plopped the old, dusty slouch hat over her braided hair and shook her head. No, she was still the same. There was just more of her.

With a dismissing shrug, she turned from her reflection, already forgetting her appearance. Her eyes glanced quickly around the bedroom. *Their* bedroom. The new house at Four Winds was even bigger than the one lost in flames. Chase had wanted more bedrooms. Room for a growing family, he had told her when the rebuilding began.

That thought almost pulled her back into Enid's room for one last look at the baby. She'd never known she could feel this way. Gem had taken to motherhood in the same way she loved Chase—with all her heart. But she didn't go in to see little Frank. Chase was waiting for her, and it was time she gave him more of her attention again.

Chase had saddled Wichita for her and left her tied to the post. At the mare's side stood a frisky black colt, the image of his sire. When she stepped through the front door, he darted away, then came trotting back, his short tail held high like a flag.

Gem laughed when she saw him. *"Buenas tardes,* Bandito. Diablo would be proud of you." She rubbed Wichita's muzzle. "How are you, girl? Is he running you as ragged as mine does me?"

She looked up as she saw Chase walking toward her, mounted on Dodge. Her heart did a familiar flip-flop as she watched him ride closer. Was it possible that she could love him more every day?

"You ready?" he asked.

"I'm ready."

"Mount up, then, and let's go."

They rode for over an hour. Gem hadn't ridden out onto the range this spring or summer, what with being pregnant and then having the baby. It was her first chance to see the wonderful recovery of the range. It would be another year or more before it would feed as many cattle as it had in the past, but that time would come.

Chase had increased their herd again, adding shorthorns from Oregon this time. It was good to see cattle dotting the range. Good to breathe the fresh Montana air. Good to look up at the mountains, black with ponderosa pines, purple gray peaks stretching to touch the heavens. It was all good. Her life was good.

They returned to the ranch house as dusk was settling over the earth.

Chase pulled up next to the bunkhouse. "Let's go in. We might even be able to round up a quick game of cards." His grin was irresistible.

A haze of blue smoke filled the bunkhouse. Gem squinted her eyes, peering at her hand. It was a good hand. Three jacks and an ace. "I'll see you and raise you two bits."

Pike threw in his cards. "Too rich for me." He ran his hand over his leathery-skinned face, then tilted his chair back and lit another cheroot.

Gem's gaze moved to Teddy. He was studying her with thoughtful green eyes. "I'm still in." He tossed in two bits.

"I think she's bluffin', boys," Chase said with a low chuckle. "Here's a five-dollar gold piece that says she is."

"That's it for me." Corky folded his hand.

Gem glanced once more at her cards. "I'm still in. I'll see your five dollars."

Teddy went out without comment.

Chase watched her with twinkling sapphire eyes. A satisfied grin tweaked the corners of his mouth. "That was the last of your money, Mrs. Dupre. Just how do you intend to match my raise?" He slowly pushed another five-dollar gold piece into the center of the table. Before she could answer, he raised one eyebrow as if in sudden inspiration. "How 'bout yourself, ma'am? I admit you're not much to look at. Not much higher than buffalo grass. But I hear you're expected to pretty up some."

Her heart quickened, just as it always did when he looked at her that special way. "I'm a good worker, sir, and not used to much pamperin'." She remembered that terrible, wonderful day they had met as clearly as he did, and she spoke her lines on cue. "I'll see your raise."

Chase's grin widened. "I'll have you know, ma'am, that I've heard it said you cheat sometimes at cards."

"Never, mister," she lied with aplomb.

He chuckled again. "Not this time anyway." He spread the four kings across the rough wood table. "Second time in my life that four kings brought me such luck."

She felt warm clear down to her toes.

"You'd better come with me, miss." Chase pushed up from the table and held out his hand to her.

Gem rose and took it, her gaze never leaving his face as he bid good night to the cowboys and led her from the bunkhouse. He paused in the frosty glow of moonlight, turning toward her with a sly grin. Suddenly he swept her off her feet and tossed her over one shoulder, taking off with quick strides toward the house.

"Chase, put me down! Chase, put me down this instant. The men will see you. Put me down, Chase!"

His only response was to chuckle. He never broke his stride, not until he'd reached their bedroom and closed the door with his boot heel. Then he carried her to the bed and dropped her unceremoniously onto it. The fall knocked her hat forward over her eyes.

"Chase, really—" she sputtered as she pulled the hat away.

He was beside her on the bed, the humor gone from his eyes but a tender smile remaining on his lips. "I lied to you, ma'am." He kissed her throat.

"Lied?" she asked, making a half-hearted attempt to sound angry, but failing.

"When I said you might pretty up some." His fingers unbuttoned her blouse. "You're already the prettiest woman between here and Texas."

"Am I, Chase?" She closed her eyes, discovering once again all the wonderful sensations that his lips and hands could stir in her.

"Gem—"

"Hmm?"

"I'm a lucky man."

She smiled, her eyes still closed. It had been luck indeed that had dealt him four kings six years ago, but it hadn't been so hard to make sure he held four kings tonight.

"As long as we're together, my love," she whispered, "your luck will never change." She drew closer into his embrace, smiling as she promised, "I'll see to that."